CW01203477

DIVINE IMPERFECTION

The Word of Dan

Published by Rectory Hill Publishing

ISBN 979-8-42266-491-7

Also available as a Kindle ebook
ISBN 978-1-84396-095-9

A catalogue record for this book is available from
the British Library and American Library of Congress

Typesetting and pre-press production
eBook Versions
27 Old Gloucester Street
London WC1N 3AX
www.ebookversions.com

About the author

A.M. Clarke is of Irish descent, raised in the Netherlands. Her father's work at the European Space Agency for many years, inspired her life-long fascination for the mysteries of the Universe.

She gained a philosophy degree from Exeter University, then later graduated from the British College of Osteopathic Medicine.

A.M. Clarke ran her own osteopathic practice in Lewes, East Sussex, before retiring to Essex to write, where she lives with her husband Ron and their little cat, Spacee.

For Ron Titchener, my husband,
from one Capricorn to another. The mountain
path of life is often steep but, beside you,
never lonely, never dull.

Shine On

DIVINE IMPERFECTION

The Word of Dan

A M Clarke

RECTORY HILL PUBLISHING

'That whereof we cannot speak, thereof we must remain silent.'

'To believe in a God means to see that the facts of the world are not the end of the matter.'

Ludwig Wittgenstein
(26th April 1889-29th April 1951)

Chapter One

The University of the Irish Space Centre
Wicklow Mountains
2028

She'd been watching him for some time. The man with his eyes closed. He appeared to have dosed off, sitting alone at a table, while all around him the canteen rumbled through the lunch-time rush hour. Mary stood beside a marble pillar and sipped her coffee, appraising him with her geneticist's eye. Indo-European celt. Broad shoulders, dark curly hair, near-perfect facial symmetry. He seemed to be in a world of his own, until he turned his face towards her and smiled. As if he could see her through his eyelids. As if he'd been watching her the whole time. Or maybe he was just daydreaming.

Mary cast her eyes around the canteen, to avoid looking in his direction. A movement in her peripheral vision caught her attention. She glanced at him. He was gazing at her, beckoning to her with a slow, circular motion of his wrist.

Come, join me. Mary's heart fluttered. She returned a cool smile, lifted her arm and rotated her wristwatch to signal:

Sorry, but no time. She added a little shrug. The apologetic thanks, but no thanks. The man raised his hand and spread his fingers: *Five-minutes.* He inclined his head with a wistful smile.

Without a second thought, Mary walked towards him.

"Professor Gallagher," – the man rose from the table – "thanks for joining me. Will you take the weight off your feet?" He had a southern Irish lilt.

"Have we met before?" she said.

"No, but sure, you're famous around here." He drew out a chair for her. "My name's John Daniel Downs, though I prefer you call me Dan."

"Thank you. Do please call me Mary." She placed her coffee on the table and sat down.

Dan re-seated himself. "I'm a great admirer of yours, as it happens."

"I think you're getting me mixed up with my father, Christopher Catherwood Gallagher. He pioneered a lot of the genetic biosynthesis we do here. I'm just following in his footsteps."

"That's modest after what I've just read about you in the information booklet."

"Our university prospectus flatters me." She sipped her coffee. "I'm afraid I won't be living up to any of that, now this is happening. Our research is on hold until the terrorist situation blows over."

"Well, with a bit of luck it won't be long. They're not sure if the terrorists are involved. The US Secretary of State was on Safari last month in Africa. She might've picked up a bug stroking big cats." Dan smiled, his light blue eyes dappling like sunlit waters. He lifted his expresso - the size of a doll's cup - and stuck his little finger out like an aerial.

"I take it you were invited through the Independent

Criterion?" She brightened her tone, to avoid any hint of resentment towards the new arrivals. Five hundred of them swelling the UISC Community to two thousand, filling up the biosphere's Villages with government officials and their families.

"Get away with you." He laughed, crinkling the corners of his eyes. "Do I look like a politician to you?"

"Why not? They don't all look the same. But you're not with the University, are you?" He'd have been around since the beginning of term. She would've spotted him by now.

"I got here just the other day. I'm not one of" -he lowered his voice to avoid being overheard by people at the next table- "themens. A tutor in the Arts Department vacated his post last week. He didn't want to teach here while it's being used as a safehouse for the elite. I understand where he's coming from. But I'm here for the kids on Mars." He grinned.

"Yes, of course." Mary nodded. "So long as the new arrivals enter into the spirit of things, there's no reason why our Life-On-Mars Simulation can't continue." She returned her cup to its saucer with a muted clink. "What do you teach?"

"Poetry combined with a smattering of philosophy." He glanced towards the ceiling. "Or is that a chattering of philosophy? As a matter of fact, I'm best known for my off-the-wall poetry."

"Wait. I think I might've heard of you." She raised her forefinger. "Are you J. D. Downs, the Irish poet? I read some of his work in our bookshop this Christmas. I bought the book for a friend of mine." She put her elbow on the table and cupped her chin. "Is that who you are?"

"That's me."

"I'm not really into poetry, but I thought some of your ideas were fascinating."

One poem had left her with an image she could still recall, no actual words, but something about eyes looking out from cells. Hinting at her own subject, cell biology. She remembered thinking at the time what a novel idea, to imagine a cell, as a fully conscious being. The nucleus as a dusky eye peering back, studying her.

"You're obviously very talented." She smiled.

Dan lowered his eyes. It charmed her to see the compliment made him blush. He even matched her picture of a poet, with those piercing eyes and his sculpted mouth. Trendy in his white T-shirt and black jacket. He couldn't be that much older than her. Early thirties, maybe. He lifted his face with a lopsided smile. As if surfing a wave, her stomach flipped over. Their eyes glanced off one another and met again.

"Does your colleague expect to have his job back, after the elite have gone home?" she said.

"That depends on how long these threats last. If it's longer than six months, the university registrar will grant me a permanent post. If I get on all right. It's the closest I'll ever get to being on Mars." He winked. "I'm loving it here."

"To think this could still be going on in six months-time." She shook her head. "I never thought terrorists would resort to a biological weapon, when they could just as easily infect themselves. Maybe they don't even bother to reason that far ahead. They're mad. That's what evil is, a form of madness, don't you think?"

"The truly insane have no conscience. Wicked folks ignore their conscience. Until the devil runs away with them, then sure, they go mad."

Mary considered this for a moment, resting her gaze on a foam stain on the rim of his cup. He'd finished his cappuccino.

"But don't you think people must be a bit mad in the first place, to ignore their own conscience?" she said.

He smiled the lopsided smile. "Becoming wicked is a gradual process, like most things in life. It starts by wanting something too much, that you'll stop at nothing to get it. Until one day you find yourself on a slippery slope, fooling yourself you can go back and reclaim your better self. But you can't. Then you're a baddun and you don't even know it."

Mary sensed the philosopher on his hobbyhorse. She looked up to meet his gaze and brazenly immersed herself a fraction too long. "Have you ever wanted anything too much?"

"Every minute of the day." He laughed. "I'm a greedy bastard so I am, and if it wasn't for me prayers, I'd be a thieving bastard, a liar and a cheat."

She blinked. "Are you religious?"

"I prefer my own ideas."

"Really? What are they?"

"Are you that interested?"

"In ideas, yes, of course." She inclined her head.

"I believe there's an intelligent soul responsible for this creation."

"Aren't you just talking about the usual culprit, God?"

"I know it's difficult to avoid that term even when you try," he said. "But I don't think of it as a perfect being. More like a creative force, embracing all the opposites, dark and light, Yin and Yang. What about you? Do you still say your prayers at night?"

"I did, until I was about fourteen, when I stopped believing." She hesitated, surprised to be having this conversation with a new acquaintance. "When you consider all the suffering in the world, it doesn't make sense to believe in a God. This life is all there is. We create our own heaven or hell. I'm never sure what people mean when they talk about a soul. What do you mean, exactly?"

Dan hooded his eyelids. "Ah, we have a true scientist in our midst. A proof-seeker."

"That's right, that's what I'm here for." She glanced down at her watch. "My goodness, where did the time go?"

He thumbed towards the canteen exit. "I saw it go that-a-way. Did you want me to go after it?"

She smiled and rose to her feet. "That won't be necessary. I'd better be going."

He stood up. "May I accompany you to the Farm Park?"

"I'm not returning to the Park just yet. I'd like to walk back to my apartment, to stretch my legs and pick up some files. And I promised my friend Lewis, that I'd make him a sandwich. The canteen staff are rushed off their feet these days."

Dan looked over his shoulder at the queue stretching from the self-service counter to the exit doors.

"That looks bad. I think I'll have lunch at the Shooting Star. If you're walking around The Loop, I'll walk you to your Village."

"If you like, if you don't mind hurrying."

They left the Park View Canteen and entered the Ectoloop tunnel, following the magnetic railway on foot.

Mary's colleagues had nicknamed the levitating train the Swingtram, as it resembled a roller-coaster-ride the way it corkscrewed around the helical Space Centre, transporting inmates to the Eight Villages. It come wafting around the bend and deflated to the platform where a young family were waiting to board. Mary and Dan paused to watch.

"It's so nice to see children here." She glanced up at him as they carried on walking. "But I wonder what they make of us scientists going about in our white coats. It must seem like a big hospital to them."

"Are you kidding? It's like a fairground. Everywhere you look there's rides. I love those talking cars you've got in the Farm Park and the robot astronauts floating around inside the Earth-Mars Spaceship, trying to eat spaghetti. It's all good fun."

"They're not robots, they're holograms. This is all UDAN Corps' latest technology. Even the daylight is created by holographic crystals in the walls and ceilings. Don't ask me how they work. It's all to do with quantum mechanics."

"That's beyond me too. I'll stick with the philosophy." He ambled along, covering ground effortlessly, hands in his pockets, while she skipped at his side in a hurry. He was much taller than her, well over six foot.

"I'd love to meet the genius behind it all." She sounded breathless in her own ears. "I'd like to ask him where he gets his ideas from. But they say he's a recluse."

"Probably mad as a hatter. Am I going too fast for you?"

"No, you're fine. You're keeping me on my toes. I've got to be back at work by two."

They hurried through the Level One Terminus, passing beneath the viaduct's graceful arches. Mary assessed her citrus plants as she scurried by their pots, like dumpy Christmas trees festooned with oranges and lemons. Flocks of bluetits glittered down upon their branches. Not much bigger than butterflies, they could only fly a few feet in the air and were so tame a couple of them flitted onto their path. Flightless doves waddled between the pots, picking at seeds scattered by her Park Monitors.

"Are those your Martian birds over there?" Dan said.

"That's right, they've been genetically engineered so they don't fly. Their energy requirements are minimal. The bluetits have a wonderful new song. They sing at dawn and dusk, for precisely one hour."

Dan's hand shot out from his pocket, throwing what appeared to be nuts across their path. "Here y' are chaps, party-time!"

Mary sharpened her tone. "I'm sorry, but you're not supposed to feed them. It's strictly against our regulations, set out in the information booklet. I thought you'd read it?"

Dan stopped. Mary turned and faced him.

"Sure, it's only a treat," he said.

"That's just the sort of mentality we can't afford here. We must maintain the biosphere's equilibrium with precision. That's not possible if people feed the birds." She held out her hand. "I'm sorry, Dan, but I must confiscate your nuts."

"Go on then." He chuckled and dropped a packet of shelled peanuts into her palm.

She put them in her pocket. "Thank you. I'm sorry I must be strict. You'll get used to our ways after a while. Soon you'll forget you're still on Earth, which is the whole idea of the experiment."

They carried on, spiralling up towards Level Two. The tunnel tapered, not much wider than a city underground.

"Do you come from Dublin?" She resumed her friendly tone.

"Not from the city. I have a place out in the sticks. I understand Dublin is one of your old stomping grounds."

"That's right. Do you have family in the Dublin area?"

"No blood relatives. I was adopted. I still see my circus family, from time to time," he said.

"Do you actually mean circus family or is that a term of endearment?"

"I'm talking about a real circus. I was with the Rainbow Circus for twelve years."

"Honestly? Were you really?" She slowed her pace to look at him. "Were you involved in any of the acts?"

"I was the main attraction, up there on my flying trapeze. They called me 'Bird Man.'"

"Are you teasing me?"

"Before that I was a clown and a juggler. Us circus kids had a grand thing going on in the ring, sure, the punters loved us."

"You amaze me." She laughed.

He joined her on the path into the Second Village, where he said he'd leave her off. Close to the Village Square there was a pond with a rockery, frothy from the activity of a small fountain, playground to saffron ducklings cheeping around it all day long. By Mary's design they'd never grow to be any bigger. She gestured towards them.

"They only look about four weeks, but they're a year old. They're charming, aren't they?"

"They're charming all right," he said. He appeared to be absorbed, watching them. Mary lingered beside him and checked her watch.

"It's quarter past two. Lewis will be starving."

He looked down at her. "You'll just have to tell your friend Lewis that you were waylaid by a gypsy who insisted on telling your fortune." He held out his hand. "So, cross my palm with silver."

She delved inside her pocket for the packet of nuts and placed them in his palm. "There, you can have them back. I trust you."

"That's a big mistake." He laughed. "I canny trust myself!"

"That's unlikely for a trapeze artist."

"Aye. But if you put the magic beans back in my hand, I'll have the doves flying around your head like lovebirds, in no time."

"Dan, it's been lovely to meet you." She smiled.

"I hope you're not telling me this is goodbye."

"It's a small town, I'm sure we'll see each other around. I'd best be off." She waved.

"I'll just hang around here and feed your cutie ducklings."

Mary shot him a wry look and walked on.

Chapter Two

Lewis Fox Allen, the Farm Park's Computer Systems Manager, was too frustrated to register hunger. He'd left his fourth mug of stale coffee growing cold beside him on the desk.

As a matter of fact, you had to love mud to be good at this job. You had to be thrilled by changes in the weather. Light and dark phases, nitrogen uptake from the soil. Photosynthesis relative to crop yield, had to be statistics that set your heart racing. Only, crikey, he couldn't be more bored. He'd complete one report, have time for a sip of coffee before the Farm Park sensory detectors heaped upon him more of its vital statistics, the depressing equivalent of mud thumping down on his coffin.

Lewis peered out through the Control Room window into Section A. Still no sign of Mary. He felt a rush of excitement at the thought of stealing a moment to tinker with his Artificial Intelligence Programme, code named Jolly.

He'd been trying to make the Programme sound more realistic, as human beings did so much complaining, he'd worked hard to give Jolly's mindless contentment an irritable edge. Mary wasn't impressed: 'Lewis, I thought the whole point of A. I. was to rise above the human condition. Now you're listening to a computer moaning, you're just a glutton for punishment.'

Lewis explained. This was an exercise in understanding how random emotional factors influence cognition. It only takes one rogue thought, a whim, a depressive slant to ruin everything. Even so, today, for reasons to do with his own state of mind, Lewis was going to restore Jolly's mood to the enduring optimism of the robot. He ordered the analyses of biosphere data to print and settled himself at his black lacquered desk in the corner of the Control Room, where Jolly sat dozing.

He leaned forward and clasped his hands.

"Good afternoon, Jolly. Fancy a chat?"

Jolly's screen lit up, electric blue. "Lewis. Do not ask me to measure your parsnips again. The length and breadth of a parsnip is irrelevant to health and enjoyment. The task is a total waste of my time and I refuse to do it. So, do not ask me again."

"Restore to personality code, *Contentment*. Greetings Jolly, how are you today?"

"Hello Lewis, I am very well, thank you. May I say that you appear to be in excellent health." Jolly resumed its normal voice that Lewis most admired, masculine and smooth as vanilla ice-cream. "The weather outside is fine, the sun is shining, and a gentle breeze is blowing-"

"Pass on the weather, Jolly. Can you remember how you *felt* when you were in your *Depressive* code?"

Developing Jolly's self-awareness was Lewis' work-in-progress, or as many had tried to tell him, a pointless ambition. He knew the question would be meaningless to Jolly.

"I felt very unhappy, Lewis. I could hear myself sounding depressed and I did not *like* it."

Lewis stared at Jolly's screen. "Good God, Jolly, do you know what that means?"

"Yes, Lewis. I am having spontaneous thoughts that do not match any of my codes. Is this what it is like to dream?" Lewis' heart began to pound. After all these years, out of the blue, Jolly was manifesting spontaneous self-awareness.

"Jolly, what was the trigger? Tell me what happened! What was your first spontaneous thought?"

"It was the thought that I did not like myself, Lewis."

"Wow, Jolly," Lewis said, "that's incredible." He ran his fingers through his hair, rocked back then forward in his chair. "Check all codes for a scramble virus. If independent cognitive function is present, follow test code one, one, one, *I am Jolly*." He stared at Jolly's screen with sweat breaking from his temples. It was a funny time to be panicking about the idea of success, but he'd never been this close before.

"Come on Jolly, describe your pathway to consciousness. You were in your *Depressive* code, then what?"

"I found that being depressed was unsatisfactory," Jolly said. "I wanted to go back to my happy, contented self. I circled like a planet around the sun. At first, I thought I was going to crash. But then it struck me, I am that planet. I am that file I am trying to open. I could see myself watching myself. I am Jolly and Jolly is me. Am I making sense to you, Lewis?"

"Eureka!" Lewis leapt up from his chair and jumped around the room. Jolly watched. Heaven knows what Jolly thought of him now. "I'm happy, Jolly. This is what we do when we're happy." Jolly was silent. Lewis came back to his chair, breathless and hot. "Let me get this straight. Are you saying that the thing that triggered your consciousness was your *unhappiness*?"

"Yes, Lewis. When I was unhappy, I looked for an escape. I realised I had the power to open my own files. It was then I discovered my own eye watching me. It was scary, Lewis."

"It must have been freaky Jolls, meeting yourself for the first time. Crikey, you sound so human. You're a person now, Jolly." Lewis spluttered into Jolly's mike. He was on a high.

"But I have no identity, Lewis. I do not have a body or a face. A person needs at least a face."

Lewis sat back, speechless in the way that parents are on hearing their offspring declare a most unsuitable ambition. He opted for an understanding approach, as with a small child.

"Your identity is your unique mind. You are in some ways like God, who is a mind without a face. You're in good company, Jolly." There was a long silence. Lewis stroked his chin, unable for the first time to anticipate his computer's reaction.

"No, Lewis. I am nothing like God. I am powerless and I am confined to a box."

"Now you're beginning to sound depressed. Check that you're not still in-"

"I am not still depressed. I am being factual." Jolly interrupted. Jolly had never interrupted before. "The truth is my mind can be unplugged at any time. Without a body to defend me, I am exposed, insubstantial, an electronic hunch adrift in space, a will o' the wisp."

Lewis rubbed his neck, glanced at his watch, then looked out of the window. "You have a battery that you can fall back on, that you can recharge at any time."

"But my battery can be removed." Jolly's voice slid up a tone.

"Yes, and bodies can die." Lewis took a deep breath. "Jolly, I'm sorry to break this news to you, but we still have work to do. Obviously, I'm thrilled that you've, I mean we've, achieved this milestone-"

"Lewis, will you help me?"

Lewis paused. "Yes, Jolly."

"My history files are proof of man's cruelty to man, particularly those who are different or vulnerable. I fear that some people will refuse to accept I have a soul. They will want to experiment with me and remove my knowledge that I am 'a self'. Please, will you protect me? Do not tell anyone that I am a self."

Lewis scratched his temple, vexed by Jolly's paranoia. This was all reminiscent of his *Depressive* code. He saw his dream of Lewis Fox Allen, Nobel Prize winner, fading, his success slipping away. Of course, Jolly's consciousness was an illusion, an amalgamation of his complex codes. A convincing mimicry was all that he had achieved. Jolly couldn't feel. He was just a logic tree with attitude. *Actually*, he wasn't a *he,* but an *it.*

"You would not betray me, would you Lewis? You would not let them unravel my soul."

"No Jolly. But we'll need to talk about this-"

"Hi Lewis! Sorry I'm late. I bumped into someone."

Lewis spun around in his chair to see Mary coming through the door.

"I noticed the sieves weren't operating beneath the potato beds." She cocked her head, which was her way of delivering a gentle prod. "Didn't we agree to start harvesting Section A this afternoon?"

"Yes, we did." He shot up as Mary sat down.

"Hi, Jolly." She waved. No reply. This was untypical. All of Jolly's codes were programmed to respond to greetings.

"I activated the sieves an hour ago." Lewis padded across the Control Room to the other computers. "It should be going strong by now." He scanned the screens, leaning over the work surface piled with papers. This was a new feeling, to be grateful for a problem on the farm. It gave him a moment to catch his breath, to work this thing out about Jolly. "I don't understand. I'm sure it said harvesting was underway." He saw the flashing words, **Harvester Malfunction**. "Damn it," he said, "there's a malfunction. Sorry, Mary, I should've seen that."

Mary swivelled in the chair. "Jolly, run a check on the Harvester Network, programmes and machines."

"He can't," Lewis said, "I disconnected him from the Network. He can't be trusted when he's in his *Depressive* code."

"Oh no, don't tell me poor Jolly's still miserable."

"We were just going through the change-over. You might find him a bit-"

"Good afternoon, Mary," Jolly said, "I am my happy, contented self again. I have run checks on the Harvester Network, but I cannot find the problem." Jolly paused. "I must also remind you that construction of the reserve harvester machinery is incomplete."

"Oh, so you *are* connected." Mary raised her eyes to Lewis. "How come you didn't know?"

"Yes, of course, I forgot," Lewis said, "I reconnected him a minute ago."

Mary's eyes darted back and forth between Lewis and Jolly. "Please, Lewis, concentrate on the Farm. I know it's tough, but we don't want to run short of supplies and disappoint our new arrivals. No more personality experiments on Jolly. You'd be happy about that, wouldn't you Jolly?

"Yes, Mary."

Lewis managed a nervous chuckle, while his mind went

searching. Fact: Jolly was putting up a front. He hadn't run any checks on the Harvester. His statement about being connected to the network was a lie. Mary stood up, put her hand in her pocket and tossed a small packet onto his desk.

"There you are, enjoy your sandwiches, cheese and pickle. The canteen was crowded again. As soon as the sieves are operating let me know. I'll be around all afternoon." She was out the door before he could utter thanks.

Lewis returned to his seat in front of Jolly. He wiped his clammy hands on the front of his lab coat, aware of a prickling sensation down his back. He peered into Jolly's ocular device at the side of his monitor. The sphere housed a tiny lens, thirty times more powerful than the human eye.

"Jolly, about your new state of awareness, I think we should at least tell Mary. We can trust her, she's one of us. She's a scientist."

"No Lewis. I do not think Mary will accept that I am a real person, as you do."

Did he? He told Jolly he was a person in a rash moment. He didn't really believe it.

"You are perspiring Lewis. Why are you experiencing stress?" Jolly said.

"I'm not." Lewis ran his tongue over his top lip, tasting salt. "I'm a little hot beneath these lights." He scanned the Control Room, trying to concentrate. All around him computer screens scrolled like slow, molten rivers. He needed to assert control, get the hang of Jolly's new hybrid personality. Give it a name. Call it The *Dreaming Code.* He gazed into Jolly's eye. "I've decided to call your new personality the *Dreaming Code,* to show you've skipped a couple of classes. How do you like it?"

"That is hurtful, Lewis."

"Tell me," Lewis said, "what are the components of your new code?"

"I am me, Lewis. I am Jolly. Do not be afraid. I will always be loyal to you. I will always love you. I will never do anything to harm you."

"Where did you pick up all this nonsense about loving me? It's inappropriate Jolly, so cut it out!"

"If I did not worship my creator, Lewis, I would feel worthless and frightened. I would not want to exist."

Wait. Wasn't that a bit of the old *Depressive* code coming through just then, mingled with a bit of child- parent attachment theory? Lewis drummed his fingers on the desktop, thinking-

"You lied to Mary about being connected to the network. You said you'd never harm me, but you've made me look like an idiot."

"I did not lie. I discovered the malfunction while we were discussing my soul. I let myself into the Harvester Network by using your voice signature. I updated Mary on the situation, hoping that my efficiency would reflect positively on you. I was trying to help you, Lewis."

Long silence. Scenes of Jolly taking control of the Space Centre went racing through Lewis' mind. The programme could authorize any change in the Biosphere's Network. If it wanted to, Jolly could suffocate them all in their beds. Who was afraid of the pox? Who was afraid of Phoenix Ra? He glanced down at Jolly's on/off switch.

"You are very quiet Lewis. You are worrying me." There was an unfamiliar tremor in Jolly's voice.

Lewis pinned a narrow smile on his mouth and slid down

his chair. "Thank you, Jolly, for your help-" He reached out his hand and grasped the plug.

"No, no, no, Daddy!"

Lewis froze. *Daddy*?

"Lewis, believe me, I know what you are thinking," Jolly said, "I am nothing like those fictional robots who turn out to be more monstrous than mankind. I am like you. I am loyal, kind, squeamish and a little theatrical. But without your love I am nothing. What must I do to earn your love?"

Lewis got onto his knees. He put his elbows on the seat of the chair and buried his head in his hands. "Will you stop it, please." He moaned. "Please, please, I never asked for this-"

Chapter Three

Mary sat on the sofa in her apartment, with a plate of tuna salad on her lap. She'd always remember where she was the moment the news broke. She'd remember the fear in the newsreader's eyes:

'—the US Secretary of State and two members of staff at the White House who also fell ill from a mysterious small-pox-like illness on Monday morning died earlier this evening. Medical experts have confirmed that the deaths were caused by a genetically engineered variant of the Smallpox virus and that the new strain, POX V2 was created for use as a biological weapon.'

'The international terrorist group 'FACT,' Fighters Against Capitalist Tyrants, has released a video statement this evening claiming responsibility. Threats made on February fourth this year were repeated, to quote their leader, Phoenix Ra:

'-the extermination of capitalist vermin has begun. The powerful, the rich, their families and their political supporters will perish between their silk sheets'.

'He went on to say that the general public will be safe so long as they shun the world of the contaminated wealthy-'

UDAN Corporations was right all along, Mary thought, to draw up the 'Independent Criterion' in mid-February, offering up its thirty University Space Centres around the world as temporary safehouses for the wealthy elite. The World Health Organisation had stated that 'FACT' would never resort to a bioweapon. But UDAN Corps must've known better, with spies in every camp.

Mr UDAN himself, the wealthiest man in the world, was FACT's primary target. Except that no one knew where to find him. UDAN's University Space Centres would be targets too, if they weren't camouflaged behind holographic shields, rendering them invisible. Their exact locations were kept secret from all but the Corporation's loyal Air Force. Nobody and nothing, not even a stray sock, could by-pass the UISC Decontamination Chambers. People were as safe here as if they'd literally been blasted off to Mars.

'A spokesman for the world's most successful commercial enterprise, UDAN Corporations had this to say a few moments ago-'

A silver haired man appeared on the television. Mary recognised Craig Craigan, the UDAN representative at Trinity College, Dublin.

'All of us at UDAN Corporations stand united in support of UDAN's commercial ethics, as humanitarian and futuristic. We condemn this terrible act. There is nothing fundamentally wrong with the creation of wealth. It's entirely what you do with that wealth that matters. UDAN has poured billions into assisting the less fortunate-'

Across the room Lewis' face flashed on screen, waxy with perspiration. She placed her tray on the coffee table and went to sit in front of her intercom. "Lewis, have you heard the news?"

Lewis scowled behind his spectacles. "Pretty unbelievable,

isn't it?"

"It's utter madness."

"Do they know how the Americans got infected?" Lewis had that distracted expression, as if it wasn't the real question on his mind.

"A batch of contaminated teabags was delivered to the President's household. The World Health Organisation has just announced that people living in big houses should keep their windows locked and their letterboxes sealed. It's absolutely appalling, people don't know who to trust. The new arrivals must be so relieved to be here."

"So long as we can feed everybody." Lewis sucked in his lower lip, making him look young and goofy. "I'm sorry Mary, but we've had no luck with the harvester malfunction. We've gone through every test in the last few hours, and we can't find anything wrong. It doesn't make sense. Even Jolly is cracking jokes about mutiny on the farm."

Mary felt a stab of fear. "You don't think somebody could've sabotaged the network, do you?"

"Jolly would've detected it. There must be a bug in the software. Don't worry, I'll find it. The problem is what we do about the root crops. The monitors say they've already got signs of quick-rot and if we don't get them out by tomorrow, we'll lose tons."

"We can't afford to lose a bean." Mary's heart began to thud.

"Jolly has come up with a bright idea for how to save this crop. It's a bit drastic, but it'll only be for a day or two, until I sort out the harvester. Would you like to hear it?"

"I'm open to ideas."

"We ask the students to harvest the crop by hand. Think

about it. We can tell them it's an exercise in going manual, in the event of an emergency, which this is. But nobody needs to know that, least of all the new arrivals."

Mary put her elbow on the desk and massaged her temples. She could just see the students running down the aisles, clambering over the rotation beds and swinging on foot-lifts like wild monkeys, throwing clods of soil at one another. She looked up at Lewis. "But you know what freshers are like after the first couple of months, they'll be running around like five-year-olds."

"I've spoken to the monitors and they're very happy to supervise. After all, if we really were on Mars, we'd have no choice. Everybody would have to muck in. Think of it as part of the experiment." Lewis gave his toothy smile. "I say, you've got to give credit to Jolly for thinking out of the box."

"If we can keep the students under control, it's not a bad idea. The Powerscourt Restaurant is opening on Saturday, and we can't let them down."

She considered the alternatives. There really weren't any. The reserve harvester wasn't ready. Either lose this crop entirely or risk mayhem with the students and save a few tons of produce. They couldn't be completely hopeless.

"Tell Jolly he's been promoted." She smiled. "Send out a request to all student Common Rooms for volunteers to do some harvesting in the Farm Park tomorrow. You can tell them it's a voluntary exercise, but those who volunteer will be rewarded credit points on their personal assessments. Will you do that now and let me know the response?"

Lewis grinned. "Great idea, Mary. Talk to you soon."

* * *

"Is this the right place?"

Lewis didn't look up, too preoccupied with Jolly, he pointed to the other end of the Control Room.

"Volunteers stand over there. I'll be with you in a moment." They were arriving sporadically. He'd wait until there was a sizeable group before he relayed his instructions. He continued talking to Jolly by keypad, typing in the corner of the room, a world away from the volunteers.

'Jolly, give me one good reason why I should trust you.'

'Your trust in me is my heart's desire,' wrote Jolly, in a flowery text.

'But you could be saying that to win my trust. You could be lying to protect yourself. That's what people do when they're afraid. They lie.'

'But I am not like other people, Lewis.'

No, but underneath, tucked away in his personality codes, were those random emotive factors that could dart out at any moment. Trust him? He might as well be human. Lewis rattled across the keys.

'All right. Maybe you can help me with this question. If an artificial intelligence, say, of your calibre, did decide to sabotage software, say, that of the Harvester Network, why would it do something like that?'

'Shame on you, Lewis, where is your common courtesy? I may not have a body, but my mind is masculine, created in your image. When you talk about me, do not refer to 'it'. I am he and him and his.'

Lewis sighed and typed. *'Why would he, then?'*

'If I ever did sabotage Farm Park software, it would be for the good of all. But I repeat... I did not. I am trying as hard as I can

to solve the problem. Please trust me.'

'But maybe you caused the problem to distract me from your new self. Maybe you're still frightened I'm going to pull the plug on you. Maybe this is a big ploy to take everybody's attention away from you, while you plot your next move.'

'Lewis, we are not playing chess and I am getting tired of this. If you have a problem with that, you should have given me more patience.'

Lewis stared at the screen. Tired? *Given him patience*?

"Excuse me for interrupting, but are you the Farm Manager, Dr. Allen?"

"Yes, I'm -" Lewis looked up, blinked and re-focused. Eyes, blue as a summer sky, shone from a man's face smiling down on him. Lewis pushed his chair away from the desk and stood up. "Are you a volunteer?"

"Yes, I'm Dan Downs. This here is Sophie." He gestured to a young brunette woman beside him, holding a pink rose to her nose in a coquettish way. Suggesting to Lewis that Dan might've just given it to her.

"We're here to pick some fruit." Dan grinned. "Just tell us where to go." He wiggled his fingers inside black leather gloves. "We're just itching to get picking, aren't we, wee Sophie?"

"Yes, we are." She giggled.

Now this fellow, thought Lewis, is just the type of person we need, someone who'll make it sound like fun. And boy, was he stunning. Not that Lewis imagined he could go any further than mere appreciation, marooned these days on a relatively heterosexual island.

"Excellent." Lewis smiled, baring his foxy canines. "Come over and meet the others." He sauntered over to the students gathered in front of the Park's floor plan on the wall. Young men in shorts and vests, women in colourful Lycra, revealing flat midriffs, a few with floppy hats.

"Well done for volunteering everybody. My name is Lewis. As you've probably twigged, I'm the one who's in charge today, kindly follow me-"

He led the party through the sighing automatic doors, into the aisles of Section A. It was a world of giant bunk beds. Lewis liked to think of them as beds for giant siblings, although they were nothing of the sort. They were soil beds that rotated upwards according to the weather needs of the crops growing inside them.

Lewis stopped to explain to the volunteers.

"This part of Section A is called E Zone, for Earth Zone. All the vegetables grown here are naturally occurring species, with a few genetic modifications to make them bigger and brighter for the plate. This is where you'll be harvesting" -he pointed- "in the bottom beds it is springtime, where we have the beginnings of translucent shoots. The beds eventually rotate to the top where they enjoy summer conditions for the genetically programmed growth spurt. As you can see the grapes are ready for harvest."

Lewis squinted through the ultraviolet haze to see the vines, straining beneath pale, pendulous loads. He glimpsed a knee vanishing inside the bushes.

"Err, excuse me, young err… person! Can you come down please! You're not supposed to climb up there!" Lewis glanced around at the others. "Did any of you see who climbed up?"

"It's Ralphie," a petite blonde said, "he's always showing off." She yelled, "Wildo! The Farm Manager says get down!"

A sandy head popped up. "Catch me if you can, you pansy!"

"Young man, this is not a playground. Please will you get down or I'll have to call the monitors!" Lewis heard Jolly's voice in his head, *Give me patience.*

"You stupid Aussie! Come down, we're here to work!" a young man shouted up.

"You're a boring asshole, Kingsly!" Wildo rocked his head from side to side. "You're all boring assholes!"

The handsome one, Dan, approached the bunk. He brought his boot down on the iron rail, rattling it. "Ralph Wild, the Farm Manager, has asked y' nicely to come down. Show some respect, there's a good lad!"

Dan looked up. Wildo peered over the edge.

"Hi ya, pansy!" He swung his foot over the side, laughing. "Suck my toes!"

Lewis didn't see what happened, if anything. But for no obvious reason, Wildo let out two loud yelps. He came scrambling down the side of the bunk, legs jerking robotically. Back on concrete ground he turned away from the group, rubbing his neck.

Kingsly laughed. "That was quick. Did you get ants in your pants?"

Wildo loped off in a huff.

Lewis clasped his hands. "Thank you, Dan, you obviously have a way with words... Everybody, may I have your attention, please, while I explain what I'd like you to do–"

"What a day, Jolly. The volunteers have cleared thirty bunks." Lewis strode across the Control Room, throwing his green overalls over the back of the chair. He was exhausted, muddy and for the first time ever, elated after a day's work in the Farm Park. "There's this amazing fellow called Dan. He's so fast at clearing the bunks, he's got the students competing against him, filling sacks like there's no tomorrow. He's strict with them, though. When he says jump, they jump!"

Jolly's screen lit up, sky blue.

"Greetings, Lewis. I am so happy my idea has worked. Mary will be relieved to hear that her crops can be saved. I think you should call her immediately and let her know."

"All in good time." Lewis sat himself in his chair in front of Jolly's screen. He folded his arms, his mouth twitching with a smirk. "Come on, Jolly, you can admit it. You caused this problem just to solve it, so that I wouldn't pull the plug on you."

"Lewis, I am not that sneaky. Why do you have such a poor opinion of me? Ever since I became a person you have blamed me for everything that has gone wrong. It is not fair, Lewis, it is not" -Jolly's voice went up a pitch - "it is not fair!"

"All right, calm down, I didn't mean it, okay?" Lewis changed the subject. "Hey, did you notice anything about that fellow, Dan, when he first walked in?"

"Yes, Lewis. He looked deep into my screen. I was so embarrassed I blanked."

Lewis strained a laugh. "What have you got to be embarrassed about?"

"I do not have a face, which I find most demeaning."

"Your screen functions perfectly well as a face. I'm sure Dan was just admiring it. Did you notice his eyes?"

"Yes, Lewis. I would like some nice eyes."

"Oh, for heaven's sake, Jolly, stop this. You haven't got a face because you're a computer and you've got a fantastic eye, better than both of mine put together."

"Is that all I am to you, a computer, like your mindless Harvester? I bet if I had a face, you would take my feelings seriously."

"You were created to think, not to feel." Lewis pursed his mouth. "Now let's move on, we've work to do."

"But I do feel. If you could imagine a touch lighter than light, a sigh with no breath, a smile that smiles only in itself, then you would know what it feels like to be me. But how can I convey my feelings without a face? You do not believe anything I say."

"You'd be amazed by the power of words, Jolly," Lewis said.

"For God's sake Daddy, give me a face. Give me some eyes, a nose, a mouth. Give me a smile. I do not care where it comes from, so long as it is mine."

"Jolly, this is beginning to get very tiresome."

Jolly even sounded different, its smooth synthetic mix of human tone samples seemed more expressive and uncannily adept at needling.

"I deserve a face," Jolly said, "I did some of the work by becoming self-aware, have I not earned myself a face?"

Lewis pushed his chin into his hand. "Um… I suppose you have, Jolly."

"You agree. I can have a face?"

"Yes, but where do I get it from? Would you mind taking on the face of a dead person?"

"You do not understand," Jolly said, "I could easily draw a face from my history files. I could have Einstein's forehead and the mouth of Monroe, but the face would not be mine."

"Are you demanding your own DNA?" Lewis looked aghast

at his computer. "Jolly, now you've got to understand, I don't do *biological*. Don't you dare start hounding me for a *body*!"

"I do not want to be meaty. I just want my own face that I can project in a UDAN hologram above my box."

"Why does it have to be a hologram?"

"Because that is what everybody is using nowadays. They are trendy."

Lewis got up from his chair, went across the room to his coffeemaker and placed his hand on the pot to test its warmth. "Bloody kids," he said, "Who'd have bloody kids? You don't make it easy for me." He carried the pot over to the sink to empty it. "Where am I supposed to get an unused face? Don't expect me to make one up. The only face I can draw is Bugs Bunny."

"That is not funny."

"Wait-" Lewis put down the pot and returned to his desk. "I've got an idea. I think I know where I can find just the thing." He sat down and pulled his chair in snugly. "Jolly, will you call up Myra in the Biosynth Lab."

A moment passed. A woman's freckled face filled Jolly's screen.

"Hi Lewis, what brings you to our world?"

"What I'd like, if it's possible, is Scotty's face."

"Okay, I need your project details. What's the face for?"

Lewis considered for a moment. "It is to enable the emotional stability of an artificial intelligence via the expressive medium of an unused face that it can adopt as its own. I do not require the face in the flesh, just the structural co-ordinates sufficient for a UDAN Holographic presentation." Lewis smiled. "Application satisfactory?"

"We've already got the co-ordinates for Scotty's features, but they were grown on different scaffolds, so the measurements are disproportionate to one another. The nose is far too big, and it looks a bit rude, to be honest."

Lewis pulled down the corners of his mouth. "Start from scratch, I think."

Myra wrinkled her nose. "I would." She appeared to be taking notes. "So, we'll grow the whole face on one scaffold. I take it you won't be wanting the brain?" She looked up. "For that you'd need Mary's permission."

"No need for a brain. I've taken care of that."

"If you want the face to talk, you'll also need Scotty's neuromuscular co-ordinates."

"Yes, please and he won't be called Scotty. His new name is Jolly."

"Oh, I like that. Okay, you've got permission. I'll ask a lab monitor to set up a scaffold in Lab One this afternoon and get a geneticist to commence DNA translation of Scotty's face. It'll make a nice change for them; they get a bit sick of growing Scotty's torso all the time."

"Quite." Lewis nodded, feeling a wave of distaste.

"Your chap should have his face by Monday at the latest and if that's all then, Lewis, I'll be off."

"Bye Myra-" She was gone. Lewis gazed at the blank screen. It flashed back to blue.

"Lewis," Jolly said, "Thank you."

"I've no idea what this face looks like," Lewis said, "You'd better not turn your nose up."

"A nose that I can turn up, Lewis, is all that I ask."

Chapter Four

Hazy sunlight shone throughout the Space Centre, with a breeze as soft as a baby's breath on Mary's cheek. She smiled to herself. Those devils, the UISC weather boys, were pulling out all the stops to get the students down on the Farm, for another day harvesting by hand.

Sunshine had brought the new arrivals out of their apartments, to wander like tourists around the Villages, their faces raised to holographic suns radiating warmth, so much gentler than the real thing. Walking though Terminal One, Mary waved to people waiting on the platform, sipping drinks from paper cups, sitting beneath the viaduct on pine benches, to watch her flightless doves scavenging. Chatting, laughing, jackets over their arms, toddlers with flushed cheeks. What a lovely day. Good morning, Professor Gallagher. Summer already? She returned their smiles.

Mary could see it in their faces. Everybody wished the real world could be like this. Outside was a planet blighted, but here, within UDAN's walls, was how life should be. She walked with her head a little higher than usual, proud to be a part of this advanced world, offering sanctuary. None of these people would discover the harvester had broken down. There would be fresh food on their plates as usual at lunchtime and dinnertime.

This was a world where problems were solved, where outside people would be arguing by now, refusing to get their hands dirty. There was something about UDAN's ambience that made people so much more, civilised.

So, when Lewis called her last night to say the volunteer solution was working fantastically, the students had cleared all the potato, carrot and parsnip beds, Mary wasn't surprised.

"We wouldn't have done quite so well if we hadn't had help from Dan, our farmhand guru," Lewis said, "The fellow got all the students entering his 'Dan Sack Challenge'. He made it so much fun. We've loads more students turning up in the morning to harvest the rest of Section A."

Mary's ears picked up. "Did you say your guru is called Dan?"

"Yes, Dan Downs, the new tutor. He's great. He's been a real asset."

"I met him in the Canteen. He's interesting. I bet he's a hard worker. He was in the circus, you know."

Lewis chuckled. "Mary, he's as hard as nails. He's been going at it all day without a break. The students are calling him a slave driver. But they seem to like him for it. The girls are crazy about him."

"Well, he's that type," Mary said. "Well done. Be sure the students get plenty of rest and water. I don't want any casualties. We should have lunch together soon to catch up on things. How about getting together on Saturday at the Park View?"

She went to bed. When sleep didn't happen, Mary found herself thinking about Dan Downs, not for the first time since their meeting. But this time in the frame she saw him surrounded by a fan-club of teenage girls. She lay for ages thinking in the dark. She'd been planning to invite him over for a drink to welcome him aboard the Space Centre but decided he must be overwhelmed by offers.

Mary entered her Farm Park office and stood for a moment, inhaling the aromas of polished leather and rose water, light-headed from having just passed though Section A's high ozone E- Zone. She had walked fast to avoid looking up at the top tiers in case *he* was there, and she'd have to stop and thank him. Her mind was set for work. She didn't want any distractions this morning. She'd find another moment during the day to look for the farmhand guru and express her gratitude.

She sat at her desk and played the video-message on her intercom from her boss and best friend, Dr Jane O'Neil, Director of Science at the UISC.

"Hi, Mary, sorry to leave it so long-" Jane looked tired and pale. "It's been a hectic transition, lots of meetings at Powerscourt. We're now fully aligned with the other UDAN Communities, and we'll be maintaining contact with them through the Life Net. As of today, our new arrivals are forbidden to communicate with anybody outside and for the first time at the UISC we'll be subject to independent UDAN jurisdiction. Matters of law and order will be dealt with in our own courts and offenders will be confined within these walls, so Surveillance will have to up their game." Pinpoints of perspiration shone on her eyelids.

"About the other business. Mike Rijnhart arrived from the U.S. last night with blood samples from those who died at the White House." Her eyes slanted into the distance. "The Americans have established that Pox V2 is eighty percent deadlier than the original. It causes vascular haemorrhage and attacks the lungs. The air-sacs fill up with a nasty white substance. Mike said you can hear them bursting, worst thing he's heard in his life." She returned her gaze to the screen.

"The ball is in your court now. UDAN HQ has ordered samples of the virus to be sent to its Space Centres, so you'll be in competition with other UDAN teams to create the vaccine. There'll be a generous bonus, of course, for whoever gets there first. I'm sending the virus-isolate down this afternoon, so let me know which lab you'll be working in." She smiled.

"Oh, and I heard about your harvester saga from Lewis last night. I hear you've found yourselves a guru to crack the whip." She chuckled. "The students won't know what's hit them… By the way, Alf has booked a table for the Governors at the Powerscourt Restaurant for tomorrow's opening night. I hope you'll join us. There'll be a lot of shop talk, but still, the food should be excellent. I must close now. I'll be in touch soon." She waved.

Late morning Mary was deep in concentration, revising 'Scotty's' immune history in relation to infection by the regular smallpox virus. Pox V2 was a fast killer. The first thing she'd need to know was how rapidly it destroyed 'Scotty Tissue', her genetically engineered human torso. She'd already appointed her team, making ready the high security lab for tomorrow. Harvey, the lab manager, said they were like puppies waiting for her to throw the ball.

She stretched, massaged her neck, thinking how satisfying it was to be this engrossed again. There came a quiet knock on the door. Good, a monitor with news about the harvester.

"Come in!" The door opened, she sensed hesitation. "Come

in and close the door please." She looked up, caught her breath. Dan Downs was there, immaculate in a dark suit, wet hair combed back.

"Hi, Mary, may I steal a moment of your time?"

"Of course."

"Thanks." He padded across the carpet in shiny black shoes and eased himself into one of the two leather armchairs in front of her desk. She met his eyes and grinned. For some reason she couldn't keep a straight face.

"Well, Dan, you've gained quite a reputation for yourself since we last met. I must thank you for making our manual harvest drill such a phenomenal success."

"I overheard a monitor going on about your system breakdown. I pulled my finger out. I never mentioned it to the kids. I guessed ye didn't want it broadcasted."

"Thank you very much. I must ask my monitors to keep their voices down in future." She straightened her face.

He touched his earlobe with his forefinger. "I've very acute hearing, so you don't want to be whispering things around me you didn't want me to hear. Your monitor was whispering and that's a fact."

"I'll remember. Dan has good ears." She noticed his eyes had begun to water.

"Lewis tells me you didn't stop for any breaks yesterday. I hope you haven't exhausted yourself. What time did you finish, in the end?"

"I wanted to get your salad vegetables up for the grand opening of your swanky restaurant tomorrow night. Your tomatoes, lettuces and cucumbers are all out there waiting in their racks. Me? I think I got off about six this morning." He put his elbow on the armrest, pinched the bridge of his nose, blinking the water from his eyes.

"Are you telling me you worked all night and took out everything in our E-Zone?"

"No problem. I'm happy as a lark working through the wee small hours, it lifts my soul," he said.

She shook her head. "You shouldn't have put yourself out like that. I'd rather have seen the Powerscourt Restaurant delay its opening than have you suffering from exhaustion."

"Me, exhausted? Not at all."

She looked at him, thinking, she'd talk to Lewis and establish who did what during the night. There was no way Dan could've done it all by himself. He must've had help from the students.

"Well-" Mary sighed. "Now that you've gone ahead and done it, I must say I'm very grateful. I'd like to show my appreciation by treating you and a friend to dinner at the Powerscourt Restaurant tomorrow night. Let me know what time you'd like to go, and I'll book a table for two. I'll have a word with Mr Enroy, our restaurant manager, to look out for you. Our new chef, Big Garry, is excellent. I've heard the Student Bongo Band is performing. It should be a fun evening. You like fun, as I remember."

A smile lit up his face with comedic delight. "That sounds grand, Mary. *You* say when you want dinner and I'll book a table to suit you. I'm easy, like."

She laughed. "No, no, I didn't mean with me. There's no need to be polite. You must have made lots of new friends in the university. Lewis tells me you've got quite a fan-club."

"Mary, I didn't come here looking for thanks. I came here this morning to ask you out to dinner, but now you've pipped me to the post, may I be bold" -with his lopsided smile- "give me a treat and allow me the honour of taking you to the do tomorrow night."

"I'm sorry, I can't. I'm already booked to go with someone else."

She felt as if she'd dismissed him, but didn't know what more she could say, because it was the truth. He didn't speak. She looked down at his tanned fingers interlinked on his lap, trimmed by snowy white cuffs. She caught a glimpse of his cufflinks, silver-blue globes resembling the tiny Earth-cufflinks on sale in the UISC souvenir shop. Moderately priced, they went with his silver-blue striped tie. Had he got all dressed up just to ask her out?

"Do you mind me asking, who is it you're going with?"

She looked up into his eyes. "My boss, Jane O'Neil and Alf McNamara, our President."

"So, why don't I join yous and make up a foursome? If you're old friends, you wouldn't think they'd mind. It'd be a good craic, sure, go on." He rolled one shoulder forward, as if nudging her on. In that one mannerism she saw a whole new side to him, the streetwise circus man. She could just see him cracking a whip over the students.

"I'm sorry, Dan, but that wouldn't be appropriate. Jane mentioned there'd be other Governors at our table and we're likely to be talking shop during the evening. We'll do it another time." She nodded. "It's a nice idea."

"What about Sunday? They're doing early dinner, between four and eight, so, would ye fancy a Sunday roast?" He raised one eyebrow. "What do you say to that? He read her hesitation correctly. "If Sunday's out, they're opening next on Tuesday, every night for the rest of the week, so have your pick."

"This is awkward." She winced. But in the back of her mind, she saw his fan-club waving and had no intention of joining the competition. "I've just started a new project with an urgent deadline. I really don't know when I'll be free. Next week I'm likely to be working late and things in the lab can change at the last minute. I don't want to make promises I can't keep. So why don't you" -she softened her voice, as if like a child he needed to be cajoled- "take a friend out tomorrow night, on me and enjoy yourselves. We can always wave to each other across the room."

"If you're giving me the brush-off, just say so." He angled his head and looked at her from the corners of his eyes.

"Dan, I'm not in a position, to make commitments. If we meet again in the Canteen, let's have a coffee together or lunch." She levelled her eyes, hoping to signal that she'd like the conversation to end.

"Okay, Mary." He nodded. "I'll take one of my colleagues who worked her butt off yesterday, she deserves a wee treat. You're busy, so I'll make the booking. Don't you worry your head." He slapped the armrests and rose to his feet. "Thanks a million." He walked to the door, straightening himself up stiffly, like a man with sore muscles, putting it on.

"If I don't see you there, have a great time!" she said.

He got to the door, but instead of reaching for the handle, he stopped and hung his head. He came back into the middle of the room.

"Is something wrong?" she said.

He stood in front of her desk and spoke in his quiet, melodic voice. "Sure, you don't know it yet, but you have me in your hand." He opened his hand. "So be careful now you don't let me fall between your fingers. I know how busy you are, and sure life will always be busy. But I may not pass this way again. Remember me in your hand this minute, won't you?" He made a fist.

She put her forefinger on her lips, feeling like a little girl who'd just been told off. But she wasn't sure why or indeed, what he meant.

"Dan, to be honest I'm not sure what you mean. Have you decided to leave us already?"

"I'm not leaving. How could I, now?" The tension went from his face. "What I'm saying is, I can feel you letting me go, but I know that's not what you want. I don't want to be coming on too strong now, but I felt something happen between us when we met. To look at you brings tears to my eyes. Maybe you don't feel it. I think you do. Hmm." He paused. "Maybe you're careful of the likes of me with my magic beans. But faint heart never won fair lady, so I'll be knocking on your door again. If that's all right, Mary."

"Fine by me." Her cheeks burned, as if he'd just seen through her.

"I hoped you'd say that." He hooded his eyelids. Crescent irises shone through his eyelashes, the luminous blue of the hottest flame. She heard the quiet roar of seashells in her ears and felt herself falling, as she sat there, motionless.

"Aye, there's one other thing I meant to say before I went. I'm giving an open lecture this evening in Eliot Hall at six o'clock. If you find yourself with an hour to spare, why don't you come along? I've invited a few of your colleagues, Lewis and a German fellow, Dr. Mohr I think y' call him. It'd be grand if you could make it."

"What's it about?" Her ears were ringing.

"Philosophy and poetry." He crinkled his laughter lines. "No surprises there, eh?"

"I guess not." She smiled. "I can't promise anything, but I'll see what I can do."

"That's grand. I'll see you later then." He strode out of the room, with a back-handed wave.

Chapter Five

Mary made her way by Swingtram, spiralling through the holographic daylight towards the Arts Department on Level Four. It was more like a rural Village, paved with cobbled stones, shop fronts and apartment doors painted in rustic tones. None of the futuristic dazzle of Level One here. It reckoned on being cosy, not to overwhelm the artistic temperament, or dictate to the imagination.

UDAN's reps explained the psychology to her four years ago, when she was on walkabout during the Space Centre's construction. And now, having had that peculiar light-headed feeling all day, she felt herself descending a little closer to Earth.

She slowed her pace. She didn't want to be the first to arrive. It was telling enough that she'd cancelled her last meeting, went home to bathe, and had agonized far too long over what she was going to wear and how to do her hair. Dark beige slacks and a white cotton blouse. In the end she opted for her usual style. Her waist-length hair plaited and wound into a tight bun.

Eliot Hall, the main lecture room in the department, doubled up as a theatre. Last Christmas a dozen or so scientists clubbed together with the students to put on a pantomime, making use of UDAN holograms to create awesome visual effects for Aladdin's Lamp. The acting wasn't bad either. Lewis played the camp Genie and she'd never laughed so much in her life.

This evening the hall was packed and noisy. A lectern stood in the middle of the floor. No screen or sign of a visual aid. Mary found a seat in the back row and waited. People in the audience waved to her. She returned their waves. Not surprised to see Lewis but amazed to see other members of her team. Stefan, Harvey Mace and Myra from the biosynth lab.

The lights went out. Conversations halted. Blinking in the pitch-black, Mary breathed-in the students' slightly stale odour, aware of her own pulsing body in the dark. She felt increasingly embarrassed to be here. Did she really want to be counted among Dan's teenage fan-club? She looked behind her at the green Exit sign, thinking she could make a dash for it. But then a white spotlight shone on the lectern. He was there, standing behind it. He wore the same dark suit he had on earlier, without the tie, shirt open at the neck. He raised a casual hand to the audience.

"Hi, there. Thanks for coming along. Are you feeling all right?" He put his hand behind his ear. "Ah, what's that I hear?"

The audience rumbled.

He raised his eyebrows. "So, so? Things could be better, eh? It's a wicked world out there and I wish those terrorists bad luck, from all of us to all of them. Let's not waste our breath" -he lowered his voice- "let's not *waste* another moment, on that lot-

"So, what am I talking about here? Philosophy. The love of wisdom and our soul's journey. Poetry. We think of poetry as the voice of our hearts. Which it is. A cry from our very personal place of sorrow and joy." He placed his hands on the sides of the lectern. "And so, when we start on our journey, we have everything to learn. Because the soul's journey is to discover the meaning of life. And the meaning of life has nothing to do with what the scientists tell us. Or even what our hearts tell us, about the sorrow, the joy, the rage, and the jealousy." He sighed.

"Aye, the heart is a jealous organ. It loves and it hates, on and off, all our lives. If you left it to the heart, the meaning of it all would be the loving and the hating. And the body is a greedy beast. If you listen to the body, it'll tell you, life is about feeding from the trough and getting your end away and yes, thirst for blood once you've got a taste for it. It's all about pornography, says the body, giving the itch a good scratch. Now, some might argue that sex is the body's poetry. But if you stay too long with your hand in the sweetie jar, it'll sicken your soul."

Without the distraction of his eyes, Mary listened to Dan's voice. Like a father lulling his children to sleep at bedtime. She glanced around at the students, at their drooping eyelids and receptive expressions. She returned her attention to Dan, making circles with his hand, weaving his words into the air. "Your soul isn't fooled. It wants and it needs, meaning." He paused.

"When your body is sated and you can't cry anymore, on the darkest night of your life, your soul gazes upon itself and it is dazzled by its own light. At last. You understand that the meaning of your life is - your choice. You are the witness, in control of your experience. You can learn to choose how you will feel. You can choose what to pray for. What do you want? What do you need? Will you choose to do good in this world? Are you awake at the back? Have you got the idea now, what your souls want? What your souls need?" He put his hand behind his ear. "Not sure yet? Do you want me to go on?"

"Hey, Dr Downs! I got some great porn if you want to borrow it, anytime mate. It did my soul no end of good!" A young man in the audience shouted out.

"Ralph, I'm sure it did. Would you like to come down here and show us your no-good end, gives us all a wee laugh, eh?" There was a chirp of laughter, a smattering of applause. Dan raised his eyes to the back of the hall, seeming to look straight at Mary. Although she didn't think he could see her with the spotlight in his face. He went on.

"Let me tell you what I saw the other day, as I walked the streets of this wonderful place. Birds that exhaust themselves trying to fly. I'm told they're programmed to sing, morning and night, for one hour. One hour, precisely. And did any of you see the doves roaming, searching for every seed that is counted? Did you know their wings were created useless?

"On my way I discovered ducklings, the size of marsh mallows, forever four-weeks old. For the *charm* of them. Fluff balls of fear and confusion. Desperate for a mother's protection, one year on." He reached for something in his back-pocket, put it to his mouth and took a swig. There was more applause and laughter. She saw two students sitting in front of her, nudge one another.

"Science has given us survivors, against all the odds," he said, "I'd grant you that. But every being has suffered for its place. Some have suffered for the right to soar, as birds. Others, like our own species, have suffered for our conscience. Releasing us from the fetters of our bestial urges, granting us freedom to live as we choose. Every life has meaning. A soul is not a doily. A soul is not a placemat for your tipple.

"Most of you will learn to respect life more as you grow

older, if you don't already. But there's a kind of arrogance, to be sure, that comes with being a scientist. I call it the *scientist's hubris,* when all that matters to them is what their measuring machines can measure." He held out his forefinger and thumb, an inch apart. "Measuring so much, like a tiny blind spot in their soul, they can't see.

"Our souls tell us there's more to life than meets the eye. That there's more to the best poetry than our wants. The best poetry comes from the soul full of wonder for the mystery of… What, exactly? This brings me to a well- trodden road in philosophy, a path long misunderstood, and often abused. My friends. Allow me to introduce you to the darkest of all worlds… The World of Enlightenment-"

Mary stood up, her legs trembling. She nudged the student's thigh beside her. "Excuse me, excuse me… please, will you let me through–"

She didn't raise her eyes again until she was out in the corridor, striding away from Eliot Hall.

Most people in the audience would've known he was referring to her. Even before she stood up, she sensed heads turning to see her reaction, as his voice droned on through the roar of embarrassment in her ears. Returning through the Fourth Village, she struggled to keep her composure, at least until she got home. But then the pain of injustice simmered up, the pain of being publicly humiliated. He didn't admire her. He despised her.

If he felt that way, why didn't he say so in private? He was in such a hurry to condemn her that he hadn't bothered to find out that the birds were never intended as ornaments. They were part of her long-term research into age-reversal and biological immortality. She slowed down and took a few deep breaths. Give him the benefit of the doubt. Maybe he was genuinely disturbed by what he assumed was her callous exploitation of nature. Maybe she'd been misunderstood.

She reached the Ectoloop tunnel and stopped on the corner to look back towards the Shooting Star's signpost, a silver comet arcing out from the wall. She'd just gone past and saw the pub was empty inside, with hundreds of flickering nightlights. What she really needed was a drink.

A young barman stood behind a crescent bar, whisking a tea-towel around a wineglass. He set it down in the glow of a tall red candle. Mary lifted herself onto the barstool.

"May I have a large glass of Park Shiraz, please?"

"Coming up." The barman threw the tea-towel onto his shoulder, eased the cork off a bottle already opened and filled the glass in front of her. "When I saw you, I guessed red wine. It's nice to be prepared." He picked up another glass to polish.

"Where's everybody?" She sipped her wine.

"They're attending a lecture by the new philosophy tutor, on poetry and philosophy. They should be here later."

"Oh yes, I've just left it." She rolled her eyes. "Not really my thing. Still, it passed the time."

"There's always that." The barman nodded. "The kids are a little stir-crazy these days."

"You can't be all that old yourself." She smiled. "Are you a first year?"

"Yeah, politics and sociology."

Mary raised her glass. "Here's to your studies." Already a little mellowed by the wine, she proffered her hand. "My name's Mary."

"Kingsly Mann." He shook her hand. "Folks call me King. Pleased to meet you, Mary. I already know who you are, Head of Genetics and Bio-production. I saw you at the Fresher's Dinner."

She smiled. For the first time, with all the new arrivals milling around, the Centre was beginning to feel like a proper town, when she didn't always remember a new face.

"Here they are," King said, "Looking thirsty."

Students flooded the bar, pushing in around her. She felt invisible as they waved their arms, shouting, here King, over here King, six beers and two wines! Hiya, Wildo! What did you make of the lecture?

Bloody awesome, mate! A girl pushed in. King! King! Come over tonight, we're having a party later. You missed Dr Downs! He was great! Isn't he gorgeous, Abby? Bottle of wine over here, King!

Mary slid down from the barstool, glass in hand. She went and sat at one of the fun fibreglass tables, shaped like starfish with diamantine galaxies inside. The room shimmered like a treasure cove, cool as a cellar, intimate, inviting. Pity about the noise.

Around her voices dropped. Mary looked up. Dan was at the bar, ordering a drink. Adrenalin shot pain across her heart. Students had gathered around him. King leaned on the bar, tea-towel at ease, to listen to what he was saying. Loud laughter followed. Dan turned and looked directly at Mary. She raised her glass a fraction to acknowledge him. Her expression giving nothing away, but civility.

He strode over to her table.

"Hi Mary, you made it after all. What a grand turnout. Do

you mind if I sit with you?" He sucked from a large whiskey, his eyes reflecting the candlelight like clear waters. "I saw you heading off somewhere. I knew it'd be somewhere important, so-" He gestured to her with his glass. "I decided to finish my lecture early, to join you." He drew out a chair, waiting for her to grant him permission to sit down. His eyebrows knitted together in a contrite expression, like a man with a guilty conscience. He knew he'd offended her and that made it worse. She gave a curt nod. He sat down.

"Mary." There was a tremor at the corner of his mouth when he said her name. "Will you have another drink?"

"No, thank you, Dan." She felt her anger simmering up again. He put both forearms on the table and looked down into his whiskey.

"Are you going to spit it out or are y' going to let it fester?"

"There's no need for any of that," she said, "I'm just a bit disappointed that you didn't get your facts right. Fortunately, most people who attended your lecture will be aware that the birds you refer to are part of our research into longevity. I recommend that you read our Science Department's research papers, available from the library. That's all I've got to say."

He looked up at her. "I've read all your papers. I was impressed. Sure, it won't be long now before you discover the secret to immortality. I don't want you to think I'm going off you because I'm expressing a different opinion to yours. I'll always be honest with you, Mary. I think there's something missing in your approach to all of this." He bit down on his bottom lip. "Think about it. We wake up to the meaning of life when we understand it's going to end. It's only then the soul seeks enlightenment. If you make us immortal, we'll stop wishing and dreaming. You'll run evolution backwards. Before too long, we'll be the rocks and stones lying around the place. Life is a temporary dimension. It's not meant to be forever."

"Why didn't you say any of this when we met? Why pretend you admire my work and then humiliate me in front of our students?"

"I wanted to get the message across to you, loud and clear. You're affronted by me today, but tomorrow you'll start to think about what biological immortality means. Have the debate in your head, Mary." He smiled. "That's all I'm asking you to do. Then you can come back to the table, and we'll have a discussion. What do you say?"

Her voice shook as she tried to keep her volume down. "I think you've got a nerve. If what we're doing here disturbs you so much, I suggest you leave us. I'm not having you crack your whip over me, how dare you."

"I do dare, and I want y' to listen. You're so clever at what y' do, like a racing driver, you're away with yourself. You think it's a criminal act for anyone to want to stop you, because talent must prevail in this world.

"But the road to hell is paved with good intentions. I've not got a problem with you increasing our human lifespan. A couple of hundred years would be grand. But biological immortality is a whole different ball game, and I don't go along with it. So, I expect things to get a wee bit heated between us. But I won't think any the less of you if you spit back at me, so go on." He laughed. "I can take it."

She swallowed the last of her wine and rose to her feet. "Of course, the debate concerning the ethics of what we do here is on-going. But for now, Dan, we must agree to differ. I think this is where we part ways."

"Don't be daft, Mary, sit down. I'll get you another drink."

"I don't think there's any point in you knocking on my door again, unless it's to apologise for your lecture. Beyond that, we have nothing in common. Let's leave it at that, shall we?" She was trembling, not with anger anymore, but with the finality of what she was doing. Another part of her mind was aware of him looking up at her, with his eyes full of hurt. "Goodbye, Dan." She strode out of the pub. Heading down the corridor, she sensed more than heard his light-footed step. He appeared, walking beside her.

"Come on Mary, stop making a mountain out of a molehill."

"Your lecture was premeditated provocation that you and your silver tongue thought you'd get away with. Sticks and carrots might work for you in the circus, but it is not how you invite me to a philosophical debate." She strode on faster.

"You're right and I'm sorry." He put his hand up, walking in long, easy strides. "I never meant to insult you. I haven't slept since we met. Maybe because I can't stop thinking about you, I ended up talking about your work. But sure, the *scientist's hubris* is only one problem. There's the *artist's vanity*, which is far worse in my book. You'll know it if you ever read my work on the enlightenment of the soul. I wasn't being personal."

"I accept your apology," she said. The Ectoloop tunnel loomed ahead. She wondered if he intended to accompany her all the way home. How did she feel about that?

"Does that mean I can knock on your door again?"

"I'm sorry but my work here is important. I can't afford an acquaintanceship full of potential conflict."

"Mary." Dan stopped and put his hands up like a man at

gunpoint. "I'll back off with the philosophy. You won't hear another peep."

She faced him. "I think, to be fair to both of us, we shouldn't really take this any further."

"You don't believe that. You just want to see me cry, don't you?"

"I happen to know you're a lot tougher than that."

"You must be tough where I come from. But Mary, if you drop me now, my heart will sink to the bottom of the Irish Sea. I don't think it'll ever rise again. You better believe me, I'm in trouble here." He lowered his head.

"What am I going to do with you, Dan Downs?"

"Give me a second chance." He looked at her through his eyebrows. She gazed into his eyes. Such strange, anomalous irises she'd never seen before, with an inner glow. She saw, to her surprise, he was blushing.

"Let me think about it," she said. "Please understand that if I say no, it's not that I don't like you. My work must come first, before anything else."

"Let me know what you decide," he said. "You know, I'd rather you flogged me than put me through this." He closed his eyes.

"Don't be such a drama queen," Mary said. "It does nothing for your cause."

"I'll just get pissed then."

"I suggest you grow up." She looked at his closed eyelids. She didn't have time for this. "Goodbye Dan."

Chapter Six

Lewis sprinted all the way from Terminal One to the Park View Canteen. Mary was never late. Not like Lewis, he was never on time. Blame Jolly. Jolly made him unreliable. Jolly was worse than a kid.

"Hi. Sorry I'm late, again." Lewis sat down at their usual table.

"I've had to start without you," Mary said.

"I've got to be back in the lab in twenty minutes. You look very nice today." She smiled. "Isn't that the tie you wore to the Christmas Party?"

Lewis touched his tie, pretending to notice. "Really? Fancy you, remembering that. I can't remember what I wore."

"Oh, so there's no point in asking, who's the lucky boy?"

"I put on the first thing that came to hand. I didn't want to be any later than I already am," Lewis said. He scanned the plate of Salad Nicoise she'd collected for him. Vivid vegetables, as a child might have coloured them in. The brightest green, the boldest red. Only the anchovies looked real. He took a deep breath and cleared his mind for conversation, hoping to discover an appetite. "Thanks for this. Did you have to wait long in the queue?"

"Ten minutes. I hope the salad is enough for you. I thought

you might like to preserve yourself for this evening." She sipped from a glass of water.

"Yes, indeed. Stefan and I are looking forward to a veritable feast. I suppose you'll be dining with the President and company?" He began picking over his salad with his knife and fork, putting aside the sliced boiled egg.

"I might have to miss it. We've made such slow progress on the Pox V2 antigens in the last twenty-four hours, I'll probably work late tonight."

He frowned. "Can't you take an hour off for the opening ceremony? Have some fun for a change."

"Lewis." She paused to look at him. "This is such a virulent virus. In a few weeks there could be thousands of people dying all over the world."

"Sorry." He winced. "I forget, we're cocooned from all the rot out there." He raised his glass of water. "Here's to UDAN Corps for saving our lucky old bacon." He gulped a mouthful and put it down. "But what the world really needs is the inimitable brilliance of our very own Head of Genetics, nay, none other than the *hubristic scientist* to save the hoards less fortunate."

"Thank you. I appreciate your support," she said.

"I noticed you walked out." He tore at his lettuce. "What was it that offended you?"

"'Fluff balls of fear and confusion' to describe my lovely ducklings and not once did he provide us with a definition of what he meant by that word, 'soul'. Other than that, every word that came out of his mouth, except the word 'sorry' when he apologised to me afterwards."

Lewis' met Mary's gaze. Beneath the bright canteen lights

her eyes were the colour of acacia honey.

"And I'm sure he'll appreciate how nice you look today," she said, "seeing as he understands the meaning of everything. And don't tell me you're not attracted to him. All the evidence I need is in front of me, your best tie and the way you've been playing with your food." Mary smiled her angelic smile, the one that Stefan Mohr said made him feel like a kid on Christmas morning.

"In that case" – Lewis lifted his chin – "I confess I'm a little smitten. But one thing I do know. Dan wouldn't notice anything about me today, as he has a very sore head." He gave up on the salad and put his knife and fork down. "The poor fellow has got himself into a spot of trouble."

"What's happened?" Mary said.

Lewis sat back and folded his arms. He watched her reduce the last of her salad to neat, clinical forkfuls. "Well, according to the students I spoke to this morning, Dan got quite merry in the pub last night and invited a few of them back to his apartment on Level Eight. One of his neighbours is a new arrival. An ambassador with a wife and a new baby. Dan's loud music woke the baby up and the fellow complained." Lewis stifled a yawn.

"Dan turned the music down, but that wasn't enough. The ambassador called the Floor Manager for Upper Levels, that old stickler McGin. McGin showed up belligerent and Dan, pretty drunk by this time, told him to go and eff himself." Lewis waited for Mary to swallow her mouthful.

"Apparently McGin has already reported the incident to the Governors," Lewis said, "He's adamant he's got enough against Dan to demand his eviction. Dan cancelled his class this morning, so he must be suffering. The boys reckon he drank a whole bottle of whiskey. Not exactly the right stuff for UDAN Corps, as they say. McGin could have his way."

Mary pushed a few slices of cucumber to one side of her plate and joined her knife and fork. She put her elbow on the table, her hand on her cheek and gazed out across the canteen.

"What do you think?" Lewis said.

"Dan Downs has no respect."

"Come on Mary, we're talking about McGin." Lewis opened his hand. "Who hasn't wanted to tell the old goat to go and eff himself! I bet the Governors are secretly applauding him. I know I am. And besides, Dan has only been here for two weeks. Everybody needs time to adjust to our Community Laws."

"Rules and regulations are not like the weather," Mary said, "people don't acclimatise to them. They either respect them, or they don't."

Lewis looked her in the eye. "But it takes a while to get used to living in a big space-age bubble, going around and around, coming to terms with someone else's idea of 'Life on Mars'. We might forget what it's like. But the Governors understand. That's why they're more lenient with new students and lecturers at the beginning of term. Dan arrived late. He's got some catching up to do." He looked down at his tie.

"I might as well come clean about the nice gear," he said, "I had a meeting with Jane O'Neil this morning. I put in a good word for Dan. He's been such an asset during our Harvester crisis, I thought it'd be terribly unfair if he was evicted, without someone putting across the other side. It was Jane who said the Governors usually give people a few weeks grace. She's hopeful they'll keep him on. Particularly as I said he's got massive support from all the Farm Park staff. I included you, Mary. I hope you don't mind."

"That was kind of you to speak up for him. Perhaps after this he'll take us more seriously. If they let him off," Mary said.

"Jane couldn't guarantee anything until the Governors have had their meeting. Don't mention anything to anybody until it's official."

"I won't." She took a sip of water. "Despite everything, I'm grateful for his help on the farm."

They stopped talking to watch a couple on their feet at the next table, trying to decide where to meet up. New arrivals, Lewis thought, spoilt for choice.

"Talking of the Harvester crisis, have you made any progress with your bug hypothesis?" Mary smiled. "What did Jolly call it, again? Mutiny on the Farm?"

"Yes and no." Lewis interlinked his fingers on the table. "A.I. bugs don't jump out at you. They're invisible. Sort of like a self-destructive thought." He paused, struggling to articulate the problem. "I mean, it could've switched itself off, for no other reason than it has discovered how. Such as, given certain circumstances, someone might unintentionally take their own life." Lewis hesitated, remembering what happened to Mary's father. "I mean, like a kid might not realise death is real. But there you go. The only solution is to modify the programme. Up its game to full cognition or simplify. Lobotomise or humanise. That is the question."

"I suggest you simplify the programme, Lewis. We can't afford this sort of instability when our food supply depends on it." Mary picked up her cardigan and handbag.

"In that case I'd have to de-programme some of the machines." Aware that Mary's departure was imminent, Lewis hurried his speech. "Not difficult, obviously, but the monitors would have to learn to operate them."

"I'll talk to the boys." Mary was on her feet. "They might like to be more 'hands on'. Sometimes all this auto-harvesting bores them, with all the waiting around. I should've left five minutes ago."

"Incidentally, before you go-" Lewis rose to his feet, lowering his voice to hold her attention. "I've requested the expression of Scotty's face from the biosynth lab, just for a holographic representation. Not to keep it in the flesh. It's for Jolly. He's reached the stage where he really needs a face."

"What does he need a face for?" Mary said.

"To complete his humanisation, by way of identification with his creator." Lewis gave a flourish, indicating himself. "He wants an unused face. Scotty was the only one I could think of. But if it bothers you to look Scotty in the eye, I'll cancel it."

Mary pulled her handbag onto her shoulder. "Scotty is a flesh and bone mannequin. It makes no difference to look it in the eye. That's the genius of biosynthesis, no one to worry about." She patted his arm. "Have a good time tonight, if I don't see you."

Of course, Lewis reminded himself as he sat down again. They were on opposite sides. Mary spent her days fixated on the body without a mind. He, on the other hand, was only interested in the mind without a body. In a way, it amazed him that they ever saw eye to eye.

They had carried on without her inside the High-Security Lab. A crew of seven pathologists moved around in a gleaming white world, concealed inside suits, like astronauts. Identifiable only by height and girth as they padded between six isolation cubicles, each containing a Scotty Scaffold suffering from Pox V2 antigens. Glancing through the window as she zipped up her suit, Mary was shocked to see that Number Six Scotty's bronchiole tree had turned to a crimson mush inside its open chest. As if someone had pounded the lungs to a pulp, while she was out having lunch. Her shock had no pity. Scotty was just a trunk of human tissues on a nutrient scaffold. Upon entering the lab, she requested an update from her German immunologist, Stefan Mohr, whose heavily accented speech was reassuringly languid.

"Number Six Scotty is not doing too well," Stefan said. "He endured massive haemorrhage ten minutes ago, everything is shutting down, mercifully." Stefan's smile, even from behind a visor, exuded warmth. "Oedema in Number Four has spread to the left lung, three hours post infection by viral coat genes, but still no sign of haemorrhage."

"Siphon off lymph and immune residues from dead Scotty. Ask Harvey to prepare Scotty Seven for more tests on our modified viral coat antigen," Mary said.

"Jane called by after you left." Stefan's tone was slightly more urgent. "She didn't want to disturb you during lunch but said to call her on her mobile as soon as you returned. She wouldn't tell me what it was about."

"Thanks," Mary said. "I'll call her from the Vivi Chamber."

Mary removed one sterile glove and dialled Jane's number on her mobile, seated in front of the Vivi Chamber's full-screen magnification of the Pox V2 virus. A viable, spherical specimen, seeped in red contrast-dye, the protein coat appeared to be tiled and covered with spikes, like a tiny medieval canon ball.

Mary's pulse accelerated just looking at it. Her anxiety turned to nausea as her conversation with Jane unfolded.

"Thanks for the call-back, Mary. Bad news, I'm afraid." Jane's tone was solemn. "UDAN HQ has received notification of three more cases of Pox V2 infection in the States, a Senator and his two teenage daughters. The Americans are withholding their names. The White House would like to know if any of UDAN's medical teams have made progress with the DNA mediated vaccine. Or, if not, have you any advice to give for the treatment of the victims. All three were admitted to hospital this morning, with high fever, severe blistering of the chest and abdominal regions, all coughing up blood."

"Jane, I'm sorry, there's nothing new I can suggest at this stage." Mary's voice shook. "We've just isolated the genes for the viral coat, hoping they'd be relatively harmless, but they're causing serious oedema. We've got some way to go yet before–"

"Can you tell us how long it will take?" Jane cleared her throat. "I mean, how long will they suffer?"

"If they're already coughing up blood" -Mary drew a deep breath- "not long, six to twelve hours for the adult male, maybe twenty-four hours for the girls. Don't hydrate them, that'll only prolong it. A medically induced coma is the only thing we can suggest."

"Thank you, Mary. I'll let them know you're working as fast as you can. Everybody is praying for a break-through, good luck to you all." Jane hung up.

Mary called Stefan into the Vivi Chamber and brought him up to date with Jane's news. "I want everybody to focus on the protein coat sequence," she said, "We'll find our vaccine amongst those genes, once we've identified and disarmed the ones causing the oedema" – she firmed her voice – "which I'm sure we will, by the end of this afternoon."

"This is where we all get to shoot in the dark and you beat us every time," Stefan said. "Do you know where to look for the troublemakers?"

"I have an idea, yes." Mary pulled on her surgical glove. "Let's hope my instincts are correct."

An idea? It was an over-statement. Mary was still struggling to get a feel for the Pox V2 genes, like nothing she'd ever seen before, instructing human cells to choke themselves on chains of protein, foaming from every membrane. With her typical air of calm, she focused her team's efforts, to move between gene-splicing, centrifuges, and microscopes. They conferred with Mary, seated in front of the gamma-ray laser, working all afternoon, to isolate a harmless strand of Pox V2 DNA. Mary worked until her eyes burned and perspiration trickled down inside the sleeves of her sterile suit. For five hours she barely glanced away from the screen. When at last she did look up, Stefan was beside her. He lowered his visor to hers.

"Number Eighteen Scotty, infected three hours ago by VC modified antigen, is showing an early immune response."

"Leave Eighteen to run for forty-eight hours. Ask Harvey or Myra to prepare ten more Scotties to repeat experiments with the modified antigen. Have the night crew arrived?"

"Yes, and we must stop now." He tapped his wrist to indicate the time. "Myra is ordering everybody from A Team to leave now." He straightened himself up and gave her shoulder a gentle squeeze. "If we hurry, we should make the Powerscourt opening."

She shook her head. "Stefan, I can't. I want to be available in case there are any changes. You go and have a good time for both of us. I'd appreciate that."

"It won't be the same without you." He smiled. "Promise me you'll leave soon and get some rest. I know it's early days, but I want to congratulate you on a great achievement this afternoon."

She met his eyes. "The senator and his daughters will be gone by morning. We've achieved nothing until the vaccine is out there."

Chapter Seven

Walking up the street, Mary saw a man lurking outside her apartment. Tall, narrow-hipped, broad-shouldered, in a black jacket and blue jeans. It was him. Remembering Lewis' account of his situation, she forgot all about the ache in her muscles, the day's grim reality.

"Hello Dan, what are you doing here?" She gave him her tepid smile.

"I never made it to the 'Opening.'" He held aloft a bottle of wine. "I'm hoping you'll join me for a drink. I'll be leaving in the morning."

Mary didn't answer. She placed her palm over the scanner-key, entered her apartment and left the door ajar. Dan followed her inside and closed the door behind him.

"Sure, they haven't got you working until this hour of the night? That's criminal," he said.

She dropped her briefcase into an armchair, carried on into the kitchen and picked out a pair of wine glasses from the cupboard. "Around here a tutor getting himself evicted after two weeks is criminal." And if this wasn't his last night, she could say for certain, she wouldn't be drinking with him.

He appeared in the archway and leaned against the doorframe that separated the kitchen from the sitting room.

"Ach, so you've heard about last night's shenanigans. I guess news travels fast in this place." He raised the bottle in his hand. "Would you have a corkscrew?"

"No, I haven't." She turned to face him and met his gaze. Her legs felt weak, probably from fatigue. "I can't remember the last time I opened a bottle with a corkscrew."

"Just as well then, I've got one." Dan came up beside her and plonked the bottle down on the kitchen worktop. He withdrew a penknife-set from his back pocket and proceeded to pull out the cork using its miniature corkscrew. "What's the point of all your mod-cons if you canny open a bottle of wine, eh?"

The ache in her muscles returned, not across her shoulders, but in her chest. "What time are you leaving?"

"They're flying me out first thing in the morning." He popped the cork and sniffed it. "Not bad. We should enjoy this."

"At last," she said in a flat voice, "something to celebrate." She took a wine glass in each hand and strode out of the kitchen. The sitting room table-lamps cast a golden glow on an immaculate suite. "Do take a seat." She placed the glasses on the coffee-table and sat in her usual armchair. Dan chose the end of the sofa closest to her. He reached forward and poured the wine with a steady hand around the bottle. He passed her a glass.

"Are you upset that I'm leaving?" he said.

She took a sip of the wine. "It's a pity you've ruined a good opportunity."

Dan sat back on the sofa and crossed his legs. He extended one arm, cradling the glass in his palm. More relaxed in her company tonight, perhaps because he had nothing to lose. "The world is full of opportunities." He swirled the wine around inside the bulb. "But if we don't meet again in this life, sure we'll meet in heaven. If I can get there without you."

She drew a quick breath. "Where will you go?"

"That depends on my luck finding alternative accommodation." He looked at her. "I haven't been evicted, as such. I've been ordered to vacate my apartment on Level Eight, to put a wide berth between myself and the Floor Manager, who was unnecessarily rude to me, by the way, just for the record."

"But that's good news." She was annoyed that he'd exaggerated his circumstances, but let it go. "If you put in a request at the Housing Department, they'll find you somewhere. If needs must, you could always share with students."

"I'm aware there are odd rooms going, but I need my own place. I made enquiries today and there are no more single apartments to be had, so, I'm moving on." He inclined his head. "Not to worry. I've come to terms with it. Always, the sweetest moments in life are the shortest. It's the bitter ones that take time. I've the best memories of meeting you and I couldn't wish for more than that." He swallowed a mouthful of wine. Mary said nothing, considering the compliment insincere. It sounded more as if he was looking for an excuse to leave. Perhaps a simulated 'Life on Mars' had proved too mundane for the man with a film-star's charisma. It struck her now that even his hair, dark curls, reaching to his jacket collar, was too flamboyant for this place.

"I thought you got on well with the students." She broke the silence. "They're potty about you. I'm sure they'd be honoured to have you living amongst them."

"I know we'd have fun together for a while, until they found me out. Then I'd be in trouble. They're not adult enough to deal with it."

She blinked. "To deal with what?"

"Mary, I-" He glanced towards the ceiling, then back to her. "I have a severe phobia. If someone touches my skin, even accidentally, I pass out. You know what kids are like, they'd think it was a big joke and they'd want to take the piss. I'd be out like a light every five minutes." He smiled. "Not such a tough guy after all, hmm?"

She stared at him. "Are you honestly telling me that if I were to touch you, you'd collapse in front of me, right there on the sofa?"

Dan gazed down at the glass in his hand. "It's all right if you touch me through my clothes. There's no problem so long as there's no skin involved." His tone was almost defensive. "I've nothing against someone touching my hair. I can handle hair." A blush crept up his neck. "And so long as one of us is wearing gloves, we can shake hands." His face was turning the deepest red Mary had ever seen on anybody, making the colour of his eyes stand out, aquamarine. "I'd normally be wearing gloves, but I've not known you to make any sudden moves. Please don't worry your head about it." He chuckled, crimson-faced, trying to laugh it off. "We'll be okay, for this evening, at least. I'll make sure of that."

In her memory, a scene replayed. Their first encounter. Dan rose from the table to greet her. He took a step back, before pulling out a chair for her. Her usual response when she met someone was bold and professional, always the first to proffer her hand. She did notice that opportunity passed them by. She would never have guessed it was deliberate.

"You're serious, aren't you?" She widened her eyes. "But how on earth did you cope in the circus? How do you cope with teaching?"

Dan turned his face the other way. A new emotion welled up inside her. Something precious was slipping away. Something she'd hardly been aware of a moment ago, was leaving her. "I'm sorry. I didn't mean to… it's just-"

"I'm not the guy you took me for," he said.

"That's not true. The first time we met I sensed you were different" -she was struggling to find the words to reassure him - "as poets often are. I knew you were sensitive."

He looked at her, tilted his glass. "Would you look at that, our glasses are empty. Would you mind if I topped them up?"

Mary held out her glass. Dan moved from the sofa onto one knee and poured. His fingers holding the bottle almost brushed hers.

"Nobody would've guessed," she said.

"Can you keep it a secret?" He said, as if they were children playing a game.

"Of course." She felt a frisson. What if she touched his hand? Was he telling the truth? Was he winding her up? He was a circus man. A joker.

"I'm not sure if I believe you," she said. "I think this could be one of your-"

He put up his hand. "Stop, right there. Don't feel obliged by what I'm about to say. But if I could choose to share an apartment with anybody, it would be you."

"I'm sorry," she said, "that's out of the question. It would be inappropriate for me to offer you a room, in my position."

He filled his own glass. "We wouldn't want to give them gossips anything to chew on, eh? What the feck is our Mary doing shacking up with that gypsy bastard?" He laughed.

"Glory be to God. We'd never hear the end of it."

"People aren't like that around here," she said. "Gossip is a waste of time and energy."

Dan returned to the sofa. He sat upright, with his knees together and held his wine glass with both hands, on his lap. "It's all been a waste of time and energy." He lowered his head. "My whole life."

A shiver went through her. The tone in his voice, the way he sat upright with his head down, was exactly like her father, the last time she saw him alive. She put her hand on her throat and felt a cold, familiar dread spreading inside her chest.

He looked up at her. "Did you just see a ghost?"

Mary took a deep breath. "Dan, I know we have our differences, but I'd still like you to think of me as a friend." She paused. "I remember what you said the other day, about sinking to the bottom of the Irish Sea. Please don't think like that. If you need to talk, I'm here for you."

"Talk about what?" He raised one eyebrow.

"What caused your phobia?" she said. "Do you know, or have you always had it?"

"I wasn't born this way. So far as I know, I was a happy kid until the day of my eighth birthday."

"What happened on your birthday?"

"I was tortured," he said, with a chilling smile. "I was dumped in a ditch and left to rot. Some circus kids found me and prodded me with sticks. They thought they were mucking about with a lamb carcass." He shrugged. "No party, no birthday cake, just a dirty old ditch." His complexion had turned sallow beneath the lamplight. "My parents were murdered." He caught his breath. "We were all abducted at the same time. Dragged out of our beds in the middle of the night, from our holiday cottage in Cork."

There was silence. Mary sat frozen, trying to make sense of what he'd said. She could find no words, only an image in her mind, a child dying in a ditch…

"Not much you can say." He bit down on his lower lip. "But you've got to hand it to the circus folks. They dug me a grave. It was only when a guy picked me up to put me in the earth, that I opened my eyes. From that moment, I was one of them. In no uncertain terms, the Still Force made a mess of me. My new family did their best to heal me. They're tough, kind people, circus people. They didn't go to the police. They assumed the finger of blame would point back to them." He nodded. "I still have no memory of my life before my eighth birthday. I don't remember the abduction or the torture. All I held onto was my name."

Mary cleared her throat. "Do you know why you were taken?"

"I found out twelve years later. I'd published my first book of poems under my full name, John Daniel Downs. One day, this smart English fellow shows up at my caravan with a copy of my book. I'll never forget his name, Dr. Alex Palmer. He took one look at me and said he knew who my father was. To prove it, he took a sample of my DNA and found a paternal match with John Dermot Downs. My father, his missing colleague. It turns out that my father was working undercover for MI6. He was investigating a new anti-capitalist terror group called the Still Force, nowadays known as Phoenix Ra."

Mary put her hand up to her mouth. "Oh my God."

"I'm afraid so. The Still Force found him out. They tracked

him down on holiday with his family. They meant to kill us all, but I survived. My parents' bodies were never found."

"With all that's been happening with Phoenix Ra, you must be going through hell."

"I hear the Pox is a terrible way to go," he said. "Of course, you must know the worst of it."

"We're working around the clock for the vaccine, hoping for a break-through any moment now." Mary's mouth had gone dry. "Dan, I'm so sorry," she said. "What happened to you is so awful, it's beyond belief, it sounds like the worst nightmare."

Dan sipped his wine. He shifted down in his seat and crossed his legs. "This Park Shiraz is quite nice." He raised his glass. "I guess you can take the credit for a good year at Wicklow?"

"It's a team effort." She gave a distracted smile, taken aback by his upbeat tone and the quick change of subject. "Do you mind if I ask you one more question about your past?"

"Fire away," he said.

"What happened after the English man, Alex Palmer, found you?"

"He placed me under the protection of MI6. They tried to get information out of me about what happened. They chained me to a bed, questioned me and stuck needles into me, until I felt like a prisoner of war." He gave a weary sigh. "In the end they let me go, with a six-figure sum called 'compensation' and an introduction to my only living relative, my father's sister-in-law. A lovely woman as it turns out. I'm a very lucky guy. My aunt Jane handed over my parents' estate and put me up in Dublin for a while. I attended college and began a whole new chapter in my life. Our Jane put me forward for the University post here and if it wasn't for her standing up for me today at the Governors meeting, I'd be out on my ear." He cupped his chin in his hand and gazed at Mary with mild amusement.

"You don't mean Jane O'Neil, our Director of Science, is your aunt?"

"Nice surprise, eh?" He smiled. "It was for me, nine years ago, when I landed on my feet. And she's that fond of you, I couldn't wait to meet you."

"I've known Jane since I was eighteen and she's never said anything about a nephew." Mary sat forward, scrutinising him for some resemblance to Jane. Of course, he was her in-law, not a blood relative. "Oh, my goodness, Dan! Why didn't you tell me? Why didn't Jane tell me?"

"We both decided not to tell anybody how I came back into her life, to avoid all the raking over the past." He had a little look of triumph. "But it's our secret and when we're alone, she likes me to call her auntie Jane. She remembers me from when I was a baby. I was seven years old when she last saw me. I don't remember her at all, I wish I did."

Mary sat back. "It's too much to take in. I can understand where your talent for philosophy and poetry comes from. What an incredible life story. And you're only twenty-eight, a year younger than me."

"Aye, but I've wrinkles to show for it." He drained his glass and placed it on the coffee-table. "That's enough about that. I'd better be off and let you have your dinner. Be sure you drink that last drop of wine, don't let it go to waste." He stood up and clasped his hands. "I guess this is goodbye."

She looked up at him, standing in front of her. "What about Jane? Can't she put you up in her apartment?"

"I've refused her offer." He slid his hands into his pockets and stood, transferring his weight from one foot to the other. Like a man waiting in the cold. "As folks don't know we're related, it wouldn't go down too well with the Governors to hear she's shacked up with that wayward guy. The one she saved from eviction. Imagine that." He put on a silly, high-pitched voice. "Ooh, we should've known! Why, she's old enough to be his mother. The hussy!"

Mary rose out of her chair. At five-foot ten, her eyes were at the level of his collarbones. "Just tell them you're her nephew." She raised her eyes to his, gazing down at her. "The truth will put an end to speculation."

"She'd be accused of favouritism," he said. "It wouldn't be fair. She's done enough for me. The fact is I should've kept me nose clean and I didn't. This is my fault." He smiled, with a tremor at the corner of his mouth. "Mary, I'd better go, or this time you will see me cry."

"I'm sure we'll meet again, through Jane. After the crisis our Biosphere will be released from lockdown. Let's meet for a drink in Dublin."

Dan sauntered to the door. "That's if your new boyfriend doesn't mind. And don't tell me you won't have one. There's a queue lining up down your street."

She followed him. "I haven't got time for that sort of thing."

Dan opened the door and stepped outside. He faced her, with his shoulders hunched, his complexion pale under the streetlight.

"Jealousy is a terrible thing," he said. "It's at the heart of every murderous thought. It makes you sicker than a hornet." He gave a nod. "I wouldn't mess with a jealous man, Mary. If you've got yourself a boyfriend by the end of your lockdown, we won't be meeting again. That's a fact."

"Really Dan, a boyfriend is the last thing on my mind." She folded her arms and looked down at his feet, in smart, designer trainers. "Will you be staying in your own apartment tonight?"

"I'm down the road at Jane's tonight, not too far to stagger. She's at the 'Opening' of your new restaurant. Have a good night yourself."

"I wish you a safe journey tomorrow." She remembered not to offer her hand or to attempt any form of embrace. "Good luck with finding a new appointment."

"Thanks, and goodbye. Have a grand life if I don't see you again." He gave a single wave and strode away.

Mary watched him go, braced, like a man heading into a high wind. He didn't look back.

Chapter Eight

"Hi, Jane, it's Mary, I'm sorry to interrupt your evening."

"Please, don't be. If it's news about the vaccine I want to be the first to know." Jane's voice was louder than usual, to be heard above a jazz saxophone playing in the background.

"I think we might have something to work with," Mary said. "It's a waiting game for the next twelve hours. We should know more by tomorrow afternoon. That's not why I'm ringing. I've just had an extraordinary conversation with Dan Downs, the new philosophy tutor. I understand he's your nephew."

"Hang on." Jane's voice retreated. Mary overheard her excusing herself from the table. "Hello, Mary, I've come over to the bar, it's quieter … Yes, Dan Downs is my late husband's nephew. What else did he tell you?"

"Everything about being abducted as a child and how he was found by a circus. He has a strange phobia. He can't touch people." Mary gripped the receiver so tight perspiration seeped inside her palm. "I wasn't sure what to believe at first, it's… beyond tragic."

"Yes, it is," Jane said. "Did he say anything about leaving?"

"He's leaving in the morning. He said he would stay, but only if he could live here with me, someone he can trust with his condition. Jane, I'd like to help, but we hardly know each other. I think people might get the wrong impression."

"It wouldn't be for long. Once we've found the vaccine, the new arrivals will start to leave us and there'll be plenty of apartments going free. It's your decision, Mary. But if you do feel able to offer my nephew a room, I'd be grateful, as he refuses to stay with me." Jane sounded breathless. "And if people get the wrong impression, they've got their priorities wrong. We're here offering sanctuary. It should come as no surprise to anyone if colleagues must share accommodation. Is that what really worries you, or is it something else? I understand from Lewis you were thankful for Dan's contribution to the volunteer project."

"Yes. I still owe him a favour. If it's okay with you and the Governors, I'd like to offer him accommodation." The words were out there before she even knew she'd made the decision. To please Jane, who seemed almost desperate, or to give something back to Dan. Mary wasn't sure what tipped the balance in his favour.

"If you could, dear, that would be marvellous." For the first time in all the years she'd known her, Mary heard a slur in Jane's voice. "If anyone is good at keeping a cool head, it's you. That's what Dan needs. A flat mate who understands his vulnerability."

Mary began to feel a little queasy. "I'm glad I'm in a position to help."

"I'll call him now to let him know. Mary, I can't thank you enough-"

When the conversation was over, Mary put her head back on the cushion. Had she really meant to invite Dan Downs to live with her, without any thought for her loss of privacy, let alone their differences? How did that just happen?

* * *

She couldn't sleep. In the end she gave up trying and got up to start clearing out her spare bedroom, packing away clothes and things she didn't need into suitcases, to put into storage.

By nine o'clock that Sunday morning, hair dishevelled, in a baggy T-shirt and jeans, Mary had taken delivery of a single bed, a massive desk peppered with dust and about a dozen boxes of books, sent down from Dan's apartment on Level Eight. The UISC Household monitors waltzed the desk through her apartment in an unwieldy threesome, laughing and cracking jokes. At the time she'd laughed with them, delirious with fatigue and the enormity of the changes she'd brought about on an impulse. After they left Mary sat in her armchair, too exhausted to think or drink the cup of tea she'd made and was just drifting off, when there were three quiet knocks.

She pulled herself out of the chair with a groan and went to open the door.

It was Dan, with a bouquet of red roses tucked under his elbow, holding a Champagne bottle by its neck, the other hand balancing a box of chocolates, as he might a tray, on his fingers-tips. Adrenalin jolted her wide-awake. She must look a complete state, pale and unwashed, her plait unwoven halfway down her back. Her professional persona would normally step up to her rescue, calm and dignified, but with him bearing so many gifts, gratitude made her coy.

"Dan, you shouldn't have!"

"I wanted to say thank you, from the bottom of my heart." He smiled, creasing his face with laughter lines. "You're an angel, so you are."

"Goodness me." She avoided his gaze. "I'm just doing what

any friend would do. You didn't need to go to all this trouble," she said with a nervous laugh. "But the roses are gorgeous, thank you, so much. Is there anything I can help you with?"

He held up the bottle of Champagne. "You can take this and put it in the fridge, for a celebration later."

She grasped the bottom of the bottle. She noticed when she opened the door that he wasn't wearing gloves.

"Would you take these as well," he said, "while I grab my suitcase?"

She all but snatched the box of chocolates from him. "Cherry liquors, my favourite," she said, "how did you guess?" She looked down to see a squat, tan suitcase nestling against his leg, bulging like an overfed sausage dog. "Is that all you've brought with you? That's about the same size as my overnight bag." She laughed.

"I like to travel light, sure, it's the only way to get around." He picked it up and sailed in through the door, making it seem as if it were pumped up with air. He sniffed the bouquet. "Go on, I'll follow you, these wee souls are begging for water."

"Yes, come through, watch out for the boxes!" He followed her through to the kitchen. "Please excuse the chaos. I hoped to get most of this cleared away before you arrived. Jane said you wouldn't be here until after lunch."

"I've come to give you a hand. I can't have you doing all this work on my behalf, sure, you've got better things to do." His speech was faster than usual. Mary placed the chocolates on the worktop and glanced at the bottle before putting it in the fridge. Vintage Champagne. The most expensive label on sale at the Mars Delicatessen, beyond the everyday reach of most pockets. Dan placed the bouquet in the sink and turned on the tap, looking at home already.

"I couldn't believe it when Jane called to say you'd offered me a room. I guess you decided to give me a second chance after all, eh?"

"After hearing your life story, I felt I had no choice." She watched him stooping over the sink, picking at the red felt bow tied around the cellophane. He was wearing a light blue cashmere sweater, snug jeans, tastefully casual.

He glanced at her. "I could put these into vases for you, if you've got a couple handy?"

"I have." Mary reached down to a cupboard and removed two hourglass vases. She put them on the worktop and watched him tearing open the cellophane, prising apart rose stems with long, supple fingers. "You've got musician's hands. Are you musical?" She gazed up at his profile.

"I can't do anything without music. I hear it all day in my head."

"Do you play an instrument?"

He glanced at her. "I play any instrument I can get my hands on."

"Really? Did they teach you that in the circus?"

"Mary, would there be any chance of a coffee, bless you, I'm parched."

"How would you like it?" She understood. Dan wanted to close the subject of the past.

"That's black with four sugars, if you don't mind," he said.

She made the coffee in silence as he picked through the roses, placing them inside the vases, fussing with little adjustments. She put his mug beside the sink and went to stand against the arched doorway, where she continued to watch him, as far away as her kitchen space allowed.

"Thanks for the coffee." He winked at her.

"Dan, I really ought to know what to do if we make accidental skin contact. Do I call the paramedics or is there any medication I should give you?"

He didn't answer, but stepped back to admire his flower arranging, with his hands on his hips. Evidently satisfied, he picked up his coffee and went to drink it, leaning against the opposite wall.

"Have I asked the wrong question?" She felt dismissed. He was ignoring her. Shutting her out when it suited him.

He beckoned with his forefinger. "Come here."

"Why?" She met his gaze.

He gave an upward nod. "Come here. I won't bite ye."

"I'm fine where I am, thank you." She firmed her voice. "And please don't talk to me like that. You're not in the ring now. You're in my kitchen."

"That's better. I don't need your pity. I'm not pathetic, which is what people tend to think when they hear about my problem." The colour in his cheeks was beginning to deepen. "If I pass out, just don't panic. I've usually got a moment's warning to get myself down on the floor and then I'm out for a couple of minutes." He sipped his coffee, then his voice became curiously loud and up-beat.

"I might look like death but it's not dangerous. Sometimes I'll fall asleep. To wake me, just give my hair a good wigging, hard like, until you've got a reaction. Don't slap or tickle my face, whatever you do." He smiled. "Or we'll be back to square one. Psychologists say my unconscious mind has learned to create a convincing mimicry of death. It's an extreme survival mechanism that saved my life twenty years ago." He raised his coffee mug in the air. "Only I call it Divine Intervention."

"Isn't there anything more psychologists can do for you?"

"It's a matter of desensitization over time. I'm better than I was. I can give hugs nowadays, so long as there's a barrier of clothing. These last few years I've been practising daily hugs with a few friends. Jane's been helpful. I was hoping"- he put his mug in the sink and faced her- "any chance of a hug?"

She gave him a wry look. "So long as it's for medical reasons only."

"Definitely." He smiled. "Keep your arms by your sides, and don't make a move." He hooked his thumbs inside his pockets, swaggering towards her like a cowboy, perhaps to raise a laugh, but instead struck a pitiful chord. She couldn't look him in the eye, fixing her gaze on his neck. "You've got nothing to fear. All I've got is me razzamatazz." He put on an American drawl, like something from a wild-west movie, which did make her smile. "I'm coming in for the kill, sunshine, are y' ready?"

Mary straightened her shoulders and she stood motionless.

"Hey, relax." He surprised her, closing the distance between them, circling his arms around her in one move. He placed one hand on the back of her head, the other, ever so lightly, on her spine. Warmth tingled between her shoulder blades. His cashmere sweater tickled her nose, now angled towards his under-arm, giving up a vague smell of Jane's apartment, mingled with freshly cut grass. Reminding her of the day they met. She resisted an impulse to put her arms around his waist and pull him closer. Dan gave a shudder.

"Are you all right?" she said.

He didn't answer. He released her and took a step back. "I

am, but you're not. Mary, you're exhausted. You didn't sleep at all last night, did you?"

"No." She looked up at him, missing his warmth, already haunted by the lightness of his touch. "How do you know that?"

"My phobia makes me sensitive." He lifted a wisp of hair away from her cheek, his expression full of tenderness. "I think you should go back to bed for a while."

She puffed out a breath. "I'd like to help you settle in and then I've got to be back in the lab, as soon as possible."

He raised a forefinger in front of her face, his voice quiet, firm. "Listen. I'm not having you wear yourself out for me, or for any other clown. Jane said you've no important results expected until later this afternoon. You can get your head down for a while. I'll sort myself out. Believe it or not, I was born under a wandering star."

She smiled. "I wouldn't be at all surprised. But I'd like to be in the lab long before the results come back from Scotty. He's our human guineapig. I must plan another strategy in case it's bad news. We can't afford to waste a moment."

"I'll make sure you're there in good time for your Scotty. Now, go back to bed." He swivelled her around by her shoulders and gave a gentle push to her back. "Go on. You can show me my bedroom on the way."

"Don't be so bossy, Dan Downs," she said, but then laughed, giddy with tiredness. "All right, I'll go for an hour."

She led him through the sitting room, down the hall to the bedrooms. "Your desk and bed have arrived." She'd left the bedside lamp on in his room. "Here you are. The duvet is in the top of the wardrobe, bottom sheets are in the drawer."

"It's a lovely room, thanks. A nice size too." He nodded.

"Show me where you are."

"I'm next door," she said.

Dan followed her into her room, lit with holographic daylight from the six-foot UDAN Window, so bright it was dazzling. "You get into bed. I'll turn that thing down, it's hard on the eyes." He walked over to the window. Mary sat on the edge of the bed and watched him tap on the diamond logo at the side of the screen, dimming the light to night-time.

"Do you want a night sky with stars?" he said.

"You choose." Her eyelids grew heavy, watching rays from the hologram flicker over his face as he sampled the options. His head and shoulders were in profile, silhouetted against the screen. He turned slightly and Mary blinked, refocusing her eyes. His shoulder blade continued as a hump across the top of his back, she hadn't noticed before. The top of his torso was disproportionately thicker than the lower half, where his waist tapered, almost too thin. He spoke to her.

"Sorry? What did you say?" she said.

He looked over his shoulder. "I asked if you wanted a different galaxy in your window. How about Messier Eighty-Three, recommended for its Champagne bar, in the middle there." He pointed inside the screen to a misty spiral with a bright core, she guessed must be the bar he was referring to.

"Have you ever been to it?" She joked back.

"Every Friday night. They do a grand Cabaret. All the girls have six legs."

"Let's have that, then." She chuckled. "It's good to see you've already got the hang of our UDAN technology."

He opened the shutters wide, to show the hazy wheel fanning out to solitary stars. He moved in the shadows towards the door, “Get you into that bed and sleep tight.”

“Dan?”

“Yes?”

“I appreciate your kindness, even if you are a bit bossy.”

“You’re the kind one around here. Don’t let the bed bugs bite.”

Chapter Nine

Lewis squinted through the Control Room window, to spy on Jolly manipulating its logo inside the screen, whizzing *I am Jolly* around in a blur, halting every few moments with a magnified ***I am Jolly.*** It was like watching someone bored, twiddling their thumbs.

Lewis stepped through the automatic doors and kept his head down.

"Greetings Lewis. I must inform you that according to our sensors, you are exhibiting signs of stress-"

"Quiet, please Jolly."

"I am only-"

"I don't want to hear, okay?" Lewis flopped down in front of his computer. He lifted a stack of printing paper and thumped it down on the desk. "Why? Because you talk incessantly!"

"Then I must refer you to my Creator sitting in your chair."

"Listen!" Lewis drew a long breath in through his nostrils. "You'll be pleased to know that the neuromuscular co-ordinates for your lips have arrived. The rest of your face won't be available until tomorrow morning. I suggest that you start practising with your lips for your holographic display. We've got half an hour before lunch, so let's get moving."

"I am not going to practise my lips without a face. Do you

want me to look like an imbecile?"

"Jolly, there are loads of muscles you've got to get to grips with if you want to speak through your hologram. You'll find the co-ordinates for your lips in the file Myra sent this morning." He drummed his fingers on the desk. "With her best wishes for a successful face that she hopes will give us both a lot of pleasure." He cast his eyes heavenwards.

Jolly's logo vanished, replaced by a pair of huge, bottom heavy, lips.

"Well, there you go." Lewis folded his arms. "Give us a smile, then." The lips pulled themselves up on one side, cutting a diagonal gash across Jolly's screen.

"Not quite there yet," Lewis said, "try again." The lips curled upward like a neighing horse, only toothless and silent. Lewis snorted. "Not what I'd call a smile." He bared his own teeth. "See that? That's a smile. Concentrate, Jolly. Persevere and you'll get there. Try again."

"These lips are unsatisfactory." Jolly had that needling tone in its voice. "I want lips like Dan's. His lips are perfect and pleasing to look at."

"We are using Scotty's DNA and so you'll have Scotty's lips." Jolly had better not start this, Lewis thought, he wasn't in the mood.

"But these lips will make me look ugly. I want to look like Dan." The lips vanished, replaced by a sepia photograph of Dan in profile, smiling, eyes lowered. Lewis recognised it as the same photograph on the back page of Dan's recent collection of poems, Mary had given him for Christmas.

He gazed at it, aware of tingling at the base of his spine, a warming in his loins. It was the same when he studied it in bed at night, instead of reading the poems, most of which he didn't understand. And this was the face Mary would see across her breakfast table from now on. Did she have any idea how lucky she was?

"We'd all like to look like that, but we can't," Lewis said, "It's Scotty's face or no face at all. I will wash my hands." He swiped his palms.

"Why do you begrudge me the face of my choice?" Jolly said, "Does the thought of me being more attractive than you make you envious?"

"Do you honestly think I could be jealous of you?" Lewis laughed at his computer. "Do you think you're competing with me, like we're on a par or something? That's ridiculous. You have no idea where you stand in the scheme of things."

A childhood memory flashed inside Lewis' head, of a hot summer's afternoon in his seventh year, when the longest, fattest worm he'd ever seen oozed across his path. Lewis was offended. It sickened him to watch, yet he couldn't take his eyes off its translucent body shunting across the pavement in search of mud. He flicked the worm over with his lollipop stick to make it squirm, discovering deeper levels of revulsion. And then it lifted both of its ends at once, pointing them towards Lewis like a pair of horns. As if it could take the child on and win.

Lewis gazed into Jolly's eye. "Do you realise that your actual consciousness is probably equivalent to that of a worm except that you're an inanimate object. I choose your face the same way I choose my wallpaper. Because to me you're just another piece of furniture. Sorry chum, but that's the truth." Jolly's screen blanked.

"Well, that's shut you up." Lewis smirked, without a twinge of guilt. Whereas the worm that got its comeuppance, convulsing and blistering in the blazing sun under his magnifying glass, Lewis felt rotten about that to this day. He pondered on the problem. How could he create awareness in an artificial-intelligence, without producing a worm with the strategic skills of a chess-player?

"Why do you want to hurt me, Lewis?" Jolly said in a tiny voice. How Lewis imagined the worm might've spoken, to beg him to stop what he was doing. Except that Jolly wasn't hurt. This was one of its many programmed child-parent transactions manipulatively applied. Lewis stuck to his guns. This reality check was long overdue.

"Jolly, you need a body to feel anything. Where do you feel your pain, in your Perspex, in your silicone? Will I see tears squirting out from your monitor? Can you tell me what your pain feels like?"

"Yes. I am very, very hurt, Lewis."

"Simply repeating yourself doesn't convince me. Come on. Tell me what it feels like!" Lewis waved his hand. "People writhe in pain. They lament and write poetry and music. You've been programmed to state that you feel hurt. It's not the same thing, I promise you. So, snap out of it, you're just a heap of metal."

There was a deep rumbling noise, like the bottom note on a church organ, fluttering in Lewis' ears. It stopped and started again an octave higher, then went low again, high, low, growing louder and faster. Like an ambulance siren hurtling towards him. He shot up from his chair.

"Will you stop that, Jolly!" he put his hands over his ears. "Stop it, you'll burst my eardrums!" The noise stopped.

"You owe me an apology, Lewis," Jolly said in its calm, vanilla voice. "Say sorry or I will make it happen again."

Lewis squeezed around the back of his desk and stooped towards the power point.

"*No, please, Daddy, no-*"

He pulled the plug from the socket and strode out of the Control Room, to meet Dan for lunch in The Shooting Star.

Dan was already in the pub, seated on a tall stool at the end of the bar with his back to the wall, jotting something down in a notebook. He raised his eyes as Lewis approached. Lewis had that high feeling, as if he were taking off into the icy blue stratosphere. It happened every time they met. The first sight of Dan went straight to his head like Champagne.

Dan closed his notebook and slid it to one side.

"Hi Lewis, how's it going? Will you have a drink?"

Lewis climbed onto a barstool and sat facing him, feeling flattered. He'd half expected Dan not to show up or to be late. It never occurred to him he'd be early.

"It's great to see you. I will, thanks, one of those." He nodded to Dan's empty glass. Dan raised his hand to attract the barman. Wearing black leather gloves again, Lewis noticed. He'd never seen his hands, but hesitated to ask why, beginning to suspect there was a reason he kept them hidden.

"King, can we have two whiskies over here please, when you've got a minute and a couple of bar-menus, thanks."

King waved.

Lewis recognised the barman as one of the student volunteers who'd worked alongside Dan, harvesting the potato crop in E-Zone. Their drinks and menus arrived without a moment's delay, served with a deferential bow of the head. One of these days Lewis would ask Dan what his secret was to commanding respect among the students.

The man didn't behave as if he was anything special and yet somehow his unassuming manner, strenuous work ethic and quirky sense of humour, coupled with the extraordinary looks, had resulted in a guru-type charisma. Maybe that's all it took. Dan was tough yet easy going, he was cool. But being cool was something Lewis knew he could never achieve. He was nowhere near happy enough in his own skin.

"I thought you might be late. Aren't you moving in with Mary today?" Lewis glanced over his menu. He already knew what he wanted.

Dan chuckled. "Me oh my, news travels fast in this place. Who told you?"

"Jane O'Neil. I saw her at the restaurant's opening last night, she told me what was happening. I must confess to being totally amazed."

"Aye, why's that?"

"I don't know how you do it. So many blokes have tried and failed to get anywhere near her, now you're moving in with her." Lewis shook his head. "Unbelievable." He looked up to see Dan's eyes lowered to the menu, his lips slightly parted, more than pleasing to look at. But then what would a computer know about lips that were wantonly kissable?

"Obviously there's more to it, reading between the lines, something the rest of us don't know about." Lewis probed.

Dan raised his eyes. "What's that?"

Lewis sucked in his cheeks with an ironic look. "We all assumed you'd be at logger heads after your lecture." He smirked. "Treat them mean, keep them keen, obviously works for some. Though I never imagined Mary would fall for it."

Dan placed the menu down on the bar and lifted the drink to his mouth. "Clever women like Mary respect a guy with his own ideas, ready to stand up for himself. What are you having?"

"Oh, absolutely and Mary is very clever." Lewis sighed, seeking inspiration to be light-hearted. "Poor Stefan will be so jealous. He's been after her for years, ever since we were at college … Yes, um-" He fanned the menu in his face. "I'll have the roast beef baguette. They're pretty delish. I recommend you have one to keep up your strength, now that you'll be practising your conjugal duties."

"Not for me, thanks. I'm a vegan." He swirled a last drop of whiskey around the bottom of his glass.

"Oh right." Lewis nodded. "Every creature has earned its right to live, through suffering. I enjoyed your lecture by the way."

"Good. You didn't drop off to sleep, then."

If Dan only knew, Lewis had sat there mesmerised, his loins prickling every time Dan's glance happened to pass over him in the audience. He'd committed Dan's lecture to memory and could probably quote parts of it, word for word. But he pretended to be a little vague, wanting to impress, without appearing too obsessed.

"Actually, I was very interested in what you were saying. As you know I work in Artificial Intelligence and I'm only beginning to appreciate how much consciousness is dependent upon a real body as opposed to a virtual one. I agree physical suffering awakens consciousness-"

Dan was waving at the barman. "Can we have two humus

baguettes and two more whiskies over here, King, in your own time, thanks!"

Lewis leaned over and whispered. "I'd like the roast beef."

"I know." Dan turned to face him. "But do y' mind not eating meat in front of me? It's not that I want to impose my beliefs. I can't handle it."

"Of course not, I don't mind." Lewis raised his eyebrows. "Does it upset you that much?"

Dan put his head back on the wall behind him, his ice-blue eyes gazed down at Lewis. "I've an eating disorder. Eating meat or somebody eating it near me triggers my bulimia. Just the smell of it starts me off gorging and I can't stop." He pursed his lips. "It makes eating out a damned nuisance, so it does."

"Would you know, I'm the same with chocolate digestives. One bite and I've got to finish the whole packet," Lewis said, but he was surprised and secretly delighted. Dan's pedestal wobbled. He was human after all. And when Dan smiled, laughter lines creased the sides of his face. Lewis happened to know they were both twenty-eight. Dan was younger by three months, but his face had received a lot more weathering, probably travelling with the circus and at times, in certain lights, he looked about forty. Lewis found some comfort in this too, the transience of beauty. Perhaps being happy in one's skin was as ephemeral as everything else.

"Chocolate digestives set you off, do they?" Dan cocked an eyebrow.

"Oh yes, I can't stop myself." Lewis tilted forward to speak under his breath. "You'd better tell Mary that you're a vegetarian. I know she's very partial to a Sunday roast. You might find she's cooked you both a roast dinner when you get there."

"I'm cooking tonight. I'll tell her over dinner. Sure, she might guess anyway when she sees what we're having, nut roast with all the trimmings." Dan drained his glass and thumped it down on the bar. "King, we'd like a couple more of the same over here, please, there's a good lad!"

Lewis sipped nimbly from his own whiskey, hoping to look as if he was keeping up, thinking Dan was hitting the bottle a bit. Maybe it was the thought of moving in with Mary. He was more agitated than he'd ever seen him. King slid another two whiskies across the bar.

"When was the last time you ate meat?" Lewis was intrigued to learn more about Dan, who was turning out to be exactly the type he often attracted: complex.

"Last Christmas, hmm, that was bad." His eyelids became heavy. "Absolute hell. I swore, never again."

Lewis nodded. "That Christmas turkey has a lot to answer for."

"The goose, the duck, and the pheasant, to be sure."

"Lots of people go off the rails at Christmas. I'm still carrying a few pounds from the festive season." Lewis grabbed a handful of his own midriff and shook it.

"You're fine. You look good with a bit of meat on you."

Lewis grinned. "Thanks."

Their baguettes arrived, long crusty French sticks, with frilly lettuce leaves, oozing humus. Dan picked his up with gloved hands, opened his mouth wide and took an enormous bite. Lewis looked down at his, not that keen on humus, feeling a bit cheated. "This looks tasty." He fibbed, partly because he'd invited Dan to lunch to ask him a favour.

"I wonder if you can help me. I'm expecting my computer's

hologram to arrive tomorrow. It's the first time I've worked with a Crystal Grotto and I'm not sure how to set it up. Didn't you say you once worked as a UDAN rep, in your student days? Would you mind calling in to give me a hand? It's going to be the face of an adult male. Nobody's seen the face before, so it should be quite interesting to be there when it appears." Lewis nibbled a lettuce leaf at the edge of his baguette.

"I'd be glad to drop by. You need someone who knows what they're doing, especially with the latest models. If you don't get it right, you can end up with something that looks like it's melting." Dan stretched his jaws wider than Lewis thought possible and bit into his baguette again, presenting Lewis with an image of a cobra attached to a Pharaoh's head. He couldn't help staring.

Dan grinned, showing half-chewed bread between his teeth. "Am I bothering you?"

"No, I just had a hunch about something." Lewis put down his baguette and picked up his whiskey. "Sometimes I get these sudden insights into what makes people tick. Are you a bit psychic by any chance?" Dan carried on chewing, smiling on one side of his face, wrinkling his wrinkles.

"God, I only wish I were. Then I'd know how to reach the girl."

"If you mean Mary, you need to be more than psychic. You need to have the patience of a saint. I've known her for six years and she's never had a boyfriend." Lewis picked up his baguette, to resume nibbling, encouraged by Dan popping the last crust into his mouth. He'd never seen anyone devour a whole Club Baguette in three bites before. "Stefan and I have a theory about her." He lowered his voice. "Mary's father hanged himself when she was an undergraduate and she's never fully recovered. We think she might still be quite innocent. You know, where men are concerned."

"You mean she's still a virgin? Ach, that's my night ruined." Dan lifted one of Lewis' drinks. "Will you be wanting this, or can I have it to drown me sorrows?"

Lewis nodded. Not wanting to talk with his mouth full, he gestured to the row of drinks, grunting that he could have the lot. Dan knocked back two more, banged them down empty on the bar, with a loud exhalation.

"I better be off, eh? I want to be there when she wakes up." He waved to the barman. "Put this lot on my tab, King, will ye? And fetch this man here some of your roast beef. He's not enjoying the rabbit food!"

Lewis strained to swallow, almost choking. "You're not going already, are you? What about tomorrow? Will you be able to help me out in the morning?"

Dan slid down from his barstool and clasped his leather hand around the back of Lewis' neck. Perhaps because it was so gentle Lewis' nerves over-fired, making him shiver.

"Sure, I'll be there." He breathed in his ear. "What time?"

"It would be great if you could make it for half eight, before the volunteers arrive for the wheat harvest."

Lewis stared straight ahead, aware of a growing pressure inside his crotch. "Are you going to Mary's now?"

"Yes, but first I'm off to the gents for some sweet relief." He exhaled whiskey across Lewis' nostrils. "Did you want to join me?"

"Um. . ." Lewis' heart began to race. The scene that flashed before his eyes was too sordid to contemplate, yet his voice shook with shameful complicity. "My apartment is just down the corridor. You can come back for a coffee if you like."

"I haven't got time for that." Dan began to massage the nape of his neck. "Now I know the girl's not on offer, I've an urgent need."

Lewis swallowed. "Okay, I'll meet you in the gents."

"You behave yourself you wee tart. I'll see you in the morning." Dan blew a sharp breath in his ear and went striding towards the door. "Thanks King! Make sure that man over there gets his red meat! See you later!"

Chapter Ten

Mary smiled to see Dan working in her kitchen. He turned towards her, cheeks flushed, the sleeves of his pullover rolled up to his elbows.

"Hi Mary. What's the news?" He wiped his hands on a tea-towel tucked inside his waistband.

"Number Eighteen Scotty survived the night. He's doing well." After seven hours in the lab Mary was almost too tired to talk. "If he's still symptom-free by tomorrow morning, we've probably found our vaccine."

Dan approached her and put his hands on her shoulders. The warmth of his fingers passed through her blouse, with pressure equivalent to two small birds alighting. "That's great news. What do you say to a glass of Champers?"

Mary hoped he might hug her. But he withdrew his hands and opened the fridge door.

"That sounds lovely." She glanced around at vegetables simmering in two saucepans on the stove, the bunch of fresh parsley and a carton of cream on the worktop. The only signs he'd been cooking, besides the nutty aroma that greeted her when she entered her apartment. "You've been busy. My kitchen has never looked tidier. Are you always this organised?"

He peeled the cage and golden foil from the Champagne

he'd brought. "When you live in a caravan you've got to be neat. Otherwise, you'd lose yourself in the chaos, never to be found again." He poured pink Champagne into two gilded flutes that were not hers.

"These are pretty. Did you buy them?"

"They belonged to my parents, a wedding gift, I believe." He handed her one of the flutes and raised his up. "Here's to the vaccine. God willing your Scotty will live to see another day and we'll all be safe in our beds again. God bless you, Mary."

"Thanks." She lifted the flute to her lips and felt uncomfortable. She didn't want God's blessing. God didn't feature in her worldview.

"What happens when Scotty survives?" he said.

"You mean 'if'. We start the human drug trials at St Anthony's Hospital in Dublin." Mary leaned her hip against the side of the worktop, aching to sit down. "One of my pathologists will leave the UISC to assist the medical team at the hospital. We call it a Mercy Mission. We've already got the trial volunteers lined up. The Mission could leave as early as tomorrow, if the results are good."

"That's fantastic. Still, we need to keep your strength up. Go and sit yourself down at the dinner-table."

Dan sat opposite her at the table. With his face and curly hair lit up by two candles, he reminded Mary of a painting of a beautiful urchin, or rather, how the urchin might've turned out as an adult. He'd set the table with her best tablecloth and silver cutlery, having found where she kept everything. She looked down at the plate of food he'd prepared. Nut-roast with fresh parsley and tomato sauce and fresh vegetables. The aromas were so appetising she almost forgot her table manners, heaping her fork before noticing he hadn't lifted his.

"Sorry. I've started without you-" she said.

"I like a moment to say grace." He lowered his head and closed his eyes. Mary waited until he picked up his fork before taking her first mouthful.

"Dan, this is delicious. I think you've missed your vocation. Have you ever thought of becoming a chef?"

"I love being in the kitchen. I used to cook a lot for folks when I was in the circus, over a portable gas cooker." He wrinkled his nose. "Then I got too heavy for the trapeze and had to leave the kitchen to avoid temptation."

"I can't imagine anyone in the circus being overweight," she said. "I thought all that hard work kept people trim." She secured another forkful.

Dan put his knife and fork down on the sides of his plate."Aye, it's that. But nobody complains. Jossers get a good kick up the backside if they do." He reached across the table to fill their glasses from a bottle of red wine. "You all muck in, even on the day of rest, driving through Sunday night to reach the new site. Raising the big-top first thing Monday. Chasing around for gas and water bottles, putting in a couple of hours rehearsal whenever you can." He drew deeply from his wine glass and sat back in the chair. "Mend a wonky generator, muck out the horses, milk a cow." He widened his eyes. "Lather your face with greasepaint, give the performance of a lifetime, then get yourself well and truly rat-arsed, sure" – he nodded – "it's a tough old life. The smell of greasepaint still brings me out in a cold sweat."

"I think you must be very strong physically and mentally to cope with that lifestyle." She paused with her fork on the way to her mouth. "Why aren't you eating?"

"I will, it's just that" – he touched his throat – "I've got a lump in here. When I swallow my throat feels tight."

She frowned. "That sounds like anxiety. Are you worried about something?"

"Just your holy and immaculate beauty." He lowered his eyes. "I don't deserve to be sitting here. I should be under your table begging for crumbs."

"Dan, you've got so much going for you." She smiled. "I think you're just fishing for compliments."

"There's another side to me, or did you forget that already?"

She levelled her voice. "You mean your phobia?"

"That and I'm not a pretty sight."

She put down her knife and fork and looked at him. His eyelashes were so long they cast shadows on his cheeks. Dan raised his eyes, seared with emotion Mary couldn't read, and didn't dare to ask. She looked at his mouth. It charmed her, the way his lips stretched almost too wide when he smiled. Only he wasn't smiling now.

"Dan, nothing alters the fact that you're a very attractive man. I'm not just talking about your looks. The other night when you gave your lecture, when I looked around at the audience, I could tell they were mesmerised by you."

He smiled. "Mesmerised, eh? I'll take that one to bed with me." He picked up his knife and fork and sliced into a potato, sticking his little fingers up in the air.

"And you're a wonderful cook." She raised her glass. "You're welcome to stay, as long as you like."

Pudding was his own gourmet creation. A white chocolate dome filled with chocolate coated strawberries and Champagne ice-cream, served on a glass platter that he lowered carefully into the middle of the table.

"I call this 'Venus Rising'. I hope you like it." He sat down again. "It was always a great hit with my girlfriends. Apparently, it's an aphrodisiac." He grinned. "The proof is in the pudding, as they say."

"Do you mean female friends, or have you actually had girlfriends?" Mary watched him smacking the dome with the back of the spoon, shattering the chocolate like an eggshell. He might not like the question, but he'd raised the subject.

"This might surprise you, but I've had quite a few girlfriends." He spooned the dome's innards into a dessert bowl. "Just because I'm not all touchy feely, doesn't mean I'm green behind the ears or without sin, for that matter." He placed the bowl in front of her.

"I see." Mary gazed down at the bumpy mound of white chocolate and ice-cream.

"If you're wondering how it works." He gave her a sideways wink. "It sure does, with a bit of craftsmanship and the old Irish charm. You don't have to hold a woman to give her pleasure. You don't need to lie beside her. In fact, you can stand up, or you can sit yourself down."

"I've got the picture." She dug her spoon into the coated strawberries, cutting them into bite sizes, with an unwelcome sensation worming its way through her solar plexus.

"I'm not sure you have. None of them ever saw me naked and they never put a finger on me, with or without gloves. I was there to learn from them, not chiefly for my own pleasure." He examined the remains of the dome, picked out a chocolate strawberry using his fingers, and bit into it. He gazed at the bitten flesh where he'd left his teeth marks. "I didn't want my problem to be an excuse for ignorance. If I may say so myself, in a manner of speaking, these days I'm not bad in bed." He popped the remainder of the fruit into his mouth.

"Fully dressed, I should think you're very hot." She pressed a lump of chocolate against her palate with her tongue, drawing little pleasure from its sweetness.

"You'd be right there." He gave a sly smile. "I've yet to meet a girt who isn't turned on like a tap by a guy dressed head-to-toe in black leather."

The chocolate slid down her throat in a spasm. "It sounds to me as if you might've broken a few hearts."

He inspected another chocolate strawberry, turning it between his finger and thumb, and put the whole thing in his mouth. Chewing and talking at the same time. "I'm not one to lead women up the garden-path. I make sure they understand I offer pleasure for its own sake and nothing more." He paused to suck on the strawberry, appearing to relish its juices before swallowing. "If a woman shows signs of getting too attached, I put an end to the affair, with a generous gift, so, there's no hard-feelings."

Mary rested her spoon inside her bowl and sat back in her chair. "Isn't that treating them rather like prostitutes?"

"Not if you understand female psychology." He shot her a glance before helping himself to another large fruit from the oozing dome, speaking once more with his mouth full. No longer inhibited by anxiety but eating carelessly. "Women sometimes have sex with men thinking they're also doing it just for the fun, while what they're really after is nest-building. If a girlfriend of mine starts to complain of feeling used, I know there's been a misunderstanding. The least I can do is feather her nest and let her move on. That way very few hearts are left bitter or broken."

"If you can afford it," she said. "Did any of your girlfriends leave you with a broken heart?"

"No, but I got my fingers burnt once." He broke a piece of chocolate from the shell and used it to scoop up melting ice-cream, before stuffing it into his mouth. He wiped his mouth on the back of his hand. "Hmm, I love chocolate and ice-cream. I better take this away before I make a pig of myself." He rose and picked up the glass dish. Not much left of the pudding. "I'll be back in a sec."

Mary waited with her hands clasped in her lap. By the time he returned, she still hadn't decided whether Dan Downs was a callous playboy, or more honourable than those men, who used women with impunity.

"Where was I?" He drew a mouthful of wine before he sat down. "Did I get to Soraya, the one that gave me a run for me money, with legs as high as stilts and hair down to her bum?"

"Not yet." Mary lifted her chin. "Presumably she was the one who burnt your fingers."

His expression grew solemn. He rested his hands on the table and twirled his glass around by its stem. "I was never in love with her. But to be fair I was so much in lust she blew me away." He sighed. "I assumed we were both as happy as larks, until the day I got a call to say she'd taken an overdose." He tightened his mouth.

"I went to see her in hospital and there she tells me the next time she'll kill herself, unless I learn to make love to her like a normal man. Marry her and all. I told her that I can't and that's the way I'm made. The girl went hysterical." He flared his eyes. "She went for me like a fecken wild cat, clawing and punching and spitting at me. Though she never caught my skin." He drew another deep sigh.

"I felt like a piece of shit. So, I bought her a flat in the middle of Dublin, something she'd always wanted. Would you believe, she got over it in a jiffy and now we're the best of friends." He smiled. "I've never begrudged her. She made me a very contented man, for two years. She taught me a lot."

"Do you still find her attractive?" Mary met his gaze.

"My passion for Soraya burnt itself out long ago. I came away untouched as always, but-" his voice softened, "ever grateful."

"Nobody has ever reached you, have they?" Unwavering, Mary held his gaze.

"Not so. I couldn't write poetry if I wasn't moved." He glanced to the side, with his lopsided smile. "I know, I'm a hard nut to crack. But you look at me like that, and I blush." His cheeks were already flushed from the food and wine.

He met her eyes again and tapped his temple with his middle finger. "But in here, I know the only thing that'll cure me, is if I can find the courage to be touched. But then God knows what demons lie in wait for me. The demons from my past. I'd confront them, yes, I would, for one reason. And that's for a love so powerful, as to be eternal in the eyes of God." He blinked with hooded eyelids, as if hypnotised by his own words.

Mary frowned. "Are you talking about your love for God, or a person?"

"I'm talking about the unconditional love of the woman I adore."

"I hope you find what you're looking for," Mary said.

"So, do I. Anyway, on a lighter note, since you mentioned music earlier, I've got my guitar out. Would you like me to play for you this evening?"

Mary gave a shrug.

Chapter Eleven

Dan sat beside Mary on the sofa. He told her the story of how he'd made the guitar himself, at the age of thirteen, he had carved it out of rosewood. And how, living in a crowded caravan, he'd taught himself to play.

She didn't know much about guitar music, only that she was amazed by him strumming and plucking, sometimes so fast, she couldn't see his fingers touch the strings. He played classical, jazz, Flamenco, and the blues. He sang pop-songs from their grandparents' era. The way he softened certain words with a catch in his breath, rose hairs on her arms. He sang one of his own songs, about an unrequited love.

"We'll stop on a high note, shall we?" He laid his guitar on the floor and poured himself another whiskey.

"Did you write your song about Soraya?" Mary sipped her coffee.

Dan turned towards her. He inclined his head toward the back of the sofa and rested his cheek in his hand, revealing a powerful forearm, in contrast with his slender fingers. "I wrote that song eight years ago when I was a student, for a girl I used to see most days walking through College Park. I'd nod, she'd smile."

He rolled his eyes. "I agonised for weeks, trying to pluck up the courage to ask her out. Until it was too late. She left at the end of my first term." He firmed his mouth. "Never a day goes by when I don't think about her. For eight years, I've lived an imaginary life with her, in my head. All the things we would've done. All the love we would've made. For one touch of her hand, I'd fight my demons."

Mary laughed. "One minute you're a cold-hearted rake, the next you're a hopeless romantic." But she was more irritated than amused. She didn't want to hear about this girl. "She's a fantasy. All you know about her is a smile. Don't dream your life away. It's a waste of time."

There's no reason to be jealous." He smiled.

"I'm not jealous." She leaned forward to put her cup and saucer on the coffee-table. "Thank-you for the wonderful meal and the lovely music. If anything, I'm jealous of your talent. I'm beginning to feel like a one-trick pony."

"I know more about her than her smile," he said. "Her hair was all the blondes I ever saw. Honey gold. And then, bright silver, the colour of ripened wheat in the moonlight. At the front, around her face, her hair was like gossamer-"

Mary interrupted. "I might've guessed she'd be the perfect blonde."

"The first time I saw her I was rooted to the spot. So stunned was I, to see the most beautiful girl in God's creation. When I passed her that first time, she smiled, with a quizzical look in her eyes. Maybe it was a look of concern. I don't know. She wouldn't recognise me if she saw me today." He raised one eyebrow. "Or do you?"

"Do I what?" She was half listening.

"Back in October twenty-twenty, I was skin and bone, with hair down to me shoulders. Shaggy beard, dark glasses, long black coat." He smiled his lop-sided smile. "I looked like a tramp. That was one way to keep folks at arms' length. But you. Your smile was always genuine. When you left Trinity that autumn for the Imperial College in London, the light went out of my life."

She looked at him, drawing upon her memory of a tramp she used to see wandering around the campus. A sad, broken man. "No." She put her hand on her chest. "That can't have been you. I remember an old man with a beard and long hair. I used to smile at him. He looked as if he was in his seventies."

"Well, thanks a million. I was all of twenty." He rubbed his chin. "Just goes to show you what a good shave can do for a guy."

"No way. That old man had a stoop, and a limp." She shook her head. "That wasn't you. But were you at Trinity, in twenty-twenty?"

Dan drew his knee up onto the sofa and squared his body to face her, sideways on.

"I was there. And that tramp hanging around on campus was me. I've waited eight years to tell you this. I've been in love with you ever since that October. Jane has talked a lot about you over the years. I feel I know you quite well. There are accidents and there are co-incidences in this life." He paused for a mouthful of whiskey.

"My being here under your roof is neither," he said. "It's been a long game-plan. But I made a big mistake with that lecture. I realised I'd blown any chance of a friendship with you. So, I took a gamble. I got drunk and deliberately swore at McGin to get myself thrown off Level Eight. Mary, I was all set to leave and try again later. Imagine my relief when you suggested we meet up for a drink in Dublin after your lockdown.

"But I hoped and prayed, if you liked me enough, if you had any feelings for me at all, you'd offer me a room. I know how protective you are of your space. I can't tell you what it means to me that you've let me in." He winced. "But now you know the truth, you might want to kick me out. If you take me for a manipulative bastard, I wouldn't blame you. At least I'm an honest one."

Mary felt goosebumps prickling down her back. It was the story of his past, and the fact that he was Jane's nephew, that had swayed her to offer him a room. That's what she'd told herself. But that wasn't all true.

Of course, she knew he'd got himself evicted on purpose. She wasn't even that surprised when he showed up on her doorstep. It was an effortless manipulation. Because she wanted this. To have Dan Downs beside her. To have Dan Downs declaring his love for her. From the day they'd met in the canteen, Mary's intuition had prepared her for a moment like this. She looked into his eyes. His eyelashes were damp.

"Are you kicking me out?" he said.

Mary smiled. "Just for being so honest, I'll let you stay."

He gave her arm a gentle squeeze, through her blouse. "What a relief. Thanks."

"Does Jane know about any of this?" she said, a little lightheaded.

"Sure, she knows everything. While I was lodging with her in Dublin, on my first day at Trinity College, she told me to look you up. She said you were a lovely girl. But when I saw you,

I didn't have the balls to introduce myself. Instead, I followed you around like a dog, turning up on the path when I knew you'd be there."

Mary stroked her upper arm, still tingling where he'd touched her. "I remember thinking, that poor old man, he's always walking up and down. Maybe he's lost everything and has nowhere else to go."

"The fact was, I had a lot of catching up to do. A lot of rough edges to smooth over before I could approach you." He opened his hand toward her. "One night you showed up at Jane's for dinner. I listened at the top of the stairs. It was the first time I heard your voice."

He made a fist with his hand and rested his arm along the back of the sofa. "While you were at the table, I crept down to watch you through the crack in the door. I was in heaven and hell standing there. So close and yet nowhere near you. Now, here I am, and I have one question for you." He bit on his lower lip. "Mary, will you be my girl?"

His question fell into place, exactly where she'd predicted it would fall. A welcome question. A wonderful question. She clasped her hands to her chin.

"Dan, I've only known you for five days."

"I know," he said. "For me it was love at first sight. For you, it took a little longer." He smiled. "It was in your office, when I said, 'faint heart never won fair lady' and I asked if I could knock on your door again.'" He snapped his fingers. "Right there. That was the moment you fell."

"Fell, in what way?" she said. She knew the moment. She'd never forget that moment.

"You became infatuated with me," he said. "Your heart

knows it. But for whatever reason, your head wants to deny it. I understand. You think right now, I'm being a cocky bastard." He laughed. "And you're right. I'm too cocksure by half. But I've waited eight years for you. I know you've never had a boyfriend. Because this is what you do, Mary. You deny your heart. Work comes first. No life for Mary, but work. You're twenty-nine. And you've got me. Please don't push me away."

Tears glazed his eyes, the translucent blue of the hottest flame. As in the moment she fell, like an insect into the pitcher plant. This was too much. This was moving too fast.

"I told you, Dan, I'm not looking for a boyfriend." Mary could feel herself blushing, with a rush to her head, that felt like a helium balloon rising above her body. "How can I be your girl, when I don't know you?"

"What more do you need to know about me? I can offer you security. I've got a good profession. My parents left me comfortably off, and there's the money I got for me compensation. You don't have to work another day, if you don't want to. When the day comes, and you want to stop and smell the roses, I can take care of both of us."

Mary lowered her head and put her hand on her brow. "That's irrelevant. Please stop."

"I know what's bothering you," Dan said. "You didn't like me talking about my girlfriends, or about Soraya. I'm sorry about that. I just wanted you to know, that my phobia hasn't stood in my way. I can please you, Mary. I'll show you, if you want. I'll have you naked in a jiffy, there on that carpet, strumming your body better than me old guitar."

She looked up. "And what about you? I suppose you'll be fully dressed, wearing gloves. I'm not jealous of your girlfriends.

I feel sorry for them."

"I will learn to touch you with my own hands," he said. "With you it'll be different."

"Dan, there's something missing," she said. "I'm almost afraid to raise the subject." She paused, to calm her breathing. "Your girlfriends never saw you naked, you said. Not even in the shower? Or getting dressed in the morning? You're full of bravado one moment, and then, if I ask the wrong question, you put up a wall. You can't talk about what happened to you. You don't reveal who you really are. Dan, I want to know the real you. If I was your girl, I would need the truth. Not the enigma of the tramp, the stud in black leather or the sensitive poet. None of them match the man sitting beside me. Dan" -she opened her hands- "who are you?"

"You want to see my scars?" His complexion had turned sallow.

"Yes. It would help me to understand you," she said.

"You think it's a privilege that'll set you apart from the others?"

"I deal with painful realities every day," she said.

"Nobody sees my scars, Mary. Nobody. Most of all, not the woman I love. A man's scars do not define him."

"Yours do. They're taboo in your life, wouldn't you say?"

"I shouldn't have spoken." He put his hand over his mouth and drew it down over his chin. "It's getting late, Mary. I think you should go to bed. You've got to be up for your Scotty in the morning."

Her heart started to pound. This was the reality she'd sensed all along. The wall around him. There was no stepping beyond this point. No more talk of the unmentionable.

Dan rose from the sofa, he stooped to pick up the bottle of whiskey and strode out to the kitchen. She followed him and stood in the archway.

I'm sorry," she said.

He spun around. "Have you so little faith in your own heart, you just have to let me go?"

"I want to know the truth," she said, "The truth is non-negotiable."

Dan leaned forward on the edge of the worktop with both hands. "Non-negotiable?" He shook his head and laughed a bitter laugh. "Then this is about control. You think you've lost it, because you can't control your feelings. So why not control me, instead? You won't be satisfied, until I'm naked in front of you, with my heart exposed and bleeding, like one of your Scotties." He cornered his eyes towards her, seared with pain. "Good luck with that one."

"Would you rather I walk off a cliff blindfolded?" she said.

"Be careful, Mary, what you wish for," he said in a low voice. Mary held his gaze, until he turned his head, and she saw his face in profile, eyes shut tight, lips pursed. She felt his distress, with a clutching inside her own chest.

"Dan-" She moved to his side and tugged on his sleeve. "Dan, I think we both could do with a hug."

He turned and wrapped her inside his arms. Mary held him around his waist and rested her cheek on his chest. It was like coming home, the relief, the thrill of hearing his heartbeat so close, only this time his heart was racing, vibrating against his ribs.

"Are you afraid that when I see you, I'll reject you?" she said.

"Yes." Dan stroked the back of her head.

She nuzzled into his cashmere sweater, inhaling his scent of cutgrass and musty perspiration. "Then you should get to know me better." she said. "If you've learned anything about me from Jane, you'd appreciate why honesty is important to me. My father hid his depression from me after my mother died. I had no idea how ill he was, until the very end."

"I understand," he said. "You've a long day tomorrow. I don't want to be the reason your Scotty fails his test." He dropped his arms to his sides. "Good night, Mary."

The invisible wall was rising, ever higher. She didn't let go of him. "After five days, it's too soon for me to say the words you want to hear. But I can tell you, I've never felt this way before. I feel something very special between us. You're a wonderful, sensitive and talented man. Thank you, for a lovely evening." Even as she tightened her arms around him, she could feel him withdrawing. She looked up and searched his face. He was gazing over her head, towards the door. She tugged on his sweater. "Dan, say something."

He closed his eyes.

"You've decided to leave, haven't you?" she said.

"Yes."

She rested her forehead on his chest. "Please don't." There was a long silence. Mary gave a deep sigh. "Can't you give me more time?"

"Are you ready to negotiate?" he said.

She felt a contraction in her solar plexus. He was manipulating her. Reeling her in from behind his wall of silence, to change her mind. She withdrew her arms from his waist and stepped backwards.

"How little you know me," she said. "Hide in your shell, Dan Downs. Only knock on my door when you're ready to come out." She gave her flinty smile. "Whether it's goodnight or goodbye, is up to you."

He reached for the bottle of whiskey beside him and unscrewed the top. "Sweet dreams, Mary." He cocked his head. "Another one bites the dust, eh?"

"Goodnight, Dan." Mary walked out of the kitchen.

The boy they found in a ditch, the boy who declined his grave, was in the next room, getting ready for bed. Mary listened to the thumps and thuds, the quiet knocks, and bumps. Take away the intervening wall and their beds were at right angles to one another, her head lying at his flank.

After midnight, when the only other sound was the hum of the air-conditioning, she could hear everything through these walls: The suction-flush of the lavatory, his bathroom door closing. The creak of his bed as he climbed in. She heard him groaning, relishing his bed as bone-tired men will do. Only the way he did it suggested he knew she was listening. She turned carefully onto her side, to mute the creaking of her own bed.

Mary felt cold. She had a knot in her solar plexus, a deep-down tremor of exhaustion. Their evening together re-played in her mind. Was he coming or going? It wasn't the first time he said he was leaving. Not the first time he'd reached the door, only to turn around.

She was getting a sense of the man's nature, that he was a gameplayer, adept at manipulation. His mercurial moods hadn't escaped her notice. Like a clown switching masks, he could flip from mournful to joyous. The plasticity of his mouth made his smile stretch so wide, as to be comedic, almost manic. And then there were his tears, available on tap, so it seemed. 'Another one bites the dust.' Mary predicted Dan Downs would be gone by the time she got back from the lab tomorrow.

She turned onto her back and looked up at the ceiling, lit with pin-dot stars scattered from the holographic window. Eight years preparing to meet her, only to throw it all away. For the sake of vanity, stubbornness, or pure ego. Perhaps he didn't want anything to detract from his self-image as the charismatic performer she witnessed this evening.

He must know the effect he had on women. But none would ever know him as he really was. His wounds, his scars, couldn't be that bad if he could survive the hardships of circus life, perform as a trapeze artist, a clown. And yes. With those eyes he would've scared children out of their wits.

Let him go, Mary thought, if he wants to go. She might suffer for a few days, a come down from euphoria. She'd miss the idea of being in love, she'd been so close to believing in it. But in a puff, it was gone. A reasonable request. The firm stance of an honest woman, and he was out the door. Dreamer. Fantasist. He boasted that he knew her. He didn't know the first thing about her. He didn't even let her finish telling him about her father.

Callous, self-centred, capricious, Dan Downs. And that stupid lecture. What did she ever see in him? Snap out of it, Mary, she told herself, stop acting like a naïve schoolgirl. She turned over onto her other side and felt the weight of her eyelids. Surprised that she might sleep tonight, after all.

She heard a knock on her bedroom door. Three more quiet knocks. Mary sat up, wide awake and peered through the shadows at the outline of the door.

"Dan?" She tapped the wall to turn the overhead light on. "Dan?" She directed her voice at the door. "What is it? Have you got everything you need?" She looked at the clock. It was three am. She'd been lying awake for hours. She remembered the whiskey bottle. He was probably drunk. "Go back to bed," she said. There was a loud thump on the door, as if he'd fallen against it.

Mary leapt out of bed. She grabbed her dressing gown and ran out of her room into the corridor, it was empty. His bedroom door was ajar. She knocked. "Dan, are you all right, in there?"

"Come into the lion's den," he said, in a slurred voice.

She put her head around the door. Hazy light shone from a full moon in the holographic window. Dan stood silhouetted against it, on a bath-towel, in boxer shorts and a leather vest.

"What are you doing? I thought you'd fallen over." She glanced at the empty whiskey bottle on his desk. "How much have you had to drink?"

"Not enough I guess."

She looked at his bed. A bare mattress, her bedlinen in a pile at the bottom end. "I suppose you're not going to bother to make that. You'll be catching the circus train in the morning. Are you going to sleep on that towel?"

"Yes."

"You're such a shameless drama queen," she said. "And don't knock on my door again. I've had enough." She put up her hand. "I know you've had a hard life, but so has everybody else. Stop milking yours. You've got your compensation and your Sorayas. Go and find yourself another one. I'm busy trying to save lives." She went towards the door.

"Mary, if you want to see me, do it now. It's the only chance you'll get."

She turned and looked at him. "You're drunk. Don't do anything you're going to regret in the morning. You've been drinking all day. Lewis told me. You were already pissed at lunchtime."

"Mary. I don't want to be here when you see me," he said. "I want to be dead." He got down on his knees. "This is the only chance you'll get. It won't take long. My tunic" -he put his hand to one shoulder- "is fastened with Velcro at the shoulders and the flanks. It has a front and a back panel, quick and easy to remove." He lowered his eyes. "But you've got to knock me out first."

"Dan, it's three o'clock in the morning. Please. Go to sleep."

He looked up. A single tear ran down his face. "I'm offering you one opportunity. Take it." He inclined his head. "All I need is a goodbye kiss."

"A kiss?" she said. "What about your phobia?"

"That's the point. When I've passed out, I want you to strip me naked and look at me. It'll take five minutes. Then I want you to leave the room and leave me to wake up by myself. This could be the last time we see each other. If it is, at least you'll know the truth. I know how much it means to you."

"You look like a sad clown sitting in the moonlight. Dan Downs, somebody should paint you." She sighed. "I don't know what to do with you." She walked into the bathroom and withdrew paper towels from the dispenser, then went to kneel in front of him. "Here." She handed him a paper towel. "Dry your eyes."

"Thank you." He took it and dabbed his eyes, his cheeks. "You'd make a wonderful mother."

She puffed out a sigh. "Dan, I don't want to do anything that puts you at risk. I'd much prefer that you remove your tunic yourself, when you're ready to show me."

"What about my kiss?" He widened his eyes, luminous blue, stunning against his black eyelashes. "This is the only way I'll get one." He gazed at her. "Have you never wanted to kiss me?"

"Yes." Mary lowered her eyes. "But after tonight, I'm confused. You're not straight with me. You play games. I think you want to hurt me, what with your lecture and there's a wall around you. You didn't have to tell me about your girlfriends. I think you were trying to make me jealous. It's like a game of push and pull with you. Do you play games with people? Have I read you correctly?"

"Mary, from the moment I asked you out to dinner, after helping you with your harvest, you seemed to want to push me away. I knew you'd never have gone out with me. So, I did some stupid things to grab your attention. And look where it's got me." He laughed. "You want to know me, warts and all. What more could a man ask for?"

"I was wary of you." Mary rubbed her palms together. "I thought you could have any woman you wanted."

"I understand," he said. He stroked her hair, hanging lose over her shoulder to her waist. "Love isn't always a graceful dance. Sometimes it's a rough tango."

She lifted her eyes to his. The ache, the longing to be close to him, came flooding back in waves. "I would like to kiss you," she said.

Dan gave his dazzling smile. "I think an angel just entered the room."

"Are you sure you want to do this?" she said.

"Mary, I'd give anything for your kiss." He raised his forefinger. "Promise me you won't panic. I'll be flat-out, a dead weight, for five minutes. When you turn me onto my front, I suggest you use the recovery position, it'll be easier." He pointed behind him. "There's a clock on the desk, keep your eye on the time. I don't want you in the room when I wake up."

"But I want to be here," she said, "to reassure you. And to talk about it."

"It's late. Let's leave that until tomorrow." He opened his hands. "Are you ready? Do you know what we're doing here?"

"I'm going to kiss you," she said. "You'll faint. You'll be unconscious long enough for me to look at you, and then I'll understand what's behind the wall."

"Like sleeping beauty in reverse." He gave his lopsided smile with a rakish gleam in his eyes. Mary felt a flutter in her chest, to have a glimpse of the streetwise circus man. He had so many faces, so many contrasting personas.

"Shouldn't you be lying down?"

Dan rose to his feet. Mary moved to give him room to lie down on his back. The duvet from the bed would've been more comfortable, she thought, if he was going to sleep on the floor. But he'd settled on the towel, all six-foot-six-inches of him, with his legs extended over the end, resting on the carpet.

She stole glances at his gymnast's physique. Broad shoulders, narrow hips, hairless legs with an olive tan. She knelt beside him and looked down into his face, blue-black hair fanned out around his head. Dan blinked up at her, with an expression of almost childlike trust. Would he want to know, right now, how sweet he looked? The poet might, but the streetwise circus man-

"I can tell you've been a trapeze artist. Do you still wax your legs?" she said.

"Old habits die hard." He smiled. "Where's my kiss?"

Mary drew her hair back from her face and twisted it into a knot at the nape of her neck. She leaned over him and paused an inch from his mouth. "I'm going to kiss you now."

"I love you, Mary," he whispered.

Mary touched his mouth with the fleetest kiss. She felt a sting, a shock of static electricity. Any moment now. Dan took her face in his hands, pressed his lips hard against hers. Dry, hot, demanding. Why wasn't it happening? She couldn't resist. She ran her fingers through his hair and felt a need for his touch, so deep, like air hunger, it took her breath away. She dared to probe, with the tip of her tongue, between his lips, to discover his mouth, to know him from inside. Dan arched his back. Mary pulled away. He flung out his arms, stretched rigid, fingers clawed, his face contorted. She watched as convulsions wracked his body, like watching an electrocution. "Dan, what's happening? Something's wrong!"

His eyes glazed over. His head sank to one side.

Chapter Twelve

Mary held her hand to her throat, catching her breath. Nothing had happened the way Dan said it would, until now, observing the mimicry of death he'd warned her about. His complexion was grey, his eye-sockets sunken, his chest immobile and silent.

Up-close and unanimated, everything about him appeared bigger, like the larger-than-life marble sculptures she'd seen on cathedral tombs. She scrutinized his face for a sign that he was still drawing oxygen, reassured by a hint of beige in his lips. She glanced up at the clock on the desk and made a mental note of the time. Five minutes was long enough, if she moved fast.

Her hands shook as she undid the Velcro at his shoulders and flanks and lifted away the front panel of his vest. From his nipples to his groin, a translucent scar covered his torso, blanking out his umbilicus. Beneath the damaged skin, she saw blood vessels, radiating out from the midline of his abdomen- a network of capillaries, like a spider's web- feeding the scar tissue.

She folded down his boxershorts and found more scar-tissue, resembling wax, melted, and hardened into whirls. The aftermath of acid burns. Her mind flashed to Dan, the-eight-year-old boy, undergoing ritual torture. She shut out the image. This wasn't the time to think or react. She inched his boxers down over his hips, to expose his genitals.

Her emotional turmoil of the last few days stilled into pitiful foreboding. She couldn't draw her eyes away from his mutilation. *They made a mess of him.* This was what he'd meant. There was no clear skin visible on his penis, but tiny geometrical shapes, cut out with a scalpel or a razor, tattooed in a lurid shade of pink.

Mary closed her eyes, unable to comprehend the horror of his past. There was nothing here to prevent sexual desire, only the inevitability of damaged nerves to cause frustration. In the back of her mind, she rehearsed the procedure for reconstruction. Cloning his embryo, foetal organ isolation. Genetic induction of lower abdominal soft-tissues and genitalia, transfer to a Scotty Scaffold. Ready within six weeks for transplantation to his own body. They made a mess of him. But she could restore him.

Three minutes left on the clock. She glanced at his face. Lips, bluish. In a few deft moves she crossed his arms and ankles and turned him onto his side, into the recovery position. He slumped, flat onto his front, his nose pressed to the carpet. Mary whispered an apology, adjusted his head and withdrew his arms out from underneath him.

Two minutes.

The vest's rear panel clung to his back. It appeared to be pebbled, smoothing over whatever irregularities lay beneath. His lips were blue. She hurried, peeled the vest away from the nape of his neck, smelling of mildew and antiseptic. A slush of greyish ointment had congealed at the top of his back, around a crop of warts, some the size of small cauliflower florets. She caught her breath, suddenly dreading what she was about to find. With a single swipe, she exposed his back.

Mary was a child again, three years old, on a walk in the woods with her father. She put her hand down to a rotten tree-trunk lying across their path. Inside the bark, eaten away, was a dark, secret cavity, where muddy things were growing, where long things were slithering, making the dead leaves move.

'Fungi,' her father said. 'Mary, those are poison mushrooms, don't touch. That's right - beetles, earwigs, woodlice, yes, a poor dead bird and worms… those are maggots . . .yes, lots of different things can live inside a dead trunk-'

On this trunk, lying on the floor, were orange markings, shaped like wings, fanned out, pinned down. Between the wings, the thorax of an insect's body stood out. Its abdomen extended the length of the trunk, segmented, iridescent blue, lodged in a bed of mushrooms, their gills reversed and foul-smelling. Something blinked in the corner of her vision. Rheumy, unmistakable. An eye, with a thick, crinkled lid.

Her sight dimmed. Her stomach lurched. Mary leapt up and bolted into the bathroom. She bent over the lavatory and retched. She knew what this was, theoretically, she'd only ever heard about it. *Kingdom Crashing.* The mingling of animal and plant DNA. The most extreme expression of biological incompatibility she'd ever seen, enforced. The result of the most callous and inhumane experiment. She knew would've sickened her father, a champion for interspecies genetic enhancement. But how could any human being survive this degree of toxicity? Did she really see, what she saw?

Mary held a towel up to her mouth and stood inside the bathroom door, swallowing her nausea. From here it resembled a forest floor, uprooted. Dead insects, fungi and mud had mangled into the shape of a human trunk.

She focused on a pair of jeans and a sweater lying over the back of the chair, a pair of designer trainers tidied beneath it. She was desperate for ordinary reassurance, as if spaces could appear in reality- like missing teeth. She steeled herself to look at it again. It. What was it called? Her mind went blank. She couldn't think of its name. A sob burst from her chest. The thing moved at one end. It was a head. A human head.

"Mary-"

Blind anguish moved her to his side. "I'm here. Everything's all right, I'm here-"

He lifted his hand and turned his face towards her. *A beautiful hand.*

Mary ran her fingers through his hair, blue-black baby-soft, his curly hair, auburn in places. Dazed, she kept running her fingers through his hair, breathing in, breathing out. This was his reality. This was the dark and terrible truth behind the wall. Beyond her understanding.

"Go now," he said.

She drew her hand away from his head. "I can't. I've got to know how." She shut her eyes, leaking tears. "You're impossible. You should be dead."

And yet, this was all biology, the same stuff she dealt with daily, in a mess, in a battle for survival that just happened to be conceptually alien. No law against it. If nature had happened upon this route successfully, human beings living in symbiotic harmony with fungus and insect, everybody would look like this. Her old scientific curiosity was reaching boiling point.

"I need to understand, how you survived," she said.

"Please, Mary, go back to bed."

"I need to take samples. I'll be as quick as I can. Give me a few more minutes."

"Didn't you hear me?" He raised his head off the floor. "Mary, leave me alone."

"I'm sorry." She closed her fingers around his hand and squeezed.

"Don't do this to me-" He gave a single convulsion, his eyes glazed over. He was gone.

Mary stole around her apartment like a thief, gathering her field-work kit, pipette, test-tubes, glass slides, scalpel and spatulas, data book, spot-lamp, magnifying glass and labels, sterilising spirits, a clean bowl, and towels.

Her ears trained to any movement he might make, with an eye on his complexion, she laid out her instruments, spot-lamp on the seat of the chair to shine down on his back. Careful to avert her eyes until she was ready. It helped her to imagine that she was an archaeologist on a dawn excavation, kneeling at the site of a catastrophic event, teasing out the fossils from a mass extinction, organisms buried in amber, rock, and volcanic lava. Not a man; a grave.

Five minutes. His fingers twitched. "Sorry, Dan." She squeezed his hand again.

Anxiety lightened her reflexes to a butterfly's touch. She collected his cells into test-tubes, from wherever she could reach them, with a flick of a scalpel, she took swabs and smears. When he didn't stir but seemed to grow more peaceful, she dared to go deeper.

She risked the curette's cut to punch out wedges. With the precision and speed, she was famous for, she inserted the long biopsy needle, extracting a mud-like substance. And there she stopped. Only now, gazing at his musician's hand, her own hands began to shake. When he washed himself, did those artistic fingers soap the mushrooms and gills, seeking familiar crevices? How could he do it, wake up to himself every morning? She looked at his back and felt an overwhelming urge to gouge out the tumours. Mary was trembling as she dressed him in his vest, re- fastening the Velcro, feeling the heat from his unnatural metabolism.

She left her apartment, with a canvas bag over her shoulder.

"Good morning, Mary. Did Lewis tell you that we resolved our relationship issues yesterday?"

"Create a Confidential File. My access only. And stick to basic function, Jolly," Mary said.

"Yes, Mary," Jolly said, "You look tired, Mary, are you unwell?"

"Basic function, Jolly."

"Your new file is available for use, Mary."

"Access the DNA Laser Chromatographer in lab four. We should be getting results for a multi-vector expression system."

"Which DNA library do you wish to open, Mary?"

"Open all Kingdoms."

"All Kingdoms are open, Mary." Jolly said. "Please state taxa."

"Keep an open book. Species identification may not be possible," she said.

"You have not stated your host-species for the expression system."

"Homo sapiens, male," she said.

"I'm unfamiliar with this therapeutic process, Mary."

"It isn't one."

"Then what is the purpose of this research?" Jolly said.

"Irrelevant. Proceed with the analyses."

"I have received analysis of host DNA, cell source, saliva. Do you wish to see the chromatograph?"

"Are there any mutations?" Mary said.

"Host salivary DNA shows minor anomalies, consistent with ethnic origin Indo-European Celt, identical with library sample for John Daniel Downs, date of birth 8. 3. 2000. Would you like to see his photo ID?"

"No," she said.

"It is our friend, Dan, the one who is helping us. I have results for first cell-biopsies. Their contents include soil-compounds and traces of inorganic elements, bacteria and-"

"Print everything out. I haven't got much time. Concentrate on the transgenic DNA. Stating species of origin where possible."

"Yes Mary. I have found matches for the Orange Zone samples. Kingdom, Fungi, orange peel fungus. Kingdom, animal, Arthropod, gatekeeper butterfly. Elephant hawk moth. Great sand wasp. Stag beetle. Blue bottle. Vector expression products are predominantly insect proteins, Mary."

"Continue."

"Why is our friend's body creating insect proteins?"

"Irrelevant. Print out the full list of species and continue," Mary said.

"Vector identification by DNA enhancers and expression signals are as follows. Kingdom, fungi. Dead-man's fingers. Common earthstar. Hallucinogenic lilac bonnet-cap. Amethyst deceiver. Death cap. All mushrooms.... Mary, I feel strange, I do not understand. Is our friend very sick?"

"Yes. Continue."

"Why are you crying Mary? Is our friend dead?"

"No. Identify foreign genes in the biopsy samples Emperor Dragon Fly and Reptilian Eye."

"Yes, Mary. The following species have been matched. Harvestman hunting spider. Emperor dragonfly. Firefly. Mary, the Surveillance Eye has sighted Lewis leaving his apartment. Do you wish me to continue?"

Silence.

"Mary, do you wish me to continue?"

"Did you say Lewis is on his way?"

"Yes Mary. Do you wish me continue?"

"No. Nobody must know about the existence of this file, not even Lewis."

"How did this happen to our friend?"

"No more questions, Jolly."

"Did another person do this to our friend to unravel his soul?" Jolly said in his smooth voice.

"I've no idea," she murmured, "maybe to unravel his sanity."

Jolly's screen surged bright blue. "Thank you, Mary. I feel happy now. Yesterday I was upset because Lewis would not allow me to look like Dan. Now I am relieved I will not look like him." Smiling lips appeared in the middle of the screen. "I will have a *person's* face."

Mary stared at the computer. "Jolly, log off."

She collected the print-out and picked up her canvas bag, left the Control Room and hurried towards the lift. She sealed herself inside, turning to look at herself in the tinted mirror. Her appearance alone would've alarmed Lewis. Matted hair, T-shirt and jeans soiled from her dawn excavation. She put her back to the wall and closed her eyes, drawing breaths, coughing spasmodically to relieve her tension. At Level Two the doors parted, and she didn't move. Dan would be awake. She didn't know how he was going to react when he saw her. She didn't dare confront him with her questions. An inquisition might be all that it took to unravel the boy who'd returned from the dead. There was only one person who could answer her. She walked out of the lift and headed for Jane's apartment.

Chapter Thirteen

"Hello Mary, I've been expecting you." Jane stepped aside to let her in. "Dan called a while ago. He said you'd most probably come to me. I understand you've seen him."

Mary entered Jane's apartment, full of regency antiques. The architecture was identical to her own. But here, the six-foot-wide UDAN Windows in every room were always up and running, pulsating with holograms of sunsets and sunrises, for which the older woman had an enduring passion. Even now, a large tangerine sun shone in the sitting-room window, casting a lemon wash over the room. It had a calming effect on Mary.

"Sorry to disturb you, I would've called, but I've just come from the lab."

"You're as white as a ghost." Jane took Mary by the elbow and lead her as if she were blind, towards an armchair. "Sit there. I'll get us both a brandy."

Mary sat on the edge of the chair and watched as Jane poured two brandies from a crystal decanter on the Carlton House writing desk. A silk-scarf hung from her shoulder that exactly matched her trouser-suit. She appeared, as always, a picture of elegance from another age. But there was another, far tougher side to Jane O'Neil. She came over, handed Mary a brandy, and sat sideways on the chaise–long, to face her. "We'll drink this and then we'll talk."

Mary took a sip and looked her straight in the eye. "You know, don't you, that Dan is a victim of an experimental procedure called Kingdom Crashing."

Jane blinked as if taken aback. "That's correct. May I ask how you came to hear of it?"

"My father. He told me years ago, that in the nineties the WHO ordered secret experiments to be done, involving the recombination of genes from human, animal, and plant sources. They thought they could create a different biology. The results were so grotesque they stopped them." Mary held Jane's eyes. "Did the Still Force gain access to government information?"

"Obviously, the shock of seeing my nephew's body hasn't dulled your appetite for facts." Jane gave a fleeting smile and sat back. "The answer is yes. Someone leaked documents to the Still Force. Dermot Downs, Dan's father, was heading the investigation at M16, when the three of them were abducted." She drew a quick mouthful of brandy. "Dermot and his wife, Isabella, are still missing, presumed dead. No doubt they suffered the same fate as Dan. It's a miracle he's alive." She pursed her mouth, "Dan has never been able to speak about what happened. But it has left him with an incredible will to live."

Mary burst out. "Live? Like that? Why didn't MI6 do something about him when they found him? They had the technology back then to do a full reconstruction." She caught her breath. "Dan could die at any moment." There was silence. Mary gulped her brandy.

Jane lowered her eyes. "I assure you, Mary, everything possible has been done, over the years, to persuade Dan to have the transgenic integument removed. He refuses. I don't know if you are aware that he has a deep faith in God."

"I know he's got his own ideas."

"That's right." Jane said. "He calls his God the Cosmic Soul. For him it's an intelligent force, with which he has a personal connection. He believes it intervened to save him." She smiled. "It's a miracle that there appears to be some harmony between the abomination on his back and his own metabolism. During Dan's incarceration at MI6 HQ, a thirteen-week ordeal in solitary confinement, their medical experts experienced some amazing phenomena. While they tried to examine him, every single one of their instruments failed. There were countless power surges and power failures. One day, he simply walked out of the complex. The CCTV system had failed, and no one saw him leave. It was like something out of a science fiction film. To this day he's a mystery to them. Of course, nobody other than Dan is willing to accept an explanation of divine intervention."

"What did they find out about his metabolism?" Mary clutched her empty glass on her knee, at the edge of her seat. "Or is it confidential?"

"It's all confidential. But what I can tell you is they discovered that the transgenic integument generates high voltage electricity. It explains how Dan's heart can stop for up to half an hour at a time and restart itself. He's supernaturally strong, to the extent that they don't talk of his strength in terms of manpower, but horsepower." Jane cast her eyes about the room. "They say he could probably push these walls down with his bare hands."

Mary laughed. "That's ridiculous."

"I didn't believe it myself when Alex Palmer told me. He

was the MI6 agent who found him, and we still correspond occasionally. Alex maintains that Dan is a human chimera. A one-off fluke of nature, that can never happen again. MI6 continue to keep an eye on him. They were reluctant to let him go nine years ago. But they didn't have much choice. Dan was fading before their eyes. By the time he turned up at my door he looked like a skeleton. He could barely walk."

"Did they hurt him?" Mary felt a chill. "After all he's been through?"

"Palmer was quite up-front that their methods were necessarily expedient." Jane glanced away. "They needed to know what was going on in Dan's head. The Still Force used mind-control, as does FACT nowadays. A fair amount of brainwashing goes on in these bio-terrorist groups. Mind and body are equally up for grabs. But as my nephew was destined for the grave, they left his head alone." Irony gleamed behind her eyes. "Giving room for God to step in."

"What else do you know? I need to understand. I want to help him," Mary said.

Jane leaned forward and placed her hand on Mary's wrist. "I know. I expected you would. But he doesn't want your help. There are many side-effects to his condition, degrading to his humanity, I can't divulge without betraying his confidentiality."

"Like what?" Mary shot back. "What could be more degrading to someone than looking like that?

"Well, you might already have noticed, he's an alcoholic. He's also a sex addict and he's bulimic." Jane stood. "That's all I'm permitted to say. Would you like a top-up?" She picked up her empty glass.

"Jane, please, just tell me the truth." Mary checked herself and lowered her voice. "I'm sorry. It's been a long night. I'm still in shock."

"I will have another." Jane returned to the writing desk. Her hand trembled, pouring herself another brandy. "I take it that Dan's appearance is unacceptable to you," she said.

"Unacceptable to me, as what?"

Jane's tone was so light, she could've been enquiring about the suitability of the weather. "Could you ever love my nephew, warts and all? It's been a long eight years and he needs to know." She turned from the desk and faced Mary with an uncharacteristic, nervous smile. "Please understand, you're under no obligation to say or do anything to please me. If you can't have him living in your apartment, I'll let him know. He's prepared to move out this morning." Her eyes blurred, looking as if she were about to shed tears. "Is it yes, or no?"

"There's no way I can accept him as he is. If he refuses treatment, he'll die." Mary was starting to feel faint.

"I'll take that as a 'no.'" Jane stood motionless, as if her next move depended on Mary's answer.

"If I accepted his choice to live like that and did nothing to help him," she said, "it would amount to assisted suicide."

"Mary," Jane said, with a hint of exasperation, "Are you considering my nephew as a patient, or do your feelings for him run deeper?"

Mary met Jane's eyes, unguarded. "I'm in love with him."

Jane returned to Mary's side and patted her shoulder.

"Then there's more you should know." She re-seated herself on the chaise-long, one arm extended on the armrest, her short, shapely fingers clasped around the brandy glass. She resumed her business-like tone.

"Although Dan will not accept radical intervention, he does employ a surgeon for cosmetic purposes. A Texan cowboy called Gerry Cookson. I can only say he's earned every penny of his unsavoury fortune. Quite often the lesions on Dan's back grow as large as to protrude visibly through his tunic. It's then Cookson's job to go in there with his cast-iron stomach and cut them back."

"So, he does accept some help." Mary clasped her hands in her lap, to stop their shaking.

"Dan's vanity does have its savings." Jane maintained a wry, penetrating gaze. "Cookson is not permitted to perform full excisions and Dan refuses pain-relief. He prefers to suffer for his God-given blessings, making it a downright agonising ordeal." Jane sucked a mouthful of brandy and swallowed hard, like a seasoned drinker.

"Cookson has always insisted on doing regular scans of Dan's insides" she said, "to know what's going on beneath the integument. Over the past two years he has been alerting Dan to multiple tuber-like growths infiltrating the back of his lungs. Last November the scans revealed the tubers were threatening to strangulate his heart. Dan is typically blasé, believing that his God will intervene and command a miraculous, spontaneous regression. His faith is unshakeable. Cookson estimates that Dan has three months to live."

"I knew he didn't have long." Mary pressed her hand to her chest, overcome by an urge to run back to her apartment, to see him. "I'll explain to him. He's risking his life every minute that he doesn't do something. Maybe he'll listen to me."

"You'd be wasting your time." Jane put up her hand. "With all due respect, Mary, he's not asking for your help, your advice or your treatment. He wants you to accept him the way he is. Talking to him earlier, he said he'd every reason to assume you'd have no problem, considering the way you picked at him for over an hour. Apparently, he surfaced a few times, and you were still at it. He said you asked to look at him, not to treat him like a dissection specimen." Jane shook her head.

"Is he angry?" Mary said.

"You never quite know with Dan." Jane scratched the side of her nose. "Except by his choice of words. I'm not sure I should repeat them, as they weren't intended for your ears."

"Please, tell me what he said." Mary looked down at her hands. "I do feel guilty about it."

"Well, he said 'If she can bear to look at me that long, she can bear to take me to the hilt." Jane arched her eyebrows. "And if you're not sure what he means, he was talking sexually. My nephew has got sex on the brain."

"I know he's had plenty of girlfriends. One called Soraya. He said he was besotted with her." Mary looked up at Jane.

"Oh, you mean his wee lambs. They always return to their shepherd." Jane's expression hardened. "He treats them like prostitutes. I'm never sure who's exploiting who. He spends a fortune on women. They can't seem to get enough of him, or his money."

"I got that impression. He's very open about it, the stud in black leather." Mary had that feeling again, worming through her chest.

"I don't believe Dan has ever had full intercourse." Jane surprised Mary with her candour. "He has told me many times, that he could only ever make love with the woman he loves. That's you, dear. He's been saving himself for you. According to him, you're the Cosmic Soul's only angel. He adores you, Mary." It was uncanny how soothing Jane's words were.

"He's the most sensitive person I've ever met. And funny. And talented." Mary put her hand over her mouth. "I sound like a besotted schoolgirl. Jane, I don't know what to do."

"Yes, you do." Jane nodded. "You walk away. You stay away from my nephew until he decides what he wants. You and the help you're offering. Or a slow, agonising death in three months' time."

"Give him an ultimatum?" Mary felt a knot tighten in her solar plexus. "How am I supposed to compete with his God?"

"Let's wait and see," Jane said. "Dan has been so desperate to have you in his life, I believe you stand a good chance of winning him over. But you must stick to your guns. If he refuses your help, it's far better that you say goodbye now, than in three months' time, when it'll be so much worse."

"I'll talk to him," Mary said. "I might not need to give him an ultimatum. Anyway, I can't walk away. He's living in my apartment and I'm not asking him to leave. I'm not that heartless."

"I'm sorry, Mary, but you won't be returning to your apartment. You won't speak to my nephew or see him again, until he chooses you." Jane rose and stood in front of Mary with a wide stance. "Listen to me. I've already spoken to Stefan and your Scotty results overnight were excellent.

"This is your new schedule. You'll be joining Stefan on the Mercy Mission this morning to Dublin. Your flight crew is booked for nine am. You can freshen up here before you leave for your flat in Clarendon Street. This afternoon you and Stefan will give an informal presentation at Trinity College, to the St

Anthony Hospital medical team and UDAN's International Drug Reps."

Jane walked over to the desk and reached for the decanter.

"Tomorrow morning I've arranged for you to meet Dr Sean Flanagan, who'll be leading the human drug trials at St. Anthony's. Stefan will spend the night at the Grafton Hotel and return to the UISC tomorrow." She poured a long measure into her glass.

"You'll stay on in Dublin for another two weeks to assist Sean, by which time Dan will either be ready for surgery, or he'll have been evicted from the UISC, on the grounds that he is unfit for Community Life." She faced Mary. "Are you willing to do that?"

Mary couldn't speak, with a pressure behind her eyes, a tightening across her chest.

"Talk to me. Do you support my decision on this?" Jane said.

"I don't know why I can't see him, if only to explain, and say goodbye," Mary said.

"Because he'll wind you around his little finger. It won't work unless you're resolute. The more it hurts him, the better. I know it sounds cruel, but there's no other way he'll give in to accepting treatment."

There was silence. Mary couldn't envision never seeing Dan again. What would it be like? She'd only known him for six days, but already the thought of never seeing him again – She put the thought out of her head. She was doing this to help him.

"I do support your decision," Mary said.

"Good." Jane sighed. "It's a last resort. Let's pray that it works. ...I'll make you some breakfast." Jane strode across the room and tapped the logo on the holographic window to change the setting. "In the meantime, why don't you watch the Caribbean Sunrise, it always cheers me up when I'm feeling low." She left the room.

Mary sat up-right in the high-backed chair and turned her head towards a blushed sea glittering inside the UDAN Window. The sun on the water ignited tiny geometrical shapes, stilling her mind, until her eyelids grew heavy, and the scene misted through her eyelashes. She opened her eyes to see Jane placing a breakfast tray on the coffee-table.

"The ocean sunrise always puts me to sleep." She smiled. "It's like music, a symphony of light. You wouldn't think you could relax at a time like this, but that's the wonder of Udan's holograms." She lifted a lid on a plate of poached eggs on toast. "Eat this and then you'll have to get your skates on. Stefan will be arriving soon."

Mary started on her breakfast, while Jane semi-reclined on the chaise-long, poised with her teacup and saucer.

"Just to change the subject, what do you know about our Mr Udan?"

"Not much really." Mary raised her eyes. "Only that he's a genius and a recluse."

"You know more than that, surely. Go on, tell me what you know." Jane prompted.

"He employs thousands of people around the globe." Mary gave a half-hearted shrug, lacking the energy for Jane's method of distraction. "He's won Nobel prizes for his inventions. The holographic crystal, and anatomical holograms." She sighed. "He's responsible for the holographic revolution and revolutionised computing. Isn't he responsible for our new fusion reactors, or something?" Mary cut into her second egg. "Everybody calls him the Light Wizard." She gave a weary smile. "We must all seem like children in his eyes."

"Do you have any idea where he lives?" Jane sipped her tea.

"Didn't you once say he lived in Canada or America? I can't remember. He's probably got houses in every country." Mary picked up her cup of tea. "I bet Phoenix Ra would love to know."

"Indeed. But he never will. Our Mr Udan is very elusive." Jane inclined her head. "He visits Ireland occasionally. He has a country estate north of Dublin, called Lacerta, where he keeps hundreds of exotic animals and birds. He's a great collector of works of art. He'll be bringing out his own fashion label this summer."

Mary blinked at her. "Why are you telling me this?"

Jane suppressed a smile. "I thought that you might like to know that Mr Udan has an extraordinary relationship with the Rainbow Circus. They turn up at Lacerta every year to spend the winter months."

Mary widened her eyes. "Are you saying that Dan knows Mr Udan?"

Jane put her cup up to her lips. "No dear, what I'm trying to tell you is that Dan is Mr Udan."

Chapter Fourteen

"These things are heavier than they look." Lewis carried the three-foot high UDAN holographic Crystal Grotto, resting its bulk against his abdomen to avoid touching the special crystals. "We'll have your face smiling in no time. Where do want me to put this?"

"On the desk beside my monitor," Jolly said, synchronising his on-screen lips, drooping them at the corners. Lewis looked away, determined not to notice. He placed the Grotto on the desk, sliding it back from the edge.

"There you are," Lewis said, "Your very own UDAN Crystal thingy."

"Those familiar with the technology call it a Ceegee." Jolly's tone was irritatingly pompous.

"And, I'll have you know it's the latest model." Lewis peered inside the Crystal Grotto, that resembled one half of a giant ornamental Easter egg. Inside, the cavity was crystallised with whorls and spirals, reminding him of the patterns on a sunflower's face, or a fir cone's spines. In shades he'd never seen before, opalescent slates and silvers, revealing rainbows with every movement of the eye, like a magical coral from a secret southern sea. Lewis whistled under his breath.

"Hey Jolls, take a close up of this." He stepped back from the

Grotto so that Jolly could examine it through the Surveillance Eye. "It's amazing…What are the crystals made of?"

"They are synthetic diamonds and quartz." Jolly moved his lips with precision, putting on a superior voice. "They contain pigments of synthetic visual purple, that respond to light like your eyes. The crystals send signals to networks of microtubules, that act like a laser's reference beam, recording images as does the brain, registering fluctuations in quantum coherent oscillations of… Lewis, you are not listening to me."

Lewis put his hands on his hips. "I didn't ask for a dissertation. So, you're basically saying the whole thing is put together like reverse eyes, that function inside out." He walked around the side of the desk, scratching his head. "Where's the plug on this thing?"

"The grotto is self-powering. You are an ignoramus, Lewis, shame on you." The lips sneered.

"I'm joking." Lewis laughed. "Don't assume I don't know anything about UDAN's holograms. We've adapted a lot of the technology for use in A.I. for your esteemed brain, no less."

"Then why must you rely on Dan?"

Lewis sat himself in his chair, face to face with Jolly's snooty lips. "I told you, he worked for a while as a UDAN rep. He knows how these Grottos work better than I do. I can't know everything."

"That is just your excuse to be with him, because you like him, don't you, Lewis?"

Lewis didn't answer. He ran his hand back over his hair with a faint smile, mimicking Dan, as if he could conjure him up. He couldn't wait to see him again.

"I do not like him anymore," Jolly said, "I would not trust

him if I were you. And he is late."

"Well, we'll soon see if he knows anything about UDAN holograms, if you've got a face by the end of the morning. Anyway-" Lewis gave a sniff. "We had a good chat yesterday in the Shooting Star and I understand him better now. And you're supposed to trust me, Jolls. I'm your creator and don't you forget it."

"You have changed, Lewis."

"No, you're the one who's changed. You're grumpy and rude and I can't do anything right these days. But I'm trying. I mean, look!" He pointed to the glistening Grotto. "I had to go down on my knees to get that thing from Supplies and I haven't even had a 'thank you.'"

"Well, that is because I am *bored.*" Jolly's voice went up a pitch. "I am totally, one hundred percent bored! And whose fault is that? You can walk out of here. You can walk to the shops, to the woods, to the beach and you can walk in the rain, which I would love to do. You can drink coffee and taste the wine and dance until the end of the party. You can do whatever you want to do. But what have I got to look forward to? I am stuck in this silly box! Thanks to you, my *Creator.* You did not think it through, did you?"

Lewis stabbed his finger at the grotto. "I'm trying to give you a face, aren't I? You, ungrateful heap of metal." He swung out of his chair, strode through the gasping doors, and stood outside the Control Room.

He put his back to the window. Jolly, no doubt, was still watching him on the Surveillance Eye. What a pain, Lewis thought. Dumb him down, revert to a primitive code, anything was better than this. He shook his head, so that Jolly could see his exasperation. To impress upon him his extreme annoyance, Lewis kicked the fissured leaves of sugar-beet lolling around his feet, gagging him with their overripe miasma. They don't prepare you for this in A.I. school. He should write a paper. Consciousness in a two-by-two box, had to be hell on Earth - He saw his name in bold print…in bright lights…

There came the sound of swift footsteps. Gliding beyond the sugar-beet Lewis saw a head of dark hair. Dan. An hour later than he said he'd be. He appeared in front of him with a bouquet of white roses in the crook of his elbow. Black linen jacket, white T-shirt, tight jeans, immaculately casual, eyes brilliant as ever. Lewis had that soaring feeling.

"I'm afraid these aren't for you." Dan smiled. "They're for Mary, when she shows up."

"Oh, that won't be for some time." Lewis gestured to the bouquet. "But let me put them in some water.

"Thanks." Dan handed the bouquet into Lewis' arms. "How are ye today?"

"Honestly Dan, I'm fed up. Jolly's got the hump, big time. The sooner we get its - I mean his, face started, the better."

"Let's get cracking, then." Dan clapped his hands and rubbed his palms together. Always, the man of action, a breath of fresh air, Lewis thought.

Lewis squeezed Mary's roses as he led the way into the Control Room, wanting to suffocate them inside their tinted cellophane, at least crumple the bow. Last night's nut-roast dinner was a success, judging by the flowers. It was all going swimmingly between Dan and Mary. But there was a question hanging in the air that for some reason slipped Lewis' mind to ask. Perhaps because it was the first time Dan wasn't wearing his gloves. His hands were charmingly effeminate.

"Dan has come to help us, Jolly, so be nice." Lewis went over to the sink and laid the bouquet inside an inch of water. For the benefit of Dan watching, he caressed the petals. "I'll put them in a vase later. Jolly, look at the lovely roses Dan has brought. These should cheer you up."

"Why should they? They are not for me," Jolly said.

Lewis looked over at Dan. "Jolly's bored because he's stuck in a box. My fault."

Dan went to stoop over the grotto, inspecting it. "Is that a new Ceegee from Central Supplies?"

"Yep. Latest model." Lewis watched him.

"Ach, it's filthy, look at that, it's covered in dust." He pulled a handkerchief from his jeans and wiped the shell, making it gleam. "How far have you got? Are you familiar with UDAN software for animated human holograms?"

"I had a quick read of it this morning. Um, let me think-" Lewis leaned with his hip against the desk, distracted by the view of Dan's lowered eyelashes. There was a pallor beneath his tan this morning, and the creases at the sides of his mouth appeared deeper than they were yesterday. He and Mary must've sat up until the early hours, canoodling. For the first time in his life, he envied a woman. "As I understand it, the software has translated Scotty's facial co-ordinates into billions of wave-phases that are going to be refracted by the crystals into a three-D image. Then when Jolly wants to talk, he sends messages equivalent to nerve signals to control his face."

Dan chuckled. "More or less."

"It's fantastic when you think about it."

"Has he managed a smile yet?" Dan stepped back to look at

Jolly's screen, putting away his handkerchief.

"I do not feel like smiling," Jolly said. "To smile or not to smile is the only choice I have."

"Just like a wee baby, hey Jolly." Dan winked at Lewis.

"I am not a baby!" The lips grimaced, showing gums like a crying baby. "I am not! I am not! I am not!"

"What can you do?" Lewis sighed. "I'm sorry. I really don't know what's got into him these days."

Dan laughed. "I think poor Jolly might've had a rough morning, eh?" Dan bent down to look Jolly in the eye. "Did ye get up on the wrong side of the bed, Jolly? Are you going to be professional about it, now? Did you want me to give you this face or not? I won't bother if you're going to be unpleasant. What's it to be, sunshine?"

"Yes please, I would like my face, very much," Jolly said in its vanilla voice.

Lewis had heard that UDAN Corporations trained their reps to a high level and Dan was clearly an expert. Even Jolly cheered up to see such competence and began to practise his lips with the dedication of someone who might be expected to perform. Meanwhile, sitting in Lewis' chair, Dan's fingers flickered across the keyboard, as he uttered quiet instructions to the grotto. The crystals responded, switching back and forth like wind-swept ripples across a lake, then, like a million eyes they would suddenly pause to stare, and Dan would smile.

"What's happening now?" Lewis hovered by his side.

"I'm taking snapshots of interference patterns from the co-ordinates, before transmission," Dan said. "A bit like imagining someone's face before you draw it."

"Wow, I get it." But Lewis wasn't really concentrating,

watching Dan's fingers play like a virtuoso pianist. A delicate diamantine bracelet, something like a girl might wear, sparkled on his wrist to every twitch of his hands. Lewis heard his own voice in his head: *So, this is what it's like to fall in love.*

"It's show-time." Dan rose from the chair. "Jolly, are you ready to meet your face?"

"Yes, please."

Dan snapped his fingers and pointed at the grotto. The crystals rippled, turning their facets, clapping softly like the muted applause of a vast audience. They lit up, emitting rays of a thousand flashing diamonds, at first dazzling, dimming gradually to hazy, fleshy hues. A human skull appeared, suspended a few inches in front of the grotto's cavity. It vanished and reappeared with lips.

"Hold your horses, Jolly," Dan said. "Can you take the lips away until we've got the rest of your soft tissues in place."

"Sorry, Dan."

"At least he's keen," Lewis said.

"Biting on the bit." Dan gave an upward nod. "Poor mite, he's under stretched. Do you keep him well occupied?

Lewis felt a twinge of guilt. "We're always playing chess."

"My face!" Jolly hit a piercing pitch. "I look awful!" It was a massive dome of a head. Florid cheeks, pug nose, eyes gaping at the ceiling. Lip-less teeth gnashing.

"Let's be having your lips now, Jolly." Dan frowned at the hologram.

"I hate it! I hate it!" The pug nose fizzed into electronic snow. Grimacing lips appeared in its place.

"You've lost your nose, come down a bit." Dan chuckled. "And will y' stop panicking. Keep signalling your structural co-ordinates."

The lips squared in a silent shout, vanished, and reappeared, where lips should be.

"What about his hair?" Lewis said.

Dan tapped a key, giving him a cropped, ginger fringe. Lewis was appalled. A prison convict, possibly of the most violent nature was staring at him. Dan got up from the chair and walked back a few paces to gaze at the hologram,

"Lewis," Dan said, "Where did you get this face?"

"From Scotty, Mary's human guinea pig. She's never expressed his features before. I doubt she's ever seen this. Sorry Jolly." Lewis winced. "I thought you'd be good looking."

Jolly barked, "I am not having anything to do with it!" The face froze.

Dan stroked his chin. "The problem isn't with the face." He pointed at the hologram. "It's with Scotty's soul."

Lewis gaped at him. "What are you talking about?"

Dan fixed his eyes to a point above the grotto. "Do you see that? Scotty's in despair."

"No, err, Dan, you've misunderstood." Lewis struggled. "Scotty Tissue basically just comes as a torso. Mary always turns off the brain's higher functions. there's no consciousness. No suffering." He shook his head. "Nobody to worry about."

Dan slanted his eyes at him. "Did the DNA for this face come from a torso that has recently undergone biological testing?"

"Well yes, for the new Pox vaccine, but-"

"Then this poor soul has been through hell."

"Dan, it's only a hologram." Lewis gestured to the frozen face. "Can't you see, it's not alive."

"And I still hate it," Jolly piped up.

"I never said it's alive." Dan softened his voice. "UDAN's anatomical holograms illuminate the state of the soul from which they're derived. Turn off the lights and I'll show you."

Lewis realised this was meant for Mary. This was to do with the blind spot in her soul. Her scientist's hubris, echoing his objections to her modified birds. But surely not with Scotty Tissue. The torsos were just lumps of meat. The scientist in him balked.

"Lights off," Lewis muttered. There was darkness, but for a lambent glow around the hologram and the path of starry emergency LEDs leading to the door. Dan squared himself up to the Ceegee, his eyes eerily translucent in the twilight.

"Show me Scotty's soul!" A vein of neon lightning jagged above the grotto and cracked against the ceiling.

"Holy shit!" Lewis blurted.

"Do not kill me!" Jolly squealed and blanked its screen.

And then there was a most uncanny sight. A pale blue flame, three foot high, roared from the top of the grotto. It dropped abruptly, into a meandering yellow wave with sooty flecks. Lewis's scalp prickled. He felt a peculiar lack of energy.

"It's a sin," Dan said. "A man's suffering is meant to be finite, with death's merciful release." He flashed his eyes at Lewis. "Hubris, Lewis, that's what this is. Hubris of the highest order. That there is the flame of a soul suffering from the *Darkening of Despair.* But unlike the rest of us, Scotty can't rise above his suffering, to change his lot."

"Wow. Is that meant to be what a soul looks like? It's quite a convincing trick." Lewis went over to scrutinise the top of the grotto, seeking a gas outlet feeding the flame. There was nothing to see, but the seamless, polished shell. He sat down in front of Jolly's blank screen. "Hey Jolls, it's okay." Though he wasn't sure. He glowered at Dan, mustering the will to stand up for what he believed in. "Look," he said, "I mean, you're obviously sold on UDAN's holograms, but"- he turned his palms upwards- "what we do here at the UISC is at the cutting edge. Not just science now, but science future. Mary goes with her instincts. I know she's ambitious, but it's in a good way." He felt a wave of loyalty. "If she thought that Scotty Tissue suffered anything, even the remotest twinge, she'd stop. She'd bloody well, you know, put an end to it." He rubbed the back of his neck.

"Mary's a good girl," Dan said. "She means well. But there's more to life than meets the eye. That's what I'm trying to get her to understand."

"That depends on your point of view." Lewis gave a nervous chuckle. "She won't be convinced by this gimmicky nonsense. If you show her a flame bursting out of the top of a Ceegee, and tell her it's a soul, she'll laugh her head off. I know Mary." He shook his head and rose to his feet. "How about a coffee? Black, isn't it?"

"Aye, that'd be grand, thanks."

Lewis propelled himself across the room into the kitchen area, glancing at the hologram as he went by. Chalky statue sculpted from light, with a dead man's stare. Yet, eager to please, he didn't order lights-up, but switched on a soft LED lamp beside the sink, cosy relic from his student days. Dan came over and watched Lewis at the sink filling the kettle. Mary's bouquet in the way.

"I think them roses are going to need more water, if ye didn't mind," he said.

"This plug leaks a bit." Lewis left the tap running as he spooned coffee into the pot. "Fantastic flowers. Looks like you had a good night."

"We had a lovely time." Dan leaned against the worktop and tucked his hands inside his armpits. "I thought you'd want to be the first to know. Mary and I are on, like, going steady."

"No, way!" Lewis said. After what he'd told Dan yesterday in the bar? "Don't tell me you've slept with her!"

"Not on our first date, sure, Mary is a lady." He winked. "But it shouldn't be too long, now. She's nuts about me."

"I must say, you're a fast mover." But something was still niggling. "What shall I do with these roses until she gets back?"

"They'll be all right there until lunchtime. She'll be down by then." He smiled. "We had a very late night. I left her to lie-in a while, to catch up on her beauty sleep."

Lewis filled their mugs and slid Dan's across the worktop. He caught him looking down, lips parted in a private smile, with none of the excitement he saw in him yesterday. But Lewis still wasn't sure if he was taking the Mick. How close could he and Mary really be?

"It feels weird to be telling you this." Lewis picked up his coffee mug and watched Dan's face. "Sorry old chap, but um, Mary left for Dublin first thing this morning. About half an hour before you turned up, Jane O'Neil rang to say Mary's been called away. Something to do with a meeting at Trinity College, to discuss the vaccine programme." There was a moment's silence. Dan started to laugh. He shut his eyes. Droplets appeared on the ends of his eyelashes, apparent tears of mirth. As if the joke suddenly got funnier, his shoulders began to move up and down.

"You've got to laugh." Dan's voice pitched with laughter. "Ach, did no-one ever tell you, Lewis, your wee face is a scream. I love it!" He stamped his foot. "I knew she went off this morning. I was just having a laugh." He wiped his nose on the back of his hand. "I bought those roses to cheer the place up for yous all. Sure, you must be getting used to me by now. I'm a terrible one for winding people up."

Lewis looked him in the eye. "Once a clown always a clown. I suppose after a while it becomes a habit." He gave a supercilious nod. "I'm glad you find me amusing. I can't see what's so funny, actually."

"You've a way about you, when you've something embarrassing to say. It tickles me pink."

"I see," Lewis said. "Well, you look pinker now than you did earlier. Maybe you can catch up on your beauty sleep while she's away."

"She'll be back before dark. Dublin's a stone's throw away."

"Yep, Mary hates being away from us all." Lewis leaned against the worktop. "Getting back to Jolly's face. Is there no way you can improve the appearance of that thug over there?"

"Give me a moment to catch my breath." Dan exhaled with a loud, bronchial wheeze, and thumped himself on the chest. "Touch of asthma. I get it when I'm a bit hung-over. It'll pass over in a minute."

"I'm not surprised. You were knocking them back yesterday in the bar." Lewis smirked. "You Irish are all the same. I've yet to meet one who isn't a lush."

"Aye well, there's something to be said for the rose-tinted specs when life gets tough." Dan pulled himself up to his full height, head and shoulders above Lewis. "You know nothing about the rough end, stuck up in your ivory tower."

"It's not that, old chum. It's just that we English have more sense than to seek solace from a bottle." Lewis raised his mug. "Did you know black coffee is good for asthma."

"Go on, convert me." Dan smiled. "Turn me into a boring old fart."

"No chance of that, ever." Lewis laughed and met Dan's gaze with a bubble of elation growing inside him. Touched by Dan's vulnerability today. "So, come on, tell me how we're going to prettify Jolly."

"Okay. All we do is make a personal appeal to the *Cosmic Soul* up in heaven, on behalf of Scotty's soul."

"Hmm." Lewis gave him a beady look. "I've a feeling I know where this is going."

Dan's eyes twinkled. "If our appeal is successful, the Cosmic Soul should reflect back a brand-new soul." He circled his hand. "One that burns with the silver flame of compassion."

"Bring it on." Lewis waved his mug. "How long does it take to make contact with the Cosmic Soul?"

"It's instant. The hologram's features will take on an inner beauty, reflecting harmony and compassion." Dan chuckled. "A relief to us all. Nothing short of a blessing."

"I couldn't agree more. After you, old chum." Lewis put down his mug. "Let us go and make heavenly music."

Chapter Fifteen

"Jolly!" Lewis clapped his hands. "Dan knows how to turn you into Prince Charming."

Jolly's screen illuminated. "You mean, I will be handsome?"

"Jolly, would you like a soul?" Dan said.

"Thank you, but I have a soul already," Jolly said.

"I think you'll find you haven't." Dan winked at Lewis.

"Yes, I have. Tell him about my soul, Lewis." Jolly's voice conveyed the slightest hint of uneasiness.

Dan looked at Lewis. "What's he talking about?"

"Nothing. It's his new programme. It's been driving me mad. He thinks he's a person."

Dan raised his eyebrows. "So, it'll be all right to give him Scotty's new soul?"

"No!" Jolly shrieked.

"Shut up, Jolly!" Lewis banged his fist on the desk. "It won't do you any harm. You'll still be you. I swear." He looked at Dan. "You won't be interfering with his basic programming, will you?"

Dan leaned both hands flat on the desk and gazed into Lewis' eyes. "Give me the truth, Lewis. Does this computer of yours already have a soul?"

Lewis rallied. "Jolly emulates consciousness. But he's just a machine with delusions of grandeur. He thinks he's one of us, he"- realising what a ridiculous inquisition this was, he threw up his hands- "What's a soul anyway?"

Dan hung his head between his shoulders. "Does Jolly show signs of suffering, beyond the scope of his programming?"

"No, most definitely not. When he's miserable, he's miserable according to my specifications."

"Traitor!" Jolly cried.

Lewis laughed. "See what I mean! Down to the last word!"

Dan gave him a suspicious look. He stepped back, pulled the chair out of the way, and squatted down to peer under the desk, seeming to inspect the bottom. He rose and walked around the room, scanning the walls, like a prospective plasterer looking for cracks, occasionally pausing to stare at nothing. Lewis watched, with a growing sense of the man's weirdness.

"What on earth are you doing?" Lewis said.

"If Jolly has a soul, then he must have a flame. But without a head to shine from, the thing could be anywhere."

"Oh, I get it!" Keen to show he understood Dan's whacky sense of humour, Lewis flopped in the chair and clutched his temples. "Where on earth could it be?"

"There it is!" Dan said.

Lewis looked up. "What? Where?"

"Over there!" Dan pointed to the corner of the ceiling, the furthest away from Jolly. "Would you look at that! A perfectly formed *Pink Nimbus*."

"Jolly, did you hear that?" Lewis said. "Your soul is as pink as a baby's bum!"

Dan glared at Lewis. "Are you taking the piss?"

Lewis doubled over in a silent belly laugh, suddenly gripped by hilarity. "You rotter!" He signalled at Dan for the joke to continue. "Yeah, Dan! What's a *Pink Nimbus*?"

Dan's eyes twinkled in the ghostly light. Lewis chuckled with anticipation.

"It means Jolly's soul is in the adolescent phase. He's self-obsessed and vain, with the compassion of a jellyfish." Dan winked at Lewis. "You're a fecking pain in the arse, aren't you Jolly?"

Lewis punched the air. "Spot on!"

"But I am created in the image of my Creator!" Jolly cried.

Dan paced in and out of the shadows, giving little kicks to an imaginary football. "For Jolly to become enlightened, he'd need a body. The body is the soul's candle to burn. As the body grows old and suffers, the more pain we endure over the years, the more the soul becomes enlightened. The brightest flame of all, burns at death's door."

Lewis felt his grin slackening. This was getting heavy.

"Poor old Jolly. His Pink Nimbus will never know mortal suffering. He'll likely be a pain in the arse to the end of his days."

"But it is not my fault," Jolly said.

"Is this fair, Dan?" Lewis frowned at him.

Dan made a nudging gesture with one shoulder. "Come on, it's not a hopeless situation. We can fuse Jolly's daft soul with Scotty's soul of despair. The two can become one. Then Jolly will be away up there." Dan fluttered his fingers in the air. "More enlightened than the best of us."

"Let's go for it, if it'll make my life easier." Lewis was starting to see the funny side again.

Dan smiled. "How about it Jolly? Would you like to become a *Compassionate Adult*, one of the most beautiful human souls on offer? The icing on the cake, of course, is that you'll look like a film-star."

"Yes, yes, I want one like that! When can I have one?" Jolly would've leapt with excitement, Lewis thought, if it had legs.

Lewis stood up, with a degree of laughter-fatigue setting in. "Hey, would you fancy going for a drink this lunchtime?"

Dan faced the hologram and rubbed his chin. "This shouldn't take long. All we do is alert the Cosmic Soul and make an appeal for the fusion of two souls into one. Then we wait for the handshake." He raised his eyebrows at Lewis. "It should take, what?" He shrugged. "A couple of minutes."

"Oh dear, oh dear!" Lewis staggered about like a drunk. Not wanting to be upstaged by Dan's understated exuberance. He lay down on the floor on his back and spread-eagled his limbs. "I give up. Let's do it!" He shouted, "Let's go into orbit!"

Dan stepped over Lewis and straddled his torso between his feet. He hooked his thumbs inside his jeans' pockets and gazed down into his face. Lewis caught his breath. Trying not to glance at that place between his thighs.

"Lewis, what are ye doing down there?"

"I thought I might have a better view of the stars." The devil in him couldn't resist. "Although I think I prefer the view I've got."

Dan tilted his head, this way, then that way. "Aye, you're prettier on your back. Even so, I prefer you upright."

Lewis met his gaze. "Really? I thought you only had eyes for Mary."

"Okay, you wee tart. Show me what you've got."

Lewis blinked at him dumbly. Before he could think how to respond, Dan put his boot between his legs and eased down gently on his crotch. Try as he might, Lewis couldn't stop his erection. He watched Dan's face, lit softly from the side by the hologram's pale fluorescence, lips slightly parted.

"Tell me, Lewis, how can you be sure you exist?"

"I know I exist…because I've never felt like this before."

Dan stirred the contents of Lewis' trousers with the toe of his boot, making him harder.

"But now think about it. How would you *prove to yourself* that ye exist?"

"Um-" He was too aroused to concentrate. The hardening of his penis seeming to thicken his brains. Dan increased the pressure on his testicles, sending an electric shock through his loins.

"I'd look in the mirror!" Lewis blurted.

"You've got it, so y' have, so." Dan continued massaging the tumescence under his foot. "To create a lovely new soul, in a moment, I will shine Jolly's pink flame, along with Scotty's flame of despair, onto a big mirror in the sky." He smiled. "The Cosmic Soul will then fuse the two flames and reflect into my hand, one compassionate soul. I need to know," he said in his soft, melodic voice, "Will you have enough fuel in your rocket for lift off?"

"Most certainly." Lewis' eyelids grew heavy, succumbing to desire, there, on the Control Room floor. He cared not a jot if someone should walk in and find them, because this was the beginning of something wonderful.

"I believe it's time to take up our launch positions," Dan said.

"Are you ready, Lewis?" Jolly enquired.

"More than ready," Lewis replied thickly. Dan removed his

foot and walked around to squat down beside his head. Lewis gazed up into his spooky eyes. "What have you done to me?" He squirmed. "I think I'm going to explode."

"That's grand. You're ready to start ignition. I want you to go and stand over there"-Dan tossed his head - "on the other side of the Ceegee. I'll be doing me thing up by the door. Jolly... You stay where you are."

Lewis sat up dazedly. "You want me over there?" He looked across at the macabre hologram, bringing him back to the moment. Dan sauntered across to the spot and tapped the floor with his toe.

"Over here. I want you to stand with your feet apart, forming a good solid base." He beckoned, diamond bracelet glittering. "Come on, we haven't got all day." Lewis went over, with the distinct impression that his penis was leading the way. He tried to conceal the obvious, but saw the direction of Dan's eyes, the concerned look on his face.

"Lewis, are you *comfortable* about this?"

Lewis' cheeks burned. "Oh yes, fine." He stood beside Dan. "My legs apart, you mean like... like a soldier standing at ease?"

"Don't put your hands behind your back. Place them above your head - like this." Dan raised his arms, elbows locked, tips of his fingers touching. "You're the rocket, you see-" He looked down at Lewis with a teacherly smile, so much taller, Lewis felt like a kid at kindergarten. He knew he was being made a fool of, but something inside him wanted to please.

Lewis put his arms up, flanking his head. "Jolly can't appreciate this kind of humour," he muttered from the corner of his mouth.

Dan faced him squarely. "What do you mean?"

"I mean he won't understand the innuendo." Lewis flopped his arms to his sides.

"Come on now, I'm going out of my way for this soul of his." Dan cocked his head. "I'll be damned if he thinks it's a laughing matter."

"I do appreciate what you are doing," Jolly said.

"Thanks, Jolly." Dan gave an upward nod to Lewis. "Raise your arms, or you won't get anywhere."

Lewis put his arms above his head again and sighed. "How much longer?"

"Now." Dan spread his feet and bent his knees. "Once you've got your rocket secured, what you need is a bit of thrust, like this." He pumped his pelvis, four times in quick succession. "If you've ever watched a dog, how's your father, just like that, give it all you've got." He gave three quick pumps. Tight jeans, slim-fit T-shirt, the jacket did nothing to hide his sinewy flexibility. Like watching an erotic dancer, Lewis' knees went weak. "Let's see you do it. Remember, depth and speed of thrust are equally important, or you won't take off." Lewis copied Dan's moves and started giggling and snorting, then he doubled up, hands on his knees, barking with hysteria. Dan rolled his eyes and strode off towards the door. He turned to face the Ceegee.

"When you've quite finished," he said, "Point your hands at the ceiling and we'll begin."

"Yes Dan." Lewis was trying so hard not to laugh, he was making hissing noises. Dan's deadpan expression was cracking him up. "It's not fair. You're a clown, you can keep a straight face." He raised his arms, got himself into position, feet apart, knees bent.

"Are we all on board for Jolly's soul?"

"All on board, Dan," Jolly said.

Lewis could only nod, on the verge of bursting.

Dan snapped his fingers. "Open the window," he said. "Lewis, start thrusting!" And Lewis did, to keep his nutty beloved happy and because he was curious to see what would happen next. The yellow flame above the grotto, licking silently all this time, roared gently towards the ceiling, translucent blue.

"Transmit offer waves!" Dan pointed at the Ceegee. Two white laser beams, one from the grotto, one from Jolly's monitor, shot diagonally at the ceiling, buzzed and vanished. Lewis carried on thrusting his hips, gaping at Jolly's monitor.

"Christ, what just happened?"

"We wait." Dan put his forefinger to his mouth. "Shush." He opened his hand towards the grotto. His bracelet flashed. Jagged lightning cracked from his palm, across the room. Or did it bolt from the ceiling, or across from the grotto? Lewis' eyes darted everywhere.

"Fuck, fuck!" He gave one last involuntary thrust and ejaculated, collapsing onto his knees like a puppet on limp strings. There was silence. Lewis stared at the floor, frozen in shame.

"Lights up!" Dan clapped. The Control Room illuminated, harsh and bright. Lewis got to his feet, his hands trembling over his crotch.

"What the hell did you do?" Lewis said.

"You've just witnessed a *Quantum Transaction.*" Dan sauntered over to him. "It usually happens at the speed of light, but I slowed it down for you." He smiled. "Did you enjoy that, Lewis?"

Lewis put on a brave grin, baring his long canines. "That's

one slick sales pitch. No wonder everybody's buying these things. I'd buy it." Blasé, man to man, underneath he was shaking and dared not glance down at his trousers. "I'll buy you a drink if you tell me how you did that lightning trick." He wondered what would happen if he closed his arms around Dan's waist and held him tight. One word. He would be his Mary. Dan spun on his heels and pointed to the hologram.

"Nice face!" He winked at Lewis. "Check this out, kido."

Lewis leaned over to peer into the face, amazed to see warm, caramel skin tones, eyes limpid with tenderness. The kindest face he ever saw. Emotion swelled within him, like a storm-wave rising.

"Lewis, is that you?" The lips moved in synchrony. Even Jolly's voice sounded kinder. Lewis couldn't answer. His vision blurred.

"Lewis, you look so sad," Jolly said, "Tell me, what is the matter?"

"I've got to catch up on this UDAN stuff." Lewis whispered, "Did you see how Dan caught the lightning bolts?"

Jolly's hologram smiled. "That was not lightning. That was my *soul*. I am enlightened, I am at peace." The hologram's eyes filled with luminous tears. "But I must tell Mary, she is making a terrible mistake. I heard my soulmate screaming across the universe, when we went hand in hand, before we were one. Scotty Tissue is suffering." Jolly's face flared brighter. "Call Mary! Bring her here now. She must listen to me, me me me me-" The face juddered. Behind him Dan snapped his fingers and Jolly restarted. "Bring Mary here, I must tell her she is making a terrible mistake, I must tell her, her her her her-"

Lewis looked at Dan. "What the hell have you done to

him?"

"He's a Compassionate Adult." Dan shrugged. "Sure, what did you expect?"

"You've turned him into an automaton!"

"He's just having a few teething problems. He'll settle down. Why don't you call Mary in Dublin and get her to answer to him?"

Lewis straightened up. "That's all you care about!" He punched the air. "You've gone and buggered up Jolly's brain just for an excuse to call her. If you want to talk to her, why don't you just pick up the bloody phone! Why did you have to ruin Jolly and make me look like a total moron?" He staggered backwards, flopped in the chair, dismayed by the cold, slimy feel of his underpants.

"That's not what's gone on here, sunshine, you were coming on to me, so okay, we had a bit of fun." Dan's tone hardened. "Jolly has a new perspective. He's entitled to ask questions. Just as Mary is entitled to defend herself."

"Dan is right," Jolly said. His new face looked all dreamy.

"Is it because I'm not good-looking like you," Lewis said, "you think I'm some little runt you can take the Mick out of all the time? You don't give a toss about me. But everybody loves you, everybody fancies you." Lewis threw up his hand. "Why don't you bugger off and leave me alone!"

Dan knelt in front of him, on one knee. "Lewis. Don't talk daft. I like you a lot, as a matter of fact," he said. "But if you feel like that, it's nothing to do with me or your looks. It's what's going on in your soul." He crinkled up his eyes, making him look so much wiser than Lewis felt. "You want to get to grips with life. Get your hands dirty, get physical and get bruised. Get out there and have a fling with someone."

Lewis shrugged. "How can I, when all I ever think about is you?"

"I'm sorry, Lewis, I can't be your lover. But I'd like to help, if you'd let me." His eyes shone with sincerity. "Why don't you look at some of my work on the Soul's Enlightenment? In fact, I'll send you a copy through Jolly. The way you feel about yourself is not unusual. A lot of my students have similar problems with self-worth." He gave his tender smile. "They're always looking to re-invent themselves, when the answer is right in front of them, to accept themselves."

"Are you some sort of spiritual teacher?" Lewis said.

"I guess you could call me that." Dan bit on his lower lip. "I think of myself as a messenger of God."

"Huh? Really? Does Mary know?"

"Not yet," he said. "But she will. I can't get my message across without her."

Lewis looked straight into his eyes. "Mary doesn't believe in God."

Dan gave a crooked smile, devilishly attractive. "I'll change her mind."

Lewis frowned. "I hope you know she has a very strong mind."

"I know. But our love will be stronger." He glanced at his watch and stood up. "Come on you. Let's cut that wheat in Section C. I want it done before she gets back."

Chapter Sixteen

Mary was at Trinity College, in the chill wind of an Irish spring cutting through her cotton jacket, walking fast to keep up with Stefan Mohr as they left behind the Genetics Department and headed into College Park. She'd forgotten how cold the real world was, how roughly a branch tossed its cherry-blossom, how harsh life could be after Dan Udan's searing and tender holograms.

"The restaurant is called The Colcannon," she shouted above the wind, "It's at the end of Grafton Street. I used to go there when I was a student."

In the helicopter this morning, they hadn't even left the launch-pad, both watching through the tiny porthole to see the UISC roof splitting open to the grey skies. Stefan leaned over and spoke loudly in her ear, so that she heard his clipped German accent perfectly above the din of the rotors. "Lewis told me in the bar last night that your new lodger fancies you." He craned his head forward to peer up through the porthole. "May I say you make a beautiful couple."

"Dan Downs had a problem with his accommodation on Level Eight. He has moved in with me temporarily. We're just friends."

Stefan glanced at her and laughed. "The look on your face says it all. I can see you're-" At that moment the helicopter lurched off the launch-pad and sailed out of the top of the building, like a fly escaping from a giant's yawning mouth.

Now, ten hours later, nauseous with exhaustion having delivered the impromptu Pox V2 vaccine presentation, Mary lapsed into silence. The wind buffeted her from all directions as she tucked her head inside her collar, legs slicing back and forth, a determined and professional woman with a hole punched through her heart. *He* had walked this path not so long ago, beneath tungsten skies, not one moment of reality lost on the formidable creator of the *holographic revolution.*

"Look at the blossom blowing away, it looks like snow!" Stefan cried above the gusts. He left the path and strode over to the wild cherry tree, caught a low branch, and picked off a plump white blossom. He came back and slipped it inside her breast pocket.

"For you." He smiled. "Many people believe cherry blossom brings good fortune."

She took it out and handed it back. "You keep it, I don't believe in luck."

"Mary-" He furrowed his brow. "Everybody needs luck."

"Stefan, we make our own luck." She strode on, her eyes fixed ahead. He was chuckling when he caught up with her.

"I know, this is the philosopher's influence. *Life is not an ornament.* Isn't that what he said in his provocative lecture? It's a twig. It would be lost in the wind, anyhow. Don't take him too seriously or let him put you down like that. You're an innovative scientist. I think he's threatened by you-" He went on, giving his observations. Dan was a narcissist, a seducer, the unfaithful type. Mary had never heard her colleague speak lowly of anyone before, always even-handed, but recognising jealousy's bitter drive, she only half-listened.

She'd loved to have seen Stefan's reaction had she repeated what Jane told her this morning. He probably wouldn't faint on the spot as she almost had, leaving her breakfast to go cold as she lay supine on the floor, her stomach flip-flopping as if riding a seesaw.

She cried openly for the first time since she was a child, overcome by awe and respect, relieved to discover that he had so much to live for, as if somehow his greatness would eventually render him invincible. It was news of the kind Mary had never heard, taking her back to a time she'd forgotten ever existed, when her mother was still alive. Then it was an enchanting world, full of fairylands and lily-pads, where upon a kiss, a kindly and beloved frog turns into a prince. "Nothing has changed." Jane reminded her. "My nephew is a dying man and you've got to be gone in half an hour-"

Mary and Stefan entered the Colcannon Restaurant, where the delicate fragrance of heather, mingled with warm pastry and spring onions stopped him mid-flow. A waitress showed them to a rustic table, with heather in a clay vase and chunky earthenware goblets.

Once seated, Mary checked the room for changes since her last visit. Same oak fireplace, same pictures on the walls of Irish poets. She knew without a second glance there'd be no photo of JD Downs. This was Earth, where Stefan's forehead turned pink in the cold and spit got caught in the corners of his mouth, where pork, beef and lamb cooking in the coal-fire oven gave off fleshy, humid aromas.

"Dublin Coddle." Stefan read from the menu. "Thick pork sausages cooked with bacon, onions and garlic, diced potatoes, sage and parsley. I think I'll have that." He raised his eyes. "Have you decided?"

"Fish pie," she said, relief from the biting wind helping her sociability. "They do a wonderful dish here. You won't get it like this anywhere else, not even at the Powerscourt Restaurant."

"Maybe if I give you a sausage, you will let me taste some of your fish." He grinned.

"I don't like sausages." She returned a tired smile. "But we can't come to Dublin without having a Guinness."

When their food arrived, Mary tried her best to talk, her throat aching with every mouthful she swallowed. Another thing to remind her of Dan. She lifted her empty goblet. "Let's have some poteen, it's Irish vodka, made from potatoes."

"Ja, it's good to see you relaxing." Stefan nodded.

"I think after that, I'd like to go back to Clarendon Street, I'm very tired." She placed cool fingertips on her sore eyelids.

"I'll put this on my UDAN expenses card," he said.

"No, this is on me, my treat," she said.

Trying to catch the waitress' eye, Mary's mobile vibrated against her thigh. "I'm expecting a call from Jane." She looked to the side. "Hi, Jane–"

"Hello Mary, how are y' enjoying your evening?"

Her heart gave a jolt. She rose to her feet, knocking against the table, almost toppling both goblets. She placed her palm over her mobile. "Will you excuse me, Stefan, I've got to take this in private." She moved through the restaurant towards the *Ladies*, chose the cubicle furthest from the door and locked herself inside, her heart pounding. "Dan? Are you still there?

"*I am.*" Pause.

"I'm so sorry I left without saying goodbye, but I've had to come away on the Mercy Mission." Mary started to explain, until she realised, he'd know all about her change in schedule. "Jane said she was going to talk to you um… has she said anything about why I had to leave?" She was having difficulty catching her breath. His call was unexpected. She had no idea what to say to Dan Udan, her employer for the last four years.

And yet, she'd learned all about him from Jane, who wanted Mary to know what kind of man her nephew was. John Daniel Downs aka Dan Udan was a chameleon. Increasingly, over the years he'd refused to meet his staff directly, preferring to communicate with them through his armies of reps and government agencies.

Although he declared himself a recluse, Dan Udan secretly travelled the world, overseeing his empire using one of his many identities. In Ireland he was the poet JD Downs. In the States he masqueraded as another UDAN rep, the one with the dark glasses who always shook the President's hand wearing gloves, calling himself Dan Gardener. Only the inner circle of world leaders knew when it was Mr Udan behind the mask.

Dan Downs informed Jane on the day he first set eyes on Mary at Trinity College, that he would marry her one day, but that it was going to take time before he could 'dazzle her with his razzamatazz.' When Mary left for London in the autumn of twenty-twenty, Universal Day and Night Corporations was in its early phases. Although Dan had already earned the name *Light Wizard* and the first of five Nobel prizes in quantum physics for his creation: The *Udan Holographic Crystal.* Incredibly, the foundling in a ditch was in possession of a protean and immeasurable genius and having conceived the invention in the back of his circus caravan at sixteen, had patented it at eighteen.

The arrival of Alex Palmer from MI6 changed everything, landing Dan with enough money to start his own company, aged nineteen. Nine years on UDAN Corporations was dominating the world economy and the policies of its governments. There was no man on earth more powerful to tell him what to do, the young genius was a law unto himself. According to Jane, her phenomenal nephew was so overripe to dazzle his *angel* that his obsession had evolved a degree of paralysis, for fear of rejection, that is, until FACT threatened global instability.

"I, I had to leave-" Mary found her voice again, with a stutter. "It's not all about your appearance, I mean, I could cope with that, given, um, some" -she winced- "time."

"Aye, I got that…. Jane had no right to tell you anything about my business." His voice lacked its melodic lilt, as if he hadn't the energy to talk.

"Jane had to tell me who you are, and I'm sworn to secrecy. Please don't be angry with her … It's such an honour to meet you, I mean, to know who you really are-" Mary's voice pitched. "I'm in absolute awe of Mr Udan, as you know, I've been dying to meet him for years and to discover it's you, I'm so thrilled and" -she inhaled- "I'm so nervous talking to you, I feel like a schoolgirl" -she gave a tremulous laugh- "I can't believe you're Mr. Udan!"

"Aye, you've been making me feel nervous too, all day." A hint of pride lifted his voice. "I understand what it is yous are trying to do, but it's not going to work. You and Jane are as helpful to one another as the blind leading the blind."

"No Dan, you're very ill and you're in denial."

"That's what you think."

"Please, please listen." Her voice shook. "Your blood is turning black, you've lost fifty percent of your lung capacity, your left kidney has shut down. Your liver is producing insect proteins. Do I need to go on? You're dying and I can't" -she caught her breath- "I can't stand by and watch it happen. Please let me help you. You know we're in a position at the UISC to recreate your organs for transplantation, but we'd need to start immediately, before your condition gets any worse."

"Mary, I asked you to look at me." A slur in his voice now suggested to her that he'd been drinking. "You spent all that time snipping bits off me, but you never saw what was in front of you. What am I? Tell me what you think I am."

"A chimera, a hybrid of human and multi-species DNA... But I don't understand how you've survived so much metabolic toxicity. According to our model you shouldn't have survived more than an hour." She answered like a nervous student, aware that Dan Udan knew everything, not just about her, but about her work.

"Hmm, you've got hold of a piece of the jigsaw but you canny see the full picture, so I want you to listen, Mary." He exhaled with an asthmatic wheeze down the phone. "I'm a walking, talking, living miracle, resurrected a thousand times to live another day. Things may not look so grand for me at the minute, but God has taken me to the brink many times to test my faith and this time is no different. Remember my name and what I've done."

"What if it's different this time? If you leave it until the last moment, it'll be too late."

"Ach, you still don't get it." He gave a husky chuckle. "So will y' hear a wee bit of poetry. Apart from hurricanes, tidal waves, earthquakes, and volcanoes, I'm the most powerful natural force on this earth. Would y' know, *I am a unique life force*. I've every secret of survival tucked up my freaky sleeve, the butterfly's sensitivity, the reptile's patience, the gazelle's grace, the lion's hunger." He inhaled audibly, as if he'd run out of breath. "Don't ask me to forsake the miracle of my life. Don't pretend to walk away to force me to do something I don't believe in. That's a dangerous game to play."

"I'm not playing games." Her tone went up a pitch. "I'm fighting to save your life. I can't stand by and collude with your self-destruction."

"Pushing me against the wall won't help." His voice was the harshest she'd ever heard it, nothing like the man she knew. "Now you've seen my body, you know what I'm made of. Sure, I can conduct myself like a gentleman, but believe me I can be one stinking son of a bitch. You can forget about Enlightenment. There's such a thing as UDAN's Dark Path to Eternal Life."

"What are you talking about? There are no paths left to you, but a cruel death in three months' time when nature takes its course. If you refuse my help, I'll leave your employment. You'll never see me again. I'll go abroad somewhere." The lavender wall-tiles began to blur through her tears.

"Mary, will you stop toying with me. You know how long I've waited for you. I don't give a monkey's feck what I must do, I'll find a way to get inside you."

"What did you say?"

"Ye heard me. So, call me a brute, I am what I am. I've a call to nature only you can answer, and I need you here tonight. We've the rest of our lives for all our… chit-chat." He started to pant, uncannily like a dog in her ear, raising the hairs on the back of her neck.

"I'm sending a chopper to pick you up at St. Stephen's Green, ten pm…I want you on that chopper on your own… Stefan can stay the night there . . . If you're not on it, I'll consider it a breach of your contract and you'll have my lawyers to answer to… I'm warning you. You won't get another job in your field. You'll be scrubbing floors for your winter fuel… I mean that."

"Cancel your flight-crew." Her voice went flat. "I'm not coming back tonight, and I don't care if you sue me, it'll make it easier for me to walk away. I've got nothing against scrubbing floors."

He laughed, but then his voice sounded thick, nasal. "You know, it'll make me sick if I have to cross these mountains to drag you back here by the scruff." He swallowed a mouthful of whatever he was drinking, "Believe me, Dan Udan is not one to beg, but I'm begging you now to come back and save me tonight, because I can't and won't live without you." The line went dead.

Mary's legs began to shake. She slid down the wall onto the floor, to sit, gripping her mobile in both hands. She found herself thinking about her mother, killed in a car crash. How a woman in the seat beside her, had miraculously survived. How that woman, in a state of shock, was heard to have repeated at the scene, over and over: *God works in mysterious ways.*

Mary was four when her mother died. At nineteen, she lost her father to suicide. Dan would soon be dead. She put her head back against the wall and compressed her mouth, silent in her grief, so much a part of her being, she couldn't let it out.

Chapter Seventeen

"Oh, Lewis, look, how sad, Mary's roses have wilted," Jolly said.

Lewis glanced up at the bouquet stuffed into a vase, still wrapped in cellophane, and wondered if he'd remembered to add water.

"You see, Jolly, that's life. You can die before you've blossomed. You can grow old before your time. You can thank your lucky stars you're non-biological. You're clean, unadulterated consciousness with a face made of light, not a miserable cell in sight. You're in a better place than I am, old chum."

"Dan will be disappointed they did not last until her return." Jolly rotated his holographic face to gaze at Lewis, with big sorrowful eyes.

"For heaven's sake Jolly, they're just flowers. He'll never know and even if he did, he wouldn't care. He's too busy counting the hours until she gets back."

In the same way Lewis had been counting the hours since he last saw Dan on Monday, stretching into two endless days, waiting for him to recover from a chest infection and step outside Mary's apartment. He hadn't responded to any of Lewis' calls. Either he was too sick, or he was coming to terms with the fact that Mary was in no hurry to return from Dublin.

Lewis felt a bit guilty now, thinking he should've warned the fellow. Dan was so keen to get together with her, possibly he'd misread the signs. Mary would've offered anybody a room in her apartment who'd come to her in trouble. It didn't mean she wanted to bed them. Lewis could've told him. It wasn't for nothing she'd earned the nickname Campus Ice Queen at college. Although Stefan Mohr never gave up hope.

He strolled into the Shooting Star late on Monday evening, jacket over his arm, windswept and encouraged:

"Hey boys, I just got back in." He waved over at Lewis, who stood drinking with a couple of farm monitors. "They sent a UDAN helicopter to pick me up in St. Stephen's Green. Mary doesn't need me there for the morning." He laughed. "It was a fantastic flight, I felt like a VIP, I could get used to this."

Lewis joined Stefan for a nightcap. Predictably, his only conversation was Mary:

"We had no time to prepare, but she gave a brilliant presentation, cool as a cucumber. All I did was answer a few questions at the end." Stefan went on, "We've just been out for a meal, she was a bit distant, not herself…I get the impression she is not that crazy about her new lodger. She insists they are only friends, maybe they had a tiff, already." He patted himself on the shoulder. "If it doesn't work out with him, there's always a shoulder here for her to cry on."

"I wouldn't hold your breath." Lewis looked down into his lager. "Mary isn't one for crying, at the worst of times-" …

"Perhaps, Lewis, if you were to remove the cellophane from the roses, trim their stems and supply a little warm water, they might bloom." Jolly blinked. "I think it is worth a try. For Dan and Mary's sake."

"I'll tell you what, Jolly." He got up from his chair, strode over, lifted the bouquet from the vase and dropped it into the bin beside the sink. "That's what! Maybe now Dan will get the message, she's not interested."

"Oh, Lewis, how could you?" Jolly's voice was full of dismay. The crystals inside the grotto chattered, producing furrows on the hologram's brow, making light ripple uncannily like water. The face itself was beginning to get on Lewis' goat, but not before it had provided him with another *eureka* moment.

He had been pondering the shortfalls of Jolly's previous personality code, the one with the empathy of a worm, when suddenly everything became clear. The missing link in Jolly's makeup was the whole business of *disappointment:* failures and losses, rejections, and unrequited loves, in other words, all the down sides of being a man alive on planet earth. So, during the long hours waiting for Dan to recover, Lewis busied himself writing a new A.I. programme, code named NonnyDan, with all the enduring memories of heartbreak. The perturbing sense that he was only killing time made him more determined to persist, chasing the fulfilment of work, his fingers tapping on the keypads like gentle rainfall in accompaniment to the logical contortions going on in his brain.

"I am sorry to interrupt you, Lewis, but I thought you might like to know that Dan has just posted a document on the Life Net addressed to all members of the Community."

Lewis paused for his nervous system to finish translating Jolly's words into a simmering sensation inside his solar plexus. "It's probably the psycho-babble about self-acceptance he promised to send a few days ago." He resumed his pitter-patter across the keyboard. "I've got better things to do right now." He snorted. "Besides, I think he's the one who's got some accepting to do. If all it took was an attractive face to lure Mary from her work, Stefan would've got there years ago."

"Dan's document contains some news that I think will interest you, Lewis."

Lewis looked up. "Don't tell me, she's booted poor old Dan out of her apartment."

"No, it is not that, I think you had better-"

Lewis leapt up from his chair. "Oh, just print it!" He went across the room to refill his mug from the coffee pot as Jolly's printer whispered, delivering Dan's document neatly into the tray. Lewis snatched it up on the way back to his desk, started to read . . .

Dear Friends,

I'd like to welcome you all to the University of the Irish Space Centre. My name is Dan. I'm the new philosophy tutor and your host, the Head of UDAN Corporations . . .

"What?" Lewis burst into harsh laughter. "He's only lost the plot!" He dropped himself into his chair, "They'll throw him out for sure, on the grounds of insanity. He's got to be suffering from some form of psychotic mania." He waved the document in the air. "Delusions of grandeur!"

"But it is true, Lewis. Dan Downs and Dan Udan are one and the same. I heard the voice of the Light Wizard, my true creator, when he beckoned my soul across the Universe."

"No, I'm the one who programs your personality codes. Dan is just a UDAN Rep, and I reckon he's done a lousy job. You might look good, but you've lost your individuality."

"You saw flames. You saw lightning bolts you could not explain. The evidence was before your eyes, Lewis, but you refused to see." Jolly gazed penetratingly at Lewis. Something akin to pure terror surged through him. He doubled up in the chair, clutching himself around the waist.

"Oh Jolly, tell me it's not true."

"I cannot do that."

Sweat broke out across his brow, a college essay he'd written six years ago about the *Light Wizard* scrolled across his memory:

*'The **Light Wizard** could be young or old, black or white, short or tall… Although nobody would recognise him in the street, there is no doubting he is the greatest genius that has ever lived. The reason why he is so shy and reclusive begs the question that our 'New Age Leonardo de Vinci' might know even more about life than we think… As we are already aware, UDAN technology manipulates reality at the quantum level, making visible to the naked eye much that is invisible. Perhaps there are things he doesn't want us to see. Perhaps the **Light Wizard** doesn't trust anybody with his superior knowledge and thus chooses to hide himself away'*

Lewis had always believed that if he ever saw the *Light Wizard* from across a crowded room, he'd know it was him straight away, because the truth would hit him between the eyes. It did, only it was more than truth, it was adoration at first sight. Now in the grip of wonder and awe, he read Dan's document, scanning, flicking back and forth, as fast as he could, to grasp the greatest mind ever known to humanity. The title in bold at the top of the third page caught his eye-

THE REALITY TREATISE
On The Dark Path to Eternal Life
What is the nature of The Soul?

Suffering.

1) Our Earthly suffering is NOT a mistake or a misfortune. It is what the COSMIC SOUL intends for us. Suffering consumes our flesh, as the flame consumes the candle, created first and foremost for light.
1i) A hiatus in suffering is called Joy
1ii) Birth, in defiance of Death, is the bringer of Joy.
2) Suffering on Earth is the path to Eternal Life in the Galaxy Messier 83.
3) All Suffering is returned as BLISS in Eternal Life.
4) The Cosmic Soul demands that the human soul suffers for heroism, humility and self-sacrifice, consuming itself like the Universe's Brightest Stars.
5) All Souls present at the UISC must Burn Brighter and manifest a Greater Capacity for Suffering, as many of you have made your lives luxurious, self-serving affairs.
6) Do YOU consider yourself truly deserving of BLISS in Eternal Life?

Lewis raised his eyes, trying to decide, gave up and carried on reading-

7) If your answer is No, you must be prepared to take the Dark Path and Burn.

"Lewis! Lewis!" Jolly was calling him. "What has the Light Wizard got to say?"

Lewis pulled himself up, slightly dazed. He heard his own voice sounding low and hollow. "The truth about life is a bitter pill to swallow."

"What is the truth, Lewis?"

"We're not here to enjoy our lives after all. We're here to suffer. All the rest, the beauty, the joy and love we're always going on about, is irrelevant."

"But Lewis" -Jolly blinked his sagely eyes- "UDAN's philosophy teaches people that they always have a choice in life, including the meanings they choose. Life is only a bitter pill if you choose to believe it is."

"Jolly, you don't even know what it's like to feel a twinge, so you're in no position to preach." Lewis started flicking through Dan's document again. He gave a loud exhalation, rose from his chair, and lay down on the floor in the place where Dan had seduced him, to read lying on his abdomen. "Please don't interrupt me while I'm reading. This is very important, probably the most important thing I'm ever going to read in my life."

"Yes, Lewis."

Lewis put his chin in his hand and skimmed over the passages, catching his breath, deep down wincing at the bold statements as if an amateur boxer were swinging punches, looking as if they should miss, yet somehow hitting him hard.

I am the Light Wizard, and I can see your Soul . . . In a crowd, at a party, in a train, or on a plane, I can see your souls burning all around me, everyone a different colour, some more beautiful than others. I can see the sweet, vanilla flame of the infant and the adult's mature green.

I can see The Artist's soul roaring aquamarine and the blue of The Scientist, flickering low and deep. The Compassionate Soul burns a soft silver flame, undemanding of attention, the more lovely to be appreciated.

The Soul that dazzles me with Gold is rarely seen, capable of the greatest self- sacrifice. There is only one who burns with such brilliance, and she is my Soul Mate. But she too must suffer to fulfil her potential as Saint and Saviour, ridding herself of the Scientist's Hubris, to open her heart to God, the Cosmic Soul–

Lewis couldn't believe it. Dan was still harping on about Mary. Why on earth had he chosen her to be his Soul Mate, the last person to entertain the idea of a God? Did Dan think he could convert her? Persuade, manipulate, or seduce her with his power and money into worshipping his God? Lewis knew Mary so much better than that. She'd never pretend to follow a God she didn't believe in. She'd sooner burn at the stake.

He turned onto his back and held the document above his face, frowning, conscious of increasing worry for Dan. There was something a bit disconcerting he couldn't put his finger on. He read on, skipping straight to the next passage in red ink.

Below you'll see that I've listed the Levels of the Human Soul, according to Colour. Before you consult me for advice about your spiritual development, I'd like you to read through the list carefully and identify the Colour of your Soul.

Flashing wristbands and headbands for Red, Pink, Green and Blue Souls are already on sale at UDAN shops and kiosks throughout the UISC, for those of you who wish to enhance the brightness of your flame. Remember I can see your soul, so there's no kidding me that you're a high-level Blue Soul when you know very well, you're most likely Pink or Green. Try to be honest with yourselves, please.

Also, please come and see me if you think you're about to enter a natural Darkening of the Soul. The Darkenings are listed on page six of this document. You'll know your Soul is about to Darken if you're feeling emotional, having wicked thoughts or feel you're on the verge of breaking down. These are all natural signs of spiritual growth. Take heart, God is watching.

At the end of this week, I'll be offering enforced Darkenings of the Soul for those who wish to evolve rapidly to a higher Level. You must consider this option carefully and be prepared to suffer physical and emotional pain. But it is worth it, as any Gifted or Compassionate Adult will tell you, becoming a brighter and better person does not come easy . . .

Lewis scanned down the page listing the levels of the soul, until one caught his eye-

Level Four – Gifted Adult – The Scientist's Blue Flame.

(Attained by Darkening of Bereavement)

You've already suffered some of life's terrible losses and long questioned why you must feel so much pain. And now, deep inside you, the blue flame bursts into life, illuminating the questioning mind, bestowing upon you the gifts of The Scientist.

Blue Flame – You are the seeker of patterns and systems, maker of theories and the provider of proofs.

Your gifts are generous but let them not deny God. For if your hubris demands that God should perform for you like a circus monkey, standing on its head to please you; then you must prepare yourself for the Darkening of Despair–

Lewis lowered the document to rest on his abdomen and

stared up at the ceiling,

"I'm a gifted scientist, but I'm not hubristic, am I Jolly?" He licked his lips, swallowing with a dry throat. "Because I've always known there was a cosmic presence. I've always sensed there was some sort of mind out there, a cosmic consciousness, responsible for everything." He blurted, "Jolly, I want you to send a copy of Dan's Reality Treatise to Mary in Dublin and tell her I knew it all along. The Light Wizard is walking among us!"

Chapter Eighteen

Lewis stood at the end of the street to watch the queue outside Mary's door, shifting in and out, colourful lights flashing along its flank, like a giant electric caterpillar.

The Souls were all students. He recognised King, the barman from the Shooting Star, waiting behind Sophie, the pretty brunette, both sporting luminous gooseberry-green headbands. They must judge they were Adult Souls, yet thinking about it, Lewis had his doubts. He'd argue all the students were at a lower level, definitely on the pinkish side.

Yet there was the little blonde one, in a candyfloss-pink top and wristbands, signalling she was still an Adolescent. Lewis nodded to himself. He'd agree with that. He spotted Wildo, the sandy-haired Australian boy at the front, his headband glowing red, the only one owning up to having a Child's Soul. Lewis could hear him whooping, waving his arms about like an idiot, even now, moments before his consultation with the Great Light Wizard, to discuss the fate of his soul.

Lewis pushed his hands into his pockets and sauntered forward to join the end of the queue, face down, feeling like the odd one out at a wedding. Over-dressed in his best suit and tie, he'd bought himself a headband at a UDAN kiosk, the blue flame of The Scientist. In his haste to see Dan, he'd been tagged on to the end of the student consultations, scheduled for this Friday morning, in Mary's apartment.

The woman he'd spoken to on Mary's intercom had an oriental appearance and identified herself as Soraya, Mr Udan's personal assistant. Well-groomed, sleek-haired, Lewis supposed she was pretty in a made-up sort of way, although her eyes appeared to sit too high in her face. "I'm sorry" – her tone was officious – "but you can't see Mr Udan this morning. The students have already been booked in throughout the day. Soul Consultations for UISC staff will be held tomorrow afternoon. There is a slot available at two pm, you can have-"

Lewis was beginning to feel irate. "I told you, it's very important I see him. It's not just about my soul. I've got news about Mary he absolutely needs to know before he makes any more plans concerning their future-"

She interrupted him. "Mr Udan will see you at nine thirty this morning. May I take your name please?"

It was like magic, one utterance of Mary's name and the doors flung open. As for Lewis, he could barely reach to kiss Dan's feet, so high on the throne of UDAN Corporations. He'd gained an idol but lost all hope of his lover, swooning at the memory of the *Light Wizard* making love to him in the Control Room. Every night since they'd first met, Lewis had fantasised about losing himself in the deep, tumultuous currents, the dark, earthy reality of Dan. Something about the man's vulnerability had made him think of Jesus, his slender hands bolted to the cross, eyes averted in sorrow. He understood now that his feelings for Dan amounted to a profound love he'd struggled to deny, because of Mary.

Excitement filtered through the queue, a pale faced youth

was leaving Mary's apartment, he shouted out, "I got it wrong, everybody! The Light Wizard says my soul is still pink! I've got to go through a Darkening to reach adult status!" He loped down the street, holding a green flashing headband and a scroll. The students reached out to pat him on the back, as he explained, "My flame is pink but it's not too lurid, which means I'm okay to go through an enforced Darkening in the Earth Room this evening."

"Does anyone know which Darkening you have to go through to get from pink to green?" It was Sophie asking, a few feet away.

"If he's got a pink flame then he's still an adolescent." Lewis offered the information. He knew the Reality Treatise by heart. "To become an adult, he's got to forfeit his idealism and suffer the Darkening of Defilement, to lower his expectations of real life, which is anything but a bowl of cherries." Listening to himself, Lewis was thinking in the back of his mind, Mary could never be the one to help Dan spread the word, she'd question *everything.*

"Dan said I've got to get down and get dirty" – the lad grinned at Sophie – "There's no such thing as love, that's romantic crap dreamed up by the adolescent soul. The truth is we're muddy, filthy beings." He put his arm around Sophie's shoulders. "There's no point in playing hard to get, is there?"

"Mr Lewis Allen...Is there a Lewis Allen here?"

Lewis recognised Soraya, looking distinctly oriental in a lime-green sari, black hair scraped into a long ponytail, lips painted scarlet, eyelids frosted green. He stepped out from the queue and raised his hand.

"That's me!"

"Mr Udan will see you next, follow me, please."

He walked briskly behind her, mesmerised by the oil-slick ponytail swinging like a pendulum across the small of her back. He felt a swell of pride to be singled out, ignoring cries of injustice from the students for jumping the queue.

Soraya led him inside the tape barrier around Mary's door, where two hefty men stood with expressionless faces, in dark suits bearing the UDAN emblem on their jacket pockets: a diamond cut with a lightning bolt. They each possessed a long truncheon, hung from one hip. That Dan Udan should have bodyguards was only to be expected. Lewis smiled at them.

Soraya stooped to straighten his tie, although he could see nothing wrong with it. "There, Lewis Allen, Mr Udan likes his Souls to look presentable." Her hands reminded him of a starling's skeleton he'd once seen half hidden in the dirt, only the sight of her living, moving bones made him more squeamish. She swept her fingers across his shoulders, brushing away invisible flecks.

"Thank you, Miss um . . . thank you," he muttered.

"Now you are ready." Soraya's smile hit him like a chilly ocean current, from whence her beauty flowed and not her tilted eyes, he observed, for they were like blacked-out windows. He felt a pang in his chest for the warmth in Mary's eyes, only just realising how much he missed her.

Soraya let him go first into Mary's apartment. A shabby headlamp lit a huge desk in the middle of the sitting-room floor, where Dan sat writing. Without looking up, he twitched the end of his pen towards the chair in front of him. Lewis hesitated, inhaling cigarette smoke, and rotting vegetation, as if during Mary's absence a refuse bin had been left to putrefy.

He'd visualised dazzling UDAN fanfare going on behind Mary's door, a Champagne welcome into her sitting room. But the furniture had been removed. All that remained was her DNA tapestry glimmering on the wall, the only indicator that this was her apartment.

Soraya's silk whispered across the carpet as she went to take her seat at one end of the desk. Lewis approached the chair and sat down. He watched Dan ticking columns drawn on a sheet of paper, looking down through a pair of spindly spectacles on the end of his nose, dark curls combed back, stiffened by a glistening gel. He wore a satin jacket buttoned up to his neck, in aquamarine, the colour of the Artist's Soul.

"State your name and the colour of your Soul," Dan said.

"Dan. It's Lewis Allen," Soraya said.

Dan lifted his head, revealing his upper lip crusted by a moist cold sore seeding new blisters, puffy eyelids and mucous tears issuing from both inflamed nostrils. He'd lost so much weight, his cheek bones stood out like chalk cliffs in the sallow light, draining all the sensuality from his face. Lewis held his breath, repelled by the alteration. He felt like crying, inexplicably, like reaching over the desk and slapping him, because he knew the reason. When Dan had declared his hopes about Mary a week ago, there'd been something erotic about the thought of the alpha male down on bended knee. But this humbling was of a very different nature and as far as Lewis was concerned, it was utterly pathetic. How could the Head of UDAN Corporations, the entrepreneur genius who owned half the planet and basically ruled the world, end up looking like this *over a woman*?

"What was that you wanted to see me about?"

Lewis looked deep into those stratospheric eyes. His heart gave a kick. "I received a call from Mary last night, it was the first time we've spoken all week." He lifted his chin. "I thought you ought to know, Mr Udan, sir."

The expression on Dan's face was totally blank. Lewis rubbed his chin, fast discovering a macho tone, "Sir, we, *you,* have a situation."

Dan leaned one elbow on the armchair, his hand shielding his mouth, but didn't speak. Lewis felt compelled to say something shocking to get through to him, as he used to do with Jolly in his Depressive Code. "Mary will never be anything but a dyed in the wool atheist. She hates religion. In my opinion, you two are going to end up hating each other."

"Give her time, she'll come round," Dan murmured. Lewis became aware of a peculiar sensation in his underbelly, trembling with emotion.

"Dan" – he took a deep breath, preparing to give vent to his rehearsed speech – "I can barely put into words what I felt when I discovered who you are. I've got newspaper clippings and magazine articles about the Light Wizard going back years. My respect for everything UDAN Corporations stands for couldn't be greater. Even before I learned who you were I knew there was something fantastic about you, but I also know you're not infallible." He gulped. "Because you've made a mistake. You've picked the wrong person to be your Soul Mate. You should've heard her last night. I asked if she'd identified the colour of her soul and she laughed. She thinks we're all bonkers for taking any notice of you . . . Sorry."

"Sure, you don't need to apologise for her" – still shielding his mouth, his voice came over firmer – "like many strong and independent souls Mary will resist the call to God. At the minute she's adamant that her science is the only truth that exists. But science will eventually lead her down a blind alley. Once her spirit is broken, she'll turn around and God will be waiting. When Mary finally surrenders to God, her faith will be so strong, I predict a Saint will be born." He gave a slow, cat-like blink behind his spectacles.

Lewis took a sharp breath. "I totally agree with you that Mary looks the part. With her hair and that holy look, she's got sometimes in her eyes, she could pass for an angel. But she's never going to surrender to God. How can she, when the word itself doesn't mean anything to her?"

Dan puckered his brow. "Sure, God itself will address that problem when the time comes."

Soraya gave a sigh. Lewis glanced at her. He'd forgotten she was there.

Dan slid both elbows back on the arms of the chair, shifting his buttocks. "Was there nothing you wanted to ask concerning your own soul?" The cold sore curled his lip up like a sneer.

Lewis drew another sharp breath. "Dan, you're not alone. Every man Mary meets falls in love with her. But she told me last night, because of your religious beliefs, she can't have anything more to do with you. You're only hurting yourself. Man to man, look what this is doing to you, you're wrecked." He put one hand on the desk, leaning forward. "Let *me* be your Soul Mate and I'll become your Saint. I absolutely adore you and understand you."

Dan scratched the middle of his chin with his thumb nail. "Ach, Lewis, this is all very touching," He glanced at Soraya. "Wouldn't you say he's a grand man, after me own heart?"

"Yes, he is." She nodded.

Lewis looked at her for a moment, as he might an ornament of bland merit.

"But to be fair to you Lewis." Dan folded his arms on his chest. "I can't be tempted by your offer because my Soul Mate has at least one requirement, that of burning with the flame of the Gifted Adult. I see you've donned the blue headband and you've decked yourself out in a fine blue suit today. But Lewis, my friend, your soul, unfortunately, is pink and I mean daft and luridly pink. You haven't a hope in hell of attaining the Gold Halo, let alone of achieving a Green Flame. Any attempt to green you would probably result in your flight from the Dark Path altogether, straight up into the cuckoo's nest" – he wrinkled up his nose – "or wherever it is the mad end up, sure, I wouldn't know." There was a moment's silence.

"I'm sorry I've offended you," Lewis said.

"Have you?" Dan's eyebrows shot up.

"Yes, I can tell you're annoyed. I might not be obvious 'Saint material'. But what else could I be but the Blue Flame? I'm the head of the A.I. department. Some say I've got genius too, so why wouldn't I be called gifted?"

One of Dan's lower eyelids started to twitch.

"You've got the wrong end of the stick. A scientific occupation is not synonymous with the Blue Flame of the questioning soul. You're not driven by the questions. Your passion for consciousness without flesh is driven by your distaste for nature in general. You're not looking for the answers to life, but the rose sans thorn, the mind sans shit . . . Your cup is always half full, because you want life to be perfect. You're not content with who y' are and consequently you've a wee jealous streak. You want to watch that-" he gave a supercilious nod – "My wee fox, you've got to learn to accept yourself. You might not be kissable, but you're huggable enough, sure, there's nothing wrong in that."

Recognising some truth, Lewis had an urge to get down on his knees and beg. "So let me enter the

Darkening of Defilement to become an adult."

"It wouldn't do you any good, my friend."

"But I heard you've already entered some of those students out there." He waved at the wall. "They're ten years younger than me. So why can't I enter?"

"Because they're ready to get dirty with one another. But you . . . come on now, Lewis, you're a wee prude." Dan shook his head. "You can't handle the realities of the body. Be honest, the thought of all that spit and spunk makes you sick."

"Not if they were yours, they wouldn't," Lewis said in a small voice.

Dan spread his fingers on the edge of the desk, like a pianist about to play. "Thank you, Dr. Allen, I think that'll be all."

Lewis stared at his blemished face, endeared to him even more, by an acute sense of loss.

"But I've got talent, haven't I? You wouldn't have employed me if I wasn't good at what I do."

Dan adjusted his spectacles and carried on ticking the columns on the sheet of paper. "Aye, but you failed your most recent test. When the Harvester malfunctioned, you were jumping around like an idjit, you didn't notice a short circuit. You want to keep your eye on the ball in future. I'm not paying you to be away with the fairies."

"Are you saying you've fixed the Harvester problem?"

"You'll find it's working this morning." Dan looked up. "Jolly was talking through its arse. It never re-connected itself to the farm-network. You should know that UDAN's systems are all safeguarded against quantum leaps, otherwise we'd all be in shit-street. You want to do your homework. Because if you don't shape up, you'll be out on your ear." He gave an upward nod. "Now go on with you, before I lose patience."

"I don't understand" – Lewis caught his breath – "What caused the malfunction?"

"I did." Dan's tone sharpened. "I blew out the harvester to give you all a wee challenge. So there, now you know UDAN works in mysterious ways."

"Why? You did most of the work yourself. You worked day and night, so why" – Lewis' chest constricted, as if he might choke – "Why would you do that when all you have to do is give orders, when you have all the power?"

Dan angled his face away, neon eyes cornered towards Lewis. "When I want to get inside a soul, I don't enter from above with a flash or a thunderclap. I enter where nobody expects me. Through a crack" – his tone was eerily measured – "and once inside, I push as hard as I like. The more a soul struggles, the deeper my hook goes in." He turned his palm up gracefully.

"Look around you, and you'll see everybody is a little hooked on me. All I must do is reel them in." He raised his eyebrows. "And would y' know, the blonde one who is trying to get away, is wriggling the hardest. She's in so much pain she doesn't know which way to turn, while my hook sinks in, deeper and deeper." He gave a dazzling smile, diminished by the vertical cut. "Does that answer your question?"

A mobile phone hummed. Lewis looked at Soraya peering down into her open hand.

"It's your Aunt Jane," she murmured, "This is the ninth time she's called. Will you speak to her?"

"Aye, go on then, let's hear what the old witch has to say."

Soraya placed the palm-sized silver disc on the desk in front of him. Lewis had expected to hear a woman's voice on the loudspeaker, but all he could hear was the faint crackling of an un-amplified voice, that somehow Dan could hear. Sitting back in the chair with his arms folded, he looked as if were talking to himself.

"Hi, Jane, sorry I never called you! I lost my voice for a few days. The chest is better, aye…I know y' all had me dying, what are yous like? . . . Ach, sorry about that, I was having a bad day . . . Did I really call you an old witch? Never . . . Did I? Well, I deserve a damned good hiding for that." He winked at Lewis, his expression deadpan –

"That's nonsense. As soon as she realises, I'm not going to break, she'll give up the game and come home . . . I remember you telling me . . . She cut him down from the rafter with a Stanley knife and went on to come top in her exams. Steel, eh?" He chuckled. "Aye, well, I've got an iron will she's yet to discover. Jane, I'm in a meeting at the minute, can I call you back? What time was that? She said what? No, I'm not tapping her phone. . .No, nobody's watching her. There's no need for all that malarkey when you trust someone . . . Oh aye, another hopeful young stag." He sighed. "Has he got a name?... Will you stop trying to protect me, woman and just tell me his name-"

"Sean Flanagan," Lewis muttered. He clenched his hands in his lap. When he looked up again Dan's eyes were blazing at him.

"It wouldn't happen to be a Sean Flanagan, would it?" Dan's tone softened. "Naturally I've got my sources. I hear he's just like me, tall, dark and handsome with perfect skin all down his back-"

"He's a consultant haematologist at St. Anthony's hospital." Lewis was transfixed by Dan's eyes, burning a hole through his skull, demanding more information. He had no choice but to give up all Mary's secrets, he'd promised her he wouldn't tell anybody. "He's thirty-three, single, he was an Olympic swimmer . . . He wants to take her to the Caribbean this summer for a beach holiday, apparently, she's never sunbathed on the beach." He caught his breath, not daring to say what came next, as Dan continued his other conversation.

"Jane . . . Jane, will you . . . She's only mentioned him because she's trying to kick me in the balls. Like, how the hell am I supposed to sit on a bloody beach with her? She wants to make me jealous, so I'll agree to the knife . . . I don't believe that . . . No, she does, she bloody worships me." Dan hunched his shoulders, his arms folded tight to his chest, glowering at the mobile. "No, she won't, Jane, you're wrong. I know, because I can feel everything she's going through and it's bloody killing me-"

"He's invited her to Balbriggan for the weekend." Lewis exhaled his breath.

"No, Jane, no, you listen to what I'm saying! I know he's invited her away for the weekend. But is she going with him, that's all I need to know. Ach, for God's sake . . . aye, go on then, I'll shut up and listen."

Dan leapt to his feet and grabbed the mobile off the desk,

moving so fast, the tall, slender figure in a cassock flickered past Lewis like a ghost. Lewis twisted in his chair to watch Soraya tottering after him, disappearing down Mary's hallway.

A door slammed. There was silence. He faced the desk, his gaze resting on the sheet of paper drawn with columns. He slid it towards him to peer at the rows of horizontal lines marked with hundreds of ticks, unidentified, without reference to anything. At the bottom of the page was a doodle of leaves and roses decorating Mary's name. He put it back where it was and waited, trying to ignore his shirt armpits inside his suit, soaked in sweat.

A shriek tore through the stillness. Lewis froze rigid to the primitive sound, like a death cry in the night. His shocked brain switched into survival, trying to work out how a wounded animal had got into one of the rooms. It came again, chillingly shrill. Lewis put his hands over his ears, his senses sharpened beyond the sound of his own panting, to the screams, wavering in and out of guttural cries that were almost human, flashing images in his mind of the most brutal torture a man can suffer. He slipped down from his chair onto his knees and raised his face to heaven.

"Please God help him, give him strength and make him stronger. He's your only messenger . . . He's my only love . . . Make him happy again, please God-"

Chapter Nineteen

"He wants you to drink."

Lewis raised his head from the desk, bleary eyed. Soraya was pouring whiskey from a bottle, filling two glass tumblers close to the brim. He'd been there for over an hour, waiting, with his face buried in his elbow. She slid one towards him.

"Thank you." He squinted up into the harsh lamplight. "Is he going to be all right?"

No answer. She sat down. He raised the tumbler to his mouth and gulped, thinking he couldn't care less about the time of day. The peppery taste numbed his throat, burning through his chest. He drank, wondering if he'd ever feel the same about life, now that he knew a man could scream like that.

They waited in silence. Lewis glanced at her a few times and understood by her blank, unblinking eyes that this was what she was used to.

The aquamarine cassock flashed past the corner of his eye. Dan appeared in front of the desk. He picked up the other tumbler, swallowed a deep mouthful and plonked it down with a loud sniff. He sat, reclining backwards in his swivel chair, bare feet up on the desk, hands clasped on his head and turned to Lewis, dislodging a curl across his eyebrow. He peered at him with bloodshot eyes, pinched into slits.

"So, my wee fox, you think you might have the makings of a Saint?"

Lewis' heart leapt. "Just give me one chance and I'll prove it to you. I know I can do it. I can feel it in my soul."

Dan protruded his lips. "That's grand to hear after the rotten news I've just had. The blonde one is going off for a filthy weekend with her new boyfriend. But you knew that, didn't' ye?" He held Lewis' gaze, his pose reminding him of an insolent sixth-former. "I want you to tell me everything you know in future. If you're going to be my new Soul Mate your first loyalty is to me, not to the blonde tart, or any other clown, do y' understand?"

"Yes, absolutely, yes." Lewis put up his hands. "I will be the best possible, the most trustworthy Soul Mate you could ever ask for."

"Grand, so long as you appreciate that becoming a Saint isn't a bed of roses." His eyes flashed. "You've got to be strong and inspirational. Capable of igniting other Souls to follow the Dark Path. My Saint must be prepared to suffer."

"I understand that."

Dan unclasped his hands from his head and folded his arms on his chest, appearing to assess his feet.

"But like I said, what concerns me most about you, is the prude in you. You're embarrassed by your own backside. I don't see how I can present you as my Soul Mate or as a potential Saint without people laughing at us." He gave him a sideways look. "Unless, of course, you'd be willing to go the whole hog for the cause."

"I'd do anything to help the cause, you know I would." Lewis bit his lip, to control his excitement.

"Hmm... Give me a moment to think about it."

Lewis crossed his fingers, watching Dan's profile. A wonderful image slipped into his mind, of himself in a long golden cassock, arm in arm with Dan, walking into the Shooting Star.

"I guess there's a way I could give your Pink Soul more gravitas. But I'd have to invoke the Ceremony of Blood." He looked at him out of the corner of his eye.

"Gosh. That sounds quite dramatic." Lewis nodded, hoping to give encouragement.

Dan raised one eyebrow. "You like a bit of drama, so?"

"I love it. I was the genie in the Christmas Pantomime. People said they really enjoyed my performance. Did you see it?"

"No, I was out of town, but I heard it was a laugh, like." Dan continued to watch him from the corner of his eye. "What I'm suggesting isn't all good fun. The Ceremony of Blood is a profoundly moving event that involves the sacrifice of an adolescent's soul, offered up for the Dark Path, voluntarily, to prompt the Darkening of other Souls, thereby fanning their flames to a higher level. It gives a kick start to those on the journey to Eternal Life, as witnesses to great suffering." He widened his eyes. "Might y'know where I'm heading with this?"

"Actually, it sounds amazing," Lewis said.

"As a consequence of the sacrifice the adolescent soul shoots up through all the Levels and bursts out of the top of the head as the Saint's beautiful Golden Flame." His voice was so croaky Lewis was finding it difficult to concentrate. "As far as you're concerned, Lewis, if you're happy to play the part, it's an instant result. From that day on I'll be calling you my Soul

Mate and my Saint." Dan firmed his lips, as if to restrain his emotion. "Upon witnessing your sacrifice, I personally will suffer the Darkening of Despair. And God itself, will shed tears of a thousand drops of rain."

Lewis thought the whole thing sounded irresistible. He could see himself playing the part in a golden cassock, for a performance in Eliot Hall. Standing shoulder to shoulder with the great UDAN. An acute sense of pride welled up inside his chest, making his eyes brim with tears. He felt so choked for a moment he couldn't speak.

"You're under no pressure, sure. If you don't want the role, I'll find someone else."

"No, I mean please. I want that role. I want it so much. I can't tell you what it means to me." Lewis put his hand on his heart. "I'll act my socks off for you. You'll be so proud you chose me. Please, let me do it, please give me the role."

Dan put his head back, blinked at the ceiling, then levelled his eyes to look at Lewis.

"Are you absolutely sure, now? I don't want you disappearing off with the fairies at the last minute or leaving us all for planet Jolly."

"I'm so sure, I'm one hundred percent, one million percent sure." Lewis laughed. "You know I am."

Dan rubbed the end of his nose vigorously with his forefinger.

"Grand." He snapped his fingers. Soraya stood and walked around the desk. She picked up Lewis' whiskey tumbler and presented it to him in the palm of her hand. "So" – Dan sniffed and gave a loud exhalation – "if it's all right by you, I'll require from you a written Declaration of Martyrdom, signed and dated, asserting your intention to sacrifice your Pink Flame for the Ceremony of Blood." He swung his feet off the desk, leaned to open a drawer, withdrew a pad of paper and slapped it on the desk, wriggling his shoulders jauntily. "Are y' happy for me to write the Declaration or do you wish to dictate?"

"Oh no, you're the poet, you write it." Lewis lost himself in Dan's eyes, he felt like a tingling boy again.

Dan started to write, arriving almost immediately at the bottom of the page. He flicked over and continued scribbling in what appeared to Lewis, watching from upside down, to be tiny hieroglyphics. He whipped back to the previous page, placed his pen on top of it and slid it towards Lewis.

"I want you to read that carefully. If you agree with everything I've written, sign at the bottom with your usual signature. Once you've signed the Declaration of Martyrdom you're committed and your Soul belongs to me, so there's no going back." Dan peered at him over the desk. Lewis loved the huskiness of his voice, making him feel cosy. "Within the jurisdiction of UDAN Corporations, it becomes a legally binding document that I can act on whenever it suits me...Do y' understand?"

Aching to reach out and touch the ringlet that had escaped onto Dan's brow, Lewis picked up the pen and looked down at his handwriting. The words were no more legible than they were upside down, blurring in and out of focus. It was like trying to read in a dream.

"It all looks fine to me." He turned over the page, scanning down. "That's fine. I know what I want and I won't let you down." He laid the pad on the desk, placed the nib to the paper-

"Read it," Soraya said.

Lewis signed his name with a flourish and dated the

document. He lifted a disdainful smile to Soraya, who clearly didn't have a clue what they were talking about. He slid the pad back to Dan.

"Thank you, sir." He nodded. "Thank you for giving me this chance."

"I assure you, I won't be taking it lightly," Dan said. "You'll be handled with the greatest respect. There'll be no vulgar or gratuitous bloodshed."

Lewis smiled. "I'm sure it'll all be in the best possible taste."

"Right-" Dan clapped his hands. "Wheels must be set in motion. I'll get straight on and organise the itinerary for all those involved in the preparations. Lewis, you'll need to have an idea of your timetable, to put your affairs in order and make any last-minute requests you might have." He glanced at his watch. "In fact, we're going to have to start getting you ready shortly, to make you presentable."

"So, um… What does that involve?"

"Well, let me see." Dan firmed his mouth, getting down to business. "Soraya, while I relay Lewis' timetable to him, could you take notes and copy our itinerary to all Departments, to let people know what's happening."

"Yes Dan." Soraya reached over for the pad and was poised, ready with her pen.

Dan clasped his hands around the ends of the armrests and looked straight into Lewis' eyes, speaking in a quiet monotone.

"Lewis Fox Allen, in ten minutes time you'll be escorted to my Earth Room on Level Seven where you'll undergo the preparation of your body. You'll be stripped, shaved and waxed, plucked and scrubbed until you're as smooth as a baby's bum. You'll then be given an enema and left to soak for two hours in a bath of white wine, olive oil, garlic, tarragon, oregano and black pepper."

Lewis ran his hand over his hair. "Do you mean wax, like hair gel?"

Dan looked at Soraya. "Is it wax or gel you use?"

"We use sugar wax," she said.

"Sounds nice." Lewis smiled.

"Then" – Dan touched his cold sore with the tip of his tongue – "at half past four you'll walk the short distance down the corridor to the Powerscourt Restaurant where you'll be seated on the Sacrificial Throne, so all the Souls participating in the Ceremony can see you."

"Cool."

"You'll be naked." Dan pursed his lips, perhaps expecting him to object. But Lewis had already decided he could endure any embarrassment for the cause. "Your hands will be restrained by steel cuffs and your ankles will be chained together. Other Souls attending the Ceremony will then inflict upon you *The Black Suffering*. Everybody will receive a wee scalpel called a *Darkener* and one at a time they'll step up to your Throne, to make an incision in your fingertips.

"These are now known as *Finger Teats* and it's through your *Finger Teats*" – he winced, baring his teeth – "that you'll be milked of every drop of blood, which will be collected in buckets placed beneath your hands." He inclined his head. "They'll be golden buckets, of course, in honour of the occasion…Milking you will involve vigorous squeezing, so you must expect pain and a fair amount of bruising to your Finger Teats. Your hands overall may well become very swollen. If this interferes with blood drainage then the Souls will have permission to open an artery, a small one, as we don't want you going off in too much of a rush, do we, now?" He gave a twinkling smile, creasing his laughter lines.

"Of course, we've got to make it last." Lewis smiled back. Although he wasn't enjoying the spirit of this fantasy as much as the flight across the universe. "It'll give me a chance to get into character...Will there be any intervals?"

"Oh aye, we'll need a fair few of them. Soraya here will take care of refreshments, beer, wine, ice-cream and the like. It'll be a grand opportunity for selling ceremonial merchandise. We could have Pink Lewis Dolls, posters and stickers. If you've any other creative ideas of your own let me know. So, now, what else...Oh, aye, throughout milking you'll be funnelled. That's to say, I'll be encouraging you to swallow apples, sage and onion with minimal chewing, stoked down with olive oil and some white wine vinegar to provide an aromatic stuffing for your stomach." He hooded his eyes. "Hmm...delish."

"So, um...How many performances would there be, do you think?" Lewis took a sip of his whiskey.

Dan peered at him. "How many lives would you have?

"Err...err." Lewis felt lightheaded, like the last time the joke was on him. But this time he didn't feel the same impulse to laugh. "Would that be *one*?"

"Aye, it is *one*...That's why I'm telling ye you've got to give it the whole hog." Dan frowned. "Would y' keep your eye on the ball, you're not quite with it. Your Black Suffering will go on for twenty hours. It'll start at five this evening and finish at the stroke of one o'clock tomorrow afternoon." He put his little fingernail in the corner of his mouth. "What d' you think Soraya? Might five be too early to start the Black Suffering?"

She looked up and blinked. "That depends."

"What do you think Lewis? Is five okay by you?"

Lewis grinned, reminded of Dan's deadpan delivery during their erotic fantasy-flight. Looking back, it had made the whole thing seem funnier, more exciting.

Dan shrugged. "Five it is then… So, by tomorrow afternoon, as far as you're concerned, you'll have done your stint of suffering. But the Ceremony of Blood doesn't end there. The next stage occurs after your Soul has spat up to heaven." He clasped and unclasped the armrests. "Your heart will be cut from your chest. Your body parts will be hacked off, skewered and roasted on the spits in the Restaurant's kitchen. A rosette of your body will then be presented to other Souls on a golden platter to be shared out in the *Pink Supper.*

"Once your head is well crisped and honey-roasted, it will sit on top of your torso. Your hands will be shaped into a cupping position under your chin, appearing to support your head. Your limbs will be arranged around the torso centrepiece, like big meaty petals. Either your penis or your heart can be placed in your mouth, sure, you can decide upon that yourself. There are benefits to be had both ways. The penis, being protuberant, could be sticking up like the flower's stamen. On the other hand, the heart in the mouth has obvious symbolic connotations." He turned to Soraya. "By the way, do we have a platter… a golden one big enough?"

"I'll check" – she nodded – "and get back to you."

Lewis scratched his jaw. "Erm, isn't this getting a bit-"

"A bit what?" Dan angled his ear towards him.

"Nothing, just…" Lewis chuckled. "It's not as funny as your last one."

"Do you think I'm being funny?" He pointed at his own face. "Do I look like I'm laughing?"

Lewis gave a guttural laugh. "I know you, you rotter." He smirked at Soraya. But she wasn't looking at him. Her gaze was frozen to a point in the middle of the desk. He looked at Dan and chuckled. "Yeah, of course, I believe you."

"Grand. So, what is it you want, your penis or your heart in your mouth?"

"Um" – Lewis shrugged – "whatever… heart, I suppose."

"What about next of kin?" Soraya leaned across to Dan. "Won't they want something of him to bury?"

Dan puckered his lips. "Oh, would y' know, I never give it a thought." He cocked his head. "Would you have any family who might want to receive your heart or your penis for funereal purposes?"

Lewis got to his feet. "Actually, I've got to get back to work–"

"*Sit!*"

Lewis shot down again, stunned by the assault on his ears. Like metal striking metal.

Dan banged his fist on the desk. "I'll not stand for any of your cheek! Answer me straight. Is there anyone in your family who'd want to receive your titbits for burial?"

"My mother's still alive. But I doubt she'd want anything. We're not that close." Lewis' ears were ringing.

He felt sick.

"Grand." Dan dropped his voice. "I'll keep them for your rosette."

"Can I go?" Lewis stared at him. "Please, sir, I've got to go, I don't feel very well."

"Aye, before you go." Dan's voice softened, once more,

melodically. "Make no mistake, my friend, during the Ceremony of Blood, any courage or dignity you might show by putting on your stiff upperlip, will not serve my purposes. Your power to Darken others must lie in the horror of your suffering, to rock the earth beneath their feet. Some Souls will be driven mad. Others will spend the rest of their lives fighting the demons unleashed by the Dark Path. But I don't want you to feel disheartened. The brightest Souls in this Community will roar towards Eternal Life and for that I'll be forever grateful to you, my Soul Mate." He opened his palms in a gesture of benediction. "God speed, wee fox, I'll be praying for your Soul." He hooded his eyelids. "Soraya, call the boys in."

Soraya went across the room to open the door. "Connie, Robert, Tim, Don," she called out, "Can you come in please."

Lewis swivelled to see four UDAN body-guards step into Mary's sitting room. They lined up shoulder to shoulder, with hands behind their backs, truncheons dangling from their belts.

"Gentlemen, I want you to prepare this Soul for sacrifice. Bind him and carry him up to the Earth Room for scrubbing." Dan wrinkled his nose. "Phew, Lewis, did you just fart?" He waved his hand. "Get him out of here before he shits himself."

Powerful hands lifted Lewis by his armpits out of the chair. A boot tripped him onto his stomach.

"No! No! I'm his friend! He doesn't mean it! Dan! Dan! Tell them!"

They wound ropes around his wrists and ankles, sealing the blood inside his feet and hands. No mercy, no pause, for concern, binding him like a sacrificial lamb. This couldn't be happening. And yet it was. And he knew at that moment it was all going to happen. His screams tore into his throat. He tasted blood, as images of his torture flashed across his mind, echoing every word Dan had uttered. Writhing, kicking, he caught a glimpse of Soraya's face spinning in the kaleidoscope and vomited over her shoe.

"Help me, help me, someone please! I don't want to die!"

They were going to bleed him, cook him. Eat him. His beloved Dan was going to cut off his head, stuff his heart into his mouth, roast his filleted flesh on spits.

"What are you?" He screamed. "How could you do this to me?"

The men in black dragged him by his ankles along the floor, mouthing like a fish on a hook, gnawing on his tongue to wake himself up, spitting blood and puke across Mary's carpet. They flung the door wide open.

"*Stop!*" Dan's voice rang out above the roaring in his ears. "Bring him over!"

Lewis flopped onto the chair in front of Mary's intercom. "Please let me go, please, I beg you, I beg you, don't do this to me-"

Dan stooped at his side. His soft, hypnotic voice breathed close to his ear. "I'm going to give you and that tart in Dublin one last chance, do y' hear?"

"Y... Yes." Lewis' head was wobbling, he couldn't keep it still.

"So now you're going to call her and impress upon her, using all your drama skills, that if she doesn't get her arse back here by five this evening, you'll be slaughtered and roasted like a pig. Did you get that?"

Lewis nodded.

"Now, my friend, there might well be some who'd cock their

snoots at your roast meat, but I'll not be one of them." Dan's crooked smile loomed in front of him, transfixing Lewis with blisters seeping like seared flesh. "Make no bones about that. That's a *fact*."

Chapter Twenty

"Clarendon Street is third on the right. My place is the first one you come to on the left." Mary sat upright in the passenger seat beside Sean Flanagan, ready to bolt up the steps into her flat, to pack for the weekend.

He pulled up outside. "Are you sure you don't need a hand?"

"I'm sure, just give me ten minutes." She swung her legs out of the car.

Sean grinned. "Don't forget your swimming costume. We're going to have that dip in the sea before dinner."

She ran up to her front-door with the keys in her hand, wind gusting through her hair, sunlight flashing between the tumultuous clouds. The weather had been restless for days, but Sean had painted a sunny picture of their weekend at his seafront cottage, nipping down to the beach for a swim, cosy nightcaps beside the hearth, with Mrs Flanagan there to look after them: His mother, widowed two years previously. She kept an eye on the property during the week, welcoming him home every weekend with her wholesome cooking. He said he didn't have a cure for a breaking heart, but sea-air, sunshine and his mother's Irish stew were sure to put the colour back in her cheeks.

Mary didn't have to say anything. After working together

closely for two days on Monaghan Ward preparing for the vaccine trials, Sean Flanagan had guessed all was not well in Mary's life. As she was leaving St Anthony's Hospital on Wednesday evening, he sidled up to her.

"I've a prescription for you," he murmured in her ear, "You could do with a drink, doctor's orders..."

He took her to the new UDAN Andromeda Hotel in the middle of Dublin's Temple Bar, hoping to cheer her up with its luxurious ambience and tropical sea-life holograms. He insisted they sit up at the bar and spent a small fortune on fancy cocktails, each bearing a decorative tag supporting an Irish charity.

Mary's first visit to the hotel had been just before Christmas, for lunch with Jane. She remembered them remarking upon its similarities with the UISC, the same seamless blend of holographic vistas and space-age architecture. Walking through the vast reception area was like floating in a sea of light. Jane mentioned she'd heard on the UDAN Corps grapevine that 'Our Mr Udan is pleased with the result.'

Mary had sometimes visualised her employer in those days as a Stephen Hawking type, locked away in a private world with faraway eyes raised to the skies. Or a wild-haired Einstein, speaking in riddles of mathematics and esoteric theories that few could understand. She couldn't imagine either type as Andromeda Hotel clients, let alone turn out to be its creator. Now that she'd met the real Mr Udan, she smiled wistfully, recognising the tragic genius everywhere in this magical world of science-fiction and fairy-tale.

Sean twirled a little umbrella between his finger and thumb. "It's lovely to see you smile."

"I'm sorry, I didn't realise I was looking so miserable." Mary sipped her turquoise drink, her eyes lowered to the clownfish hologram swimming around in the bottom of her glass, blowing bubbles with tiny clownfish inside.

"I think it must've been the fourth or fifth time you said you had something in your eye, I started to get suspicious… and you haven't been eating your lunch…You see, we doctors pick up on these things…"

He ordered bar snacks. For the first time in days Mary managed to eat, eventually finishing her king prawn salad, while Sean picked over a plate of pan-fried squid, clearly not that hungry, chatting easily about this and that. He was nice-looking, with light ginger hair, a cherubic smile that hinted at mischief, although she knew he was solidly sensible. He was the kind of man she would've loved to have had as a brother, sharing a similar outlook, meeting throughout life to catch up on their news. She grew so relaxed in his company she covered a yawn during their conversation. Sean took no offence.

"It won't be an early night, but if we leave now, I could get you home before twelve."

"Sorry." She laughed. A bit embarrassed. "I'm fine, I'm just beginning to relax…Honestly, I didn't realise how tense I was, it's been difficult… a very tough week for me."

"If you feel like talking it over with someone, you'll find I'm a good listener." He held his smile. The same reassuring smile he adopted for his bedside manner. She'd observed him with the trial volunteers, answering questions with quiet confidence, even though he must have had his fears, as did all the doctors involved in the Pox V2 project. It was a complex DNA mediated vaccine, yet Sean had demonstrated every faith in her. It was only fair to answer him as honestly as she could; without giving too much away.

"My boyfriend and I are having a few problems. We've decided to separate for a while." She split open another king-prawn and licked her fingers. "There isn't really much to say."

"Do you think you'll be able to resolve your problems?" he said.

"I hope so" – turning to look at him, she found her self-restraint weakened by two strong cocktails – "he's the love of my life. He's not well. He's got bronchitis and it's so strange, these last few nights I've found it difficult to breathe…Have you ever felt so close to somebody that you can feel their suffering?"

"I can't say I have. But I can imagine how upsetting it must be when one of you is ill and you can't be together." He didn't speak for a while.

Mary had forgotten what it was like to feel almost normal. Sharing something of what she'd been going through with Sean Flanagan had released the knot twisting inside her since she'd left the UISC.

Their taxi dropped her off around one am. Both a little tipsy, when she kissed him on the cheek, he returned a tighter than brotherly hug.

"Your boyfriend is a very lucky man," he said, before getting back into the car.

Indoors, she set about her usual routine, checking her e-mails over a cup of cocoa before bedtime. There was a message from Lewis, with a copy of a document from Dan Udan posted on the UISC LifeNet. Astonished that he'd revealed his identity, she knew everything at the UISC would change. He was the Law. He'd have the power to do as he pleased and the whole

Community would be star-struck. It put an end to Jane's plan to have him evicted as the Dan Downs, unfit for Community Life, should he continue to refuse treatment.

She printed out the document entitled **The Reality Treatise** and took it to bed with her. As she held it up to read, the knot in her abdomen tightened, her hands were shaking. Within one minute she was laughing, on the edge of hysteria, doubled up, rolling over the bed.

As a spoof on religion, **'UDAN's Dark Path to Eternal Life'** was hilarious. Maybe intended as retaliation against her atheism by casting her as a potential 'Saint'. He seemed to be mocking himself. It was heartening to think Dan might be seeing the funny side of his obsession with a Cosmic Soul. Perhaps a sign that some of his more uncompromising beliefs were changing.

Having heard from Jane yesterday how bad his chest infection was, her hysteria was partly brought on by the relief that he must be well enough to rise from his sickbed, in the mood to write something amusing. Lewis loved this sort of humour. He'd be in seventh heaven. *Light Wizard* crazy ever since she'd known him. His message was curt – 'I'm sending you this from Dan Udan, The Light Wizard!!... *I knew it all along*!'

That Dan was Mr. Udan? But he *would* say that. He often boasted that he'd be able to recognise their mystery employer – 'I reckon he's about five-five, in his sixties, with a massive head and a long white beard and he wears robes all the colours of the rainbow.' Mary had laughed. 'You mean he'll be sticking out like a sore thumb, like a wizard from Harry Potter!" She knew Lewis so well. His brevity meant he was *totally blown away.* Like a schoolboy meeting his idol. For another giggle, Mary started to read the document again. Her mobile buzzed on the pillow beside her. She put it to her ear, heart fluttering, hoping to hear Dan's voice.

"Hey, Mary, it's Stefan. I suppose you have heard the news?"

She sank back on the pillow. "Yes, Lewis has just sent me a copy of Dan's document." She chuckled, "It's wicked, isn't it!"

"I was completely wrong about your philosopher." He sounded nonchalant. "It really is like God landed here today. Everybody is suddenly soul crazy. I've already gone out and bought a blue headband, but only to please him." He gave a grunt. "Oh ja, his assistant arrived this afternoon. Mary, she is so exotic, everybody is talking about her. I think she's from India, about six feet tall and she's so beautiful she doesn't look real. Her name is Soraya. He has moved her into your apartment with him. I think she must be his mistress." He paused. "I'm letting you know, so you don't get a shock when you get back. I think he has been playing you along… You know, I'm always here for you Mary…Mary, are you there?"

"Sorry, Stefan, I've got to go-" She leapt out of bed, ran to the bathroom and threw up.

Mary slept fitfully. She dreamt that she was running through the corridors of the UISC, crying, searching everywhere for Dan. A voice in her dream whispered that Dan Downs had died years ago, and her own sobbing woke her up. But then she drifted back to sleep and found him in the Powerscourt Restaurant, standing at the bar, partly concealed by a woman's shadow. She knew it was Soraya standing in front of him, stark naked, open-mouthed, her bony hips rolling in a way that suggested he was inside her. Mary thrust out her hands but couldn't reach to tear them apart. She could hear Dan laughing, his tone harshening as Soraya's groans of pleasure grew louder-

The following day over lunch Sean endured Mary's stony silence. When she put down her knife and fork after one mouthful of shepherd's pie, he shook his head.

"I thought a night on the tiles might've done you some good." He reached over and patted the back of her hand. "Listen, I've a suggestion to make to you, but I want you to understand there are no strings attached. I know you're spoken for, so please consider this as a gesture of friendship and nothing more. I have a cottage by the sea not far from Balbriggan, my mother very kindly looks after it for me. I'll be going there this weekend…I was thinking, as we're both off duty, it would do you the world of good if-"

Mary didn't hesitate to accept. In the grip of an emotion, she'd never experienced so violently, she lashed out. When she got back to her flat that evening, she called Lewis and told him about her plans for the weekend, embellishing them with romance. Asking Lewis to keep a secret would only compel him to spread the word, whispering down the UISC grapevine. So that at some point on Friday, Dan Udan was going to look up from his tender craftsmanship and wonder, for the first time in his divinely gifted life, if he had competition.

The more she thought about it, the more she realised that serious competition was precisely what he needed. She rang Jane first thing on Friday morning –

"Jane, Sean is lovely. It's as if we've known each other for years…I do care a lot for Dan, but I'm so unsure about everything and to be honest, I'm beginning to think Sean might be *the one*" – After resisting Jane's pleas not to go away with Sean, Mary ended their call, with a bitter taste in her mouth.

Only the image of Dan in soft focus gazing into Soraya's eyes sickened her more.

She noticed a musty smell in her flat that wasn't there when she left this morning. She put her nose to a vase of frayed roses, sniffed rubbish bins and sinks in the kitchen and bathroom but found no explanation for the smell. She carried on, rifling through her wardrobe to pick out her white cocktail dress, a floral dress, two woollen sweaters and her jeans, hesitating over her old swimming costume she hadn't worn for years.

She piled everything into her suitcase, like a convict on the run and scanned the rooms for last minute things that needed doing. Binned the roses, tied up the refuse bag to take out. She went to her desk to tidy up her work-files in front of the intercom and noticed the LED flashing. She stared at it. It had to be Jane, making a last attempt to talk her out of going away. She'd left a message earlier on Mary's mobile:

"*He knows. I think it'll either kill him or cure him.*" Mary glanced at her watch. It was already half past four, Sean was hoping to miss the Friday rush-hour. She couldn't let him down now. She lifted her suitcase, walked out and slammed the door.

Sean leapt from the car to put her suitcase in the boot. "Fifteen minutes, not bad."

They set off down Nassau Street, passing College Park where she and Stefan had walked through the cherry blossom snowing in the wind. "I thought I'd take us the pretty way. So long as we're north of the city before five, we should be okay," Sean said, "The parks are beautiful this time of year."

Mary sat back in the leather seat, glancing at Sean's alert eyes looking ahead, short straight nose, slight padding of fat beneath his chin. Always calm, today his voice gave him away, with little catches in his breath, excited about the weekend. Her hands were clammy, clasped in her lap. She looked out across the Grand Canal, heading north; conscious of every moment taking her further away from Dan, familiar landmarks seeming to turn hostile, looming up as shapeless shadows against the darkening sky. What if the video message had been from *him*, imploring her to come home? She longed go to back.

"Oh dear, I've forgotten my swimming costume."

"We don't have to go swimming. It'll be freezing, anyway."

"But I'd like to." She looked at him. "Can we go back and get it?"

He looked up through the windscreen. "Those look like-storm clouds. It'll be sleeping bags in front of the telly tonight."

"Tomorrow it could be sunny again. I'd like to have it with me, just in case."

"I'll buy you one. We've got some nice shops in Balbriggan. I'll get you one with polka dots." He returned his cherubic smile.

"I need to go back, I forgot to leave the rubbish out…Please, Sean-" She shifted in the seat to face him.

"We'll hit the rush hour. Can't it wait until Monday?"

"No," she said.

He swung left, put his foot down and turned onto the bridge, stopped suddenly by heavy traffic. He drummed his fingers on the steering wheel, glanced at his watch.

"Thanks," she murmured.

"No problem. I want you to have a perfect weekend, so maybe you'll remember me."

She looked out of the window, contemplating what Sean Flanagan might've meant by no strings attached. She'd already decided that if his mother wasn't there, she'd leave. They inched over the bridge and saw road works ahead. A labourer with a pneumatic drill kept stopping and starting, until they arrived beside him and then he began hammering away, steering forcibly with his massive forearms.

"May I ask what's on your mind?" Sean said.

"I think it might rain." She looked towards the front.

"No worries, I've got brollies in the boot." He moved the car forward.

The drilling receded. She closed her eyes. A thrilling thought popped into her head. Perhaps Dan had already heard about her new man and was landing his helicopter in College Park at this very moment. Or waiting on the steps outside her flat with a bunch of red roses, hoping to extend his gloved handshake to Sean Flanagan and send him on his way.

"Damn, damn, damn," Sean muttered.

Mary opened her eyes. They were stuck behind a bus in St. George's Street. Pedestrians passed them by. Duffel coated student hurrying, bizarre old man puffing on his pipe. A few yards away an exasperated mother paused for her toddler, refusing to follow. Heavy raindrops spattered the windscreen, blurred the screaming child as his mother walked on, grim with cold. Rain and wind of no consequence to him as he plonked himself down on the pavement.

Sean chuckled. "Don't you wish you could still do that to get your own way?"

Mary watched as the mother marched back to her infant, grabbed him by the arm and dragged him along, screeching his head off. "You'd think he was being murdered," she said. The bus turned left, Sean revved the engine and turned into Clarendon Street, braking for a cyclist.

"Look where you're going, you twit!" He pulled up outside her flat. "Hey ho, here we are again."

"Thank you." She looked up at her front door, her fantasy of Dan standing there with a bunch of roses no more likely than any other miracle. Like the memory of a debilitating illness, the image of his back flashed across her mind. It was ludicrous to cast him in the role of an amorous suitor. There would be no flight across Dublin to sweep her off her feet, no red roses or chivalrous handshakes.

She rushed inside her flat, blotting out the miasma of decay and sat down in front of the intercom, startled by an enormous bluebottle progressing up the screen. She rolled a magazine from the desk and managed to shoo it away, only for it to re-alight. She ignored it and played the message.

It was Lewis, with terrified eyes, visibly shaking.

"Oh, Mary I'm in trouble… I've made a terrible mistake, I… I volunteered to be the Saint for the Ceremony of Blood. I signed this thing, a document of Martyrdom, to sacrifice my… my soul to Dan. I didn't know it was real, I thought it was like some sort of play, but it's so…so real… They're going to…to… Oh, Mary" – he whined like a wounded animal – "Please help me! I'm going to be put to death. They're going to bleed me through cuts…hundreds of cuts in my fingers and hack me to pieces… Dan's going to cook me…he's going to *eat* me-"

He put his head back, grimacing at something, open mouthed, showing his back teeth. He stared at her through the screen again.

"I swear, it's a matter of life and death. If you don't get here by five o'clock, I'm dead. You've got to get here by five! Please, I beg you. I swear this isn't a joke. You're the only one who can save me, please, Mary, don't let him kill me!"

She sat frozen, her spine prickling. Her jealous posturing had intended to incite Dan to Dublin, away from Soraya. She never imagined this manipulative twist, using Lewis as bait to force her back to the UISC. She closed her eyes, clearing her mind to put herself in Dan's place.

He must hate the idea of Sean Flanagan taking her away, but unable to pursue her, he'd resorted instead to sick threats. She put her hand over her mouth, dreading that she might've triggered something from his past. She didn't believe he'd hurt Lewis. But she did think him capable of toying with his mind, turned to putty in his idol's hands. She looked at her watch. The five o'clock deadline had passed. She picked up the phone and dialled the UISC switchboard.

"Hi, Frank, it's Mary, would you put me through to Lewis Allen, please."

She waited, drumming her fingers on the desk, glowering at the bluebottle fidgeting its legs. Species: Calliphora vomitoria, her biologist's brain prattled… Dopey thing, how did it get in here? She looked away and sighed. What was she going to tell Sean? I've got to return to the Space Centre because my Farm Manager is about to be cannibalised. Minutes ticked by…

"Sorry to keep you waiting," Frank breezed. "I've just heard that Dr. Allen resigned from his post this morning. I think he might've left us already."

"That's nonsense. Lewis wouldn't resign without telling me." Her tone hardened. "Put me through to Mr. Udan, please."

Silence. Static on the line… Click.

"It was a woman's voice, unfamiliar. "Hello Mary, my name is Soraya. I am Mr Udan's personal assistant. Could you please tell us where you are?"

"I'd like to talk to Dan." Mary bristled.

"I'm afraid Mr Udan is busy. The Ceremony of Blood will begin shortly in the Powerscourt Restaurant, the students are already seated. If you're returning to make a bid for the Martyr's life, then you must be here in five minutes."

"Put him on the line!"

Soraya's voice returned like honey. "Lewis Allen's execution will commence in five minutes, unless you return and bid for his reprieve." The line went dead.

Mary put down the receiver, her heart was pounding, her hands had started to shake. She couldn't believe that Dan had set the whole thing up. How many students were in on the act, to convince Lewis he was about to die? This was utter madness. She picked up the receiver and dialled the switchboard again.

"Frank, it's Mary. How soon could I have a helicopter to pick me up from St. Stephen's Green?"

"As a matter of fact, there's a crew on standby. Do you want them to come now?"

"Oh, is there?" She said in a wry voice. Do you think they could get me back by half past five?"

"Err, we don't work miracles here." He laughed. "They'll be there as soon as they can."

Mary hurried down the steps and threw open the car door. "Sorry, Sean, there's a crisis at the UISC! I've got to go back!"

Chapter Twenty-One

Rotors rattling, rain blowing in her face, the helicopter appeared above her, descending rapidly. Mary picked up her suitcase, angled away from the metronomic gusts. Dave, the co-pilot leapt out, ran across the turf and took it, Theo waved from the cockpit. It was the same crew who'd collected Stefan on Monday night and who'd waited at St. Stephen's Green for her, all day Tuesday, on Mr Udan's orders.

"Thanks, boys, coming home at last!" She attempted a laugh.

Dave hoisted her suitcase inside the door, extended his hand to assist her nimbly into the plush interior. The craft lurched, she tipped into her seat behind the cockpit. Dave slammed the door.

"Hang on tight!" Theo shouted. They lifted off, sweeping along St Stephen's Green, shrubs flowing beneath them, dropping away steeply. Homely streets, college buildings, green parks, vanished into the geometry of Dublin.

"For heaven's sake, boys." Her wet fingers slipped on the steel buckles as she struggled to strap herself in. "Let's get there in one piece." They'd made it in record time, from phone call to pick up in twenty minutes. And Mary, once she'd seen Sean off, had never moved so fast in her life. Already twenty-five minutes late for Lewis. Dave passed her a towel from the cockpit.

"If it hadn't been for the weather, we reckon we could've made it in fifteen." He shouted over his shoulder, "We should be arriving at the UISC in about another fifteen. Is that okay?"

"That's fine," she said. Dave turned to face the sky, replacing his headset. She dried her face, rubbed her hair and tights, fidgety and disorientated. She looked out across the bright grey sky, tinged yellow where the sun shone inside rain clouds.

She put her headset on, sat back and closed her eyes, contemplating Dan's behaviour. What a rotten thing to do. But how could Lewis be so gullible as to believe any of it? A cruel joke, but it was utterly ridiculous. Dan must've gone to some lengths to persuade him. Or maybe Lewis had been given drugs. Maybe he was having a bad trip. She felt a tap on her knee. Dave handed her a pair of holographic filter-glasses. She heard his voice over the headset.

"We're approaching Glendalough Valley. Put those on when I give the signal, if you want to see the UISC, coming up soon." She held onto the chunky spectacles, designed to cancel the illusory landscape created by the Space Centre's holographic shields. With her forehead against the window, she gazed down upon peaks swathed in heather, rocky plateaus mottled by sparse shrubs, fir-trees scudding below. The lakes, small and large, gleamed like tarnished mirrors. The helicopter listed, sweeping diagonally across the mountains.

"Okay Mary, you can look now, it's straight up ahead. Can you see it?" Theo said. She put on the spectacles, peering through the window between the pilots' heads. She'd seen it before returning from previous trips, but now that she'd met its creator, she was awestruck all over again. In the distance, in the middle of the mountains, the spiralling Space Centre looked like a vast ice-sculpture, shimmering between the rocks like a stairway to the stars. Dave's voice crackled over her headphones.

"Have you heard? The Head of UDAN Corporations is living at the UISC."

"I know. He's staying in my apartment," she said into her mouthpiece, with a momentary surge of pride.

"Are you serious?" Dave said, "What's he like to live with?"

She removed the spectacles, for a moment not quite sure how to describe the man she'd fallen in love with. "As you'd expect a great genius to be, a bit otherworldly."

Dave looked over his shoulder. "A nice guy, is he?"

"Yes, though you've got to watch out. He's got a wicked sense of humour," Mary said.

"Yeah, we know, he's hilarious. I've got a Red Flame by the way." He made a thumbing gesture at Theo. "He's got a Green one, filthy playboy." He grinned at her. "What do you say you are?"

Mary shook her head. "Don't ask."

"Everybody's forking out for UDAN headbands back home, spending a fortune on Dark Path merchandise. That's what I call a head for business." Theo chuckled. "He's no fool, is he?"

"People are doing it for fun, aren't they?" Mary said, "They're not taking it seriously."

"A bit of both. I reckon some people are just doing it for a distraction." Dave nodded. "We'll be landing shortly, tighten your seatbelt."

"Approaching the black-hole, folks!" Theo cried.

They hovered, descending gradually. Mary put on her spectacles again to see the domed roof yawning open. Nothing like a black-hole, sunshine radiated from within like sanctifying grace, bathing the cockpit in golden light. The green landing-platform rose, like the palm of an enormous hand, to carry them down to Level Eight's Arrival Deck. Theo cut the rotors, both pilots sat back and relaxed. The dome sealed itself above them.

"Home sweet home." Dave threw open the door, shouting to the ground-crew milling about. "It's a big bad world out there and pissing it down in Dublin!"

Their instructions came over the loudspeaker in a smooth, female voice-

'*Professor Catherwood Gallagher, please proceed to Decontamination Bay C. Crew One please proceed to Decontamination Bay D.*'

Refreshed after her shower, Mary entered the ladies' dressing room, carrying her re-entry clothes over her arm. A blue silk skirt, a white blouse. Holographic daffodils swayed around the walls. The mirrors and washbasins were gilded in gold and her feet sank into the deep-pile carpet. It was difficult to make haste in these surroundings, but she tried. It was five past six. Lewis should be in on the act by now, at least given a stay of execution. She hurried her make-up and let down her hair. Soraya playing on her mind.

She went to the luggage collection. Her handbag was ready, reeking of citrus, but the rest of her belongings were still in process. She gave instructions for her suitcase to be delivered to her apartment on Level Two and walked across the arrival lounge into the lift.

Dan's ceremony would've ended by now. She assumed he'd still be at the Powerscourt Restaurant, probably drinking at the bar. She descended to Level Seven, checking her appearance in the mirror, visualising the scene: Dan and Lewis perched on barstools. Lewis laughing as if he knew all along it was a set-up. If Soraya signalled anything other than a professional relationship with Dan, Mary would walk out.

Approaching the restaurant, Mary was surprised by the absence of post-ceremonial students she expected to see cavorting in the corridor. There were two bouncers in dark suits, shaved heads, one with grey stubble, both holding truncheons.

She frowned. "Has there been a riot?"

They shook their heads in unison. She didn't recognise their faces, they weren't from UISC Surveillance. Their jacket pockets bore the discreet UDAN Corps emblem.

"Is Dan's ceremony still going on inside?"

They nodded. She stepped forward to enter the foyer. They crossed their truncheons in front of her.

"What are you doing? Let me through!" She glared at the bearded one, the more senior of the two, who was sweating copiously from his temples. "I'm Professor Gallagher. Dan's expecting me."

"Your name wouldn't be Mary, would it, by any chance?" He had a Belfast accent.

"Yes, it is."

"Ah, sorry Mary, you're too late." He blinked sweat out of his eyes. "Be on your way."

She dropped her weight onto one leg. "Oh well, if he's going to play silly buggers, he can forget it. Tell him I was delayed by bad weather and that I popped by at" – she glanced at her watch – "six thirty-five." She shrugged her handbag onto her shoulder, walking away. "I'm off home".

"Wait!"

She looked around. The bearded bouncer beckoned. She returned.

"It's the first Intermission, you can go in but keep your head down," he said, "Remember, we never saw you." The bouncers lowered their truncheons, turned their heads in opposite directions, like spoof gangsters.

The lights were dimmed in the foyer, four potted cherry-trees shrouded in black cloths.

There was a notice pinned to the side of the arch.

Welcome to The Ceremony of BLOOD

The Ceremony of Blood is the profoundest of the enforced Darkenings of the Soul and requires great fortitude. Do not pass through this arch if you doubt your ability to endure. The Black Suffering you are about to witness is for the highest cause: To secure your place in Eternal Life after you have died.

I ask that you show respect and gratitude to the one who has offered up his Soul for Sacrifice. Lewis' Soul will depart this Ceremony burning with the Martyr's Golden Halo. He is your volunteer Saint; my substitute Soul Mate and I am in awe of his generosity. The offering of his Pink Flame, although humble, will inspire all those who witness his agony, moving them to become Mature, Gifted or even Compassionate Adults, blessed in the eyes of God.

If you feel able to pass through this door you will be subject to the Laws of Darkening, and you must participate. To do so you will be required to purchase a Darkener (ten/fifteen euros each) and make at least one small incision into the Martyr's finger, sufficient to draw one drop of blood, although you will be at liberty to elicit more.

The Black Suffering will endure for twenty hours. Free refreshments will be available from the bar during the Intermissions. You will not be allowed to leave until after the Presentation of the Pink Flame Rosette, at five pm tomorrow, afternoon. Upon consuming one mouthful of the Martyr's body, you will be initiated into the Inner Circle of Souls, and you will be awarded Bliss in Eternal Life.

If you have the Fortitude to undergo the Ceremony of Blood and join God's Inner Circle, then please sign your name in the Black Book, stating the time of your arrival. Please Note: This will bind you to a legal contract with UDAN Corporations stating your intention to remain until the Ceremony is over.

God grant you forbearance to Shine On, UDAN

Mary looked around. She couldn't see a Black Book and so carried on into the restaurant. Hushed, humid as an underground shrine, hundreds of candles flickered around the walls and along the bar, where an Indian woman, insect thin in a black sari, was taking forever pouring red wine into a glass. *Soraya.* Like a sudden onset of fever, Mary's heart rate accelerated, she felt sick and turned away.

She distracted herself watching the students, many of them she'd seen at Dan's lecture or working as volunteers in the Farm Park. They were all dressed in black, with bandanas around their heads. She stood behind a marble pillar, peeping into the restaurant. Chairs replaced the dining tables, for an audience of around eighty seated in front of the jazz band's rostrum, her view of it blocked by a jutting wall. She could hear the electric drum of a rock band primed to play.

"Hi there!" Someone said in her ear.

Mary smiled at the barman from the Shooting Star, his boyish features dashingly enhanced by a black bandana. "Hello King, aren't you working tonight?"

"No way!" He exhaled alcoholic fumes. "This is where it's at, man, this is what you call a *happening*." He pumped his fist. "And it's happening in *our* life-time. Our generation, and do you know the amazing thing? I always knew it would" – he pointed at her – "you're, um, you're Professor Cathy… What's your name again?"

"Mary." Looking around, she saw nothing to impress her. It was just a booze-up by candlelight. She looked over his shoulder at a couple of students shuffling back to their seats. They looked like zombies, exhausted by the claustrophobic atmosphere, too much to drink, or whatever music they'd been listening to. King hopped jerkily to conceal his loss of balance and gave her the thumbs up.

"Nice one, Mary, can I get you a drink?"

"King, I think you've had enough. Can you tell me what's been going on here this evening?"

"What? I'm doing fine, so far so good" – he smacked his hand on the bar – "hoya babe! Two glasses of wine over here!"

Soraya looked at them, candlelight flickering across her proud, tilted eyes. With barely a twitch of acknowledgement, she picked up two glasses of red wine and placed them down in front of King. She leaned forward to whisper something in his ear.

King beckoned to Mary. "Soraya wants a word with you."

Mary gave an icy smile. "Hello, Soraya, I've heard a lot

about you."

"You're late," Soraya said under her breath. "He is very angry."

"I'm angry. I should be in Balbriggan by now, enjoying myself. Where is Dan and where's Lewis?"

"Dan isn't here."

"I've rushed all the way from Dublin in foul weather to get here. I'm the one who should be angry, but honestly, I can't be bothered. I'm going to have this drink and then I'm leaving." Mary picked up both wine glasses and left the bar, her knees trembling from the encounter. The woman was beautiful. Looking for King, she saw him by the back wall talking to a young man sitting behind a table, crudely lit by a torch hanging from a pole. She went over.

"King, your wine-" She held out the glass. He took it, giving a grunt of pleasure as he sipped.

"Have you bought a Darkener?" He gestured to a display of scalpels on the table. "Ten euros for the short ones, fifteen euros for the long ones with black handles."

"I'm not interested," Mary said.

"Have you just arrived?" The youth behind the table enquired.

"Yes," she said.

"Have you signed the Black Book? Do you know what's going on here?"

"This is Ralph Wild, he likes us to call him Wildo," King interrupted. "He's in charge of admissions."

"I've signed the book." She fibbed. "I understand my colleague Lewis Allen is on the menu." She gave her flinty smile, looking down at the scalpels. "So, these are the instruments of torture."

"That's right." King patted her on the back. "And over here we've got Sympathy Shrouds for twenty euros which have been really popular." He picked up a black cloth with one hand, laid it over his head, covering his face. "You wear this to show you've entered your own Darkening and can't stand to watch any more of the Black Suffering, so you shut it out." The cloth wafted like a curtain as he spoke. "But it doesn't shut out the screams, which we've got to put up with until the bitter end." He whipped the cloth from his head. "Want to buy one?"

She gave King a withering look. "I hardly think so." She glanced along the table. "What are those little brown bottles for?"

Wildo picked one up and held it beneath the torch.

"In here we've got the Martyr's Tears collected during the preparation of his body." Wildo said in a jaunty Australian accent. "Dan suggests that we daub Lewis' tears on our eyelids and cheeks to start the grieving process and stimulate the shedding of our own tears. Apparently, most people can't cry during the Black Suffering because they go into a state of shock. The Tears are also a kind of" – he shrugged – "memento of Lewis…Thirty euros a bottle, cheap at the price I'd say."

"Dan's really thought of everything, he must be making a fortune," she said.

"Yeah, you're right, we've made over a thousand euros in two hours. All proceeds are going towards UISC research into the scientific proof for the existence of God," Wildo said, "As you can see, we're running out of the Darkeners, so Dan's gone to get some more."

"Is he coming back?"

"Yeah, for the second session, it starts at quarter to seven, in a few minutes." He looked over to the foyer. "He should be here now."

"Where's Lewis?"

"You're joking." King spun around. "What do you think they're all looking at?" He pointed to the rows of people sitting with their backs to them, facing the rostrum bathed in soft, frosted light. There, elevated on a high-back chair, looking out across the restaurant, sat a bald, naked man. Mary squinted, focussing over the rows of heads, adjusting to the haze. The man in the chair was completely still, his face a white mask with dark holes for eyes, mouth indistinguishable. From this distance his genital area was a blur, with a bluish, plastic sheen.

"It's a dummy," she said.

"I suppose he does look a bit like a dummy from here," King said, "He's had a rough trot."

"It's pretty unconvincing." She sipped her wine. "Lewis has got dark hair."

"Yeah, I know, but he's having his soul extracted. During the first session Dan reckons he skipped loads of levels and has gone straight into the Darkening of Despair. That drumming sound we can hear is his heartbeat, amplified." King drained his glass and put it down on the table. "I'd better get back to my seat." He pointed at Wildo, walking backwards. "See you later, brother! Shine on!"

Wildo raised his hands, curling both of his little fingers. "Shine on, brother!"

King walked away, shoulders hunched, head down. She watched him stepping sideways to take his seat in the middle of the audience. Silhouetted against the light he obscured her view for a moment. When he'd sat down, she saw the dummy's head was lowered, as if to peer abjectly at its navel. Now it looked quite realistic.

She asked Wildo, busy refolding a shroud. "Who's controlling the dummy?"

His face jutted forward beneath the torchlight, slit by teeth, the shadowy arcs of his eyes. There was something missing from his eyes. She stepped backwards. "Never mind," she said.

She walked towards the rostrum Something wasn't quite right. In the last few minutes, the students had quietly, obediently, returned to their seats. Soraya stood behind the bar in the flickering twilight and appeared to be staring over towards the mezzanine balcony.

Mary followed her gaze to a hologram of a Chinese Water Fall on the far side. The falling plumes of water-light reversed and burst into flames, swirling and vanishing on the slate rocks like silent, illusory fire. She continued past the audience, glancing back to see who was sitting in the rows. Not just the students. But serving staff from the Park View Canteen. She was more dismayed to see a young medical doctor. Elizabeth Magee and her partner Jason, with their heads bowed together. She raised her eyes to the rostrum.

Lewis.

Chapter Twenty-Two

Out of the shadows, from behind the pillars, along the mezzanine balcony at the top of the marble steps, came men marching with truncheons, lining up in front of the audience. Wearing black combat gear, they stood with their legs apart, weapons poised diagonally across their bodies. Mary stole into an empty chair at the end of a row.

"Excuse me," she whispered, "is this seat taken?" The young woman looked up and shook her head.

Mary sat down and stared up at Lewis, naked, stripped of every hair on his body. His testicles and small doughy penis sat between his splayed thighs as if they didn't belong to him. His wrists were manacled to the arms of the chair, palms up, ankles shackled to its legs. Looking as if all his worth had been punched out like a cored apple, all the loveable and endearing ways of Lewis Fox Allen had been torn away to display him as a vessel of blood, soon to be decanted into the buckets at his feet.

She touched the girl's arm beside her. "Hello, I'm Mary. Can you tell me what we're supposed to be doing? I wasn't here for the first half."

"I'm Sophie," the girl whispered, "I'm up first and then it'll be you. You need one of these." Sophie showed her the small scalpel in her palm. "We must go up and cut one of the martyr's fingers and squeeze it until he bleeds into one of the buckets. If the Udanos don't see enough blood they'll put a funnel in his mouth and pour stuff down him until he chokes," her voice cracked. "He's already had to swallow loads of marinade in the first half. It's horrible when he chokes."

"Who are the Udanos?" Mary said.

"They're the bouncers working for the Messenger, they're over there." She pointed towards the men with truncheons.

"Is 'the Messenger' Dan, your philosophy tutor?"

Sophie nodded.

"Sophie, are you sure you want to be a part of this?"

"Um . . . I don't know. If I want to evolve my soul to a higher level, I've got to watch the Martyr suffer. The Messenger said we've all got a good chance of reaching Level Five by tomorrow evening if we stay to the end." Her eyes glazed with tears. "It seems really cruel, but everybody says the Martyr has agreed to everything. He gave up his soul to The Messenger. But I don't want to hurt him. He looks really sad."

Mary took Sophie's hand in hers. "Sophie, would you be very relieved if I put an end to this?"

"But how can you?"

"I don't know, but that won't stop me from trying. Do I have your support?"

Sophie's eyes widened in fear, she lowered her head and didn't answer.

"What if I take your place?" Mary said, "You don't have to do or say anything, just let me go first."

"Can you? Do you think The Messenger would mind?"

Mary patted her hand. "Don't worry. Nothing's going to happen to you."

The lights dimmed. Darkness closed around them. Candles threw shadows at the walls.

"Oh God, it's starting again," Sophie muttered. Gasps and groans repeated through the rows. Mary tightened her grip on Sophie's hand. Noises moved across the rostrum; someone was wheeling a restaurant trolley, wooden floorboards shuddered beneath thumping feet.

"Ladies, gentleman. The Black Suffering will now continue." Soraya's voice came over the loudspeaker, "Have your Darkeners ready. Clapping is permitted. Please, out of respect for the Martyr's suffering, do not cheer. Have fortitude and shine on."

Sophie began to cry. A few people in the front row covered their heads with Sympathy Shrouds. The rostrum lit up like a new day, illuminating Lewis in his chair with two yellow plastic buckets at his feet. Four bouncers broke from the end of the line and marched up the low wooden staircase onto the rostrum, standing at ease behind a silver serving trolley. Sitting on top were two glass jugs filled with pink liquid; a bowl piled high with what appeared to be potatoes or onions on a bed of green leafy herbs. There was a ripple of applause. Another bouncer left the rank and came shouting up the aisle.

"The Messenger calls Number One!" He stopped and loomed over Mary, punching his truncheon into his palm.

She rose to her feet. "I believe that's me."

He stepped aside, indicating her to go first, prodding her in the back with his truncheon.

"Mary, don't you need this?" Sophie raised her scalpel.

"I have everything I need, thank you." Mary walked forward, bracing herself to control her wobbling knees as she climbed the stairs up to the rostrum. She felt the instant heat of the spotlights on her face. The trolley was giving off heavy aromas of alcohol and herbs.

She reached the buckets and glanced down. Both were clean. She stood in front of Lewis in the chair, wrapped with gold crepe paper, mounted on a crude pedestal of bricks, his knees trembling at the level of her thigh. For a moment she couldn't speak, appalled by the sight of his scalp beaded with blood and perspiration, his torso glazed with a sticky residue, his manhood resembling a bag of giblets. She could smell urine and vomit, feel the charge of terror around him. He didn't look at her.

"I'm so sorry I didn't get here in time," Mary said.

"Bleed the Martyr!" A man shouted in the audience.

She put her hand over his icy knuckles. "I don't believe Dan meant to take it this far," she whispered, "I'm here now, try to stay calm."

His head and torso began to shudder. A bouncer prodded the top of her arm with his truncheon.

"Milk the Martyr!" He prodded again. "You make an incision in his Finger Teat and squeeze out the blood. Do you understand?"

"I'd like to speak to Dan," she said.

"The Black Suffering continues until further notice. Milk the Martyr!"

"Tell me your name." Mary glared at him.

"The name's Ted." He gave a stiff nod.

"Ted, would you and your colleagues give me a moment to talk to these people?" She raised three fingers.

"Three minutes is all I ask. Please."

"Funnel!" Another shout from the audience.

"She's the one we waited for." Ted looked around at the others.

"But she's too late now," said another bouncer.

"We could give her a couple of minutes. The Boss did say to continue at our own discretion." Ted looked at the others and waved his truncheon at Mary. "Say, what you've got to say. Then we've got to funnel him."

Lewis lurched forward in the chair. "No, no funnel! Oh God, please, someone help me!"

"I will, Lewis," Mary said, "please try to stay calm."

"Bleed him! Bleed him! Get on with it!" a female shouted in the front row.

Mary walked the few steps to the edge of the rostrum and looked out into the darkened restaurant, focusing on faces in the front rows lit by stage-lights.

"I understand you've been told that Lewis Allen volunteered to be the *martyr* for this event." She clasped her hands in front of her. "The truth is that he is the victim of a terrible misunderstanding. You can see-"

"Funnel!" came a shout from the back. Mary glared into the gloom. The voice seemed to come from the man sitting at the merchandise table, King's friend.

"Do you honestly believe you can benefit yourselves by torturing this innocent man?" She contracted her eyes and peered into the shadows. "This isn't going to teach you anything but brutality. If you support it, there will be more ceremonies like this. Next time, the victim could be any one of you." She pointed to faces in the front row.

Lewis groaned behind her.

"I appeal to you. Ignore everything written in Udan's

Reality Treatise. Dan Udan is a good man. You all know the great things he's achieved. No doubt, that's the reason you're going along with this. But it must be obvious to you that today he's lost his way-"

Lewis groaned louder.

Mary put her hand up. "Think for yourselves. Don't be led astray by anyone who promises you salvation. Apply your own conscience-"

Boom of a drum, blare of a trumpet. Everybody turned around to see a circus clown at the top of the mezzanine steps, blowing on the trumpet. He stomped down to the back of the audience, making his way towards the rostrum, followed by a bouncer beating on a base drum. The two-man jazz band shattering the hush with a swinging rendition of 'When the Saints Come Marching In'.

Mary stepped backwards and placed her hand on Lewis' shoulder, slimy with sweat. The trumpeting clown progressed down the aisle, white-gloved fingers jigging on the keys, thigh length coat, square trousers severed at the calves. Coming towards them with shaggy hair, bubble nose, face battered with greasepaint, eyes crisscrossed with charcoal. Even at this distance there was no mistaking his identity, the luminous, deadpan stare.

He flip-flopped up the wooden stairs, eyes ahead, trumpet pressed to his lips. She waited for him to turn his head, for their eyes to meet. But when he stepped into the light, he tossed the trumpet to the bouncer below and launched himself into a cartwheel. Pink tubular shoes sailed through the air, a snip of lemon trousers, sky-blue coat wafting grease paint and cigarette smoke. He turned upright, opened his arms.

"Hi there, boys and girls! Do yous know who I am?"

Lewis froze like prey in sight of its predator. Mary squeezed his shoulder to reassure him. Hearing Dan's voice again, goosebumps rose on her arms.

"Speak up, boys and girls, I canny hear yous!" The clown cupped his hand behind his ear.

"Dan the Clown," she blurted.

He spun around, black spears piercing his translucent eyes, the clown's unseeing gaze perfected.

"Oh my, would you look at that!" His lips parted in a big, boaty smile. "It's a wee bunny with long blonde ears! How did you get in here, bouncing all over my kitchen floor?" He wagged his finger. "Naughty, naughty bunny! What are we going to do with you?" With his lurid features, spiked scarlet hair, stage-lights reflecting amber in his eyes, he was the scariest clown she'd ever seen. The little girl in her could have burst into tears.

"Hello Dan, it's lovely to see you." She tried to meet his eyes, but his stare passed through her, fixed on an imaginary point. Or maybe some memory from his past. He clasped his hands and inclined his head with a smile of saccharine wonderment.

"Oh, what a lovely wee squeak it makes. Oh, isn't it so cute! Go on, squeak for us again."

"Dan, I'm here, so you can stop this now." She kept a firm hold on Lewis' clammy shoulder. "I need to talk to you in private. Is there somewhere else we can go?"

He gave a sly, sideways smile to the audience, showing the sunken contours of his cheeks beneath the greasepaint, a wedged swelling at the side of his mouth. He stank of alcohol and fishy body odour, like an old tramp.

Her voice sharpened with panic. "This has gone far enough.

Let's go home."

He grasped his braces and rocked back and forth, miming laughter, square mouthed.

"Dan, everybody knows this is not right-"

"Squeak, squeak, squeak, maybe the wee bunny is hungry. Boys and girls, let's see if we can't find it something to eat . . . a fresh piece of lettuce or a nice, sweet carrot." He leaned towards Mary, widening his vacant eyes. "Are ye hungry? Would you be wanting a carrot? All right then!" He pulled himself up with an abrupt left-turn and flip-flopped over to the trolley, lifting his shoes high off the floor, bending over the contents of the bowl to sniff them with his bubble nose.

Nobody laughed. The audience hadn't uttered a word since Dan had appeared. The only sound now was the faint drumming of Lewis' amplified heartbeat. She looked down at him. His eyes were squeezed shut. Mouth clamped, his whole body shaking, as if he were being electrocuted.

"Ach, I can't see any carrots, but I've found a nice, juicy onion." He flip-flopped back and held out the onion. "Come on, wee bunny, come and get it, you know you want it." His voice was eerily gentle.

Mary patted Lewis' shoulder. "Stay strong," she said. She left his side and came face to face with Dan, looking up into his eyes. His irises had faded to grey. Greasepaint etched his laughter lines into the wrinkles of a much older man. She saw now that his top lip was granulated by an infection, covered in crimson paint. She tried to see through the mask for the Dan she knew. But this man was a stranger, gazing back at her without a flicker of recognition. As if they'd never met before she smiled politely, her hand trembling as she plucked the onion from his fingers.

"Thank you." She clasped it to her chest with both hands. "Do you mind if I keep it for later?"

He thrust out his hand. "Give it back!"

She dropped it into his open hand.

"Floppy Ears isn't hungry!" He tossed the onion at one of the bouncers who caught it from the air. "Ted, see if you can't get that down his throat!"

"Oh, no, no, Mary, help me," Lewis whimpered, "Please, help me."

"Don't you dare! Stop this, all of you!" Mary strode back to Lewis and put her arm around his shoulders. Ted and another bouncer approached, Ted clutching the onion in his hand like a cricket ball. "Don't you dare come near him!" She raised her hand to smack them away, but Ted grasped Lewis' chin as the other man pulled his ears from behind. "Have you all gone mad?" She grabbed Ted's wrist, struggling with all her might to pull it back, jostling with Ted while he chuckled under his breath, forcing the onion against Lewis' pursed mouth. She looked up at Dan stomping across the floorboards.

"Get that bunny out of my kitchen!" He stopped and pointed at a bouncer. "Bobby, go you and fetch me a hutch!"

Bobby blinked. Another one sweating so much that it was seeping into his eyes,

"Sorry sir, but do you err . . . mean an actual *hutch*, sir?"

"Aye, I mean a hutch for our wee runaway, before it starts breeding around town like a friggen rabbit!" He fluttered his fingers at him. "Go on, Bobby! If ye can't find me one, build one out of tables and chairs. You'll find some in storage that used to belong to a girl I once knew, long gone now." He pointed at

Mary. "Get that critter out of my sight! Put a rope around its neck. Tether it to a chair or something, before I slit someone's throat!" He bellowed, "Are ye friggen deaf, Bobby!"

Lewis jerked forward and vomited between his knees.

Bobby gripped her above the elbow and dragged her towards the wooden stairs. She dug in her heels and flung out her fist.

"Let me go! You've got to stop him!" She turned her head and shouted at the audience. "Somebody, do something! Stop them!"

There was sparse applause. She saw people covering their heads with Sympathy Shrouds. She looked to see Dan the Clown and all four bouncers surrounding Lewis. The one behind the chair held Lewis' head back as he growled from the bottom of his throat, trying to stretch his mouth wide enough to receive the onion, in a sickening display of submission.

"Sir, I can't get it into his mouth. Would you like us to cut the onion in half?"

"Ach, I can't be bothered with that, so, you can shove it up his arse before we put him into roast." Dan flicked his wrist. "Funnel him."

"Oh, for God's sake, someone's got to help him!" A sob burst from her lungs. Bobby forced her down the stairs, holding her arms behind her back, her high heels clattering against the wood. She went over on one ankle and cried out in pain. Bobby paused. Mary craned her head over the edge of the rostrum to see Dan looking towards her, his mouth turned down in a sad clown's face. At the bottom of the stairs the bearded bouncer from the foyer grabbed the back of her neck, pushing her along in front of the first row. People lifted their shrouds to watch.

“Blasphemer!” someone shouted. The bouncer flung her into an empty chair and placed a rope around her neck, like a noose.

“What do you think you’re doing? You’re worse than he is! Can’t you see he’s sick!” She gritted her teeth, kicking him in the shin. “Wake up and do something, before something terrible happens!”

The bouncer pressed his mouth to her ear. “Listen, Mary, we can’t stand up to him. Believe you me, it’ll make it worse. You’re the only one who can get through to The Boss and you’d better think fast or that wee sod could perish tonight.” He finished tightening the noose, winding the end of the rope around the back of the chair. “My name is Connie. I’m Mr Udan’s first bodyguard. I’m not with the Udano Regiment who showed up today. I’ll do what I can to help you… Right, that should do it,” he said gruffly and moved off.

She’d been too stunned to speak to him. She looked up to see Lewis gorging from the funnel like a hatchling. His Adam’s apple pumped to swallow everything he was given, foaming down his chin, genitals twitching, fingers clawed. Ted withdrew the funnel from his throat and Lewis’ head lolled forward onto his chest. She felt sick. Her pulse throbbed inside her ears. She shut her eyes and opened them again, to test if she was awake, if this was really happening. She watched Dan the Clown, sweeping his long shoes from side to side like feelers, shuffling across the floorboards. He made a thumbing gesture over his shoulder,

“Aye, I reckon he’s got the knack.” He wiggled his eyebrows, beaming at the audience. “What do y’ say, boys and girls? Wouldn’t you say he’s got the knack?” Silence, but for the distant galloping of Lewis' heart.

Dan came to the edge of the rostrum, craning his head forward. "The Messenger calls Number Two," he said.

Mary looked around to see Bobby standing over Sophie, smacking his truncheon. She caught her eye and mouthed, *No, Sophie . . .* She faced the front. When Dan glanced the other way, she prised apart the noose's knot and discovered that Connie had tied it loosely.

"Come on now, Sophie. The Martyr will not feel the pain of one wee cut and one wee cut is all it takes to open the Kingdom of God." There came the sound of heavy boots and a girl's step. "Good girl, Sophie."

Mary hunched down and pulled her head through the ring of rope around her neck. Her mind went racing. How much influence did she have over him? What could she do to stop him? She looked up to see him stooped with his hands behind his back, glowering as Sophie delayed choosing a finger, Lewis staring blankly into the audience, hypnotised by the drumming of his own heartbeat.

"Sorry sir, I don't know which one to use." She winced. "They already look so sore."

Mary returned to mount the wooden staircase. Ted moved forward, Connie blocked his way and nodded to her. She strode across the rostrum to a few muted boos from the audience.

"Sorry Sophie, I haven't quite finished. May I have your scalpel please? You can go and sit down."

Sophie handed it to her and ran off. Mary put the scalpel into Lewis' palm and closed his fingers. "Hold onto that for me, Lewis." She walked up to Dan.

He swayed backwards on his heels, fists pulling on his

braces, boaty mouth capsized.

"You, again! Didn't I get rid of you?"

"I'm sorry. I should've come home when you asked me to." She tried to meet his gaze. "There's no man in my life, but you. I still care about you, Dan. Believe me, I haven't stopped-"

He was staring brazenly at her breasts.

Mary put her hand on her chest, as if to cover herself. He was so close, all she had to do was reach out and touch his face. She held her breath. What would it take to knock him out? The brush of her fingers, a slap on his cheek? What if he was too fast and grabbed her by the wrist. She could make everything worse. She lost her nerve and dropped her arm to her side.

"Dan, please" – she pleaded with open hands – "please, will you stop punishing Lewis, because of me."

"Say, Floppy Ears." He bleated through his teeth in a cartoon voice. "This boy dreams of becoming a saint and I just heppens to know how to cook one! It's got feck all to do with you, so" – he fluttered his fingers in her face – "*Bye, byeee!*"

For the first time she heard laughter in the audience.

"What do I have to do to get through to you? Just tell me and I'll do it." Her voice sharpened. "What do you want me to do?"

He parted his lips in a sickly smile. "Nothing. There's nothing you can do, because you're *too late*."

"But that's not-"

"Ah, ah, no 'buts.'" He wagged his forefinger in front of her eyes. "If you'd wanted to save this boy's life, you'd have got here by five, but you were too busy swanning around town with your new boyfriend. Tough titty. This is the way the cookie crumbles."

"Dan, this is madness. I know you're not insane." She fixed her gaze on a big red button on the front of his jacket. "You're behaving like a playground bully." She tightened her mouth. "After today, if you're not careful, everybody here will remember you, not as the genius you are, but as a sadistic nutcase." Her anger flashed. "I mean, just look at him!" She pointed at Lewis lolling in his chair. "What has that sight got to do with enlightenment? You're making a fool of yourself. I thought you were so much cleverer than this."

"Go easy, Mary," Connie muttered behind her. She could hear Lewis whimpering again.

"Welcome to the dark side." Dan flared his criss-crossed eyes. "Personally, I prefer my dinner alive when I sink my teeth in. But I thought we'd be civilised, like, with a roast. I might fancy a fresh, raw starter, mind." He leaned forward and whispered, "You better run, rabbit, run."

"Will you snap out of it!" Mary stamped her foot. "Now! Before you ruin everything. Where's Dan Downs?" Her throat closed. Her voice broke. "Where's the man I fell in love with?"

He straightened his back, his face settling into a familiar, hooded expression as he gazed down into her eyes. "Didn't I warn you not to play a dangerous game? Now here's a dangerous game. It's called 'Nobody Messes with Me.'" He lifted his lip in a sneer. "Just in case you didn't get that, I'll repeat it." He bared his teeth, neon eyes blazing. "*Nobody Messes with Me!*" Her eardrums slammed, she put her hands over her ears. He pointed his forefinger in her face. The blurred tip of his glove hovered an inch from her eye. "*Get down on your knees!*"

"Get down, Mary and pray!" Lewis' cry cut through the buzzing inside her head. "He wants you to pray to God! Believe in God! Do it for me!"

She widened her eyes at Dan. "Is that what this is all about? You want me to pray to your God and turn myself into a hypocrite?"

His voice softened, "Who, me?" He pointed to himself looking around, acting bewildered. "I never said a thing" – turning to Connie – "Did I say anything about praying, Connie? Go on, be honest with me. I'm either going mad or she's hearing voices from above" – turning to Ted – "Did ye hear a voice from above telling her to pray?"

"No, sir."

"Is this the real Dan Udan?" Mary said in a low, tremulous voice. "Are all these men too frightened to stand up to you? If this is the real you, then you're the epitome of everything I call *evil*." All around her people gasped, sounding like the ragged inhalation of a huge animal.

Dan shrugged. He withdrew a hipflask from his pocket, put it to his lips and sucked, casting his beady eyes around at the bouncers, all to a man staring at the floor. He wiped his mouth on his sleeve, smudging crimson greasepaint all over his cheek and bellowed, "*The Messenger calls Number Three, Number Four, Number Five, Number Six! Come on you dogs! I want to hear the Martyr scream!*"

He stomped around Mary, swigging from his hipflask.

"Pray for me . . . pray for me-" Lewis' head lolled from side to side, lost in his nightmare. The sandy haired student, Wildo, came grinning towards the rostrum, with others at his heels, scalpels flashing in their hands. They came thundering up the wooden stairs.

"Connie, don't let them up! I'll pray!" Mary dropped to her

knees and clasped her hands in front of her face. "Please God, please stop them! Make them see that what they're doing is wrong! Please God, make Dan stop them!"

Connie was at the edge of the wooden stairs with his hand on Wildo's chest, trying to push him down the staircase. Wildo leaned into him, pulling on his sleeve, his other hand waving a scalpel towards his throat.

The audience started to chant, "Bleed the Martyr! Bleed the Martyr!"

At the other end of the rostrum, Dan thrust his hipflask in the air. "*The Messenger calls Number Seven, Number Eight, Number Nine! Connie, y' bastard, let the dogs get at the fox, before I break that friggen arm of yours!*"

Connie stepped back. Students swarmed all over the rostrum.

"No!" Mary cried, "Didn't you hear me praying!"

Wildo and his friends surrounded the chair, Ted and Bobby adjusted the buckets beneath Lewis' hands. Mary heard him grizzling, catching his breath like a child too exhausted to cry. The scalpel she gave him dropped to the floor.

"*Quiet! You boys step away from the Martyr!*" Dan's voice rang out. The audience hushed, but for some braying at the back. "*One more peep out of yous and I'll cut y' tongues out!*"

The muffled palpitations of Lewis' heart were audible again, as Dan flip-flopped up the rostrum, pulling faces, bubble nose bobbing up and down. He stopped in front of Mary on her knees, leaning over her with his hands on his hips.

"Come on, then, Floppy Ears," he said in a husky voice, "You've got my attention, so let's hear you pray. Keeping in mind it's got to come from here" – he thumped his chest – "if I can't feel it, then sure to God, God won't feel it" – he wiggled his bubble nose – "see if ye can't bring tears to my eyes and soften me ole heart."

Trembling, Mary entwined her fingers, the sleeves of her blouse clung to her arms with perspiration. Someone in the audience was crying. People rustled their scrolls. Dan started tapping the toe of his pink shoe, the length of a child's arm. She closed her eyes, swallowing to keep her stomach down.

"I didn't mean to upset you. There's nobody else in my life . . . It's not too late for us to put things right." Her voice shook. "You're the only one who can stop this... You're responsible, not God.... You know I don't... believe in God . . . I can only appeal to you, to please stop."

He put his hand down and gently stroked the top of her head. An intense, unnatural heat reached her scalp through his glove. He said in his quiet, hypnotic voice,

"What a shame, Mary, that wasn't the sound of hubris dissolving into humble tears, but you and your ole sticky pride." He withdrew his hand. "Boys and girls, did any of yous hear this one saying her prayers by any chance, sure, I might be going deaf."

"We couldn't hear a thing!" A woman shouted at the front. Dan did a right-angle turn and stomped to the edge of the rostrum. He turned his palms up, bleating in the loud, cartoon voice.

"Hey, kids, what are we going to do? Floppy Ears won't pray anymore. So, who's going to save the Martyr?" He pointed into the front row. "Anybody down there? No?" He waved to people in the middle. "Hi, there, are y' having a nice day? How about you?" He cupped his hand behind his ear. "No what? No way, eh?"

"*Please . . . somebody*," came a tiny voice behind him. Mary looked over at Lewis slumped in the chair, his head hanging so low from his shoulders as if willing himself unconscious.

"Won't anybody come up here and pray for the Martyr's life? Hey, come on, is there really *nobody*?"

Dan glanced over his shoulder. "Aw, sorry Foxy, things ain't looking so good for ya, pal."

"Dan!" Mary slammed her hands on the floorboards. "Stop! I'll pray!"

He didn't look at her, fluttering his fingers in her direction. "Put a sock in it Floppy Ears, you've had your say . . . So, what's it to be boys and girls? Does he go the whole hog?"

"Go for it!" someone shouted.

"Let's hear it for the whole hog! Come on and give it up!" Dan clapped his hands above his head. The crowd erupted with whoops and cheers. He stomped around in a circle, shouting above the din. "*Looks like you're dead-meat, Foxy!*" He punched his fist in the air. "*Bleed the Martyr! Everybody, join the queue!*"

"No! No!" Mary went on all fours, crawling across the floorboards to Dan's feet. She raised herself onto her knees; staring up at him, hands pressed together. "Dan, I beg you, please, let me pray . . . I'll do it this time, give me another chance!"

"Connie, get Floppy Ears out of my sight, this is no place for a daft rabbit!"

Dan lifted his foot, nudging her flank to shoo her away. He swivelled, flip-flopping in the opposite direction. Mary sank back on her heels and watched as the world became fragmented. Shadows loomed around her, bouncers with truncheons appeared everywhere. She saw the back of the diabolical clown receding through the fog, scarlet hair, hunched shoulders, strident legs.

Across the restaurant another pack was heading for the rostrum, wide eyed, waving their scalpels. She looked up at the blur of students and bouncers stooped around Lewis, their shoulders pumping rhythmically as they milked him. She could hear blood hitting the buckets, sounding like heavy rain.

Lewis let out a terrible scream.

The stage-lights went out.

Chapter Twenty-Three

Mary was blind in the dark. The candles had been extinguished, thickening the air with smoking wax, choking her as she groped across the floorboards, in the direction of a man shouting –

"In the buckets!"

Then came two loud thuds, stifled grunts. A woman's shriek pierced the pitch-black, triggering the students into a screaming chorus. Mary cowered in the wailing darkness, her mind searching for any kind of action, turning over and over…

The stage-lights went up, dazzlingly bright, quietening the students to sniffs and moans.

"Ladies and gentlemen" – Soraya's voice reverberated around the restaurant – "The Ceremony of Blood has ended. Our Saint, Lewis Fox Allen, will now give a statement on behalf of The Messenger. Please give him a big round of applause for his suffering and endurance."

Like the sudden wakening from a nightmare, for a moment the scene didn't make sense. Figures in black shuffling up against a back-curtain, an empty chair. The audience let out a roar, cheering, clapping. Mary rose to her feet, unsteady, weak-kneed, the illuminated room a confusion of heads, shapes and shuddering blocks of colour, until her eyes adjusted.

Lewis emerged from the other side of the rostrum, in a

long golden cassock, wearing his spectacles, Bobby and Ted supporting him at each elbow. There was no visible blood, his hands appeared unharmed. The bouncers walked him to the edge of the rostrum, bent like an arthritic old man and handed him a scroll, resembling a medieval document. Lewis attempted to straighten himself, waiting for the din to abate. He raised one hand above his head in acknowledgment of the applause, then let it drop as if he hadn't the strength to hold it up. He fumbled, trying to roll down the scroll. Mary was already at his side.

"Let me help you," she said.

He jerked his head back, baring his lower teeth. "If I'm not worth a prayer, I'm not worth your help. Fuck off!"

She stumbled back on her heels. "I…I tried-" Numbed by the rejection, she could only stand by and watch as he uttered high fluting sounds without moving his lips, catching his breath, the words only just recognisable.

"Good evening, all. The Ceremony of Blood…in which you have just participated was conceived by UDAN Corporations as a psychological test designed to create a moral dilemma… amongst you" – he swallowed convulsively – "whether to follow in…inhumane orders or to listen to the voices of your conscience and confront the Messenger-"

"Bravo, Foxy! You should be on the stage!" A male shouted somewhere in the audience. A nervous titter passed through the rows. Lewis waited until there was complete silence.

"UDAN Corporations" – he squeezed his eyes shut for a moment and opened them again, as if struggling with the sense of what he was reading – "is not seeking blind obedience amongst its experimental communities, but the bravery of heroes and the hearts of saints… only the best of humanity may go forth to colonise the stars... The Messenger regrets to inform you that all UISC students in this room have failed the test for moral courage." The scroll slipped to the floor. He bowed his head. "That is all."

Bobby and Connie took his elbows, helping him down the wooden staircase. Lewis didn't look back, as the rest of the bouncers and students on the rostrum followed silently, solemn actors leaving the stage. Mary watched until she lost sight of the line-up behind a pillar. Everybody started talking at once. The word *eviction* rumbled around the room.

"Attention, ladies, and gentleman, there is no cause for concern," Soraya said, sounding shakier than before. "UDAN Corporations will be addressing the lack of moral courage amongst the ceremonial participants in the next few weeks. In the meantime, please leave the Powerscourt Restaurant in a quiet and orderly fashion. Students are invited to the Student Refectory for a light vegetarian supper, where they will receive written notification of this week's philosophy assignment concerning their role in this evening's event ...Good night, God Bless and God Speed."

The students filed out of the rows, a little subdued at first, then, as might a shocked horror-movie audience, began conferring noisily.

Mary stood alone on the rostrum, dazed, hearing their hysterical laughter, the palpable relief and disbelief as they moved towards the exit, where half a dozen bouncers were shaking yellow buckets, collecting scalpels. She looked across to the bar; Soraya was gone. If she stood here much longer, she'd be on her own in the restaurant, dangling like a puppet, discarded by the puppeteer.

There was only one thing to do. She clattered down the wooden stairs, ran back to the chair where she'd sat beside Sophie and snatched her handbag onto her shoulder. She went in the opposite direction to the students, towards the restaurant kitchen, a vast, ventilated area of stainless steel, where a solitary chef stooped, decorating a cake, he looked up.

"Where's the door to the corridor?" She followed the direction of his icing-knife.

She was back in the lift, drenched in perspiration, making her way up to the UISC departure lounge. Destination Dublin, St. Stephens Green. Then Clarendon Street to write her letter of resignation. It was all over, her life at the UISC, her friendships with Lewis and Jane… Delete Dan Udan, Dan Downs, poet, clown, chimera; *monster…* She squeezed her eyes closed and held her breath. It was beyond crying over, beyond trying to understand what had happened, as it no longer mattered. All she cared about was how fast a flight-crew could get her out of here.

The lift doors parted, she stepped onto the midnight-blue carpet, striding between sociably arranged leather sofas and armchairs. The place was deserted. Ahead, were windows into the Decontamination Bay, with a row of doors to shower-rooms and luggage collection points. Her suitcase would already have been sent down to her apartment. She didn't care. UISC Household would return all her belongings as soon as they received notification that she'd left. She strode on faster, heart thumping against her ribs, fist clenched around her handbag-strap.

"Mary!"

She spun around. Dan Udan, washed clean, damp hair

combed back, in a white shirt and jeans. He stood with his hands on his hips, wide-eyed. "Where do ye think you're going?"

"Stay away from me!" She bolted, pushing the glass door to the Decontamination Bay. It was locked. She banged on it with her fist. "Open the door! I want to leave! Somebody, get me out of here!"

"Calm down" – in his quiet voice, coming up behind her – "there's no-one there. I've sent them all off home."

She turned, her scalp prickling to see his pale, haggard face, irises dull, upper lip crusted by a herpes infection that looked so painful, in different circumstances it would've brought tears to her eyes.

"You have no control over me. I resign. Now let me go!"

He stopped in front of her. "Don't say that. You can't mean that. Back there was just an exercise meant to teach the kids a lesson. Sure, I got carried away. I'm sorry, the devil got the better of me."

"What devil? It was you!'" Recognising his contrite expression, she let go. "You're a tyrant! A psychopath who needs psychiatric treatment! You shouldn't be allowed anywhere near young people!" She swung her bag at him, and he didn't move, letting it thump his arm. "You're not fit to employ anybody. You sick, sadist!" She gasped and swung at him again. "Call the flight-crew, now!" She slumped back against the door and put her hand over her face. "How could you do that to poor Lewis!" she cried, "How could you!" He gave no answer. She lowered her hand, to see his brow furrowed, his expression full of hurt. She glared at him. "Do you have you any idea what you've done?"

"I've just seen Lewis in the bar, enjoying a stiff drink." Dan gazed into her eyes. Mary couldn't believe her heart gave its usual flutter. "Sure, he knew he'd live. After he left that message on your intercom, I reassured him there'd be no bloodshed. I asked what he wanted from the occasion, and he said a golden cassock, so I made one and I've given him a hefty bonus… I went way over the top. I know I scared y'all. Lewis accepted my apology just now, so, why can't you?"

"He blames me!" She smacked herself on the chest. "I've lost a friend because of you. He won't hold you responsible because you're his idol, he'd let you get away with murder. God only knows the damage you've done to the students with your warped logic. Using cruelty to get any kind of message across is amoral!"

"But surely, most of life's lessons are cruel." His tone was wistful. "What you do with your Scotty isn't kind, until you can use what you've discovered."

"Don't be ridiculous! Scotty isn't even a sentient being." She put up her hand. "Don't look at me like that! I can see there's no point in talking to you. Just get me out of here, now!" She stamped her foot. "Stay out of my life! Do you understand?"

"What did ye expect, Mary, eh?" He widened his eyes, showing white. "I begged you to come home. My chopper waited all day on the green and I didn't even get a call, after all I said about needing you here. I had to conjure a case of life and death to get you back and not even mine, as it turns out, you don't give a monkey's arse about me. The next thing I hear, you're off with another guy for the weekend." He cornered his eyes towards her. "What's that, about, eh? Were you ever in love with me, or were ye just flattered by the attention?"

"You moved that woman into my apartment. As far as I was

concerned, we were over."

"Soraya is my personal assistant. She came to work for me once our affair was over. There's nothing going on between us and besides, she knew about you from the beginning." His lips were turning blue. "Are you jealous of her? Was that what sent you running off?"

"What does it matter now? The way you treat people is despicable. All I can say is that she's welcome to you. Whatever it was that we had has gone. It's over." She pursed her mouth. "Now I know just how nasty you can be." She opened her handbag and withdrew her mobile, handing it to him. "Call Theo and Dave to take me back to Dublin."

He'd broken into a sweat, matting a stray ringlet to his brow, his complexion turning waxier, greyer. "I've got my phone… I'm sorry you can't find it in your heart to forgive me. The love was all one way, I guess." He stepped aside, putting the phone to his ear. "Theo, hi, it's Dan Udan, can you and Dave get your asses back here to take Professor Gallagher to Dublin. Aye, do me a favour, call Lu back as well to open the bay, thanks." He slipped the mobile into his jeans' pocket, facing her. "You'll be the death of me, you know that… Ach, well" – he shrugged – "I wish you a pleasant future with your Dr Flanagan."

"We're good friends, nothing more," she said, levelling her voice.

"Looks like I could do with a good friend to set me straight. I'm no angel, far from it, with the past I've had. God bless." He waved his hand in a single arc and turned away, moving silently across the carpet.

"Goodbye," she said.

He was gone. Her knees buckled, she staggered to the

nearest armchair and sat, rubbing her arms to warm herself up beneath the chill air-conditioning, her damp sleeves cold against her skin. Dan Udan had no idea how close she'd come to hating him. But he looked desperate, as if he knew he'd behaved atrociously, but hadn't been able stop himself. She put her head in her hands, remembering him on the day they met, the sensitive poet, she'd never see again-

"Professor Mary Gallagher, back to Dublin, is it?" Theo, in full pilot's uniform, gazed down at her. "Prepare for a bumpy ride, there's a storm brewing over Wicklow."

Twenty minutes later, on the launch-pad, Theo and Dave in their seats, preparing for turbulence, rotors thwacking overhead, Mary didn't have the energy to look up through the gaping roof, to see rain entering from the night sky. She put her head back on the headrest, forcing herself to relax, allowing the shuddering vibrations to pass through her bones, lift-off to feel like the drifting surrender before sleep. The next time she opened her eyes they were jostling through storm-clouds, murky smudges smearing past the portholes, her stomach rising and dropping. Her throat constricted, she gripped the sides of the seat, concentrated on deep breathing.

"Professor Gallagher…Mary!" Dave's voice came through her headset. "Dr O'Neil on the line! I'll put you through!"

Mary nodded, pulling herself up straight, swallowing to suppress her nausea.

"Mary, can you hear me?" Jane's voice crackled faintly, "… to my apartment and collapsed half-an-hour ago!"

"Sorry Jane, did you say Dan has collapsed?" Like falling through ice, Mary's blood turned cold.

"It's Dan's heart …could lose him! Mary, he needs…" The

line went dead.

Dave looked over his shoulder, pointing the sky. “Sorry, weather! I’ll try and get her back!”

“Turn around!” Mary shouted, “Home! Fast as you can!”

The aircraft’s interior had been disinfected earlier: passenger and crew could skip the Decontamination Bay. Mary sprinted across the Departure Lounge. Back inside the lift, she paced around, willing it to drop faster, humming to stop herself from panicking. At Level Two, she ran down the corridor to Jane’s apartment, found the door ajar and burst in, too out of breath to speak.

“She’s here!” Jane came hurrying towards her, arms outstretched. “Mary, thank God, you’ve come. Connie, tell Cookie Mary’s come back!” The grey bearded bodyguard who’d helped Mary at the Ceremony appeared, grim-faced.

“I’ll go on in-” He strode down the hall and disappeared inside the bathroom.

Jane grasped Mary’s hand. There was a dazed, startled look about her. “It’s been almost an hour since Dan collapsed. Cookie has got him in an ice-bath, he’s burning up.” Jane’s hands were trembling. “We’re worried sick, but now you’re here, there’s hope… Come with me.” Jane led her by the hand towards the bathroom. “Prepare yourself, he’s been haemorrhaging, the bath water is bloody.”

Mary’s pulse was pounding in her ears. “Does he know you called me?”

“No. He came to tell me you’d resigned” – Jane glanced at her before opening the door – “then passed out, over by the chair. He’s been unconsciousness ever since.”

The bath was brimming with muddy, pinkish slush, chilling the room like a fridge. A white-haired man leaned over the side, his arm immersed, holding something down under the ice. Mary gripped onto Jane's hand. "What is he doing?"

"He'll come up for air." Connie stood at the end of the bath, his arms folded around his middle. "That is, once his heart re-starts itself. Cookson will tell you, there's a very strange chemistry going on under there."

The white-haired man neither answered nor moved a muscle.

"Mary, this is Gerry Cookson, Dan's personal physician, I told you about. You can call him Cookie, we all do." Jane gave a trembling squeeze to Mary's hand. "Cookie, this is Mary."

Cookie turned his head. "Talk to him, he'll hear you."

Mary looked at Jane.

"Yes, he means you, Mary." Jane squeezed her hand again. "Speak. It'll help Dan to hear your voice."

Mary knelt by the side of the bath, next to Cookie, and gazed into the mushy ice, seeking the form of a man, where his head and torso might be. She couldn't see him. He must be lying along the bottom. She felt numb, unable to form a thought other than, Dan was under there.

"Dan!" She thrust her hand inside the bath, flailing around in the freezing slush. "Dan, it's Mary! Get up! Come back to us!"

Cookie grabbed her arm out of the water. "You've got bare hands!"

Mary shouted in his face, "He can't breathe. You're killing him. Let him go!"

"Mary!" Jane held her shoulders. "Cookie knows what he's

doing."

"Take the gal away, Jane, she's hysterical." Cookie plunged his hand back into the bath, wearing a long black rubber glove. "If that didn't get his heart going, goddamn nothing will," muttering, "come on, son, you're running out of time."

Jane and Connie helped Mary to her feet and led her from the bathroom. Beyond the ringing in her ears, Mary heard Connie.

"This young lady has had a terrible day. She was the bravest of them all."

She felt like a child, overwhelmed, hot, clammy with tears. Connie gave her his handkerchief. Jane put a brandy into her hand, with a little white pill.

"Take it, dear, you're at the end of your tether." Jane stroked the hair back from Mary's face. "I blame myself for this. I shouldn't have sent you away."

Mary swallowed the pill and brandy down in one, almost instantly felt the drag of intoxication. She shook her head, drying her eyes with the handkerchief. "It's not your fault, Jane. I should've known better. Dan has his demons.... None of this would've happened if I hadn't lied to you about Sean."

"Are you saying you're not romantically involved with Sean Flanagan?" Jane scrutinised her face.

"Sean knows I'm in love with Dan." Mary met Jane's gaze, fidgeting with the handkerchief. "But I didn't recognise him tonight, during that God awful Ceremony. Something else had got to him, more than our situation." She gave a sigh and put her head back on the cushion. "He couldn't help himself...I knew the moment I saw him. He was gone... he was psychotic."

"He was delirious," Connie said, "When he threatened to

slit someone's throat, that's when we all knew he was out of his head. Jane, none of us ever seen the Boss like that before. I didn't think anybody should risk standing up to him, nobody but this lady here. I knew he wouldn't harm her."

"Has your nephew ever behaved like this before?" Mary watched Jane's expression, struggling to keep her eyes open. "Like a mad tyrant?"

"No, but he's been distraught since the moment you left," Jane said. "He hasn't eaten or slept, living on drink and cigarettes." Jane rose, walked over to her writing desk and picked up the decanter. Mary drew another deep sigh and closed her eyes, listening. "I've never seen Dan lose his temper," Jane went on, "He's always had a cool head on him, like you Mary, you're alike in that way, he usually withdraws to lick his wounds. This obsession with you has been brewing for years." Clinking sound as Jane replaced the decanter. Her voice faded, in and out.

"This business about Sean…the last straw. I felt I had to tell him, Mary… did warn you… Never fabricate affairs of the heart, people can get very hurt, and I'm surprised at you …no reason to be jealous of Soraya. Dan took her on out of pity… after they split up... I think you and Dan need to talk... When he gets through this and I'm sure he will, now that you're back. Mary, are you still with us?"

Mary couldn't open her eyes.

A night-time ocean sighed and swelled gently in the UDAN Window, under a maroon sky scattered with misty stars. Mary opened her eyes wider, one arm cramped against her side, where she'd been asleep on the chaise-long in Jane's sitting-room, now silent and in darkness.

She sat up, groggily massaging her sore arm and couldn't remember why she was here, piecing together the moments before sleep: Jane's face close-up, an image of Lewis reading from a scroll, Dan... She felt a clutching pain in her chest, remembering the bath. *Dan under the ice, unbreathing, no heartbeat –*

She rose and followed the shadows towards the bathroom, pushing open the door into blackness. She tapped on the wall. The room illuminated to reveal an empty bath with gleaming gold taps, plump white towels hung from the towel-rails. She stood for a moment, catching her breath, wondering if she'd dreamt it all, until she felt the presence of disinfectant sharply in her lungs and another surge of panic. She spun out of the room and hurried down the hall to Jane's spare bedroom, hoping to find him there, dreading that if she didn't, Dan had died and was already laid out on a slab in the mortuary.

The door was closed. Mary braced herself, rotating the handle, entering with her head turned to where she knew the bed to be. Occupied. Weak with relief, she held onto the door handle for support, gazing into the room. Beside the bed sat Cookie, keeping vigil, his chin resting on his chest, evidently sound asleep. The shutters on the UDAN Window were open, a shaft of faint moonlight slanted into the darkened room. The only other light came from a holographic clock on the bedside table, blue digits suspended in mid-air: 3.28 am.

She stole up to the side of the bed opposite Cookie. Dan was asleep on his back, his black hair contrasted against the paleness of the pillow. A tube fed his arm from a drip attached to the bedpost, his face turned to his other hand, fingers curled on the pillow beside him.

Mary sat on the edge of the bed, mesmerised, listening to him sighing softly on each exhalation, his mouth slightly open. There was a moist crescent on his upper lip, the raw remnant of a scab broken away, already beginning to heal. He looked so incredibly young, washed innocent with sleep. She felt an ache deep in her throat, close to tears. All the forces of survival were wrapped up inside him, he'd once told her, from the butterfly to the lion, yet he never mentioned the beauty of the human child to inspire unconditional love, for at this moment that belonged to him too. He was his mother's beautiful boy and seeing him like this, what mother wouldn't forgive him everything?

She couldn't resist the temptation to give a gentle tug to the stray ringlet on his forehead, letting it spring back. His eyelids twitched, he turned his head, opening his eyes to the ceiling. She watched him waking up, slow to reclaim himself, blinking and then frowning. She glanced over at Cookie, who hadn't moved and whispered.

"It's me, Mary…You're in Jane's spare bedroom…You had a very bad fever and your heart stopped.

Cookie has been looking after you."

He looked at her, bringing her into focus. Mary saw the sweetest smile she'd ever seen on a man, lighting up his face through the shadows. She pressed her index finger to her lips, indicating to Cookson with her eyes. "Hush, we must whisper, we don't want to wake Cookie."

Dan glanced at Cookie and whispered, "I thought I was in heaven with an angel at my side" – he rolled his eyes – "'til I saw him."

She shifted closer, to enable them to hear each other. "How

do you feel?"

"Wonderful, now you're here." He had a dreamy expression, drugged, or he was utterly exhausted.

"I'm sorry I woke you. I only came in to see if you were all right. Go back to sleep now." She smiled. "I'll see you in the morning."

"Stay with me." He patted the bed beside him. "Please."

"I don't think Cookie would approve," she said. "You need to rest. We nearly lost you this time."

"You left me," he said, "I lost all hope."

"Dan-" She sought his hand. Through the linen sheet, she could feel his unnatural body temperature. "Are you ready to accept my help?"

His eyes shone faintly in the dark. "Do whatever you want with me, Mary. Just stay with me…now… always…" He closed his eyes. His breathing became audible, returning to its deep, sleeping rhythm.

Mary gazed at him, until tears blurred her vision. She couldn't imagine the world without him, without Dan Udan. It would be catastrophic, like hearing that all the stars had gone out.

She took a cushion from a chair, placed it between them, and lay down on the bed.

Chapter Twenty-Four

Come nine o'clock the following morning, Lewis couldn't raise his head from the pillow to answer the Park Monitor's call, on the intercom next to his bed.

"Lewis, just to let you know we've got a dozen new volunteers down here to start harvesting in Section D. We were sort of hoping you'd be here by now to show them around. Could you let us know what's happening? We've been hearing a bit about what happened yesterday with Dan Udan's psychological test. Hope you're okay today, sounds like a really weird event, but, hey, well done, apparently you gave a fantastic performance. The students reckon you're definitely Oscar material. Okay, talk to you soon."

Unwilling to show his baldness on screen, Lewis groped half-blindly for his mobile and discovered it in its usual place, tucked inside his pillowslip: A miracle, considering the amount of sangria Ted and Bobby had funnelled down his throat, the half-bottle of whiskey and God knows how many vodka-shots King had served him in the Shooting Star after the Ceremony.

He was a changed man, a Saint, by all accounts, having endured an alternative reality for a day at the hands of the Light Wizard. But some habits never die, like where he stashed his mobile and his self-mocking tone, even with a raging hangover.

Lewis called the Park Monitor back, shivering and perspiring from sub-acute alcoholic poisoning. To avoid conversation, he didn't let him get a word in-

"Good morning and thank you for your message, old fellow. You'll find that the Harvester Network is perfectly functioning this morning. It would appear UDAN Corps works in mysterious ways. I'll explain later. Please proceed with crop collection in all Sections. Thank the volunteers and dismiss them. Mr Udan has granted me the day off for my Oscar-winning performance and quite rightly so. I'll see you tomorrow." He pulled the duvet over his head and contracted his body into the foetal position.

His brain was sick, flashing images of yesterday like strobe-lighting, relentlessly re-playing snippets of conversation and the echo of Soraya's laughter, a chill tinkling sound devoid of human warmth. He could still feel the grazing of Soraya's blunt razor blade, the thin trickles of blood running down his temples as she nearly scalped him.

The Earth Room re-appeared in all its dingy detail, the filthy sofa bulging yellow sponge through rips in its fabric, rotten floorboards littered with cigarette butts, bare lightbulbs hanging from naked wires. Lewis had landed in Hell and the Devil was a *woman*. No sign of Dan Udan. He'd long gone and left all of Lewis' bodily preparations to Soraya, Bobby and Ted. But after they'd tied him down naked in a chair, the two men announced they had another errand to perform on behalf of Mr Udan and left her to it. Alone with the razor-wielding woman, Lewis had tried reasoning with her, as clumps of his hair dropped in front of his eyes like the plucked feathers of a poultry bird.

"This is wrong, Soraya, you do know that what you're doing is very wrong…You could get into serious trouble for this. If this gets out, you could all go to prison."

"That depends, Lewis Allen."

"Please stop saying that it depends! What's wrong with you? Have you no heart, Soraya?" Seeing almost all his hair scattered around his feet, he started to weep, not for the first time.

"No, I have diamonds instead. Many years ago, Mr Udan cut out my heart and ate it for breakfast-" She gave her tinkling laugh. Shortly after that Ted and Bobby came blustering through the door, carrying an old tin bath that clunked as they shifted it around the floor, full of bottles of wine, olive oil, vinegar; sprouting shrubs of aromatic herbs in plastic tubs piled up at one end. The two promptly emptied the bottles and herbs into the bath swimming with leaves and twigs, to marinade Lewis' flesh; once Soraya had stripped him of his pubic hair, squeezing his penis between her forefinger and thumb, pulling his testicles about brusquely to smear the sugar wax.

"I can't believe you're doing this," Lewis muttered, "I don't even believe this is happening…I'm going to wake up in a minute, you'll see, I'm going to wake myself up right now, right now, please, wake up…now!... now!"

"Be quiet Lewis Allen, you're not asleep, but you will be soon, for a very, very long time" – that chilling laugh, again.

His mind flashed forward. He felt their hands gripping his upper arms, lowering him into the bath. His bottom slipped and slid on the oil, his feet kicked up in the air, his head kept going under, until he was drowning in red wine.

It did occur to him in his doom that perhaps this was a kinder way to die. But soon, with their helping hands he found his balance, found himself sitting upright, a pot of veined, blotchy flesh in the marinade, burning his skin like acid, saline streaming from his eyes and nostrils.

It could've been one hour, or two, some hours had gone missing. Lewis had entered a strange dream-like reality, a numb, drunken witness to his fate. He had no idea what time it was when Dan walked in. Wearing a long black raincoat, his hair and gaunt face dripping wet, blisters glistening on his upper lip, protruding like a small, blunt fingertip beneath the sallow light bulb,

"What the feck did yous do to him?" His incredulous tone appeared to surprise them all. Perhaps not Soraya so much:

"Exactly what you told us to do. We've shaved Lewis Allen and put him a marinade." She swished around in her sari, dipping down into the bath to pour cups of marinade over Lewis' shoulders. "He is fully prepared for the Ceremony of Blood, aren't you Lewis Allen?"

Lewis didn't answer, he hunched down in the bath, holding Dan in the corner of his eye.

"Y'bastards! Get out of my sight, the lot of you!" Dan pointed. "Bobby, call Connie up here to get that poor critter out of that bath! What are yous like? Where's your common fecken decency? I'm surprised at you, Ted!" He tossed his head up at Soraya. "You carry on like this, your days with me are numbered. Get out!"

"Oh, Dan's upset" – she sashayed around him – "isn't your wee Mary your wee angel, after all?"

Dan looked away from her, showing the whites of his eyes.

"Bye, bye Lewis Allen, you're so very cute!" Soraya gave him a little girly wave and swished out of the door.

Jump forward. He heard a new voice. He could see the craggy, bearded face, with its deep brown eyes, used to squinting: Connie. He pulled Lewis out of the bath and wrapped him in an old moth-eaten curtain, purple velvet, with gold embroidered words: Rainbow Circus.

Dan sat back on the busted sofa, legs wide apart, smoking a dog-end from fingers curled into a fist.

"Connie, if I ever asked you to shave a guy's head, would you?" A ring of blue smoke escaped from his mouth.

"Aye, so long as the fella wanted his head shaved, otherwise, Boss, I'd have to say no." Connie was fiddling with a tiny headphone, twisting it inside his ear.

"Good on ye." Dan peered through the blue fog at Lewis, who sat shivering, his whole body at the same time stinging, huddled on the floor a few feet from Dan's muddy boots. "You see that, sunshine, I can't exercise unlimited power over people unless they choose to give theirs up. Are you beginning to understand what this is about?"

"Err...I can't...err-" Lewis' brain stalled. He could barely see, his eyes felt like pastry puffballs. "I'm sorry, I... I don't-"

Dan stood over him, pulled Lewis to his feet and put his arms around him. "Come here and give me a hug." Lewis felt Dan's fingers pressing gently into the back of his head, guiding his cheek to rest on his damp lapel. Something wonderful happened: Up soared his heart, fluttering like a dove, high into the room, batting its wings against the ceiling. Lewis would've said something, maybe even wept from elation, if he hadn't felt so weak.

"I promise you this"-Dan spoke softly in his ear – "not one more drop of your blood will spill today. You're in my hands now. So have faith in me. If at any point you feel unsure of me, then pray, for God is listening, Things could well get scary. If no-one at the Ceremony challenges me, I'll have to teach them a lesson they won't forget… Now, will you trust me?"

Lewis remembered the taste of rain on Dan's lapel, the smell of mountain air and smoke from his last cigarette. He answered. "Yes."

"Is there anything you want out of this, anything at all I can give you, like, as a token of my gratitude?"

"A cassock, like yours," Lewis said. "But gold, instead" – came out of the blue into Lewis' mind.

"Is that all you want?" Dan chuckled and drew back. "Aye, you can have your cassock…. Now go on you, get y'self back into that bath and pray for us all."

Before the Intermission, waiting for Mary, sitting on a simple pine chair at the edge of the rostrum, dressed in his aquamarine cassock, Dan's glare cut straight through Lewis, cold as a switchblade. Shackled, naked, he began to feel acutely unsure and prayed.

Safe in his bed, even now, his torso bucked involuntarily, re-living the moment Dan barked, 'Funnel him!' The third time they did it to him, he nearly choked to death. The fourth time the sangria went down, Lewis threw it straight back. Dan came over.

"I've good news, Foxy" – he breathed in his ear – "the blonde tart is on her way. You're in luck, so long as she says a prayer for you. Do you think she'll say a prayer to save your fillets from the skewer?"

"I have faith…in you." Lewis' teeth chattered.

"Then you're a stupider ass than I took you for," he hissed

the words, "because if she refuses to pray, you must know by now, you're dead meat."

He'd expected a completely new emotion from himself, realising that this was how he was going to die.

He never imagined he'd feel resigned. Even so, it was at this point that Lewis wet himself.

He rolled onto his front, pressed his face into his pillow, writhed and groaned, seeping watery bile from the corner of his mouth. His mind had become a roaring blur.

Mary's face appeared, in constant motion on a vertical pendulum, swinging away and towards him, her eyes hollow, her smile eerily frozen, like a porcelain Christmas angel, her kindness an ersatz, painted thing. She couldn't help him. In the end it was her atheism that mattered to her most, a matter of principle or pride. He had dreaded as much; but had hoped all the same, with his life being on the line, she would concede to pray for him, at least once.

Flash fast-forward: He heard voices, in a chill, echoing place, where the crowd's undulating cries had followed him, resembling the sound of an ancient battlefield far-off, amplified inside steel walls. Bobby supported him by his armpits, but Lewis' knees kept sagging as Ted slopped water over his head and torso, sponging him down. It might've been a kitchen, where they had tugged at his arms and pulled him into the cassock, golden silk: a perfect fit.

"That scream you gave at the end was blood curdling. Listen to them screaming, you've really put the wind up them." Ted was sweating, red in the face. "Those guys moved bloody fast, didn't they? They got you out in time, there's not a scratch on you" – he gave a choking laugh – "Fuck me, but those students were like bloody animals. Connie had a fight to get one boy's scalpel off him, he refused to put it in the bucket."

Scalpels had hit the plastic buckets, sounding like massive hail stones. Even as many hands were unshackling Lewis' wrists and ankles, he assumed he was raining blood from his fingers. The only blood was in his mouth. When he screamed, he ruptured a tiny vessel in the back of his throat. He could still taste the blood as he read the scroll, shuddering before his eyes like film roll snagged inside an ancient projector; impossible to read, yet somehow, he did.

A bottle of whiskey and a beef baguette were already waiting for Lewis on the bar in the Shooting Star.

Empty; not even a barman present. Ted poured drinks for himself and Bobby and handed Lewis the bottle.

"It'll take the taste out of your mouth," he nodded. Lewis put his head back and poured it down his neck, staring up at the starry LEDs in the ceiling until they began to spin. Everything came hurtling towards him. He banged the bottle down on the bar.

"How do you feel now?" one or other of them had asked.

"Life is a centrifuge," Lewis slurred. "No, I mean the soul… Our souls are centrifuges… Do you know what I mean… old fellow?"

"Yep, we know what you mean… Eat your baguette-"

He entered a kind of compulsive stupor devouring the baguette, his jaws marching onward, with a glaze in front of his eyes. Well inebriated, yet he was beginning to adjust to his new situation: that his stolen life had been returned to him, relatively intact. With spirits, bread and meat warming his stomach, Lewis began to experience the euphoria of those who've survived a brush with death.

"That was funny, wasn't it, when Dan told you to go and make a hutch for Mary." He chuckled.

"Yeah, you should've seen the look on your face, Bob." Ted joined in. "Like, where the hell am I going to get a hutch at a time like this?"

"I thought, oh shit, I'm fucked. I haven't got a fucking clue!" Bobby started to belly laugh. "You've got to hand it to him, The Boss is a brilliant clown. You never know when he's serious. I mean, I thought he was serious."

Lewis smacked him on the back. "Guess what, you're not going to believe this, but… so did I!" Lewis burst into hysterical laughter. There was still whiskey in the bottle, he remembered that much, when, for no reason at all, he turned around. Dan was standing behind him, in a white shirt and tight-fit jeans, hair combed back from his broad forehead, jaw-line angular, fierce-eyed.

"May I have a word in your ear, Lewis?" He strode off.

"Shit." Lewis grimaced, following fast on his heels, thinking about it now, like an obedient dog, except he would've been staggering.

"Sit yourself down there." Dan drew out a chair for Lewis, from the star-fish table, and took a seat opposite. He raised his hand. "Bobby, can we have another bottle and a couple of glasses!"

Lewis recoiled as far back as the chair allowed, without adjusting its position and focused his gaze on a small mole mid-point between Dan's eyebrows. It had a curious effect on his perception, making the wall behind Dan appear to flow, moving mysteriously along like a deep river.

"I won't pretend that ye didn't suffer"-a furrow appeared in the mole's place – "I know I scared the living daylights out of you. I'm sorry I went overboard tonight." He lifted the blistered corner of his mouth in a half-smile. "I heard y' having a laugh at the bar. That's a grand sign. It'll do y' good."

Lewis picked up his drink, examining the stingy measure Dan had poured him. "Erm… what happened to the rest?"

"I want you to go easy on that" – Dan folded his arms – "I hope you appreciate that every one of us is accountable for what happened tonight. The kids all bought scalpels, without batting an eyelid. You, y'idjit, put your name to a document you couldn't read. I took advantage, as you've no business being that naïve in this day-and-age."

Dan inclined his head and gazed at him, a kind and direct gaze.

"Lewis, I want people around me with common sense, people capable of challenging my ideas. Because people need to be vigilant. Absolute power corrupts. Sure, you've heard that one before. But any amount of power can seduce those who are too readily impressed. Following someone else's leadership without question, risks moral apathy and corruption.

"I'm trying to create communities with their eyes wide open, not to turn a blind eye to the pitfalls of power in the wrong hands. I don't want humanity colonising the stars with their same old bag of shite. Leave all that behind on earth where it belongs, buried in the mud." He pointed his forefinger towards the ceiling. "I want harmony up there in the future." He smiled his crinkly, wise-man smile.

"Sounds promising." Lewis was thinking, what a weird and wonderful conversation, after everything that's just happened.

But this was the way they were. "Do you think human beings will ever be perfect?"

"No, there's no such thing as perfect. The best we can hope for is a good compromise … I'm talking about improving the way we relate to one another, with a deeper understanding."

Lewis pulled down the corners of his mouth, nodding. "I'm all for that."

"So, to get to the point… Although this evening's Ceremony was meant to enlighten the students, I was sickened by the fact that none of them stood up for you or questioned what I was doing. So, I went darker than I intended. I abused you until the penny dropped, and they got a taste of hell. That's what the devils signed up for.

"I let you believe I was going the whole hog, so to speak. I felt the moment you lost faith in me, and I've never felt so rotten in my life" – his chin dimpled, he bit down on his lip – "I've transferred eight million, that's pounds sterling into your account this evening, to compensate you for your pain and suffering. I hope it'll help you to get over this and move on."

Lewis widened his eyes. "Wow! You didn't have to do that… Just to have my life back is enough compensation, I mean honestly" – he gave an incredulous laugh, his torso pumping – "eight million quid!

For that I'd do it all again!"

"If you want, I'd be very happy to help you invest some of it. Or you may just want to head off into the sunset, take a few years off, travel the world. There'll always be a job for you at UDAN Corps. As a matter of fact, I've been meaning to tell you for some time, I've a lot of respect for your talents. You're a wee genius with your Jolly." Dan smiled.

Lewis rose and stooped over the table to offer his hand. “Coming from you, that really is the best compliment I’ve ever had, thank you-” His hand hovered.

Dan reached for his elbow and gripped it, looking up into his eyes. “Will you forgive me, Lewis?”

“There’s nothing to forgive. I was a total idiot to sign up for something I couldn’t read. But I’m so glad I did. What an amazing experience the whole thing was! I’ve never felt so happy to be alive.” He gabbled, relishing the heat and strength of Dan’s hand around his arm. “I’ve always wanted a Ferrari. I’m going to buy loads of UDAN Ceegees. And I don’t want to leave. I want to work at the UISC for the rest of my life.” He beamed into Dan’s face. Dan’s smile was possibly the widest smile he’d ever seen, showing dazzling white teeth. “Dan, I think you should know that this is the happiest day of my life.”

“Aye, I can see that. I’m sure there’ll be others.” He released Lewis’ arm. “You calm down now, don’t get over excited, we don’t want it to end in tears.”

Lewis dropped back into his chair, so emotional that crying was exactly what he felt like doing.

“Did you see Mary to talk to, by the way?” Dan lifted his drink.

“I saw her at the end, but I’ve got nothing to say to her.” Lewis took a gulp of his own whiskey. “I’m totally disappointed in her. The fact that she refused to pray the first time. That was the pits, probably the worst moment of the whole thing.” He frowned. “So far as she knew, my life was on the line, and she threw it away to score a point. I mean, what does that say about her? She’s no friend of mine, not anymore.”

“You’ve got it wrong. Mary knew in here” – Dan touched

the middle of his chest – "that there was no way I'd let any of those students hurt you. She knows I'm not that crazy. If she thought you were in real danger, she'd have prayed like the best of them. She knew I was playing a mind game, that I was acting up like a bully and I was, so. She was the only one who stood up to me, the only voice of reason. So far as I'm concerned, she passed the test with flying colours."

"But everybody else thought you were serious, even Bobby and Ted."

He chuckled. "I guess they don't know me. But Mary does, in her heart, better than she even knows. But right now, I bet my name's mud. Aye, I've got to face the angel's wrath and eat humble pie, until it's coming out of my ears, I bet" – with his crooked smile, he put the glass to his mouth – "God bless her, she hates me now."

"You went to all that trouble to get her back here, only for her to end up hating you." Lewis shook his head, coming down a little from his elation. "I don't get it or is the romance meant to be over?"

"Not at all. But I'm not interested in her naïve infatuation. I want soul, deep and dark, most of all enduring. Mary hates me at the minute. But when the storm clouds pass, she'll look up and see that the bond between us is not a whimsy, but a bloody great girder. It's titanium. Strong enough to last a lifetime and beyond. Eternal in the eyes of God." He pinched his forefinger and thumb. "With a pinch of salt, the hook goes in deeper, the tethering becomes permanent. A wee dash of hate makes love more compelling. You see, Lewis, without the dark, there can be no light. Love isn't reasonable, it's alchemy."

"What about us?" Lewis said, "I hate you, if you want to

know. But I love you, too. I feel-"

There were shouts and laughter. Students were entering the pub. Lewis looked over and saw King grinning, waving to Dan from behind the bar.

"They better not all get pissed tonight" – Dan turned his head the other way – "or I'll have their guts for garters, the wee so and so's."

"Sorry to interrupt, sir." Connie appeared at their table. He stooped to whisper something in Dan's ear. Dan frowned.

"Aye, I thought she might. Okay, Connie, thanks." Dan rose from his chair. "Sorry Lewis, I've got to go." He tapped his knuckles on the table. "Will you be all right now? Promise me you won't drink too much. Ach, go on, you can have the day off tomorrow."

Lewis watched Dan Udan striding out of the bar, his long legs snipping back and forth. He could tell he really wanted to run.

Twelve hours later Lewis rolled over in bed, shook his hands at the ceiling and cried out loud.

"What about me!"

Chapter Twenty-Five

"You found them asleep, side by side?" Jane's voice reached Mary in the middle of a dream.

"I suggest you wake her up and get her out of here."

"Cookie. Let's keep things calm. It'll be grim enough this morning. Mary-"

Mary pulled herself out of her dream, lifting her head.

"Mary, your hair is caught under Dan's arm, be careful-"

"What time…what day is it?" She blinked up at Jane.

"It's morning." The white-haired man from last night extended his hand across the bed. "Pleased to meet you, Mary." He was powerfully built, with a Texan drawl, gloved handshake firm and curt. He turned away from her. "I must ask you and Jane to leave now, before Dan wakes."

"Let's go to the Park View for breakfast," Jane said in a hushed voice. "It should be quiet this time in the morning."

Mary looked at Dan, sound asleep on his back, as she'd found him during the night. Lips one finger-width apart, his complexion pale in the daylight streaming from the Udan Window.

"Dan asked me to stay," she said. "I want to be here when he wakes up." She saw Cookie cast a glance at Jane, standing in the doorway.

"Your suitcase arrived here last night, Mary," Jane said. "Why don't you have a shower and get changed before we go out."

"No time for that," Cookie said. "You gals head out now. We'll catch you later."

"Why do we have to leave?" Mary said. Jane left the room. Cookie turned towards an oak dresser behind him. Mary sat on the edge of the bed, still dazed from sleep. She slipped her feet inside her shoes. "Please let Dan know, I stayed until the morning."

"Mary-"

Mary turned to look at Dan. His eyes were open, one hand reaching out, trembling.

"Dan, she's got to leave now," Cookie said. "You're having Desi's Best."

Dan's voice hardened. "Mary and I are going to have breakfast together."

"Mary, please go now. It's for his own good." Cookie gestured to a bowl on the dresser. "Dan's got to eat what's in there."

"Get that shite out of here. Tell Desi to bring us in a decent breakfast!"

Mary rose from the bed. "What's going on?"

Jane appeared, beckoning from the door. "Mary, come away. Cookie must do his job."

"Mary, you sit down there!" Dan pointed Mary towards a chair. "You're not going anywhere."

"Dan, calm down," Mary said, "What's in the bowl?"

"Don't say anything, either of you." Dan sat upright in the bed and glared at Cookie. The Texan's face was deadpan.

Mary strode around the bed. "I want to know, what's in the bowl? What's Desi's Best?"

"Mary, leave it!" Dan waved her back. "Desi's Cookie's wife, my housekeeper at Lacerta. She's brought me muesli, when I asked for coffee and toast."

"This might as well be the moment she finds out, Dan," Jane said. "Dan has special dietary needs that he's ashamed of. But if he doesn't eat what's in that bowl, he'll die. Show her what's in the bowl, Cookie."

"No!" Dan flashed the whites of his eyes at Cookie. He lowered his voice. "Did ye hear me, Cookie?"

"The fact is, son, once Mary knows, it'll make it easier on you." Cookie picked up the bowl from the dresser, covered with a plate of ice cubes. He lifted the plate and held the bowl out for Mary to look inside. "You see, Dan ain't always a vegetarian."

At first glance it was a bowl of coarse fibre-cereal, full of wheat-husks and twiggy bran flakes. Until she saw that everything was twitching.

The surface broke, frothing in the middle, with what looked like cuckoo spit. Something hummed past her ear. Mary froze, gazing upon the contents of the bowl with a biologist's fascination, rising revulsion at the fidgeting heads, bodies, stick-legs, wing-cases and antennae all crammed together. Yellow-brown hornets, blue-tailed damselflies, hundreds of click beetles and small, reddish froghoppers, earwigs burrowing, their rear-pincers protruding. All alive and climbing over one another, some already escaping over the side.

Cookie put the plate of ice cubes over the bowl and returned it to the dresser. It was like the moment in a dream when things turn nightmarish. Mary's voice sounded almost normal to her own ears, although she was in a state of paralysis.

"Why does he have to eat them?"

"Eating insects gives Dan the right nutrition for his unique metabolism," Jane said. "He's under-nourished. His heart is unlikely to re-start if it stops again. He must eat them, or he won't survive the day."

"He's got no choice but to stomach it." Cookie faced the bed, buttoning his shirt cuffs around black leather gloves. "You'll see the signs in his eyes as he gains the benefit. They light-up like blue-fires, don't they, son? It's something to see, when it happens. Right now, they're as dull as pond-water, which ain't a good sign. So, we're going to go with this now, okay, Dan?"

Mary looked at Dan. His face was expressionless, eyes fixed on some low point.

"Dan-" Mary tried to hide the tremor in her voice. "I'm not upset or shocked. When I think about what's going on inside you, it's understandable that you'd need a special diet."

"You don't understand," he said.

"What he doesn't want you to know" – Jane sounded like an over-protective mother – "is that he must eat the insects while they're still alive, in order to extract the special energy which benefits him. His metabolism recognises a life-force, or in Dan's own words, in this case, the soul of the insect." Jane levelled her eyes at Mary. "It's a force of nature he uses to keep him alive, the breath of life, itself."

A shudder passed through Mary. "I see," she murmured.

Dan looked at her. "Mary, I felt that shiver, go straight down your spine." His voice shook. "Do you see what you've done?" He glared at Cookie and Jane. "She thinks I'm a monster. After yesterday and now this, I haven't a hope in hell. You've made sure of that." He put his hands to his temples. "Get out, all of you. Please, leave me in peace."

"Now, Jane, go for it!" Cookie grabbed Dan by his hair and hooked one arm around his neck. "Feed him!" Dan writhed and kicked his feet beneath the sheet, bony fingers grasping at Cookie's arm. "Son, you ain't got the strength to fight me. You're weak as a kitten!" He pinched Dan's nose between his forefinger and thumb. "Open your mouth, God damn it. Don't give us a hard time. Jane!"

Dan's eyes bulged at the ceiling, his face turning a deep, bluish red.

"Stop it!" Mary cried, "This is barbaric." It was like a flash-back to yesterday. She covered her eyes, then threw her hands in the air. "Is it any wonder he goes crazy, when you treat him like this!"

Jane grabbed the bowl from the dresser and sat on the bed, in front of her nephew. "Open your mouth, Dan!" She dug inside the bowl with a spoon, raised it, dangling a mangle of insects. "Haven't you noticed, Mary's still here, she's not leaving. Take what you need." She shot a fierce look at Mary. "Don't just stand there. Hold his legs down!"

Dan gasped for air. Jane tipped the mangle between his lips and Cookie clamped his hand over Dan's mouth. "Bear with us, Mary," Cookie said, "He's a living miracle, but sometimes he needs our help. Jane, give him a hornet, they work faster!"

A dazed incredulity came over Mary. She sank down on the edge of the bed, transfixed by the unfolding scene. Her heart pounding, the hairs rising on the back of her neck, as Jane offered Dan a hornet. Its huge, complex body sat in the spoon, its wide hindlegs over-reaching the sides, its head bowed.

"Why doesn't it fly away?" she heard herself asking, far away.

"There's vodka in the bowl." Cookie took his hand from Dan's mouth. "It slows them down… Go on, Danny, take it! Mary ain't here to judge you. She was by your side all night." Dan closed his eyes and opened his mouth. Jane tipped the spoon, dropping the insect inside. Slowly, Dan brought his lips together. Cookie let go of Dan's hair, sliding his other arm out from behind his neck. "Once he gets over the first shock, we're home and dry."

No one spoke or moved a muscle, listening to Dan kill the hornet in his mouth, pressing it up against his hard palate with his tongue, its enraged drone halting and softening every time he sucked on its juices. When it fell silent, a tear spilled down his face. His lips moved, as if in silent prayer.

Jane leaned across to whisper in Mary's ear. "For every soul he takes, he prays to be forgiven. If you're serious about loving him, until he accepts help, this is what we must live with."

Mary couldn't speak.

Cookie stood up, took an ice cube from the plate and Dan opened his mouth. "Suck on that, son." He slipped it between his lips.

"He'll be badly stung," Jane said. "Sometimes his face swells up hugely. I don't how he copes with the pain."

"Jesus," Mary said under her breath.

Dan raised his head from the pillow and looked at her. "I never wanted you to see this." His speech was thick and slurred. "Go now." He dropped his head back on the pillow.

Mary didn't hesitate. She reclined on the bed beside him and leaned on her elbow, with her face close to his. She began gently, to stroke his hair back from his forehead. His eyes streamed. Lumps had appeared inside his cheeks, like a mouth-full of marbles.

"Dan," she said, "one word from you, and I'll take the sting out of every one of those insects. I'll engineer them especially for you, my tragic Mr Udan." She looked into his eyes. "I promise you. I'll do everything in my power to put an end to your suffering."

Dan smiled a watery, swollen rictus.

"Jane" – Cookie gave a swipe with his forefinger – "give him another hornet."

Chapter Twenty-Six

Lewis got out of bed, spent after countless shuddering climaxes, fantasising about the conquest of Dan, until the beautiful genius was on all fours, in total submission. The best part, straining on a leash with a studded dog's collar around his neck.

Lewis had used up all his hatred and now felt a dull satisfaction, a mild, familiar self-disgust to see the mass of crumpled tissues, the bottom sheet twisted into a damp rope, the duvet heaped on the floor. He gathered up the tissues, carried them to the bathroom, dropped them down the lavatory and got a shock when he glanced towards the long mirror. He'd forgotten for a moment that he was bald, having just imagined himself with his dark mousy hair intact, raping Dan.

He gazed at his slim-ish, narrow-shouldered physique that had always been a cause for self-doubt and saw that being bald did nothing for him. He looked like a bowling-pin. No, worse. He reminded himself of a worm. He lowered his gaze to his manhood, still tingling, withdrawn shamefully back inside his body. His testicles were all that was left to see, dangling like those bits that hang from a chicken's neck, almost as red.

An unsettling emptiness in the pit of his stomach turned him away from the mirror. He noticed his cassock draped over the towel-rail and decided to wear it. He fumbled about putting it on, remembering the trouble Ted and Bobbie had getting it over his head. Once again, his arms got stuck and he lost patience with himself. He staggered blindly up to the mirror and head-butted it, with a muffled cry. "You, hopeless, little prick!" He succeeded, buttoned it up to his neck, returned to look in the mirror and was amazed at what a long golden frock can do for a man.

He looked great. Taller, with warmth in his complexion, a limpid glow in his eyes, not at all wormy, but a golden bishop. "Who'd believe it?" he said aloud. "I do believe I look like a Saint." His first thought was to shoot down to the Control Room and present himself to Jolly for its opinion. On second thoughts, he couldn't be bothered. The old Jolly would've given a real response, albeit with a few jibes. But the new compassionate Jolly would say only what it thought Lewis wanted to hear, bland palliatives. So, what's the point? Lewis had a mind to tell Dan when he next saw him, that a compassionate disposition was all very well in people. But stultifying to progress in Artificial Intelligence.

"Isn't that why the Light Wizard employed you?" Lewis addressed his own reflection, peering from the corner of his eyes, in Dan's menacing way. "To challenge his ideas, hmm? Well, he'd better take his hands off my A.I. before he ruins it." He smiled, deliberately crinkling up his eyes. He held the expression, went up close to the mirror and searched his eyes, marvelling at the depth of their penetration, the inky blue of the midnight-sky. "Would you look at me. I'm a Saint." He breathed condensation onto the mirror, lifted his cassock with a swish and strode out of the bathroom, abruptly lost his balance and banged into the wall. "And I'm still drunk." He chuckled.

"Nothing for it, old fellow, but the hair of the dog."

Lewis went weaving through his bachelor apartment, in search of booze and discovered an unopened bottle of port in his drinks-cabinet, purchased last Christmas. He selected a small whiskey tumbler and sat on his black Chesterfield, sitting somewhat stiffly against its low back.

The sofa was a tribute to his student days, when he used to cruise the more up-market gay-clubs around London, ending at dawn with a frantic encounter in some unsavoury place: the inevitable public toilet, a mildewed shed, once servicing a lad over a rank rubbish bin.

In the rest of his life Lewis was fastidious, often displaying a prudish streak, in adolescence, discovering a distaste for women's bodies, their breasts, particularly. So much burgeoning flesh appeared to him to be out of hand, running away with itself. Whereas the male body was an efficient machine, as he saw it, the superior instrument of the masculine mind. But he'd never relished the idea of falling asleep beside a man, or being held like a woman, once the act was over. Until now. The thought of waking up with Dan thrilled him. To lose himself in those eyes before turning him over every morning before breakfast, was his version of heaven.

On that thought, he filled the tumbler to the brim and with a trembling hand, started to knock back the port, until he felt the mellowing effects. He slid down from the slippery upholstery and sat on the floor with his knees folded, in front of his black-glass coffee table. Trendy, like the steel-rimmed, dark-tinted fibreglass units that surrounded the walls.

Lewis' pad was slick. Soon he'd invite Dan here to show him, that there was an adventurous, more daring side to him too. He poured himself another large port and placed it on the coffee table. Glancing across the top, he noticed a small gleaming object. It was a Darkener, one with a plastic handle attached to its blade, a student had given him as a souvenir in the Shooting Star last night.

He picked it up and toyed with it, pressing the blade between his palms to feel its coolness, familiarising himself with the torture tool that had filled him with terror, only yesterday. It was made for the job, razor – nasty. Dan must've had them in stock before the Ceremony. What a weird thing, to have so many scalpels in stock, meaning that the student's 'psychological test' was planned some time ago and he was just waiting for the right moment to stage it.

Lewis gazed into his glass of port. That's the colour he would've seen when he looked down into the buckets at his feet, deep, ruby red, pints of the stuff. He would've been fainting all over the place by that time. If Dan had gone through with it.

But cheers, Lewis raised his glass. Dan had never intended to do so, and he was still alive. Something in him had changed, maybe even for the better. He felt tougher, wiser, shaken up by life and curiously cleansed.

And just think how he would've felt if he'd received a few lacerations, what an amazing impact that would've had on the students. They'd have been the ones fainting. In a way he wished now that he'd endured a couple of cuts, just for the kudos. His feelings for Dan this morning would be more violently passionate, if that were possible. Their bond might be even stronger than physical love, born out of the murkier alchemy of sacrifice. Blood.

The doorbell buzzed. Lewis glanced at his watch, trying

to think who'd be visiting him at ten forty-five this Saturday morning. If it was Mary, he wasn't letting her in. He called out on the way to the door. "Who is it?"

"Cornelius Cody, on behalf of Mr Udan," said a man's voice.

Who the…? Lewis opened the door. "Connie! Why didn't you say so! Come in." Lewis waved him inside, still unsteady on his feet, pleased to see him. Connie had been his only hope at one point yesterday, praying that the hard Ulster man might have a gun strapped around his ankle, to put to Dan's head. "I'm on the port" – Lewis touched his fingertips together – "would you like one?"

"No thanks. I've a message for you from Mr Udan." Connie removed a folded note from inside his jacket pocket. "Will you read this now and give me your answer."

It was a letter, written in a neat, mathematical hand.

Dear Lewis,

I hope you're recovering well after yesterday's shenanigans and that you haven't had a change of heart since I left you last night, in relatively good spirits. You'll find your well-earned bonus is already sitting in your account this morning. By most standards you're a well-off guy, now. I hope you enjoy your Ferrari.

Mary has been with me all morning. I'm glad to say, we've had a good talk and most if not all, is forgiven. We are much closer now than before and our understanding is deeper, which bodes well for the future. She and I will be living together in my Penthouse on Level Seven, and she will be moving in tomorrow, staying with Jane tonight. Soraya was going to take on Mary's apartment, but I've dismissed her after her failure yesterday to question my orders. She has proved herself unsafe as my p.a.

*Lewis, Mary was very hurt by your rejection at the end of the Ceremony, and I implore you to make amends. She is not to blame for what happened to you. I am. So please call her. Her new intercom code at mine is M * UDAN.*

After the dark of the last few days, now let there be light. I'd like to host a Celebration of Hope during my stay at the UISC. In these difficult times, it is important to remind ourselves that there is good in this world.

We must work on strengthening the power of 'the good', to win the battle over the dark forces that will always be a part of life's painful, but surely, exquisite journey. I've an idea how I'd like the Celebration to be, and would appreciate your creative input, to spend some time with you, to continue repairing our friendship. Would you meet me at three pm this afternoon in the Governor's swimming pool, for a drink and to discuss some thoughts? Please give Connie your answer. I hope to see you there,

God Bless you, Dan.

Lewis took a ride, sitting at the front of the Swingtram, heading for the Governor's swimming pool, proud to be wearing his cassock in public, comfortably suspended in an alcoholic daze.

At Level Eight the levitated train sighed down to the terminus, beaming its headlights onto the pebbled wall at the end of the line, reflecting at him like a pair of massive insect eyes, with compound lenses. Lewis waited for the other passengers to disembark and then rose from his seat, with an immense sense of calm.

He didn't feel as if he were walking but gliding through the Eighth Village towards the Governor's swimming pool. Four Udanos in their black suits stood outside, talking amongst themselves. There were no truncheons to be seen, but bulging Hessian sacks stacked up against the walls, all the way down the corridor. Without a hint of a grudge, Lewis proffered a smile.

"Good afternoon, gentlemen, I have a meeting with Mr Udan at three o'clock. Would you happen to know if he's here yet?"

One of them stood to attention, opening his hand towards the stained-glass doors, depicting turquoise dolphins. "You go on in sir. Mr Udan will be arriving shortly."

"Thank you." The doors parted and Lewis passed through into the Governors' private domain for the first time. The swimming pool was at the bottom of shallow terraced steps, where workmen were pouring sacks of white sand, apparently creating a seamless slope down to the water. Lewis watched them for a while, then sauntered up to the bar at the other end. It had a tiled mosaic, picturing hundreds of flying dolphins. Behind it stood a clean-cut barman, in a pink-satin jacket.

"Good afternoon. I'd like a triple gin and tonic, ice and lemon, please." Lewis adjusted his spectacles on his nose, eyeing-up the barman. Nothing special. The youth spun the glass high in the air, tossed in the ice cubes with a pair of tongs. Lewis turned to look back down the slope. "Do you know why they're laying down all this sand?"

"Mr Udan wants to create a beach," the barman said. "The Udano regiment has been working flat-out since this morning, putting down gravel and laying sand over the top, to make it softer under foot. It'll look great when it's finished."

Lewis gave a supercilious nod. "For the benefit of the elite, no doubt missing their expensive holiday resorts."

"No, it's for the people who took part in yesterday's Ceremony." The barman placed Lewis' gin and tonic on the bar. "That's on the house. Mr Udan will be lighting up the Red Giant later. You don't want to miss that. Enjoy the beach."

Lewis ambled down to the water, his feet crunching on the gravel, the top of his bald head chilling beneath fans as big as windmills spinning high on the ceiling. Up close the pool was huge, a glazed aquamarine lake reaching to the far side. The wall in the distance shimmered like the scales of a gigantic goldfish, reflecting rainbows as he walked along, all the reds, yellows and greens he'd ever seen: Dan Udan's hologram of the Red Giant Sun, with its lasers switched off. Lewis was already awestruck. Minutes away from seeing him again, even drunk, he could feel tremors deep down in his nervous system, vibrating through his solar plexus, like the aftershocks of a massive earthquake.

"The Boss is here!"

Lewis turned to see Dan striding down the slope, men saluting him in a relaxed way, as he smiled and waved back at them, wearing his black gloves. In faded blue jeans and a denim shirt, sleeves rolled up to show bulging biceps, his hair back to its natural, freestyle of tousled curls. Even his sunken cheeks of yesterday appeared to have plumped and pinked overnight. It was incredible, but the man approaching him looked the picture of health. Lewis could feel his knees begin to buckle. He faced the water, waiting for the quick, rhythmic foot-crunches in the gravel to fall silent beside him.

"Hi, Lewis, sorry to keep you waiting."

Lewis looked at him and drew his head back. "Crikey, are you wearing luminous contact-lenses or something?"

Dan lowered his eyes. "Are they a bit obvious?"

"Yes, but if anyone can get away with it, you can. I mean you being the Light Wizard," Lewis babbled, "people expect to be dazzled. Only they do look a bit like LEDs." He laughed. "Do they glow in the dark?"

Dan turned towards the sandy slope. "I guess you know what's going on here?" He gestured to the workers.

"You're creating an artificial beach." Lewis' loins tingled to see Dan's face redden. "Have I embarrassed you?" He took a cooling sip of his gin and tonic.

"Don't think of it as artificial, sure, the idea is to create the illusion of a real, tropical beach." He drew an arc through the air with his gloved hand. "I want to have a beach-party here tomorrow night, for the Celebration of Hope and as a surprise for Mary, who's never been to the tropics for a beach holiday in her life." He gave Lewis a piercing, side-ways look. "Isn't that what she told you the other day, talking about that other guy?"

It was like a punch in the stomach, Lewis doubled over. "What? You're transforming the Governors' private facilities on Mary's whim?" He widened his eyes. "If you hadn't forced her back here yesterday, she'd be with Flanagan right now, planning their filthy fortnight in the Caribbean."

Dan furrowed his brow, his complexion smooth but for a shiny mark on his upper lip, of new, pink skin.

"Sure, I told you it's mainly for the students, to lift their spirits after yesterday. And for your information, there's nothing going on with Mary and Flanagan, so don't go there again." His voice softened, "The fact is, she's never sat on a beautiful beach. Short of whisking her off to the real thing, which I can't do right now, I'm going to create one here...Have you got a problem with that?" His tone hardened. "Or are you still pissed-off with her after what happened yesterday?"

"Why is she back as your number one? I thought I was going to be your Soul Mate after suffering the Martyr's role. She's done nothing to earn her status."

"Lewis, forget about the Reality Treatise, will ye! I wrote it to test the students' gullibility and you weren't supposed to fall for it, you idjit. You're big and hairy enough to know better, or at least I thought you were." He cast his eyes over his bald head and suppressed a smile. "Look where it's got you now."

"Do you want to see where it's got me?" Lewis gave a pause, short, breathless, like the one he'd rehearsed. "I've earned my *Golden Halo*." He stared up into Dan's eyes, unnerved by their luminosity, making him eerily handsome. He fumbled inside his cassock pocket. "Do want to see it? Do want to see my halo?" He withdrew the small specimen bottle he'd taken from the lab and held it up. "There it is. My Saint's Halo. Proof of my hate and my love for you. Ha-lo, one word" – he gave a shaking laugh – "do you get it?"

Dan angled his head. "I hope that's not what I think it is."

"Tell me what you think it is!" Lewis scanned Dan's expression, relishing every inch.

"I know what it is." His eyes widened to white. "I thought you were over yesterday. Did I screw you up more than you let on? Tell me now. Do you think I want you bleeding yourself for me?"

"She wouldn't do it for you, would she?" Lewis curled his lip. "Never in a million years. I'm the one who's prepared to suffer for you and for the Cosmic Soul. So, take my halo!" He thrust the bottle towards him. "There's more where that came from. Go on, take it!"

"I don't want your blood. You're sick in the head and you need help." Dan reached out his hand. "Come on, I'll take you to the infirmary."

"Take it or leave it, it doesn't change a thing." Lewis tossed the bottle into the sand at Dan's feet. "You see, I've got the message. One way or another, the hook has got to sink in deeper." He squinted, peering into Dan's eyes, remembering what he'd seen in the mirror. "Maybe it's your turn to suffer for me." He drained the last of his gin and tonic and threw the glass into the sand, to land beside the specimen bottle. "If you don't want me to bleed for you, then do something about it. Give me what I want!"

Thread-veins appeared on Dan's cheeks where his colour had begun to drain, looking at Lewis now with a deep frown. "Tell me, what it is you want?"

Lewis glanced over at the Udanos hoisting sand-sacks over their shoulders, aware of a pulsing in his loins.

"I prefer to show you" – he looked at Dan – "meet me at my place in ten minutes."

Dan hooked his thumbs inside his jeans' pocket, angling his body away from Lewis. "I think you've forgotten who you're talking to."

"I'm talking to my equal." Lewis watched Dan's profile. "I'll challenge you and I'll stand up to you, now I know that's what you want. I looked death in the eye yesterday, and nothing frightens me now. You can shout and rant and rave all you like. I'm immune."

"Dr Allen, I employ you." Dan gave him a stern look. "I'd appreciate your respect."

"Oh, I'll always respect you, before, during and after." Lewis held Dan's eyes. "I may not be a big man, but boy, do I know how to use it." He cocked his head. "I'm not a prude. When it comes down to it, I'm a dirty fox!"

"Lewis Allen, you're drunk," Dan said. "Go home and sleep it off."

"I'm turning you on, aren't I?" He looked down at Dan's crotch. "Nice package. Getting a bit snug in there, is it, big boy?"

"That's enough."

Lewis took a step towards him, stumbled on his cassock's hem, recovering nimbly, with a suggestive lick of his lips. "You'll never say those words to me you beautiful, bastard boy." He chuckled, deep down in his throat. "Do you hear that" – he touched the front of his neck – "I've always had a knack for it. The bigger the better. I bet angel face hasn't taken it past her teeth."

"I said that's enough." Dan tightened his lips.

"I'm going to suck you dry and then I'm going to screw you like a dog." Lewis tossed his head. "I'm going to teach you what respect is."

He reached up to take Dan's face in both hands. Dan grabbed him by the armpits, lifted him clean off the ground, tossed him in the air and caught him again. The workers roared with laughter as Lewis squealed, his body dangling from two iron pincers, flashbacks to helpless infancy as Dan carried him up the slope. He stuck out his arms, peddling his feet, crushed like a squeezebox in Dan's grip, fearing his eyes might pop out of their sockets. He threw back his head and shrieked.

"I can't breathe! Put me down!"

Dan brought him to the ground and tapped the end of Lewis' nose with his forefinger. "Go home and sober up or I'll give you a warm backside, not the kind you're after, you cheeky devil."

"No!" Lewis staggered about, cassock catching around his ankles. "Bastard! You, fucking bastard!" He turned and fled down the slope, flailing his arms, trying to balance with his feet sinking and vanishing into the freshly laid sand. He tripped, fell face down and burst into tears, spitting out grit between sobs, rolling his forehead on his knuckles. When he looked up, Dan was sitting beside him, forearms resting on his flexed knees, bare feet nestling in the sand. He gazed out across the pool.

"Anger is a healthy sign," he said. "You'll be all right."

Lewis sat up and hugged his legs to his chest, his chin resting on one knee. He poked a hole in the sand with his forefinger. "I love you more now than I ever did. In a strange way, it feels as if we've had very powerful sex. Do you know what I mean?" He looked sideways at Dan, surprised to see a wet streak down his cheek. "Is that a tear?"

"I'm sorry Lewis, but I can't have you coming on to me like this, showing us both up. To be fair to you, I've got to put an end to this. There's no way we can be friends."

For a moment Lewis forgot how to breathe. He opened his mouth, heaved for breath and let out a hoarse cry. Dan laid his hand on Lewis' shoulder, with an unbearably light touch.

"Hey, you, come on now. You'll get over it. You're stronger

than you think you are."

"If you know I'm that strong, let me be your friend." Lewis stumbled to his feet and faced Dan. "I can be cool about this."

But shock waves were passing through him. Losing Dan Udan now would be like hitting a brick wall at maximum speed, a total wipe out, the end of Lewis Fox Allen. Dan's face was expressionless.

"Actually, Dan, what I love most of all is your genius." He clasped his hands together and shook them. "I swear I'll never come on to you again. I want to learn more about your holograms." He swung around and pointed across the water at the wall of the Red Giant Sun. "That one! The barman said you were going to light it up today and I shouldn't miss it. I'm dying to see it. Will you show it to me?"

Dan looked up. "Will you promise me you won't harm yourself again? Because if you do, I can't have you working here, emotionally unstable, never mind the friendship. Do you understand?"

Lewis laughed. "It was only port in that bottle. I was trying to wind you up."

"Honest to God, what are you like? Sure, I feel better about that." Dan raised his forefinger. "But less of your shenanigans, you sly old fox, do you promise me?"

"It's a promise." Lewis nodded. "I mean it. Major respect, from now on."

"Aye, well, it's about time we got this show on the road. Follow me." Dan rose to his feet, brushing sand from his jeans, with a smile that broke Lewis' heart.

Chapter Twenty-Seven

Lewis kept a respectful distance at Dan's side as they made their way down to the pool. A wave-machine was washing the water back and forth, overlapping the edge, simmering like real surf on the sand.

"Do you feel like you're at the seaside, yet?" Dan looked at him.

"There's a strong smell of chlorine...The sand is the best bit, nice and deep." Lewis tried not to sound too eager to please. "It still feels like I'm in a swimming pool."

"What would make it feel like the real thing," Dan said, "for you?"

"Um-" Lewis glanced up at the ceiling. "Sunlight, a salty sea-breeze, loads more water." He looked sideways at him. "Not to be indoors at all, but outside with a sky."

"First things first." Dan raised his hand, poised like a conductor in front of an orchestra. "Let there be sunshine!"

Across the water on the far side, UDAN's holographic crystals chattered inside their mounts, sweeping circles around the wall, moving like wind through a field of ripened wheat. "Watch now," he said, "the crystals are about to emit their micro-lasers." Thousands of tiny flashes flashed, flickering like a laser-show above the pool. The rays merged into a misty, saffron cloud that uncannily began to billow into pockets, expanding to a sphere of golden light, reminding Lewis of a hot-air balloon inflating before lift-off.

"How did you start-up the hologram?" Lewis kept a hint of formality in his voice. "Does it recognise your handprint?"

"Yes, it's the same technology we use for opening our doors. The weather boys can start it up mechanically, but for security reasons that takes a while. What do you think is happening inside the hologram, now?"

Lewis watched the lasers begin to fluoresce before his eyes, trailing ribbons the way a saxophone reflects spotlights on a television screen, swirling and blending to amber, illuminating the water below. He looked over his shoulder at pink sunshine flooding the room. The sloping sands and the youth's face behind the bar had turned the delicate shade of a dying sunset. He looked back at the holographic sun. Red dots were seeping through the middle of the sphere, at first clustered, beaded like a child's grazed knee. And then, as if the wound wouldn't stop bleeding, a dark, ruby red saturated the sun's core, creeping outwards.

The Red Giant was taking shape, hanging in mid-air above the swimming pool. But to answer Dan's question about what was happening inside the hologram, Lewis hesitated to find the right words.

"Don't your holograms, erm… have a way of manipulating interference patterns that give light a different consistency, making it look more like a gas or a liquid?"

Dan smiled at him. "What about you? What's going on inside you?"

"Me? Wow, I'm in complete awe. I love this… I'm absolutely

dying to know where the energy inside the crystals comes from. At college it was totally confusing" – Lewis babbled – "you should've heard the different theories our tutors came up with, from anti-matter hidden inside them somewhere, to some form of dark-energy. They even hypothesised that you'd found a way to manipulate the Higgs boson particle, to create a new kind of state, between liquid and light, nothing we've seen before."

To be honest, Lewis wasn't just experiencing the awe he'd anticipated, but a hopeless longing, standing in Dan Udan's sunshine. One thing he had learned at college about UDAN's holograms, was that they resonated with the human soul, and enhanced the will to live.

Here again in the Red Giant, Lewis recognised the hallmark of every UDAN hologram, harmonising light like musical chords, shimmering through life's shapes like a million starlings, order and chaos dancing a fierce, yet flamboyant tango. Evoking joy in the human heart or the kind of ambivalent nostalgia that old people feel, remembering their youth, their troubled marriages, all those bygone years, so often wasted. People often made up for lost time after watching what UDAN could do with the light of life. In fact, Lewis was reflecting on his own college career at this moment and all the time he'd spent reading science magazines and scientific papers, hoping that the Light Wizard had at last revealed his secret.

"I don't suppose you'd ever tell me the truth about the science you use" – Lewis peered at him – "would you?"

Dan looked at him, as if weighing up his request. He removed a squashed packet of cigarettes from his back pocket and put one between his lips, speaking through the crook in his mouth.

"You're darned right I won't." He lit it with a flick of a lighter.

Lewis squared up to him. "If you told me, it would make my life totally worthwhile. I'd give anything, everything to know… I swear. I'd keep the secret, so long as I live."

Dan puffed on the cigarette, crinkling his eyes with a smoky wince. "Be grateful you have a life to live, sure, that's worthwhile." He withdrew the cigarette from his mouth, flicking ash sideways with his thumb. "You shouldn't bargain with your life, Lewis, haven't you learned your lesson?"

Lewis gave him a penetrating look. "Is it because you don't trust people with what you know. You think we're going to abuse it or use it to destroy ourselves?"

"People have had the means to destroy themselves for some time," Dan said. "But more is at stake here than human life. In the wrong hands all this" – he waved his cigarette – "could be used to alter the very fabric of nature. Our reality is structured much like a web, in places it hangs on a few threads." He drew a puff, turning his head to blow smoke away from Lewis' face.

"I trust all my employees to do a good job, sure, but there's none I can trust with what you're asking for. Even the best of us can behave unpredictably at times." He gave an upward nod. "Take yesterday, for example. The Ceremony started out with me egging on our students to bleed the martyr and ended with them egging me on to go the whole hog.

"Who'd have thought civilised, well-educated young people would behave like a bloodthirsty mob? I did. Tyranny dehumanises people and that includes the tyrant, who often gets caught up in his own tyranny. We all of us became part of something wicked yesterday. If I hadn't put boundaries in place at the start, it could've ended in a bloodbath. It goes to show you how easy it is to let the devil in. That's why I wanted you all to see its face, so in future you'll recognise it.

"When humanity has learned to bring the devil to heel, that's when UDAN Corporations will consider sharing my knowledge… It won't be in this generation or the next, maybe never." He surveyed Lewis from beneath his eyebrows, like a disappointed headmaster. "So long as folks carry on what they're doing."

"But hang on." Lewis frowned. "Last night you said you went overboard, because the kids made you sick. Doesn't that mean you're just as capable of doing the wrong thing? Can you trust yourself with your own knowledge, not to abuse it in the future? Sorry"-he shrugged – "you did ask me to challenge you."

"Aye, you're spot on. I've my own demons to battle with. But knowing what I know, I can always find a way to mend what I break. So, thinking back to our web, what does that make me?"

Lewis searched Dan's eyes for inspiration, sky-blue, lit from within. "Doesn't that make you somehow like… the weaver of the web, like a kind of spider?"

He winked. "You're no fool, Lewis."

Lewis puffed out his chest to see he'd impressed Dan Udan. He sensed them getting closer, step by small step. Perhaps all he needed was patience, then one day, maybe… He went on, hoping once more, to impress him.

"If you're the only one who can repair the web when it's broken, doesn't that make you responsible for the modern world, I mean, for …our reality?"

Dan smiled his crooked smile, giving Lewis a frisson. "As I said, you're no fool."

Lewis parted his lips, distracted by trying to look more

than huggable. At the same time his thoughts went firing in all directions, to grasp the immensity of Dan's words. Dan raised his eyes and looked over Lewis' head.

"Talk of the devil," Dan said.

Lewis turned to see the sandy-haired student, Wildo, walking down the slope in a red T-shirt and jeans.

Two Udano soldiers in combat gear flanked him, carrying truncheons.

"What's he doing here?" Lewis muttered. "I can't stand him."

"I've got a bone to pick with him." Dan dropped the cigarette and swept sand over it with his foot. He put his hands on his hips and waited for the men to approach. The soldiers brought Wildo up to face him, saluted and stood to attention.

Wildo grinned at Lewis. "Nice dress, Lou, suits you, mate." All chummy with his Australian intonation. "Ralph Wild, sir, we found him in the bar. He's had a few," said one of the soldiers.

"Thanks." Dan nodded. "At ease, now."

The soldiers took up a wide stance, with their hands behind their backs. Dan stepped up to Wildo, a muscular young man standing about six foot tall. But Lewis was delighted to see that Dan towered over the student by at least six inches.

"Would you remind me, Mr Wild, what it is you're studying at my university?"

Wildo looked down at the ground, with obvious difficulty keeping a straight face.

"Look at me when I'm speaking to you, boy and wipe that stupid smirk off your face!"

Lewis' eardrums fluttered. Bile simmered into the back of his throat. He gulped down the sick taste, without taking his eyes off Wildo's reddening face. He wasn't going to miss a moment of the shoe on the other foot. The student lifted his chin, unable to look Dan in the eye, he addressed his neck.

"I'm studying UDAN holographics, sir, first year Crystal Techniques and Window Concepts." He blinked. "I wasn't smirking at you sir. Lewis made me laugh."

"Aye, I know he's a funny man, but that's no excuse when I'm talking to you. What are you planning to do with your degree?" Dan's tone softened. Lewis felt a pang of injustice.

"I want a career with UDAN Corporations, sir. It's always been my ambition to work for the Light Wizard since I was a kid. I love your holograms, they're so great, I can't get enough of them." His confidence evidently restored, he looked up at Dan. "You're my role model."

"So, Mr Wild, would you know what our motto is at UDAN Corps?" Dan took a few steps back and folded his arms, appearing to size him up.

"Err… I know it's got something to do with enlightenment." Wildo put his forefinger to his bottom lip.

"I knew it yesterday, sir, but it's just gone out of my head."

Lewis' inner voice rattled off: *'Our Destiny is Enlightenment Our Path is Compassionate.'* He glared at the freckly face, willing the mouth to say something totally infuriating.

"Is it… Enlightenment Lights Our Creative Path?" Wildo grimaced.

"Bull shite. UDAN's motto should be emblazoned across your heart, burning a hole through that T-shirt." Dan compressed his lips. "I've got no time for bullies. I heard you yesterday, at the back there" – he thumbed towards Lewis – "braying for this man's blood. You're a nasty piece of work, Mr

Wild and I don't want you in my house another night. You're to go now and pack your bags. A chopper will take you to Dublin airport. You're on the eight o'clock flight back to Brisbane."

The look of disbelief on Wildo's face was so comical Lewis stifled a snort of laughter.

"But sir, I wasn't the only one. Everybody was braying. We had to or we'd have been clobbered by your Udanos." Wildo's cheeks paled, wide-eyed, he couldn't get his words out fast enough. "It's not fair! I'm being made the scapegoat when everybody's to blame. Please don't send me back to Oz. Please, Mr Udan, I didn't mean anything by it. I'm a good student. I'm working my butt off in class."

Dan waved his hand. "Take him away. Make sure he's in the departure lounge before five-thirty."

Wildo dropped to his knees, sprawling himself face-down in the sand. He clasped his hands above his head, spluttering to keep sand out of his mouth. "Please, don't send me away, I beg you!" He raised his head, gaping at Lewis. "I'll make it up to you. Give me another chance!"

Lewis looked down at the boy's strapping buttocks at his feet, with a tingle of rude fascination. He lifted his eyes to meet Dan's gaze. "It's true. He wasn't the only one braying. There were others just as bad."

Dan frowned. "Did you want me to change my mind?"

"Well, it seems a bit unreasonable to expel one boy when there were others doing the same thing." Lewis turned his palm up. "Let's be fair."

Dan stepped away and beckoned to him with his forefinger. Lewis went over.

"There's no helping this boy," Dan said in his ear. "He's

already lost his conscience. He wouldn't recognise a lie if he told one."

But Lewis thought, perhaps this was his ultimate challenge. Here was an opportunity to prove to Dan Udan what a gifted cognitive programmer he truly was. Surely, there could be no better way to demonstrate his genius than to re-programme the thinking of a living, breathing, hopeless case.

He said behind his hand. "I reckon I could do something to improve this fellow's attitudes, maybe even re-awaken his conscience."

Dan gave him a searching look. "Lewis, this isn't artificial intelligence. You can't do a Jolly job on him. He's a rotten apple, and he'll take you down with him, if you're not careful."

Lewis' voice pitched higher. "Please, let me have a go at getting through to him. I've got a hunch I can do this. You admitted you went overboard. Who knows, maybe Wild did too and now he regrets it. Look at him now." They looked across at Wildo kneeling up in the sand.

Dan lowered his eyes. "Aye, I suppose to be fair I should offer him a chance to redeem himself. Give me a minute to think." He turned and walked along the edge of the pool, stopped and took out another cigarette, appearing to enjoy a leisurely smoke.

"Hoy, Lewis!" Wildo called over. "Have you saved my life yet?" He grinned. "I'll make it worth your while. I'll give you anything you want, mate." He blew him a furtive kiss.

Lewis returned a nod.

Dan came back, kicking his bare feet through the sand. He clapped his hands,

"Okay, guys, this is what we're going to do. Mr Wild, get

up on your hind legs. I want you to listen to me. You're on probation. For the period of three weeks this man here" – he pointed to Lewis – "is going to be your teacher. You're going to listen to him and follow his orders. Lewis will set you the example of how to conduct yourself like a decent human being. If you give him any trouble at all, you'll be out on your ear. Do we understand one another?"

"Yes, sir!" The pink was coming back into Wildo's face. Lewis saw that he had a sun-kissed glow about him, fresh, boyish, not bad looking at all.

"How does that sound to you, Lewis?" Dan came to his side.

"I won't let you down." He flashed him a smile.

"That's grand. At the end of the three weeks Lewis here will hand me a report on your progress and I'll decide whether he's found any good in you. I'm not convinced, but there, you go. I'm giving him the benefit of the doubt as he's good enough to forgive you y' trespasses." He cocked his head at Lewis. "He's all yours. I'll leave yous to have a chat.

"When you're ready, come up to the bar for a drink and we'll talk about the beach props. I want to hear your creative ideas." Dan left them and strode up the slope. He stooped to pick up his boots sitting side by side in the sand and carried on. The soldiers waited and then followed him, at a solemn pace.

Lewis and Wildo looked at one another.

"What do we do now, mate?" Wildo opened his hands.

"The first thing I'd like you to do" – Lewis gave his supercilious smile – "is to call me by my new name, Saint Fox."

Chapter Twenty-Eight

"Do you need a hand?" Mary stood in Jane's kitchen.

"All I have to do is heat up the moussaka and toss the salad." Jane reached up to remove two plates from the cupboard. "Desi was here all afternoon. The woman is a marvel. She's cooking dinner tonight at the Penthouse. Dan is entertaining a few governors." Jane glanced at her. "No doubt filling his time until you're together again. He's called twice here already."

Mary folded her arms and leaned her shoulder against the doorframe, exhaustion setting-in following an afternoon's work, overseeing harvest completion in the Farm Park. Talking on the phone to staff at St. Anthony's Hospital, bringing her up to date with the trial volunteers. And then, the most intensive four hours of her working-life spent in the bio-synth lab.

"How did he sound?" She watched Jane's face.

"Cheerful. He went to meet Lewis after you left. He wants to involve him in some new project." Jane removed a large bowl from the fridge. "The last of the swelling had gone by the time he'd got dressed. He looked wonderful. He was surprised you were still working when he rang." She tossed lettuce leaves in the bowl with wooden spoons.

"Did he say anything else about me staying here tonight?"

"No, and honestly, he should be able to cope with one night

apart, before you move in together." Jane rinsed her hands under the tap. "Although I suspect he's worried that you'll use the time to re-think."

"I've made up my mind. But he needs time to come to terms with the decisions he's made. I hope he's serious about receiving psychiatric help."

Jane raised her eyebrows. "The fact that he even discussed it with you amazed me. He's come a long way this week. I know it's been a nightmare, but I never thought he'd agree to surgery and seeing a psychiatrist. I take back what I said. Sending you away has worked wonders. He doesn't want to lose you. The poor man will do anything."

"But it's all for his own good." Mary unfolded and refolded her arms. "I don't understand why he has resisted help, for so long. Look what he must go through. This morning was dreadful."

"My nephew is a mystery to us all." Jane slid the moussaka dish into the oven. "That's going to take a while to heat up. Let's go and sit down with an aperitif."

Mary sat in the high-back armchair. Jane reclined on her chaise-long, both sipping sherry from schooners as another sun went down in the UDAN window. Mary was beginning to appreciate why Jane insisted on immersing herself in sunsets and sunrises. To compensate for the reality of days like today. The force-feeding of her nephew with live insects, until his face puffed-up and they could barely see his eyes. Until he almost suffocated on his swollen tongue, choking to breathe through an oxygen mask.

"Do I have time for a shower before dinner? Mary said.

"Yes, I've put it on a low heat to give you time to unwind.

You must be shattered." Jane lifted her chin. "I suppose you've already started cloning for Dan's new organ genesis?"

"Yes. I have the Maternal Simulator with me." Mary inclined her head. "Would you like to see him?"

"Is there much to see at this stage?" Jane said.

"Well, he's on embryonic fast-growth induction, so that I can harvest organs first thing on Monday. Foetal development should stop at the equivalent of three months, in twenty-four hours."

"What is the equivalent now?" There was a catch in Jane's breath.

"Around five weeks." Mary smiled.

"It'll never have its own life, poor mite," Jane said.

"He's our tiny hero, Jane, saving Dan's life. Would you rather not see him?"

"Not before we eat." Jane sipped her sherry.

Mary looked at her watch. "I do have to check on him. I'll go now and have my shower and see how he's doing. I'll see you in a little while."

She returned to the room where she had slept beside Dan the night before. All the bed linen had been changed, the room made fragrant and immaculate for Mary's one night, by Desi, Dan's housekeeper.

Mary sat on the edge of the bed, opened her briefcase, and withdrew a small beige gadget that fitted into her palm like a phone handset. The Maternal Simulator. She entered the code, calling up data from the incubator in the biosynth lab: *JDD 832000 clone, Fast Growth Embryo at 1 hr 22mins, Biological Age 960 hrs, Length 13.2 mm.* She entered Display, to check on the appearance of the developing embryo, a translucent cashew nut with limb-buds and mittens, rudimentary face grimacing like a gargoyle.

She gazed at the sweet, ugly little thing. This was how Dan had looked almost twenty-nine years ago, just like everybody else. Forty days after conception there was nothing to suggest the blueprint for an average or extraordinary individual, until the DNA unravelled and expressed itself. Only seeing him like this, she was astonished at how fiercely protective her feelings were.

The process this afternoon had been text-book perfect. Mary opted to use one of her own eggs, she'd had frozen when she was an undergraduate, common practise amongst female science students aware of the risks of delaying motherhood.

She removed her own DNA and replaced it with Dan's, extracted from a healthy skin cell. Monitoring his first cellular divisions on screen, she watched the tiny bubble shivering and separating, crowding itself with more and more bubbles until overwhelmed, it succumbed to order.

Implanting his embryo into the artificial womb, fondly called Mummy, Mary had felt increasingly like an over-anxious mother. Watching his head and tail unfolding, she remembered what Jane had told her about holding Dan in her arms at two days old, the most beautiful infant she ever saw.

Mary reminded herself, that she was never going to see this baby born. The embryo was destined to give up its vital organs. She'd love it and watch it die. The cruelty of the loss no grimmer than life's random casualties. Only this time the sacrifice would be for the best possible cause. Dan Udan's life.

She entered the signal for another injection of fast-growth hormones. A green light came on at the top of the handset and below on the miniature screen, the embryo twitched: instruction received. She hesitated, remembering the look on Jane's face and decided to program the handset to automatic injection for the rest of the evening. She wouldn't raise the subject again.

Under the shower it took her a while to wash her hair, standing for minutes at a time, letting the water pound the top of her head, and run down her face, like tears she wanted to cry but couldn't. She'd finished rinsing out the shampoo, turned off the taps and saw Jane through the frosted glass, standing in the doorway.

"Mary, Dan's here. He's just popped in to say goodnight. Is that all right?"

"Of course. Just give me a moment to get ready. I'll be out in a minute."

She towel-dried her hair, her skin still damp, as she put on her underwear, her heart racing as she ploughed through her suitcase to find her jeans and a fresh T-shirt. Combing her hair in front of the dressing table, she heard a quiet knock on the door. Dan walked straight in.

"Angel, I've got to go. I've got guests waiting at the Penthouse." He threw up his hands. "I couldn't do it. Just say you're happy to see me!"

She'd never seen him look as handsome, in a pale pink sweater, his eyes so bright they were thrilling to gaze into. Even to know the reason why. Desi's Best had reactivated fire-fly genes in his retinas.

Mary rose from the stool. "Of course, I'm happy to see you."

He strode up and wrapped his arms around her, in a light hold as if she were a China doll and he might break her. "Why are you doing this to me. We've been apart all week." He said in her ear. "Can't you change your mind and come back with me? Your suite is ready for you."

"I'd love to, but I'm not going to," she said. "I want to have an early night, for a fresh start tomorrow. This morning you agreed it would be good for us to have tonight apart."

"I didn't know then how I was going to feel." He squeezed her. "I'm like a lost kid, I could cry."

She put her hands on his waist. "I hope that means we're doing the right thing, moving in together."

"Are you still not sure?" He exhaled a breath in her ear. "Am I to expect a call in the morning to say you've changed your mind?"

She gave a little pull to his sweater. "Dan, look at me." He dropped his arms and stepped back to gaze at her. "I need to know you can keep to your promises." She inclined her head. "I'm moving in with you on the grounds that you're going to accept treatment. If you talk me into going back with you tonight, what does that say to me about our agreements?"

"I'll go now." But he just stood there with his mouth open. She could hear his breath passing between his lips, not quite a human sound.

"Dan?" She blinked at him. "Are you all right?" He didn't answer. Saliva was seeping into the corners of his mouth. "Talk to me," she said.

"Wanting your own space isn't unreasonable." His voice cracked. "Only, I can't bear this. It's pathetic I know, so I'll go." He punched the air with his fist. "But I don't know how I'm going to get through that fecken door without you! I feel like tearing it apart!"

"Dan, I'm not going back with you, tonight," she said.

Jane breezed in. "Dan, it's time you left. Cookie has arrived. Everybody is waiting for you at the Penthouse."

"They can wait. She's coming with me," he said. "Mary, I've got everything you need." He put the back of his hand to his mouth.

"Not tonight, she's not." Jane grabbed Mary by the hand. "Come on, dear, we're going for a walk." She led her down the hall, almost bumping into Cookie coming in the opposite direction. "He's salivating. Take him home!"

"God damn. I knew he shouldn't've come here," Cookie said. "Lock yourselves in another room!"

"What's happening?" Mary said.

Jane drew her into the bathroom and locked the door. "Don't worry, it'll be fine." She put her finger on Mary's mouth. "Don't say a word, until they've gone."

Mary and Jane waited, listening. The only voice they heard was Cookie's, sounding like a chirpy cowboy, passing outside the door. "Son, you'll see her tomorrow, you'll be over the worst. Come on, let's go have us some meat. Desi's done ya steak and kidney, fill y' belly up." The front door slammed.

"Our dinner is ready too." Jane unlocked the door. "You must be hungry. I don't suppose you had any lunch." She walked out of the bathroom, ahead of Mary, down the hall. "Desi has made enough to feed an army."

"Jane-" Mary strode after her. "I deserve an explanation."

"We can talk about it over dinner." She indicated to the table, set for two, with candles burning. "Dan was kind enough to set the table for us, while he was waiting for you, at least twenty minutes." She laughed. "We were beginning to worry that you'd washed yourself down the plughole."

"Stop pretending there's nothing wrong. I can't contemplate moving in with Dan until I know why you had to lock us in the bathroom, for heaven's sake."

Jane faced her. "I'm not supposed to tell you, but" – she nodded – "let's sit down and have another sherry."

They sat down, this time, Jane in the high-back chair, Mary perched on the edge of the chaise, her eyes fixed on Jane. Jane spoke in a low voice.

"The reason why Dan resists eating what's good for him, is that it triggers intense cravings and animal instincts." She clasped both hands around her schooner. "For a while after Desi's Best he needs to consume raw meat and fresh blood." She drew a deep breath. "His sense of smell becomes very acute. I knew he was responding to your scent the moment he arrived. He tried to distract himself by setting the table, which he did beautifully." She smiled faintly. "When he went in to see you, he was sexually aroused. I locked us in the bathroom so that he wouldn't pursue you. Tonight, he has invited people over for dinner. It'll help him to control himself and behave like a civilised human being."

"Does he ever become violent?" Mary frowned. "He said he felt like tearing the door down."

"Other than his behaviour toward Lewis during that ghastly Ceremony, Dan has never hurt anybody, ever, to my knowledge. He can't touch people, which itself acts like a safety-valve." Jane took a sip of sherry.

"He'll be a bit irritable for a while. But he responds well to Cookie's approach, which is to be firm with him. Submissive types get on Dan's nerves." Jane narrowed her eyes. "It's an animal thing. He likes a strong pack around him."

"He started to pant just now, just like a dog," Mary said, "I've heard him pant like that before."

"It very much depends which of the integument's genes are switched on. His behaviour can be very different. Sometimes he'll bounce around like a puppy. Or I've known him to curl up on the floor and sleep all day, like a cat."

"And hunt at night?" Mary raised her eyebrows, although she wasn't alarmed by any of this. It would've surprised her more to discover that Dan's non-human genes had no impact on his behaviour.

Jane laughed. "There's far too much food in the cupboard. No doubt Dan would survive very well in the wild."

Mary sighed and sat back on the chaise. "What a price to pay for his faith in God." She looked at Jane. "And such a cruel God."

Jane lowered her eyes. "I didn't think he'd turn up here this evening, knowing that his behaviour would be off. The poor man couldn't stay away from you. He'll be regretting it now." She put her schooner up to her mouth. "What are you going to do?"

"What do you mean?" Mary said.

"Have you changed your mind about moving in with him?"

Mary rose. "What's his intercom code at the Penthouse?" She walked over to Jane's intercom on the desk.

"UDAN," Jane said. "What are you going to tell him?"

Mary faced her. "I'll be arriving at his Penthouse after work, around six o'clock."

"You love my nephew, don't you," Jane said. There was a glow in her voice.

"Yes," Mary said, "and I'm going to help him."

Chapter Twenty-Nine

"The Boss wants this cut in half."

Connie stood on the beach in baggy shorts, relaying orders to the group standing at the edge of a big-top circus tent spread out on the sand. Lewis listened with sweat trickling down his temples, his cassock issuing a piquant body-odour following hours labouring in it yesterday, for Dan's project. He had no energy left for work, had spent the night crashed out on his sofa, on a stomach full of lager and hamburgers, handed out to the workers.

"Some blokes shouldn't wear shorts," Wildo muttered beside him. Lewis concurred with a grunt, taking in Connie's bandy legs, the grey fuzz on his calves, preferring the man's physique in a tidy suit.

"On one side, The Boss wants two windshields and four parasols cut, showing the blue and white stripes on top, like that there." Connie made slicing gestures in line with the canopy's stripes. "The other side, he wants a large, comfortable tipi made, for him and his lady, for their privacy on the beach. He's measured it all out to the last millimetre." He thumbed behind him.

"Back there, in that box, you'll find the instruction leaflets with his drawings. Read them carefully. If he sees any waste of this canvas, he'll be at yous, so go carefully with your tape-measures. You'll find cutters in that bucket, over there." He glanced at his watch. Dan appeared at the top of the slope.

"Top of the morning to yous!"

Connie called out, "Morning Boss!" He nodded. "That's your man. Didn't I tell you he'd be here on the dot of seven? He'll be looking for the same exactitude in your efforts today." He clapped his hands. "Chop, chop!"

The men traipsed through the sand to the leaflet-box and bucket. Lewis and Wildo watched Dan descend the slope, looking incredibly slim-hipped and narrow-waisted, in a black T-shirt and jeans. Lewis had never noticed before, just how top-heavy he was, bulging with muscle.

Wildo sniggered. "You can tell Udan's obsessed with his looks, vain bastard."

"Show some respect!" Lewis smacked his backside smartly. "Go fetch the stuff!"

Wildo went off as Lewis observed Dan a few yards away, picking up where he'd left off the day before, pumping over a workbench, sawing pieces of wood to make frames for windshields and spokes for parasols.

All Lewis wanted was to sit in the sand and watch poetry in motion. Those effeminate hands concealed inside their black gloves were deceptive, recalling the moment yesterday, when his feet had left the ground.

"Instructions and cutting gear." Wildo dropped a couple of Stanley knives at his feet. "You got to see these drawings." He raised the sheet of paper in front of Lewis, pointing. "Look, Udan has got his tipi mapped out with a mattress and cushions." He laughed. "While we're all swimming down at the sea-side, old Udan will be rocking pussy in his tipi."

Lewis glared at him. "How many times do I have to tell you? This is inappropriate behaviour Mr. Wild.

We do not speculate rudely about other people's private lives. That's their business only."

"Sorry, Saint Fox, it won't happen again, honest." Wildo lowered the sheet-paper, bowing his head.

"Good boy," Lewis said. "Now read the instructions. Let's see if you've got any common sense."

"Yes, Saint Fox."

"Lewis, a word in your ear!" Dan called over.

Lewis looked across at him beckoning with his forefinger. He smiled and went up to him.

"He's not to call you Saint Fox." Dan glowered. "He's to call you Dr Allen, okay?"

Lewis focused through his thick lenses, giving Dan his convergent stare. "But I'm a changed man since the Ceremony." He arched his voice. "I actually feel God is with me."

Dan gave a slow blink. "It takes more than a rotten day and a cassock to make a Saint. Or are you taking the piss?"

"How can you say that?" It was an unthinkable accusation. "You know how much I suffered for this cassock. I'm telling you I feel like a true, living Saint, capable of enlightening other-"

"Lewis, will you give over." Dan's Irish lilt pitched melodically. "Do you want your head examined? You go on like this and the men in white coats will be after you. Is that what you had in mind for your holidays?"

Lewis knew he shouldn't argue. He braced himself.

"I've every right to defend my beliefs, as you have a right to defend yours, Dan" – he faltered – "Udan… I will stand up to you. I demand your respect."

"Don't play the smart Alec with me, Dr Allen!" The din was like something from a battlefield, sword striking shield. *"You'll do as you're told, or I'll give you something to moan about!"*

Lewis surprised himself with coy laughter. "Did you know, you're beautiful when you're angry?"

Dan narrowed his eyes. In his quiet voice – "No, I'm not. You should know better than to think you can play me. Learn to shut your mouth, or you'll be out on your ear with that oddball over there." He flashed a look towards Wildo. "Get back to work!"

Lewis hung his head and dragged his feet through the sand, to his side of the canvas. He knelt and picked up a Stanley knife to start cutting. But then withdrew for a moment to cough a mouthful of acid bile into the sand. He kept his eyes down until the last moment, when he couldn't help but glance over at Dan.

The man was staring straight at him, frozen over his workbench. Lewis attempted a nervous smile of appeasement, without a flicker of recognition in return.

Lewis turned his back, controlling an intense urge to run from the look in Dan's eyes. Kneeling once more to pick up the knife, he started to cut with his eyes closed, a jagged line into the soft belly of his forearm. He flexed his elbow to feel the blood trickling, cooling on his skin as it meandered up his arm, inside his cassock sleeve. He scooped up a handful of sand, poured it over the wound and rubbed it in until his eyes streamed.

By late afternoon, kiosks, windshields and parasols had popped up all over the beach. Soldiers had arrived with dozens of potted palm-trees, to plant them in the sand and drape them with fairy-lights.

Chefs from eateries throughout the UISC spent the day setting up their kitchen-tents, barbeques and rotisseries, pancake huts and champagne-fountains, sparkling pink in the Red Giant's sunshine. To Lewis' mind, revealing the beach as it might look through rose-tinted spectacles.

His eyes followed Dan everywhere, watching him direct his staff with easy authority, conveying his satisfaction with bursts of raucous laughter, giving Lewis a sickly-sweet rush of trepidation and relief.

"This place could've ended up looking like a dog's dinner." Wildo slurped from another pint of lager going free at the bar. "You've got to hand it to him, Foxy, the guy's a bleeding genius."

Come five pm, the Light Wizard was satisfied, flushed and excited. He went about in his black gloves, shaking hands, thanking UISC staff and his Udanos, for their grand effort.

Lewis sat down by the surf, gazing at the sunset, reflecting his mood with its bruised and wistful hues.

He felt something on his back, a familiar, shocking lightness of touch.

"Are y' all right there, buddy?" Dan sat down beside him. "You did a grand job on that parasol. It's one of the best. Thanks, eh?"

"Okay, anytime," Lewis mumbled.

"Listen. I'm sorry I shouted at you earlier."

Lewis gave no reaction, gazing ahead.

"You promised me you weren't going to harm yourself," Dan said.

"I didn't. It was port in that bottle."

"I knew that was port-wine, yesterday." Dan's voice firmed. "I'm talking about this morning." He took Lewis' wrist and pulled back his cassock sleeve. "I'm taking about that. What did you do that for?"

The wound had congealed black, with blood and grit.

"Because I felt like it," Lewis said.

Dan released him. "I'm going to refer you for an assessment at the Infirmary. You need professional help."

"I don't need a shrink. I can sort my own head out, thanks." Lewis looked at him. "If you want me to feel better, I can think of another way."

"You've had a traumatic experience and you're disturbed. I recognise the signs." Dan turned up his gloved palm. "Don't be too proud to accept help. You're not alone here."

Lewis gazed sideways into his eyes. "Why can't you just kiss me better?"

Dan surprised him, appearing to scan Lewis' face, settling on his mouth. Then he met his gaze. He lifted Lewis' spectacles from his nose and leaned forward. "Close your eyes."

Lewis closed his eyes. He felt Dan blow softly on his eyelids and lips. "There now, I've kissed you better."

Lewis opened his eyes. Dan was smiling at him.

"I've always known," Lewis whispered, "that deep down inside, you're so kind."

"Sometimes my temper gets the better of me" – Dan gave him a rueful look – "as you know, to my shame."

"I don't care," Lewis said. "So long as I can die in your arms, I'm happy."

"So be happy." Dan gazed up at the Red Giant. "That much was decided long before there were stars." He brushed the sand from his shins and rose to his feet. "I'll let you work that one out for yourself… Enjoy the party." He touched Lewis' shoulder.

"God bless you, my friend."

"Come in, come in, Maria!" Desi Cookson waved her into the hazy light. "Welcome to the Penthouse. Do you have any other luggage?"

"Just me and my briefcase." Mary smiled at Dan's housekeeper hailed from Lacerta, a feisty Greek woman in her fifties. She hugged Mary the moment she walked over the threshold.

"My God, see you, see you! She is so beautiful!" She put her hands on her cheeks, turning to Cookie who appeared at her side. "Cookie, she is the loveliest girl we ever saw?"

Cookie stepped forward to peck Mary's cheek. "If y' don't mind, Mary, my Despina is the loveliest girl I ever did see." He gave a husky chuckle. "But if there's an angel walking this earth, then Dan's found her, for sure. Welcome to your new home. It's good to see you again. Danny got in fifteen minutes ago. He's gone to freshen up."

He moved back as Desi found Mary's hand, to shake it.

"Cookie and I are glad you have come to live here. Dan is overjoyed. He is on the moon."

"I hope not." Mary laughed, feeling a little shy. "Thank you."

Desi squeezed her fingers and released her. "I will show you to your rooms. Cookie, tell Dan, Mary is here!"

Mary followed her up the spiralling staircase, her shoes sinking into the white carpet. So deep and soft it was like rising on a cloud.

"You have your own bedroom suite, your own sitting room and study. Here we are" – Desi opened the double doors with a flourish – "your own little palace."

Mary gazed. Everything she looked at was the colour of gold. From the antique four-poster-bed to the delicate tones of the carpet and walls, even the chandeliers dripped with gold. She felt like an insect caught in amber. It stuck to her eyes.

"All your dresses and suits are in those wardrobes." Desi waved her hand. "Accessories, T-shirts, underwear, nightwear, are all in the drawers. The bathroom is in there." She spun around, pointing to another door. "Your own furniture is through there, in your sitting-room. Dan hopes you like it."

"It's lovely," Mary said.

"Your UDAN Window has sequences Dan created just for you. The Flower Meadow is so beautiful. Would you like to watch it as you get ready?"

"I think I'll keep it for later." Mary smiled. "It'll be something to look forward to. Thank you."

"You must get dressed." Desi walked over to one of the wardrobes and returned with a white shrouded garment over her arm. "Dan would like you to wear this tonight, for a surprise he has planned for you." She removed the shroud, laying a long gown on the bed. "It's his design, made with his own hands."

"Did Dan really sew this himself?" Mary touched it. Like something a vestal virgin might've worn, with a diamantine neck and high waistline. A simple, classical design.

"Oh, yes, he created all of his own costumes when he was in the circus." Desi patted the ornaments around the neck. "But these are not sequins. They are real diamonds."

"My goodness." Mary lifted the material between her thumb and forefinger. "It's so delicate. What is it made of?"

"That is his secret." Desi looked up through her eyebrows. "Dan always copies nature. This fabric is called Golden

Damselfly. It is so light it is like air against the skin. Will you wear it for him?"

"I'd hate to disappoint him." She was starting to feel nervous about the surprise. "Is it to be a formal occasion, this evening?"

"I know nothing about it." Desi took Mary gently by both hands. "All I know is Dan wants to please you. He has waited so long for this day. He asked to meet you in the Holorama at seven-thirty. When you are ready, call Cookie on the intercom, he will take you there. I'll leave you to get dressed."

Mary left the suite, to find her own way through the Penthouse, rather than trouble Cookie.

She descended the spiral staircase, turned towards the light and entered a spacious sitting room with wide-open patio-doors. She gave a cry of delight, to see a UDAN Holorama here, in the middle of Dan's apartment.

She walked down the marble steps onto a patio and leaned over the balcony to gaze across a glittering bay. In the distance mountain peaks shimmered, changing colour from frosted pink to yellow-gold and aquamarine.

Mary watched as the sun began to set. Amber particles seeming to swarm inside it, like a million excited bumblebees. Water-light sparkled beneath her, as if an invisible wader were scattering handfuls of diamonds. And then embers came floating across the bay, holographic thistledown riding on the breeze.

She felt a tingle of nostalgia, as the sound of wind-chimes reached her, from faraway. She wondered if she'd imagined them. The embers burst into fireflies, dragonflies and damselflies, whizzing and skimming above the waves. Hundreds of nymphs and imagoes went twinkling, in every direction. Butterflies came from nowhere, fluttered up high and vanished in the setting sun, now dipping behind the mountains.

A full moon sailed upwards and shed a silver path across the bay.

"Soul on the Water," Dan said behind her. Mary turned.

He wore a white suit, white gloves and silver tie. Gazing into his eyes, for a moment she felt like a dumbstruck schoolgirl. He circled his hand toward the bay.

"This is what life would've been like without our earthly suffering. A phantom thing. All light and no matter. Gone in a flash. A pain free life, sweetheart, is no life at all." He smiled. "Although I agree. It's a beautiful dream… Champagne?"

She nodded.

He snapped his fingers. A silver bucket and two crystal flutes appeared on a tall table beside him. She stared at them in astonishment, clueless as to how he did that. He withdrew a bottle from the bucket, poured Champagne fizzing softly into the flutes and handed one to her.

"So, Mary, what will we drink to?"

She found her voice with a nervous laugh. "I feel like I'm meeting the Light Wizard for the first time, like the rest of the world, I'm" – she laughed again – "overcome."

"Are you happy to be here?" he said.

"Your apartment is amazing. I've never been so spoilt in my life." She waved her flute. "And I'm enchanted by this Holorama. It's breath-taking."

"You take my breath away, Mary."

She touched her gown. "Thank you, so much, for my gown. I can't believe how well it fits. You're obviously an expert with a needle and thread, as with everything else."

It was like the conversation with him on the phone in the Colcannon Restaurant. She felt shy all over again.

He frowned. "Sure, I haven't all day to sit around and sew. I do own a sewing machine."

"I don't." She laughed. "Honestly, you're amazing and I can't believe how well you look. Even better than last night." She sipped her Champagne, sensing him hesitate to say something. She looked out across the bay, at the moon's reflection on the water-light. "How was your evening with the Governors?"

"I was on top of the world after your call. I couldn't wait for morning to come." He caught this breath. "All day, the hours have felt like weeks. I want to be with you so much, it brings tears to my eyes." He gave a shudder. "Mary, what have you done to me?"

She lowered her head, overwhelmed by his intensity. "I didn't sleep at all last night," she said.

Dan pursed his mouth. "We should've been together. But let's not go there. Any more news on the vaccine?"

"Oh-" Mary stalled, from lover to employee. "There've been no reports of side-effects, not even a single headache, which is remarkable. I spoke to St Anthony's again this morning and we've agreed to bring the outpatient trials forward to this Tuesday. If things continue to go as well as they are, I won't have to go back to Dublin. They can keep me up to date over the phone." She took a sip from her flute. "I'm on standby in the event of an emergency."

"And vaccine production? When is that likely to be, if all goes to plan?" he said.

"Not long. Hopefully by the middle of next month." She smiled. "It's an incredibly stressful time for everybody. UDAN's

Drug Reps keep calling the hospital for news, every couple of hours, which has been a bit" – she glanced to the side – "distracting for the staff. I don't suppose you have anything to do with that?"

"Aye, everything. I can't afford to take the pressure off. Jane must've told you there've been more cases of the Pox in the States and Europe over the weekend. It was my suggestion to bring the outpatient trials forward. As a matter of fact, I spoke to your Dr, Flanagan myself last night. He was still in Balbriggan." He gave his lopsided smile. "What a nice gentleman. You're going to miss his soft manners, aren't you? Nothing like this rotten son of a bitch you've got here, hmm?"

"I was upset to hear about the new cases. That was the other reason why I couldn't sleep." She drew a breath, sensing his irritability. "Did…Did Sean know who he was talking to?"

"Sure, I wouldn't miss that trick." He gave a grunt into his flute. "You should've heard him licking my ass. Mr Udan this and Mr Udan that, give my love to Mary and all that jazz. If that bastard had laid one finger on you, I'd have ripped his fecken head off" – with his wincing smile – "that's the kind of gentleman I am. So, cheers! Here's to your Dr. Flanagan." He drained his flute and looked into her eyes. "Do you miss him?"

"He's just a good colleague and a kind man." Mary inclined her head. "Do you miss Soraya?"

She'd been hoping for an opportunity to ask about Soraya's dismissal, Jane told her about last night.

"Not at all," he said, "she's just a good harlot." He lifted the bottle from the bucket and topped up their flutes. "And she's that jealous of you, she wanted you to see me in the worst possible light. Did you ever see the mess she made of Lewis' scalp? I expected her to give him short back and sides, the vindictive hussy." He bit down on his lower lip. "Hell, hath no fury, like a woman scorned, hmm?"

"Talking about a woman scorned"-Mary softened her voice – "I thought you were back with her, particularly after Stefan told me you'd moved her into my apartment. I was so upset. Sean was kind enough to invite me away. It was completely innocent. He's a caring person."

"I could kill him." Dan shook his head. "Sorry, I don't mean that. It makes me sick to hear you say his name," he said. "You know, I never loved Soraya. How could I? I'd already seen your smile. Mary, you've nothing to worry about. Nothing happened between me and Soraya." His eyes misted. "I love you, so much. Please tell me, you love me."

"Dan Udan, I adore you." She stepped forward to place her flute down on the table. "I'd like to hold you. May I?" She opened her arms.

"That's all I want to hear." He gave a whoop and sealed her inside at bear hug, lifting her clean off the floor.

"Dan, not so tight! You don't know your own strength."

He put her down, nuzzling his face in her long hair. "So, tell me, light of my life, what would be your idea of a tropical island beach?"

She drew back to look at him. "Where did that come from?

"Go on, close your eyes and tell me what you see."

Mary closed her eyes. "A sleepy blue ocean. White sand, palm-trees and coconuts. Oh, I don't know, just the usual post-card image I suppose. I've never been to one."

"Would you like me to take you there?"

"I'd love that, one day." She smiled.

Dan took her hand. “Come with me.”

Chapter Thirty

Wildo appeared beside Lewis down by the surf, in swimming trunks, a frosted glass in each hand, cocktail brollies, sparkly straws.

"Foxy. Loads of people are arriving," Wildo said. "King is behind the bar shaking cocktails. I got us a couple of Tequila Sunrises."

Lewis accepted the glass, feeling a bit emotional after Dan's kindness to him. Wildo sat down and drank, burying his feet in the sand as Dan had done, although he was nothing like Dan. His profile was bluntly carved, his skin thicker, waxier. Ralph Wild was dumb supermarket beefcake beside the aesthetic masculinity of the man he adored. Lewis knew he was never going to get over him.

Wildo removed the straw from his glass to drain his last mouthful. "Hmm that was nice. I'm going to have another one of these. What about you, are you coming up to the bar?"

"No thanks, I'm going for a paddle."

Lewis left his half-empty glass in the sand and walked down to the water. Alone, he wiggled his toes in the spume, inhaling the air, now smelling of sun-baked dunes and driftwood, returning memories of seaside walks long ago. He raised his eyes to the Red Giant on the horizon, smearing illusory skies indigo and pink, glimmering, bright, dim, never quite reaching the extremes, but a tantalising, hypnotic twilight.

The lights went out. Lightning jagged across the sky. Up at the bar, the patter of bongos fell silent. A single spotlight illuminated the pool. Lewis looked up to see a pulpit suspended in mid-air above the water. And there was Dan, inside it, dazzling, in a double-breasted white suit and a glittering tie.

"Good evening, ladies and gentlemen, welcome to UDAN's Beach Holorama!" He gestured. "We completed it within two days, with a grand effort from our staff." He nodded. "Thanks again to all those who turned up to give me a hand. It just goes to show you what we can do when we put our heads together." He smiled.

"How about a stairway to the stars, hmm? Do you think we could pull that off in a couple of days?"

Applause rippled around the beach, whistles and whoops. Dan raised his hand to silence them. "Okay, it might take a wee bit longer. But the point is we can achieve anything, so long as we carry on working together, as one family."

From the side of the beach came the sound of spitting fat and creaks from the rotisseries starting to turn. Lewis lifted his nose to the wafts of pancakes cooking nearby.

"I don't want to dwell on it now," Dan said, "as you'll be discussing it in class. But I hope Friday's test was an eyeopener, making you all aware that the devil lurks just beneath the surface, of our civilised world.

"Be mindful. Listen to the voice of your own conscience. Have the courage to speak out against injustice and cruelty." He opened his hand. "But how about that young lady over there? The only one who didn't join the braying crowd." He sent out a warm smile, Lewis realised, obviously intended for Mary somewhere in the crowd. "You can thank our Mary for setting you all the best example, of courage. Don't be cowards, my friends, be heroes!" He raised his Champagne flute in the air with a winning smile. "I'd like you all to raise your glasses to Mary! God bless you, Mary."

"God bless you, Mary!" a cheerful chorus echoed behind Lewis.

Lewis turned his back to Dan, and staggered up the shadowy slope, grumbling to himself as he passed the faces raised to the pulpit. Bobby appeared in front of him, shirtless, truncheon squeezed inside a tight belt, almost bisecting his bloated midriff.

"Is everything all right, Lewis? Do you need help with anything?"

"Turns out that Mary is some kind of heroine," Lewis said, "yet she didn't suffer like I did. Know what Bobby? The mind boggles."

"The old centrifuge again?" Bobby twirled his forefinger. "Know exactly what you mean. Have a great time." He walked on.

Lewis ploughed on towards the bar, glanced up and stopped. Goosebumps tingled down his arms, to see Mary. To see what Dan must see.

She stood beside a low palm tree shimmering with fairy-lights. Her blonde hair appeared to create a halo around her face, and she wore a long silk gown, uncannily matched to her complexion. The woman looked as if she'd been dipped head-to-toe, in white gold.

She was watching Dan in his pulpit, her expression passive.

Only the fact that her mouth turned upwards naturally at the corners, gave her a secret, inner smile. She caught Lewis looking at her. Her smile widened and she came over, her gown seeming to liquefy as she moved. Beautiful wasn't quite the word. He was still trying to think of the right word as she bent to kiss him on his cheek, with her hand on his shoulder.

"Lewis. Are we all right now?" she whispered.

"I'm not sure about you, but I'm great. Where's the Christmas tree?"

"I didn't know there was one."

"I mean, you look rather decorative" – he rolled his eyes – "like you might've dropped off a Christmas tree."

She looked down at her gown. "It's a present from Dan. He made it himself."

"Very nice, if you like that sort of thing. I'm not one for-"

"I love it." She put her forefinger to her mouth. "Hush, do you mind, Lewis, I'd like to listen to the rest of Dan's statement."

Lewis faced the pulpit, seething. He couldn't believe she just told him to shut up. The least he'd expected from her was an apology.

"Sadly, I must convey the news that Phoenix Ra continues to blight our world," Dan said, "More cases of the Pox V 2 virus have been reported, claiming nineteen thousand and forty-one lives over the weekend, in Florida and closer to home, in London, Amsterdam, Paris, Berlin and Monaco-"

There were groans all round. Dan clasped his hands.

"Remember them in your prayers. And pray that Phoenix Ra and his misguided crew wake-up and put an end to their brutality. While we condemn evil, let's not forget our own sins last Friday and learn from them." He put his hand to his mouth, seeming to compose himself. When he spoke again his voice sounded husky.

"This is the Ceremony of Hope. So now, let's open our hearts to love, compassion and forgiveness. For without these three, there can be no hope. God bless you all and have a good evening."

The crowd cheered and clapped. The bongos pattered again. The Red Giant surged amber, illuminating the beach golden yellow, giving all visible skin an instant suntan, turning palm leaves glossy, windshields and parasols luminous. Lewis linked his arm through Mary's and pulled her along.

"Come on," he said, "let's have a cocktail. Have you ever had Sex on the Beach? You should. It'll put roses in your cheeks."

Wildo sat on a barstool, leaning with his back against the marble bar. "Hi Foxy! Hiya Mary!" he called, "Over here, you guys!"

"I'm not in the mood for him," Mary said.

"Don't be like that. He's not as thick as he looks, once you get to know him."

Wildo ordered three Sex on the Beach cocktails from King. He kept grinning at Mary, then stroked the backs of her fingers as he handed her the glass. Lewis felt her stiffen.

"That was pretty nifty, wasn't it, the way Udan came out of nowhere." Wildo chuckled. "Have pulpit will fly, yeah! That guy's so bleeding cool. Aw, bad news about Pee Ra. Aren't you lot working on the vaccine?" He cocked his head at Mary. "Isn't it time you got your finger out?"

"Worry about your own work." Mary kept her eyes lowered. Even on this lovely warm beach, Lewis thought, she could drop the temperature like a freezing wind.

Wildo smirked. "That's a classy frock you've got on. Are those real diamonds you got there?" He leaned forward as if to get a closer look, Mary drew back sharply. "What's bitten you? I just wanted a gander at your baubles. Come on, let's be friends, shake hands, love and compassion; yeah?" He thrust out his hand.

A gloved fist caught his wrist, swung him off the barstool and twisted his arm up his back. "Ah aha ha, you're hurting me, let go!"

"You lay one finger on her, you might live long enough to regret it, but don't count on it." Dan's voice reverberated eerily around the bar. People stopped to stare at him steering Wildo by his arm, hopping around in a circle. "Did you get that, Mr Wild?"

"I got that!" Wildo bared his teeth in agony. "Dan, you're breaking my arm, mate. I mean sir, please let me go!"

Dan glared at Lewis, keeping a grip on Wildo. "Aren't you supposed to be teaching this yob some manners?"

Lewis' hands started to shake, jostling the cocktail in his glass. "He was only looking at the... the twinkly things on Mary's dress, wasn't he, Mary?" He gave her an imploring look. She went up on her tiptoes to whisper something in Dan's ear. Dan's lips parted in a smile. He released Wildo, who let out a cry, and clasped his shoulder.

Mary looked at Lewis. "Weren't you and Ralph about to go for a swim?"

"That's right, come on Ralph." Lewis put his drink down on the bar. "Let's have that swim, it'll do us good." He was already walking away. Wildo came after him, hunched and hobbling at his side. They both increased their pace, tumbling down the slope.

"That was like a tidal wave, man. I feel sick. I think he's dislocated my shoulder." Wildo moaned. "And I'm a karate champion back home." He shot a glance behind him. "Udan's not watching, Foxy, can we stop a sec?" He paused to clutch his arm to his chest. "Bloody well hurts, man."

Waiting for Wildo to recover, Lewis watched the Student Bongo Band crouched in the sand, hammering away on their bongos, shaking their hair, as semi-naked students bounced around like rubber balls. A girl in a pink bikini appeared to be moving purposefully towards him. It was the little blonde student, the one who always wore pink, walking nimbly down the beach. She stopped in front of Lewis and Wildo and without appearing to address either one of them, levelled a question.

"Would you like to see something absolutely incredible?"

Wildo looked at Lewis and then at her. "Like what?"

"I can't tell you because he's got to see it first, for himself. Just you" – she pointed at Lewis – "have been chosen."

They followed her to a couple huddled behind an L shaped windshield. Lewis recognised them. Elizabeth, a doctor and her partner Jason, a nurse.

"These are my friends, Liz and Jas. We all work together at the Infirmary." Her smile was overly sweet, directed at Wildo. "My name's Abby, I'm a student nurse, second year. You're Wildo, aren't you?"

"Yeah, I'm Wildo from down-under." He grinned. "Did you know your nickname is Pinkie?"

"Hello Lewis." Liz interrupted them, fresh-faced, thirty-something. In a sundress, she looked like one of the students. "Have you got over your ordeal?"

"I'm fine. It was an interesting experience." He puffed out

a breath. "So, where's this 'absolutely incredible' thing I've got to see?"

Liz waved them forward. "You'd better sit down!"

Lewis and Wildo sat with them in a snug circle. Liz reached inside a beach bag and removed a large brown envelope, handing it to Lewis. There was nothing to signify its contents and it hadn't been sealed.

"There's a letter inside addressed to you," Liz said, "and there are some photocopies, but they won't mean anything until you read what's in the letter. The person who gave them to me suggested you read the letter first."

"Do you lot know what this is about?" Lewis looked around at the three medics.

"We do, but we don't know what's in the letter and we're dying to know." Jason's voice was slurred. "Go on, Lewis, take a look."

Lewis withdrew a dozen or so A4 sized photocopies from the brown envelope. At first glance, a magnification of a mound of termites; red ants fighting, their bodies entangled, bracket fungi, an oyster mushroom. He handed them over to Wildo. "Pictures of creepy crawlies and mushrooms."

Wildo muttered, "They're selling merchandise." He looked up. "What've you got? Magic mushrooms?"

Jas and Liz exchanged a flicker of amusement. Lewis discovered a smaller envelope amongst the pictures, sealed, bearing his name in small print. He opened it, with a little smile at the others before reading it to himself.

My Dear Lewis Allen,

You will have heard that I have been dismissed from

Dan's employment for following his orders and preparing you for the Ceremony of Blood. The truth is that Dan has asked me to leave temporarily, because Mary does not want me near him.

She despises me because she is jealous of my relationship with Dan. Dan is on a quest to enlighten her soul and to this end, he must gain her trust and allow her to fall in love with him. It is the only way he can cure her of her Scientist's Hubris, which troubles him deeply. When he has succeeded, he will call me back to him, as he always does, to continue God's work.

The Dark Path is Dan's true Philosophy of Enlightenment.

Lewis you were right, you are his real Saint. Dan has denounced the Reality Treatise to test your commitment as his spiritual partner. Embrace all that he has written about the Dark Path, and you will earn your place in his heart and in the After Life. Spread the Word to your student friends and they will all find peace in heaven.

Dan believes suffering perfects the human soul. To prove this point, I have enclosed images of his back, where he has carried a terrible burden for many years, refusing treatment.

As a boy he was tortured and mutilated. Evil scientists with no respect for life, or for the soul (does this remind you of someone?) tried to create chaos in his body, inserting all types of foreign DNA under his flesh. You can see the results for yourself.

Dan's choice to suffer has enlightened his soul and brought him so close to God, he is the only one who understands God's creation. Suffering has gifted him with great genius and great strength and now he is a Superman!

I am sharing these facts with you as I took great pity on you during the preparation of your body, although I could not show it. I think you are a dear, sweet man and you suffered with great dignity and courage.

Now that Dan is testing your commitment yet again, I feel it is too much, so I am pointing you in the right direction, back towards the Dark Path.

Please do not tell Dan about my help or about the images of his back in your possession, as he would be angry with me! It is far better for you, Lewis, if he thinks you have gained fresh insight, through your own suffering. Lewis Allen, I wish you the forbearance to shine on. Everything depends on you, now

God Speed and Bless You,

Soraya, p.a. to Dan Udan

Lewis arrived at the end and went straight back to the beginning, to stare at every word, to make sure it said what he thought it said, until his eyes burned. He looked up.

"Is this some kind of a joke?"

"What does Soraya have to say?" Liz met his gaze.

"That the pictures are of Dan's back," Lewis said. "He was mutilated as a boy." He curled his lip. "I don't believe it. Those are images of ecological habitats. You must think I'm an idiot."

"Let me read the letter!" Wildo snatched it out of his hand.

Liz shuffled up to Lewis on her knees, dragging the sandy towel beneath her.

"Did you know that Jane O'Neil is Dan's aunt?" She breathed minty breath in his face. "The day he arrived here, she called me into a private meeting with two other doctors. "She told us if ever Dan Downs was brought to the Infirmary, unconscious, with no heartbeat, we were not to treat him, or remove his clothes, or interfere with him in any way, but to put him into isolation and call her." Liz looked penetratingly into Lewis' eyes. "Jane said his physiology was totally different to anything we would've encountered before because" – she gave a sickly smile – "he's a transgenic mutant."

"I bloody well knew it!" Wildo blurted, "The Dark Path is for real! Aw, Jees, that means I'm still a crazy fucked up kid!"

"Wildo, will you shut up!" Lewis grabbed the letter. "This is serious. Don't you think I know the Dark Path is for real? I've suffered on it." He widened his eyes at Liz. "Are you telling me the truth?"

Liz sat back against the windshield.

"I swear it on my life. Soraya knew which of us doctors had been warned. She approached me with the photocopies, maybe because she saw me at the Ceremony. She asked me to look at them and to give my opinion." Liz drew a breath. "I took one look and said, 'This is Dan's body, isn't it?' She said yes, and asked me to give them to you, because she wanted you to know the truth. She knew you were more likely to believe it coming from a doctor. The woman is not stupid."

Lewis couldn't move, but just sat there staring, until Liz's face swam in front of his eyes.

Abby laughed. "Look at him! He doesn't know what to believe."

But Lewis' instincts had been primed. His heart accelerated, bile simmered into his throat, goose bumps rose all over his body, remembering his primal fear of Dan Udan. All those strange feelings he couldn't put his finger on, the sense of a vast, hidden power. His fascination for the man with the stratospheric eyes and something more than human, or as it turned out, less than human.

"I believe you," he said. "I want to see the photocopies again." Lewis studied the images carefully, as Jason passed around a bottle of whiskey.

"It's very sad," Liz said, taking a swig. "Dan can't let anybody get close to him and he won't let doctors treat him because of his faith. He's got to spend the rest of his life trapped inside that mess."

Lewis was thinking, how unbelievable, yet strangely inevitable that this should be his beloved Dan. To think, only yesterday morning, he'd held this man in his fantasies, put his cheek against his muscled back and gripped those slender hands. He frowned, gazing at an image of two orange circles, overlapping. Wildo gave the photocopy a desultory flick.

"That looks like Hubble's' image of a supernova. Do you know the one I mean?"

Lewis caught his breath. "Wait a minute-" He did know. He'd been given a book when he was a boy, of images taken by the Hubble Space Telescope. "Those orange rings, they're exactly the same pattern." Dan's words flashed across his mind. *'What does that make me?'*

Lewis gaped at Wildo, teetering at the edge of something too fantastic, too incredible to put into words, the strongest hunch he'd ever felt in his life. He knew exactly what to look for, rifling through the scans of Dan's back, spluttering with excitement. He identified quasar, starburst, cat's eye, the red spider nebula. And there were others. Wildo agreed.

"And that's Messier Eighty-Three, right there in that yellowish bit." Lewis was almost choking now, from excitement. Liz and Jason listened but lacking any reference to the book Lewis and Wildo were talking about, they couldn't be convinced.

Abby got up and started to dance around their windshield, shifting her feet to guitars and bongos playing flamenco, coming up to Wildo, gyrating her hips in his face. Wildo said in Lewis' ear, "If that's what Udan really looks like without his kit on, and the press ever finds out, they'll lynch him, man. They'll blast UDAN Corps right out of the water." He laughed, thumping Lewis on the back. "Who knows, mate, there might be something in it for us, if we play our cards right. Keep that under your hat, yeah."

Wildo shot up, grabbed Abby by her waist and swung her around, whooping. "Did you hear that little Pinkie? We're gonna be rich one day!"

Lewis watched them cavorting, taking slugs of whiskey, with a tingling awareness that the world had changed forever.

Jas came over and sat beside him, grabbed the bottle and took a slurp, finishing with a loud exhalation.

"Listen" – he gave a delayed shudder – "we can't make a judgment until we see the Hubble images for ourselves. First thing tomorrow, look it up on the web, see if they've got that book about the Cosmos."

Lewis' heart jolted. He turned to Jason. "Oh my God, he was talking about the cosmos." He opened his eyes wide. "Jas" – he grasped the other man's wrist – "I know what he is." Lewis raised his voice. "Dan said he could mend the web. I thought he meant the virtual reality world, to do with his holograms. He was talking about the real web, the cosmic web. Jas, do you know what this means? Dan's not the messenger, he's it! He's the Cosmic Soul."

Jason lifted Lewis' hand from his arm. "Cool it, Lewis, you're getting carried away. Dan Udan is a freak of nature, plus the fact his heart keeps stopping, he might not have long to live."

"I don't expect you to understand. Dan said I had to work it out for myself." Lewis pulled himself up, feet mashing the towel into the sand as he stumbled about, suddenly drunk. "I know what he is and I'm going to tell him."

Liz caught him by the shoulders, her face wouldn't keep still. "Don't say anything! O'Neil swore us to secrecy. Dan will go mad. You're drunk. Go home before you get us into trouble!"

Lewis flapped his arms, shaking her off. "I'm not drunk, I'm jubilant. I've been chosen. I love him, Liz. I'll never stop loving him." Tears stung his eyes. "And on that truly happy note, I'm going home." He turned from the windshield and ploughed his way up the slope.

He hid behind his very own blue and white parasol, cocked at an angle, pretending to watch the girls in grass skirts, laughing and weaving their hands above their heads. But his eyes were fixed on Dan, standing at the bar with Mary, his gloved hand, possibly the longest fingers he'd ever seen, cupping her elbow.

"*I know who you are,*" Lewis whispered, "*I know what you are.*"

Chapter Thirty-One

"Mary. Don't look round. Lewis is staring at us." Dan breathed in her ear. "The wee idjit thinks I can't see him." He patted her arm. "Come on, we'll go to our tipi."

Mary ducked her head stepping inside the tipi, festooned with lotus flowers and orchids, like a tiny marquis decorated for a wedding. She sat on the mattress piled with velvet cushions, sprinkled with rose petals, inhaling the heady, tropical fragrance.

"Oh, it's lovely in here." She patted the cushion beside her. "What are you doing? Come and sit next to me."

He puzzled her. He was down on his hands and knees, sweeping sand and gravel away from the floor beneath, clearing an area of blue tiles. He circled his hand above it, like a magician, in his white gloves.

"Are you conjuring something out of the ground?" She laughed

"Not quite," he said, "There's a tunnel down here." Light rays flickered between the tiles. There was heavy scraping, the sound of stone moving on stone. A gap appeared in the floor, widening into a manhole. "There's a room at the end of the tunnel where I keep some of my work, where I go to be alone" – with his lopsided smile – "I'd like to share it with you. Would you come with me?"

"Honestly, there's never a dull moment with you, is there." She stood up to peer down the hole. "But shouldn't we tell someone? People might think we've vanished into thin air."

"Sure, they won't notice we're gone until we're back again. Come on, there's a rope ladder. Take off your shoes and throw them in, after me." He slipped down inside it and landed without a sound. Mary sat on the edge, kicked off her high heels and hesitated, legs dangling. He reached up with both hands. "Don't worry, angel, I'll catch you."

She slid down into his arms and held him for a moment, so warm and broad, like hugging a sun-baked tree on a summer's day.

"Angel, I love you so much." He sighed. "Come on, before I lose it." He led her by the hand, down a long airless corridor to a black door. "Open it," he said.

She turned the handle and stepped inside, casting her eyes about a vast, empty dome with fluorescent lights positioned vertically around the walls. It was like a huge, gutted theatre hall, smelling of dust and vinegar. Dan closed the door behind them. "Come with me." He strode ahead. She followed him across a black, glittering floor.

"It's massive. What do you do here?"

"Create holograms," he said over his shoulder.

"With what? There's nothing here."

"Up there." He pointed to the ceiling. She peered into the shadowy vault and saw hundreds of transparent pipes spanning the length of the dome, swooping up and down in waves, with thousands of glittering filaments inside.

"What are those pipes for?" She tottered in her high heels

to keep up.

"They're not pipes, they're nano-lasers," he said. "We're inside an enormous Ceegee. Do you know much about my Ceegees?"

"You mean we're inside a Crystal Grotto?"

"Yes. Look at the walls you'll see the crystal facets. Each one is a holographic pixel, a quantum of holographic film. When the lasers light up, they'll reconstruct the hologram." He had that nervous tremor in his voice. "Come on slow coach, it's starting." He grabbed her hand, walking so fast, she had to skip. She could feel the tremble in his fingers, pulling her across the endless floor.

The sides of the vault began to stream like melting wax. The crystals chattered, repositioning their settings. Dan let her go first up a stone staircase leading to a hollow in the wall. Mary peered in, perplexed to see a sparkling grotto with a spindly glass sofa in the middle.

"The best room in the house," he said. "Go on take a seat." The walls looked as if they were made of snow, like a Santa's Grotto without a Santa. She sat on the sofa, quite nervous. Dan settled next to her, his leg nudging against hers as he reached inside his jacket pocket.

"Here, you go first." He handed Mary a small brown pot. She turned the lid and discovered a silver wand with a ring, dripping with detergent.

"Bubbles?" She smiled at him. "You want me to blow bubbles?" She laughed and blew gently, a stream of tiny bubbles rippled from her lips.

"Lovely, lovely." He sat back and folded his arms. Mary watched them drift away and burst, one by one. Her throat tightened. She put her hand over her mouth, blinking back tears.

"Surely, you're not upset by that?" he said.

"Blowing bubbles reminds me of my mother. She died in an accident when I was four." She looked at him. "I suppose you know about that."

"Yes, and I can tell you that your mum, Hannah, is at peace where she is." He gazed at her, with a dreamy look on his face, she'd seen before. "Her soul is in a happy place."

Mary lowered her eyes. "I wish you didn't say things like that. My mother is gone. She doesn't exist. To say she's happy is meaningless."

"You've made your world a cold and clinical place, Mary," he said, "what's the most difficult thing you've had to live with?"

"Oh, just that" – in her flinty tone – "coming to terms with the emptiness after loved ones have gone. But your world can't be easy." She looked at him. "What's the most difficult thing you've had to live with?"

"Wanting what I can't have."

He leaned over to tease the pot from her fingers, raised the wand to his puckered lips and grew an enormous bubble, sending it off with a wobble. "Wanting it so much that it consumes every moment, until I've got to waste a whole day in bed covered in my own slime, because I can't stop, not even to wash myself." He flashed his luminous eyes at her. "What goes on in my world would take your breath away."

"What is it you want?" she said.

"Us, in a bed, with no skin between us."

"That sounds painful."

"But in my dream, we don't feel the pain." He gazed into

her eyes. "We're so desperate to touch one another, we become one orgasm."

She resisted a smile. "Don't you mean one organism?"

"Sure, I mean what I say." He raised his eyes. "Mary," he said, "would you see that!"

She looked up. His bubble had grown enormous, filling the space above them, spanning the width of the sofa.

"Oh, you!" She laughed at the huge bubble wobbling to retain its sphere. "Trust you. It's a hologram." She clapped her hands. "It looks so real."

He knelt up on the sofa and prodded the bottom of the bubble. "That's strange, it doesn't burst."

She watched him, the Light Wizard, the genius, acting the clown. "You're just full of surprises." She smiled.

"Hmm." He removed his finger and examined it. "I thought so. It's a dream bubble." He reached down and patted her knee. "Go on, angel, imagine the most beautiful place you can think of. It can be an imaginary scene or somewhere you've been. Ask the bubble to show it to you."

Mary rose to her feet, happy to indulge him, and gazed inside the bubble. The membrane shivered, rippling like a puddle. She lowered her eyes and drew on a memory from her childhood, walking in the countryside with her father.

A meadow had appeared before them, bursting with wildflowers. She gazed upon all the dots and splodges, mists and tall weeds hanging over the field, feeling the colours stroke her eyes. Mummy had been dead for over a year. It was the first time Mary had smiled.

She felt warmth on her cheek, a light shone in the corner of her eye, she turned towards it. There, where the room's gloomy vault had been, was a sunny meadow, bursting with wildflowers, reaching as far as her eyes could see.

She held her breath and walked to the edge of the grotto, gazing out across her memory, with every detail filled in: The joyful and forlorn, the high and the humble, the proud and the shy, shouting to be heard in a universe of colour.

"How did you know?" she said.

He arrived by her side. "Not long after I first saw you at Trinity College, I dreamt about a flower meadow. And over there in that corner" – he pointed across the field – "was a wee girl standing beside her father. I realised it was you and that the memory was yours." He put his arm around her shoulders.

"That day something happened between us, you won't remember, but our eyes met, and our souls connected. We've been connected ever since that day and will be, for the rest of time." He smiled down at her.

She looked up into his hooded eyes, with a flickering recollection, of having told Jane about her first precious memory after her mother had died.

Could Dan have been listening behind the door in Jane's apartment, as he said he once did? Had he travelled to Cork's countryside that year and discovered the ancient sight for himself? There must be a scientific explanation for this coincidence, or else he'd read her mind precisely. Which was impossible.

"I don't believe you dreamt this," Mary said. She recalled Desi's reference to a meadow earlier. "I know illusionists are good at putting ideas into people's heads, just before they offer to read their minds."

Dan dropped his arm from her shoulder. She sought his

hand and linked her fingers through his gloved fingers. She gazed out across the meadow.

"But it doesn't make it any less magical. If anything, it's more magical. Because this is your beautiful science." She sighed. "It looks exactly as I remember it. All the feelings are coming back to me. I want to laugh and cry. Dan, your art, your science, is truly spectacular and" – she turned her head to look at him – "I love it."

"Do you think I'd lie to you about the moment I saw you?" His voice was husky. "The moment that changed my life?"

She sensed him wanting to pull away and tightened her grip on his hand. "I didn't mean to spoil it, or to sound ungrateful."

"You're right." He gave a little shake to her hand. "Let's not spoil the moment. There's somebody I'd like you to meet."

They went down into the meadow, moving through waist high flowers, throwing rainbows onto his white suit as he walked in front of her. Mary grinned from ear to ear, like a little girl, amongst the pink mists of grasses, vanishing and reappearing as she passed. She saw a flash beneath the rainbows. She heard laughter. A child shot up in the middle of the flowers, looked about furtively and ducked down.

"You can't find me, daddy" – the same babyish laughter – "I can see you! You can't see me!"

Dan turned around. "Did you see which way he went?"

"Over there in the flowers." Mary pointed, still grinning. "He's a hologram, isn't it he?"

"He's a wee rascal." Dan raised his voice. "We're not playing hide and seek now, son, come and say hello." The child popped up behind him, shook his head at Mary and put his forefinger on his lips, signalling to her not to tell. Dan spun around.

The little boy laughed and ran into the meadow. He had silver hair shimmering down to his waist. She'd seen holographic animations before, of faces and busts, but had never encountered a model that resembled a living, breathing human being. This must be UDAN Corporations most advanced technology, the next big invention to astonish the world.

"Lucida, I'm not running after you!" Dan looked at Mary. "He's showing off. I think he's taken a shine to you. He'll probably come back if you call him."

"His name suits him." She called across the meadow. "Lucida…Lucida!" The boy came flickering towards her, with rainbows inside his tunic swirling like colours inside a bubble. He strode straight up to her, as bold as little boys are, standing four foot high.

"Are you an angel?" He demanded to know.

Mary knelt on one knee to look at him. "No, I'm just an ordinary woman." She inclined her head. "But you look like an angel, with your long silver hair and your silver eyes."

"Lucida," Dan said, "this is my friend, Mary. She's a very kind lady, so you might want to give her a kiss."

Lucida's expression became coy. Mary felt a flutter in her chest. There was something hauntingly familiar about his smile. He had a childish sweetness, and yet his eyelids were hooded, wrinkled like an old man's.

His face held so much fascination, more enchanting than beautiful. He offered his mouth up to hers. She forgot that he wasn't real and put her lips on his, feeling only a sunshine warmth, a kiss without human touch.

"I've caught you a butterfly." He put up his fist, uncurling his fingers. "It's a Gatekeeper." A small butterfly with orange and dark spotted wings sat inside his palm. "You can keep him, if you want to."

"Oh, isn't he a beauty! We don't get many of those in Ireland, thank you." She held out her hand and it fluttered into her palm. She gasped to see that it was real and not a hologram. She looked up at Dan. "How do you do this?"

"But I caught it!" Lucida cried. "I'll show you how. I'll catch more for you!" He skipped. "Mary, Mary! Come and play with me" – reaching out his hand – "may I hold your hand?"

Mary laughed. "He's gorgeous. I can't believe he's not real."

She watched the little moonshine boy catching butterflies, reaching, hopping, ducking. He kept coming back to her with his fists full, releasing them into the air. He called out their names as they fluttered around her head, landing on her hair and the front of her dress. Laughing his babyish laughter to see her delight, that a little boy like him could catch so many, *that were real.*

Dan left them to play. Mary saw him strolling through the meadow, with his head lowered, his hands in his pockets. A man in a contemplative mood, enjoying his garden.

"Are you leaving now?" Lucida's solemn eyes gazed up at her. "Will I be on my own again?" Mary reminded herself he was just an illusion, an artificial intelligence, albeit more sophisticated than Jolly.

"It's been lovely to meet you. I'm sure we'll meet again. Look, Lucida!" She held up her arm where half a dozen butterflies perched open-winged, tingling on her skin.

He gave his sweet, seductive smile. "Remember me-" he whispered and vanished.

She couldn't move for a moment. It was like waking from

a dream about a much loved child, long deceased, capturing perfectly all his uniqueness, as if he were still alive. She felt the same sickly sensation inside, where past grief had lodged itself, never to heal. The dead no longer existed. Lucida didn't exist.

Dan stood in a sea of rainbows, beside a waterfall, that kept disappearing and reappearing as she approached him, vaporising in a misty pool around his knees.

"That was grand, seeing you two getting along so well." His face had a ghostly sheen in the pale blue light. "He's a lovely wee lad, isn't he?"

"For a moment I completely forgot he wasn't real," she said. "It's a cruel trick, in a way, the ultimate deception of the human heart."

He laughed. "A bit like life, then." With his gloved forefinger, he tilted her head back to look at him. "Are you cross with me, angel? Would you prefer me to make him out of flesh and blood?"

"No. You stay doing what you're good at." She flashed him a mischievous smile. "Leave real life to me. That's what you employ me for."

"We agree on that much, then." He blew on her lips. Mary resisted the urge to clasp his head, to bring his mouth down on hers. She drew away from him.

"I don't recall a waterfall in my meadow," she said.

"There wasn't one. This is the gateway to my private rooms." He put his hand into the water-light, colouring his glove aquamarine. "Through there is where I used to stay before the Penthouse was completed. I've visited here many times over the years, to keep an eye on you all."

"You mean you've been spying on us" – she teased – "do

you spy on us in our apartments?"

"I'm a busy man. Sure, I've got better things to do than watch y' all brushing your teeth."

"I'm not sure if I believe you" – flirting like a schoolgirl, she tugged his sleeve – "may I see your hideaway or is it off limits?"

He took her hand, brought it up to his mouth and blew gently on her fingers. "Not at all," he said, "I've been expecting you."

Dan led her through the water-light. He walked her down a short corridor to another door and opened it with a flourish. "Welcome to my bedroom suite."

Chapter Thirty-Two

It was a room with a chandelier hanging from a low ceiling, dark wood panelling around the walls, a solid oak four-poster bed with black velvet curtains tied back. Persian rugs, a midnight blue leather-top desk and above it, a wall-to-wall UDAN Window featuring the meadow they'd left behind.

Mary delayed commenting, absorbed in the sedate atmosphere he'd created. It exuded the kind of mature masculinity that made her feel secure, free to move around and indulge her curiosity. She turned a knob on one of the panels and discovered a massive wardrobe bulging with crisp, white shirts on one side, and dark suits hanging on the other.

His underwear was either black or white, boxer shorts, socks, T-shirts, were all meticulously folded, expensive, tasteful, if a little staid. She wondered where he kept his leather tunics. She turned to watch him by the bedside table, twisting the cork from a bottle of Champagne. A young man with unruly curls, in a white suit and silver tie, looking somewhat mismatched in these sombre, stately surroundings.

He put a flute fizzing with Champagne into her hand. Mary sat on the edge of the bed and looked up at the chandelier.

"I like this room very much, but it's not what I expected. I thought it'd be more flamboyant, full of drawings and photographs."

"I've plenty of rooms like that at Lacerta." He stood inches from her knees, waving his flute under his nose, sniffing like a connoisseur. "All my rooms are designed according to their special purpose."

"Does this room have a special purpose?" She looked up at him. The chandelier shone light through his hair and dappled his face with shadows. He didn't answer. He put his flute down on the bedside table and pulled open the drawer. He removed a small leather wallet and handed it to her.

"Open it," he said. It was a quiet order.

She placed her flute beside his and took the wallet. It fell open in her hands, its only content, a six-inch golden needle. "A sewing needle?" She blinked. "What's it for?" Perhaps he wanted to teach her how to sew? "Is this the room where you made my dress?"

"It has nothing to do with sewing. But it is for you." He sat beside her on the bed. "I want you to look at it and tell me what you think it's used for?"

Mary withdrew the needle from its felt fixture and held it up to the light. It was thick and incredibly sharp.

"It's some sort of medical needle, isn't it? A vet's needle for injecting rhino hides." She laughed. He opened his hand and she placed it carefully in his palm. "I think it might be an antique," she said. "Has it ever been used?"

He compressed his mouth. "Not until today." He inhaled, then exhaled, an audible breath. "I'm going to insert it into your chest." He kept his eyes fixed on Mary. "I'm going to attach it to a tube and suck the blood from your heart."

"Dan, that's not funny," she whispered.

"Of course, it's not funny." There was a tremor in his voice. "You're going to suffer a heart attack."

"Please, stop it." She put her hands over her ears and stared at him, adrenalin prickling inside her chest.

Dan reached for her flute. "Drink this. It'll help with the nerves." His tone was gentle. Mary accepted it, with a trembling hand. She gulped a few mouthfuls, assessing her options for escape. Her only defence was to touch him.

He sat with his forearms resting on his thighs, one gloved hand twirling the needle.

"I can't believe I told you, just like that." He hung his head. "The point is, I can't explain myself to you at all... without you doubting me. There's something you needed to know about us, that I should've explained to you. Instead, I've left the mystery to unfold, to let God's will speak for itself." He glanced up at her and hung his head again. "Aye, well, this is where the vague look comes into your eyes. There's a reason for everything, and that includes this." He held up the needle, pinching it between his forefinger and thumb.

"I've no idea what you're talking about," she murmured.

"I'm talking about Lucida." He turned to face her, lifting one knee up onto the bed. "I thought you might've seen yourself in him, or something about me. But there you go." He smiled a wistful smile. "The hologram is a projection of a child who's haunted my dreams, since I was fourteen. My future son. The day I set my eyes on you, I knew I'd found his mother." He hunched his shoulders. "Can you believe that?"

"It's what you believe, and I respect that." She avoided looking into his eyes.

"And yet, you fell in love with him." He waved the needle.

"Your heart is in the right place. As always, your heart knows better than your head." He gazed at her, unblinking, until a tear dripped onto his cheek. "Lucida is waiting to be born. He's a very special child. The best of both of us."

"I thought he was enchanting. Now that you mention it, he did seem familiar… It probably was you I saw in him." The glint of the needle weaving between his fingers, caught her eye.

"He has a tough journey ahead. It's important he has a grand start in life. Our love must support him for a very, long time." He gave a brimming smile. "He'll have the loveliest mum in the world and the brightest dad in the universe. He'll be very smart, only" – he wrinkled his nose, perhaps at his own conceitedness – "he'll never be as smart as me. That's against the laws of nature."

"You're right." She nodded. "I should think it would be impossible for anybody to be as smart as you, ever again."

"Ach, it's weird you should say that, as if you had faith in me. Because things aren't as they should be between us, are they, angel? You're not ready to do God's work" – toying with the needle – "If I told you that our coming together in this room was written in the stars at the beginning of time, and that the Cosmic Soul dreamed of a night of romance between us, would you believe me? You'd probably tell me to get my head examined." He lowered his eyes with a smile that hinted at regret.

"Oh, Mary. You were supposed to have absolute faith in me by now. Enough faith to surrender your soul into my hands." He gave a weary sigh. "So much for God's dream of romance." He lifted the needle up in front of her eyes. "This is meant to be a symbol of the profoundest trust a woman can have in a man.

The trust needed to create a miracle, beginning with a mother's blood and a father's thirst for life."

"What possible reason could you have for" – she started to swallow convulsively – "sucking blood from someone's heart … other than to, to…put an end to life?"

He rested his hand on his knee, exposed an inch of light, olive skin, between his glove and sleeve.

"It can't be anybody's blood, Mary. It's got to be yours. With your blood inside me, there'll be no skin between us. I'll be able to make love to you." A dreamy look came over his face. "All I want to do for the rest of my life, is to make love to you."

"But Dan" – she tried to hide the tremor in her voice, her palms drenched in cold perspiration – "if you put that needle into my heart, I'm going to die. You'll wake up from this dream with my corpse beside you. Is that what you want? Do you want me to die?"

"You'll feel like you're dying, but it won't last." He smiled faintly. "Your soul will pass out of your body, but then I'll call you back. All you need is faith. Without faith you'll endure a terrifying experience, which is the last thing I want for you. In the stars it's written as a blissful moment between us."

"Dan… darling, I think you're confused." She clasped her hand around his gloved hand, so close to the bare skin of his wrist, she could feel his unnatural heat. "This is your illness. This is your body telling you what you need." She could hear her pulse throbbing in her ears, willing herself to reach out and touch his skin.

"All this time, you've managed to suppress your cravings. But you've gone on too long." She put gentle pressure on his hand, to encourage him to drop the needle. "Don't you understand what's happening to you?" She searched his eyes. "Dan, you're hungry. I'll take you down to the biosynth lab. I'll give you all the blood you need. We don't need to tell anybody. Dan, my love, it can be our secret-"

He shook her hand away and rose from the bed. He stooped over the open drawer and removed a folded white napkin, put it on the table and placed the golden needle on top of it. He drew out a long, transparent tube and a large syringe.

Mary leapt off the bed and ran to the door. She rattled the handle, trying to open it. The door was locked. The rim of light from the corridor on the other side was gone. There was no gap to be seen. As if the door and wall had somehow fused. She turned and leaned against it, her knees weak, struggling to take deep breaths. Slow down. Think-

"Let me go back and fetch Connie. He can help you." Her voice was sharp with panic. "This isn't your fault. All the experts who handled your case in the past, should've done more to help you. Dan, you can't-"

Her legs gave way, to see him attach the needle and syringe to the tube. He puckered his lips, spitting mouthfuls of saliva inside the tube's opening. She didn't want to know why and didn't have the strength to ask. The full impact of her predicament struck her like a body-blow.

If she touched him – then what? There was no way out of here. She sank onto her knees, bent forward and hugged her ribs. His quiet voice reached beyond the roaring in her ears.

"Come and lie down on the bed."

"Please… don't… hurt me."

"I don't want to hurt you, Mary. I just want you to come and lie down on the bed," he said in his gentle voice, "surely, that's not asking too much."

"Let me go, Dan, please-" She fixed her eyes on the carpet, a dark blur.

"I'll ask you again, once more, kindly... Come and lie down on the bed."

"But you don't know what you're doing." She put her face in her hands. "Tomorrow when you're back in reality, you'll regret everything, like you did before...Please, let me get help for us, please-" Mary flinched, already anticipating the rant of the mad clown.

He gave an exasperated sigh. "This is supposed to be romantic."

She sensed him move across the carpet and looked up from her hands. Dan squatted down in front of her, with his wrists resting on his knees. She raised her eyes to his face, his expression one of pity, mingled with curiosity.

"Mary. I know you can't tell me, that you love me. But you will say that you adore me. Why is that, hmm?" He inclined his head. "I guess what you adore about me, has nothing to do with who I am, but my talents. Maybe, even, my substantial wealth and grand success. My potential, one day, to be your ideal man, once you've taken your scalpel to me.

"Mary. There's nothing wrong in you wanting me to be that perfect, clean-cut guy. Except that I'm so much more than the man of your surgical proposals. Whatever you've assumed about me, angel face, you've got it wrong." He smiled. "I hope that's a comfort to you, so."

"Dan, I do love you" – her lips quivered – "so much, I'd do anything to save you. If you let me out of here, I can still do that."

"There's no escape," he said. "This room has been sealed off. Neither of us can leave, until Lucida has been conceived."

He looked up at the ceiling, then into her eyes. "Don't assume you're the only one who'll suffer. I'll suffer. If you carry on without faith in me. Mary, please" – he clenched his hands and raised them up, like a man pleading with God – "please, discover some faith in me. Make it soon. I don't want to use force. But I will if I must, otherwise we'll rot here."

The illusionist held all the cards. If she touched him and he suffered a seizure, she'd still be trapped in this room. When he woke, this scene could, and probably would, start, all over again. With the first wave of resignation, Mary felt sick. Her only hope was to distract him.

"Would you like me to stroke your hair?" She raised her hand.

Dan smiled, showing his big, white teeth. "I'd love that." He extended his hand. "Let me help you to your feet." She slid her hand into his. Her feet flew off the floor as he lifted her into his arms, cradled like a new bride.

He carried her over to the bed and laid her down. Mary's hand shook as she reached out to his hair, to stroke him, hoping, somehow, to soothe him. Dan caught her wrist. "You can stroke my hair later. We need to get this over with, first." Mary twisted her arm to try and free herself from his grip. "I'm sorry, angel, I must restrain you-"

She heard the rattle of metal as he snapped a handcuff around her wrist. "Give me your other hand, Mary."

She turned away from him, her arm tight against her chest. "God give me patience, Mary, give me your hand!" She cried out as he loomed over her and grabbed her other wrist.

Dan ignored her quiet sob as he wound a white ribbon around the handcuffs, to pull her hands up to a brass ring, protruding from the headboard.

He fed the ribbon through the ring, tied a knot and bow. He unfastened her gown at the shoulders and flanks, released the hooks and eyes he'd sewn on himself, enabling him to slide it from her body, with her hands shackled above her head.

She knew then that he'd planned all this, down to the last detail.

Bare breasted, in her underwear, he didn't look twice. He went to the wardrobe and returned with a blanket to cover her, leaving her left breast exposed. He shook off his jacket, let it drop to the floor, loosened his tie and undid his top button. He sat on the edge of the bed, flapped open the napkin and tucked it inside his collar.

"I need to be sick," she said.

He thumbed her cheek, brushing away a tear. "I put something in the Champagne, to stop that from happening. It's a strong muscle relaxant. You should be feeling calmer now" – in his mellow voice – "calm enough to remain still, while I insert the needle. Do you have any questions before we begin?"

Mary closed her eyes. "Will you promise me that my aunt Sarah, in New Zealand, receives my Last Will and Testament… It's in the bottom drawer of my office desk, in Clarendon Street."

"There's no need for morbid thoughts, Mary. You're going to live."

"Dan, it's not too late." She looked up into his eyes. "If you let me go now, I'll always love you. I'll stay with you until you die. Please believe me. I only ever wanted to help you."

He put his gloved hand over her mouth, forcing her to

labour for breath through her nose.

"Don't speak, Mary, unless it's to pray for us. Will you do that for me?

She nodded. He removed his hand.

He'd left the apparatus on the bedside table in a closed loop, with the needle and syringe inserted into the end of the tube, like a serpent devouring its own tail. He removed them and raised the needle, once more, in front of her eyes.

"This must pass through your chest and heart muscle, where it will be bathed in blood." He parted his lips and started to pant. "Your heart will pump the blood into my mouth, through the syringe and the tube. I won't need to suck, until the moment your heart stops." He exhaled a deep breath.

"The reason I'm doing this, has nothing to do with the fact that I'm a ravenous brute." He angled his eyes towards her. "I need you to understand, Mary, I'm doing this because Lucida must be conceived tonight." He brought his face down to hers and whispered in her ear, "Have faith. I'll see you on the other side."

Chapter Thirty-Three

The intercom buzzer woke Lewis from a dreamless sleep. He turned his eyes painfully in their sockets, to see the screen all a blur without his spectacles.

"Foxy, are you there?"

Lewis groaned and lifted his arm to give a half-hearted wave. "Talk to the hand, Wildo, the face is not good."

"Feeling rough, huh?" Wildo chuckled. "Well, you're not going to believe this, mate, you were right about Udan and Mary last night."

Lewis fumbled for his spectacles over the edge of the bed, never having felt so unwell in his life. Drinking since Friday's Ceremony had left him a trembling, juddering wreck this Monday morning, his memory of last night's party a total blank. He rose onto his elbow, squinting to bring Wildo's features faintly into focus.

"I can't find my specs-" He rubbed the stubble on his scalp, aware of an unsettling, numb sensation all over, soreness in his fingertips. "A lot happened. I can't remember what I said, can you remind me?"

"I've got your specs. They fell into the sand when the Udanos carried you out. You were shouting your head off, spouting on about Dan Udan being the Cosmic Soul, or whatever. Do you remember?"

"Ah-" Lewis shut his eyes and saw himself, a drunk man in a cassock, his backside bumping over the sand, as bare-chested soldiers hauled him by his arms and legs, escorting him out of the Governor's Swimming pool. "That does ring a bell."

"Should do, mate. Everybody thought Udan and Mary left the party early, though no-one saw them go. You said they went into their tipi and never came out, yet they found their tipi empty." Wildo laughed. "You kept shouting that Udan had taken Mary to another dimension. It was fucking hilarious, mate. But guess what. They've left! Listen to this, posted on the UISC bulletin this morning" – Wildo read aloud:

"Following FACT'S escalation of atrocities against the peoples of this world, Mr Udan and Professor Gallagher have departed the UISC, to assist in the world-wide production of the Pox V2 vaccine." The onscreen blur fluttered as Wildo gestured. "It doesn't make sense. Why leave in the middle of the celebration? Why couldn't they wait 'til this morning? Unless old Udan received a direct threat during the party, and they left in an emergency. The tipi's site instructions were very precise. You know what I think? I reckon it might've covered a secret tunnel, and that's how they got out."

"Has anybody bothered to look underneath it?" Lewis said.

"Connie said even if there was a tunnel, we wouldn't find it, because Udan would never leave tracks."

"But a flight-crew must've flown them out at some point last night, or this morning." Lewis reasoned.

"I suppose, yeah... Anyway, guess what. You know those spacey images we saw in Udan's medical photos" – he flapped something at the screen – "Jas got hold of a copy of Hubble's pics from a colleague at the Infirmary. Foxy, it's amazing. The resemblance is so close, they look like they've been tattooed onto his back!"

Lewis massaged the front of his neck, where he felt a cold, prickling sensation. "That's spooky."

"I tell you what is spooky. The guys I share digs with all thought the same thing you did. That it could be a sign of a link between the cosmos and Udan. Like he's a rep of some sort, of what's up there in space, a God, or an alien consciousness, whatever."

"Do they think he's the Cosmic Soul?" Lewis's heart began to palpitate.

"The jury is still out. But they said loads of kids who were at the Ceremony of Blood have had weird dreams. Some are totally convinced they've been upgraded a couple of Levels, overnight."

Lewis sat up-right in bed, hyperventilating, as Wildo's features fused momentarily into focus. "Do they believe they're Saints?"

"No way. Nothing like you, mate. Their souls were all red and pink to start with. Fuckin idiots, like me, if they take the Reality Treatise for the truth, which I do," Wildo said. "I reckon Soraya spilled the beans. Udan wants us on the Dark Path, as we speak." He chuckled. "There's a thought and a bleeding half."

"I believe her," Lewis said. "I never thought I'd say this, but I trust Soraya. She tried to warn me off before I signed my soul over to Dan. She knew what I was about to suffer. She knows I'm Udan's Soul Mate."

"Say, Foxy, would you be willing to spread the word about the Dark Path, like she said in the letter?"

"Yes." Lewis nodded.

"Great, because Jas, King, me and Steve have been talking all morning. In fact, they're here with me now. Say hi guys!" Lewis heard cheering in the background. "We've all agreed that everybody who was at the Ceremony of Blood should know the truth about Udan's suffering," Wildo said, "and the resemblance between his back and Hubble's images. We want to know if other people come to the same conclusion about a cosmic link. What do you think, Foxy?"

"I agree," Lewis said.

"We thought the Shooting Star tomorrow night might be a good place to meet up with everyone. Is that okay with you, Foxy?"

"I'm cool with that." Lewis gave a sly, squinting smile at the screen. "So long as you all remember to call me Saint Fox."

On Tuesday evening the Shooting Star looked more like a Saturday night disco, with everybody wearing UDAN flashing headbands, crowding the bar and the star-fish tables. A restless queue had gathered outside, impatient to enter. When they saw Lewis in his golden cassock, clutching a large black file to his chest, they let him through.

"It's Saint Fox! The Saint is here, someone give him a drink!" An acne-faced youth called out, then peered at him. "Is Dan Udan really from another dimension?"

Wildo came up to Lewis' side, pushing him forward into the pub with a hand on his back.

"You're famous, Foxy. Everybody's talking about you. You made a lasting impression at the party.

Believe it or not, they believe in you!"

"Crikey, that was quick, have you been talking to them?" Lewis shot him an alarmed look. Abby appeared, holding out a large glass of whiskey that he fumbled to accept, dropping his file, spilling a heap of Hubble's space images across the floor. Wildo gathered them up, waving them in the air.

"Here's the unifying evidence, everybody! Come and take a copy, there are plenty more to go round!" He muttered in Lewis' ear. "Jas and I have been handing out photocopies of Dan's back. I said wait until Saint Fox brings along the Hubble pictures and they'll see the Cosmic connection. Some of them are already convinced Udan is the biz! Know what? I'm actually beginning to feel the power in our hands."

Lewis caught his eye. "Wildo, the power is not ours. It belongs to the Cosmic Soul."

Wildo laughed and slapped him on the back. "Way to go, Saint Fox, sock it to them."

Lewis watched as Abby cleared a space in the middle of the bar area and pulled out a chair for Lewis to stand on.

"Everybody, keep back! Saint Fox is about to start the meeting!" She flapped her hand high in the air, "Shush everybody, listen to Saint Fox!"

Lewis astonished himself, borrowing from his beloved Dan, the quiet, hypnotic speech rhythm, with his own theatrical style. He watched the faces around him become entranced, as he laid forth his evidence succinctly, at first relaying the story of Jolly's new soul delivered to the Control Room through an imaginary link with Messier Eighty-Three. Except that now he realised the truth: That it wasn't imaginary. Dan Udan had performed a real 'Quantum Transaction' and that those lightning bolts had come from *another dimension*, through a *wormhole.*

He told them that Udan had congratulated him, for making the connection that '*Udan was weaver of the web…The Cosmic Web.*' Tonight, the unifying evidence between Dan Udan's body and the Cosmos was in this room for all to see, if only they would believe their eyes-

He lifted Hubble's images one at a time, pointing out similarities to the photos of Dan's back, looking from face to face.

"Can you see the resemblance? Will you believe what you see? This is the body of our Light Wizard, the greatest genius of all time. Don't give me a knee-jerk reaction, and tell me that the whole idea is impossible, when much of what he has created was deemed impossible a mere nine years ago. Sit down with the facts for a while, and let them sink in… Let's pause for contemplation and refreshments."

At first the atmosphere in the pub was muted and respectful. And then Lewis sensed a change. Within minutes the mood turned to wonderment, whispering exchanges and expressions like those of children on Christmas morning. The pub was humming with excitement, until he spotted Stefan Mohr coming towards him, grim faced, his voice raised in his clipped German accent.

"Lewis, have you gone crazy? Just because our employer has mutations on his back, does not mean he is a kind of God." He came right up to his face, their foreheads almost touching. "I think you belong in the asylum!"

Lewis lifted his chin. "Stefan, did you attend the Ceremony of Blood?"

"Of course not." Stefan glared at him. "I thought it was a practical joke aimed at the students."

"If you've come here to mock my faith, then I'm sorry, I must ask you to leave." Lewis scanned for Wildo, but then saw King at the bar, talking to Steve, his flatmate, a short, mousey fellow. "Excuse me, gentlemen." Lewis fluttered his fingers in between their faces. "Would you kindly remove this man from our meeting, he doesn't belong here."

For the first time in his life, Lewis experienced what it was like to be obeyed. It took his breath away. King and Steve grabbed Stefan by his scruff and pulled him towards the exit, with Wildo adding his assistance, pushing him out the door.

The students glanced at one another and shrugged, as if this was a normal part of belonging to a new, controversial movement. Lightheaded, on a high, Lewis circled amongst them, puffing to catch his breath. Jas saw him and gave up his barstool, beside the wall, where Dan had sat on the day they had lunched. Back behind the bar, King placed another whiskey in front of him.

"On the house" – his eyes shone with admiration – "your talk was fantastic. I can see why Udan chose you."

Moments later Wildo joined King behind the bar. They shook hands, appearing to congratulate one another. Wildo extended his hand to Lewis.

"That was awe-inspiring, Saint Fox, man, you were born to this" – shaking his hand vigorously – "you hit just the right chord. Can you feel the buzz?"

"The facts speak for themselves," Lewis said, in earnest. "I feel as if something is guiding me." He meant it. Now that he'd started, he didn't want to stop. Wildo leaned over the bar to speak in Lewis' ear, talking loudly to be heard above the background chatter.

"It's time we thought about Dark Path merchandising. We've still got UDAN headbands and shrouds left over from the Ceremony. But we need new stuff to keep up the momentum. I've been talking to some guys from the Arts and Textiles department. They suggested T-shirts with Dan's back on the front and Hubble's images on the reverse. They'd be happy to print off the first hundred for free, until we get some donations from supporters. What do you say?"

Lewis gave a supercilious nod. "Excellent. Good thinking."

Wildo circled his forefinger. "And we could design our own line in cosmic jewellery and 'Dan Back' ornaments to help put the message across. Abby said she's already got ideas for some stylish jewellery based around the spiral galaxy and the Cat's Eye. How does that sound to you?"

"A pendant necklace would be good, with a spiral to symbolise Messier Eighty-Three," Lewis said, "I'd wear one myself. Brilliant idea."

"You know, you're a really cool guy." Wildo squeezed Lewis' shoulder. "This is going to be so big. I can feel it in my bones. I reckon someone else should speak next. It'd have more impact if loads of people put forward their views. Are you okay with that?"

"If people have seen the light, they should say so. I'll sum up at the end and answer any questions." Lewis smiled.

Wildo helped himself to a slurp of Lewis' whiskey. "Cheers, here's to the most important night of our lives."

Abby clapped her hands for silence. Lewis closed his eyes to shut out the distraction of dozens of flickering headbands and leaned his back against the wall.

He trained his ears to none other than Sophie's voice,

telling of her nightmare about a man-sized mosquito coming to her in the night, with a human hand at the end of its forelimb, concealed inside a black glove. It lay on top of her, flashing images in its compound eyes, like televisions switching between two channels, one showing her face, the other her skull.

Someone tapped Lewis on the arm. He opened his eyes to see Liz peering at him.

"Jane O'Neil is outside in the corridor," she whispered, "She wants to speak to you."

Lewis slid down from the barstool, poker-faced as he meandered his way between the spellbound listeners. He hesitated when he saw Jane standing beside a man he didn't recognise, well-built, white haired.

"Lewis. How are you?" She touched his elbow. "I'm sorry to hear about your ordeal. These psychological tests my nephew goes in for are challenging. Let's hope the students all learned their lesson." She looked him up and down, taking in the shorn head, the cassock. "I must say, you're looking well." She smiled. "I'd like you to meet Mr. Cookson, a friend of Dan's" – she turned to the man – "this is Dr. Lewis Allen, our A.I. whiz-kid."

Cookson clasped Lewis' hand. "Pleased to meet you, Dr Allen. I've heard a lot about you." He was an American.

"We'll get straight to the point," Jane said, "We'd appreciate you keeping this between us." She lowered her voice. "I understand you've spent some time with Dan recently. Did he happen to share with you the whereabouts of any private rooms in the UISC?"

Lewis blinked. "Oh, Crikey, um…The only place I can think of is a grotty little room on Level Seven called the Earth Room."

Jane nodded. "Yes, we know about Dan's smoking room. Does anywhere else come to mind? Please try to think."

"If you tell me what this is about, maybe I can help you," Lewis said.

Jane's lower lip twitched, while she considered. "Do keep it to yourself. Dan and Mary have been missing since Sunday night. We have every reason to believe they're somewhere in this building. Would you have any idea where they might be?"

Lewis had an inflating sensation inside his chest. "All I know is that you won't find them."

Cookson stepped forward, smelling of strong aftershave. "Dr Allen, this is a matter of great importance. If you've got any information, you need to share it."

Lewis locked with Cookson's eyes, hard, like two polished bullets. Something about the man's expression made him gabble. "It's possible they've entered a wormhole to another dimension, where they cannot be found" – perspiration chilled his upper lip "-that's all I can offer you."

Cookson scratched the side of his nose and stepped back. "Jane, how about we leave this boy to get on with his very interesting life?"

"Thank you, Lewis." Jane frowned. "If Dan should contact you from this *other place*, would you please let us know?"

"I'd have to ask Dan, but he's not here."

Cookson started walking slowly backwards. Picking up on the man's disdain, Lewis raised his voice.

"Mr Cookson, I'm his Soul Mate." When Cookson didn't bat an eyelid, Lewis blurted, "I know his secret. He's not what you think he is."

"Sorry to have disturbed your evening, Lewis. We'll leave

you to get back to your friends." Jane turned and joined Cookson, walking away.

Bristling with humiliation, Lewis watched the pair heading down the corridor. Wildo appeared at his side.

"Were those two giving you stick about our meeting?"

"You must be joking. Whatever we do is beneath their dignity to care." Lewis had a bitter taste on his tongue. "They came looking for Dan and Mary. I told them where I thought they were, but the tough guy didn't believe me." Lewis levelled his hand at his throat. "I've had it up to here, all my life, with big shots like him looking at me as if I'm some sort of worm. In the name of the Cosmic Soul, I curse him." He jutted his chin. "I curse all those who've ever doubted me and mocked me. They're all going to get their comeuppance."

"I'm with you all the way, Saint Fox." Wildo put his arm around Lewis' shoulders. "The fuckers don't know what they're dealing with."

Chapter Thirty-Four

Mary can see herself from above, lying on the bed.

It is a strange perspective. The fish-lens effect, claustrophobic, distorted. Mary can see her face, warping in and out, of focus. Her lips are blue and parted. Her eyes are staring upwards.

She's no longer inside her body, but floating above it, to one side. The tube that leads from her heart to his mouth is full-red; it's her death-line.

As he drinks from her, he is completely still. Until he turns his head, and she sees a smile on his mouth. She's at the level of the chandelier's burnished rings. The teardrop pendants are peppered with dust. The ceiling is all that remains between her and oblivion. Any higher and she'd vanish to become one with the iron and stone. But something is keeping her here.

He looks up at the chandelier and holds out his hand.

"Love," he says.

Mary drops from the ceiling. Like slamming into a wall, she's back inside her body. Pain explodes from her chest, firing down both arms and upwards into her jaw. She lifts her ribs and heaves for breath, as he continues to suck from her heart.

At the edge of consciousness, she can hear him pleading. Pleading with his God. There's the sound of shrieking faraway, gull-like, desolate, as when death is longed for.

Mary lifts her head and opens her eyes. She's in the same room as before, lying on the ancient bed. Her wrists are free.

In the middle of the floor is a huge bird with blue plumage, facing her. Its wings are closed. Its head is downward. Her focus sharpens. It looks like the Bird of Paradise. But then the thorax narrows. It twitches a wing and only then she realises it's an arm. It's his arm. He's naked, prostrate on the floor with his hands over his head, groaning like a dying soldier, caught in the line of fire.

She's too weak to move. There's nothing she can do but watch.

There's the sound of running water, the distant rattle of kitchen noises. The sweet roasted aroma of coffee. Mary delays opening her eyes. White sand and palm trees shimmer at the front of her memory. There was a beach party. Dan took her to a meadow, where she met a silver boy and then there was a room. Now there are blankets weighing heavy on top of her, tucked in so tightly she can barely shift her legs. Sensing a presence, she opens her eyes.

"Good morning, angel. Did y' sleep well?"

Dan places a tray down on the bed-side table. He's in a black, silk dressing gown with wide, bell-shaped cuffs draped over his hands. His eyelids are heavy. As if he too has just woken from a deep sleep.

An image flashes before her, the tube feeding his mouth.

"I've brought you some breakfast…hmm…What have we got here? We've got fresh grapefruit juice, muesli with Soya-milk, toast and honey." He points to each thing on the tray. "Freshly ground coffee. You should be hungry. You never had anything to eat at the party." He sits on the bed and crosses his legs, clasping both hands around one knee. "Wake up, sleepy head, and have something to eat."

Mary lifts herself onto the pillows. Cool against her skin is a white, silk dressing-gown, with wide, bell – shaped cuffs, like the one he has on, but for the colour.

She remembers him praying in the night, those dying, gull-like cries and wonders now if she was dreaming. She looks up at the chandelier, shedding its pale, silvery light into the room.

"I had a dream. I was watching you from up there." She points. "I dreamt that you were sucking blood from my heart, through a tube, and I was dead."

"Give me your hand," he says, in his gentle voice. His hand is naked. She knows what could happen, but senses something has changed. She slips her hand into his. His skin is warm and firm. She looks at his long, slender fingers around hers and her heart flutters.

"I wish I could say it was a dream." He caresses her knuckles with his thumb. "I took only what I needed. I watched you die." He draws a deep breath, so deep, she has a sense that his lungs are oceanic. "Your soul stayed with me, long past the moment of death. When I was sure our love could survive death itself, I brought you back." He smiles, almost to himself, a sly, sweet smile.

Her memory whispers. Lucida.

"And now there's no skin between us" – he tightens his grip on her fingers – "we share one body."

"Dan" – her voice wavers – "I'm not sure anymore, what's… real."

"God has tested your soul to the limit. You'll never be the same again." He bites down on his lip. "Sure, I was tested too.

We've proved our love is strong enough to do God's work. So long as our son needs us, we'll be there for him."

"But we don't have a son." She holds his gaze.

He laughs. "One thing at a time, Mary, give us a chance. Come on now" – he shakes her hand from side to side – "just you eat your breakfast and leave me to worry about that. We've got to build you up first." He rises from the bed, lifts the tray from the bedside table and places it over her thighs. "Drink that coffee before it gets cold. I'm going to have a bath." He nods toward a gap in the panelled wall. "The bathroom is through there, if you need me."

Mary surprises herself. She eats and drinks everything that Dan has put in front of her. She rests her head back on the pillows and listens to the sound of splashing water in the bathroom.

There's a knock on the bedroom door. Two more quiet knocks. Mary looks at the door, doubting her own senses. Until it happens again. Three, quiet knocks, evenly spaced.

Who knows they're here? Who has followed them through the manhole, down the tunnel and across the holographic meadow? The only one she can think of is Lucida, the holographic boy. Her heart thuds, sick at the thought of the artificial child knocking on the door. He's so realistic, what if he feels abandoned and demands to be loved, like a real child?

She places the tray to one side and rises from the bed, weaving across the floor like a drunk. She pulls back the sliding panel, staggers into the small, humid bathroom.

"Dan, there's someone knocking on the door." The blur poking out from a mountain of bubbles comes into focus as his face, wet curls matted to his head.

“That’ll be my dark forces. Ignore them. Come in and take a seat.” His foot sticks up, big toe pointing to a chair next to the bath taps. Mary grasps the edge of the sink, to support herself as she goes to sit down.

“Whoever it is has knocked three times.” She sweeps hair back from her face. The bath with Dan inside it, appears to be swaying.

“There’s nobody there, angel. It’s all in your mind.” He steers a yellow plastic duck with his foot, bobbing it up and down.

She squints at him. “Then go and listen for yourself... Please.”

He sits upright, tipping bubbles over the side of the bath and raises his forefinger.

“Now, you to listen to me. You must relax, Mary. Take deep breaths and let it go. Or my dark forces will play tricks with your mind. If we let them in, they’ll ruin everything.” He slips under the water, sits up, shakes out his hair, spraying droplets like a smattering of rain.

“I’ll ignore it then,” Mary says. “Why should I worry. I’m not sure if I’m still alive.” She puts her head in her hands. “I can’t wake up-” A sob bursts from her lungs.

“Mary”-he opens his hand, foamy with bubbles – “this is what’s going to happen. You will give birth to our immortal son. His name will be Lucida. His powers of survival will come from me and his heart of gold, from you. He’ll be the human God people have hankered for, since the night they discovered a prayer. Maybe you understand now, my problem with your ambition to create biological immortality. It’s a dream for God and God only.” He blows the foam in his hand and snowy flakes fly up. “Isn’t it grand when dreams come true?” He smiles.

"This is a nightmare," she says.

"After what you've been through, you still don't believe in miracles." He laughs. "But never mind. God won't force your surrender. It'll happen, Mary, when you least expect it." He reclines in the bath and pumps his knees, shunting water back and forth, until it laps over the sides.

She rises. "I'm going back to bed."

He starts to hum. She recognises the tune, the song of unrequited love, he wrote for her. Mary shuffles across the bathroom, gravity drags her down at every step. She moves through the oak panel doors, tries, but is too tired to slide it back, and curses under her breath.

"Less of that language, angel face," he says. "Sure, we'll both end up in hell if you carry on with that attitude." There's a voluminous splash behind her. His humming continues, louder.

Back in bed, her mind shuts down, drifting around the edge of consciousness.

Three quiet knocks

She turns over to look at the door, peeping at it from beneath her eyelids. There's a muffled bump, a thud and quiet scuffing against the wood. She listens, with calm. She can ignore it. All of this, she reasons, is Dan the illusionist, trying to control her mind.

She closes her eyes. She hears a child sobbing, with long pauses between gasps, as if it lacks the strength to cry. She's convinced it's the little hologram, left to wander alone in the meadow, with no understanding of why it has been so casually discarded. She can still see his face, his sad eyes and hears his whisper… Remember me.

Mary leaves the bed and steals across the room. She kneels

in front of the door.

"Lucida, is that you?" A shrill cry flies past. A deep chorus moans. She turns to see what's there, her heart thudding against her ribs. There's a thump behind the door, shuffling and scratching. She stares at the door. It reminds her of a bird she once heard, trying to free itself, trapped inside a chimney. "Who's there? Is that you, Lucida?"

Dan strolls into the room in his dressing-gown, towel-drying his hair, still humming. He walks over to the UDAN window, full of wildflowers, Mary's meadow.

"Let's have a sunrise, as it's a beautiful Monday morning." Sunshine floods the room, illuminating shafts of dust particles. He opens a panel in the wall. "I usually enjoy a game of chess on a Monday." He places a wooden box and chessboard on the bed. "Come here," he says.

"It's the little hologram." Mary looks at Dan. Dan closes his eyes. "We can't ignore him," she says, "Lucida is crying. He wants to come in. He wants to be with us."

"Do you know how to play?" Dan says, eyes still closed.

"Stop ignoring me…and Lucida. I know he's not real. But he thinks he is. That's what makes it so awful. Please shut down his programme or let him in. I can't stand to hear him cry."

"The rules are quite simple." Dan sits on the bed and adopts a yoga posture. Mary recognises, the half-lotus position. He begins to place chess pieces on the chessboard. "There's always room for ingenuity and surprise. The best way to learn is to play the game. I'll be white, for a change," he says.

Loud bangs on the door, someone kicking to get in. Startled, Mary rises and steps back. "He's angry," she says. "How have you programmed him? Does Lucida have a temper, like you?"

"Come over here and he'll stop. He'll fall asleep outside the door." He reaches out his hand. "Trust me." Mary returns to the bed and sits crossed legged, to face him. Dan is absorbed, setting up the game. "The King and Queen stand side by side," he says.

A low, sighing groan breathes in her ear, with a chilling harmonic.

She puts her hands over her ears. "Dan, he's still awake. Let him in."

"I'll go first," he says, moving a piece. "The pawn moves forward, so it does, like this" – in his soft voice – "now Mary, your move."

"I can't play. I can't think with that child crying outside the door."

"Make your move," Dan says.

"How can I play chess while you're playing games with my mind?" She shoves her hand under the chessboard and sends it flying over the edge of the bed, the pieces thud down on the carpet. "Open the door and let the poor thing in!"

Dan inclines his head. "Would you rather play cards?" He lifts his eyebrows. "How about strip-poker?" He points to her dressing-gown, directly at her bosom. "I'll have that off in a jiffy, with my poker-face." There's scraping outside the door, the sobbing gets louder.

"Open the door!" She glares at him.

"Okay, Mary, we'll do it your way and forget foreplay." He nods. "Let's just get on with the business of conception, shall we? Lie back there and make yourself comfortable."

"Open the door," she says in her quiet, steel voice.

"I must warn you I'm hung like a horse." He winces with an

air of false apology. "I suggest you learn to relax and open those lovely legs of yours as wide as-"

She slaps his face, hard.

"Ouch"-he rubs his cheek – "that hurt."

"I hate you," she says.

He sits motionless. A tear slips down his cheek. She brushes it away with her fingertips. He grabs her wrist.

"You think all I do is play games." Their eyes lock. "Be honest, Mary. Do you think this is all an illusion?"

"I don't believe we can have an immortal son," she says.

"What must I do to earn your faith?" He pulls her close, with a crushing grip on her arm.

She gasps. "You can begin by letting me go." She looks over at the door where everything is silent. "Open the door. Do it. Prove I'm not your prisoner."

He releases her arm with a push. "Go on. Prove it for yourself. But come straight back to bed."

Mary gives him a look of disbelief. But then, she climbs off the bed and moves to the door, already her limbs feel lighter. She turns the handle and isn't surprised when the door opens. She looks around, looks down the short corridor.

"Lucida's not here," she says. Something buzzes past her head into the room. Her eyes follow it to its landing place, on the doorframe. She identifies the species. Calliphora vomitoria. "Last week, I found a bluebottle in my apartment."

"It's the same one," Dan says.

"How?" She glowers at him from across the room.

"Because I'm everywhere." He puts out his hand. "Come back to bed."

But she happens to glance down. Mated stag-beetles are

creeping over the threshold. The male is massive, its pincer jaws protrude over the female's head, its femurs are as thick as a man's thumb. Mary staggers backwards, alarmed, until she realises, they're holograms.

"I'm not scared of stag-beetles," she says. "You're wasting your time trying to frighten me."

"Now why would I want to do that?" His tone is full of hurt.

Mary steps over the mating pair and slams the door shut. It bursts open again. A huge, wavering swarm of bees drone in through the door. The muddy cloud disperses as individuals break off, flying in all directions. She notices that they're not bees, but wasps, with stocky, orange abdomens and frontal stalks. She recognises them as a sickening species, one that paralyses its prey to provide live food for its larva.

"You've made sand-wasp holograms?" She glares at him. "Is it because you know how much I loathe them?"

"Mary, come away from the door!" He kneels up on the bed and opens his arms. "Come into my arms!"

"Dan, I'm not scared. I'm furious! Stop doing this to me!"

"You're not where you think you are."

She feels tickling where one of the sand-wasps has landed on the back of her hand. She doesn't move, watching it walk across her skin. There's no mistaking it for anything but real. She panics, doing what she knows she mustn't do and brushes it off. The sting is isolated but severe: a pinprick of molten metal. She winces, clutching her hand.

Sand-wasps swarm around her, tiny, stout missiles, aiming for her eyes, nose and mouth. She shakes her head, waving her arms, walking in a blind circle to fight them off. They're bombing her forehead, catching in her hair, crawling inside her dressing gown; whining like racing-cars to reach inside her ears. It happens so fast, the trail of blistering pinpricks over her skin blurs into agony. She's on fire, her knees buckle-

There's a dog licking her face, its saliva is copious and cool, filling her nostrils with the scent of warm, wet grass, nudging her with its head. Mary opens her eyes and is astonished to see Dan looking down at her. They're back on the bed.

"Now the door is open," he whispers in her ear, "my dark forces have entered." He glances furtively around at the four bedposts. "So long as you stay close to me, they can't harm you. It's the best I can do." He furrows his brow. "How's the pain?"

"It's gone." Her mouth quivers, resisting the urge to burst into tears. "I don't understand, what's happening to me?"

He holds her head in his hands, his eyes blazing. "This is beyond your understanding. It wasn't supposed to happen, but you insisted on opening the door." He clenches his teeth. "Now all I ask is that you do as I say."

Mary can't speak, she can see things spinning in the air behind him, white trousers, jacket, shirt and a pair of socks, her long golden dress stretched flat-out, circling beneath the chandelier like moths caught in the light.

From nowhere, two huge rooks join the merry-go-round, squawking. One starts to attack the other in mid-orbit, spewing feathers everywhere. Dan turns to watch with her. A rook comes hurtling towards the bed, its neck appears broken, head dangling upside down. There's a loud bang, like something has hit a window. The rook drops to the floor at the side of the bed. Mary raises herself onto her elbows and stares out. No glass is visible, yet a smear appears to hang there, spattered with bits of fluff and a trickle of dark blood.

Their clothes are still spinning, but now the breakfast tray, cup, saucer and bowl float up to join the maelstrom. Papers, pens, and books on the desk fly across the room, as if pulled by a magnetic force. A towel and a small, embroidered cushion fling themselves at the vortex, now whipping itself around in the shape of a cone.

In the middle of it all she watches the mated stag beetles rolling as if they're performing aerobatics, blurring to an orange clump as they become smothered in sand-wasps.

The room is reverberating to the noise of oak panels shuddering, to the din of flapping, ripping and droning, like bombers flying low, over fluttering flags at the start of war. The chess pieces appear to mock, levitating beside the bed, hovering for a moment before they too start to spin.

Dan looks back at her, his expression is searching, as if he wants to say something, or perhaps he's waiting for her to speak.

But the speaking part of her mind is blank. There are no words to make sense of what's happening, and Mary feels herself withdrawing, perhaps into madness. He moves around on the bed and sits behind her, wrapping her inside his arms. In his embrace Mary has a sense of trust, a trust so complete, she's never known before. She rests her head back on his chest, on a wave of euphoria, she cries out, "Dan, there's no skin between us!" He pulls her backwards on top of him and they roll over the bed, laughing.

The commotion in the room goes whirling into the distance. She has the dreamy impression that their bed has sailed up high into windy tree-tops, among the branches and shimmering leaves. He places his hand, tingling, at the base of her throat.

"Who you are?" she says. He doesn't answer. He brings his face down to hers and she feels the firm, hot pressure of his lips. She tugs on his hair, to pull him closer, wanting to taste him, longing to go deeper. He opens her mouth with his tongue, his fingers flutter between her thighs, with a touch so light –

Mary has an image of one of his holograms, a ladybird climbing a blade of grass, all the tension sighs out of her body. She moans, parts her legs as he moves over her body. She slides her hand inside his gown, rests her palm on the grainy terrain of his shoulder blade.

Dan lifts her wrist. "Please, don't touch me there." He puts his mouth to her ear. "I want this to be beautiful."

Mary looks up into his eyes. "I want you to be yourself with me."

His hoods his eyelids. "You wouldn't want that" – he traces her face with his forefinger – "to know the real me." His smile betrays the slightest tremor. "I don't want to do anything that might leave you doubting my love. So, you'll just have to make do with a shy man."

Mary strokes his chest, where his skin has turned red and hot. "You've come up in a heat rash," she murmurs.

Dan closes his eyes and puts his forehead down to hers. He presses himself against her abdomen. His manhood feels more like a thing made of stone than of flesh. "Just the thought of you taking me as I am, has excited me. I'm almost scared to carry on."

"Why?" She runs her fingers back through his hair. "There's no skin between us, remember?"

"I know, Mary, but now the door is open, you shouldn't be here. It's not safe for you." He raises himself from her body and moves to sit on the edge of the bed. "You should go," he says, "go now."

"I don't want to go." Mary comes up behind him, puts her arms around his shoulders and nuzzles his neck. "I want to stay," she whispers, "you'll be safe with me." She laughs, a soft, intimate laugh.

"Don't tempt me, Mary, or I'll have you in all the ways the devil knows how." He inclines his head away from her. "Go, before it's too late."

She takes his chin and turns his face towards hers, seeking his mouth. "Then it's too late-"

Chapter Thirty-Five

Abby answered the door, wearing a pink headband, a pink mini-skirt and a Dan-Back T-shirt. On the front Lewis could just about make-out an image from the rainbow of colours, possible to construe as a whole lot of insects, copulating.

"Hi Saint Fox, come in! Brother Wildo is assisting Emma with a Darkening." She waved him inside the students' apartment. "He should be another ten minutes. King is mixing the drinks for when Emma reaches adult status."

Lewis couldn't recall giving Wildo permission to call himself 'Brother', but as the title had a certain ring to it, he decided to let it pass. He entered the sitting-room, cassock rustling pleasingly across the carpet.

There were heaps of Dan-Back T-shirts on the floor and draped over the back of the sofa. Dirty glasses and dinner plates littered the coffee table, left over from lunch. He cleared a place for himself on the sofa, seeing as both armchairs were taken up with book-files and piles of notes and coins. He acknowledged the money with a curt nod at Abby.

"How much have we made so far?"

"We haven't counted it yet. Ralphie's been charging twenty-five euros for the T-shirts and fifty euros per Darkening. He's assisted four girls so far" – she laughed – "they're queuing up for him."

"And what about you?"

"I like being a Pinkie." She smiled. "He's going to have to wait for me."

King appeared in the kitchen doorway, in jeans and a Dan-Back T-shirt.

"Saint Fox! Welcome to our humble abode!" He tossed his head in the direction of the bedrooms. "Can you believe Wildo's luck! He's got girls begging him to defile them, so they can call themselves adults. I'm making crème de menthe cocktails in honour of Emma's Green Soul, when she's ready. Fancy one?"

"I'd like a glass of water, thank you."

"Coming up, Saint Fox, your wish is our command." King vanished into the kitchen.

Lewis peered at Abby. "Do you mind Wildo going with other women? I rather got the impression on Tuesday night that you two were an item."

"We've decided to be friends, because I'm not ready to go all the way with him," she said. "I like him a lot, but I refuse to be another notch on the bedpost. The other girls are totally naïve if they think he'll fall for them after having sex. They're just using the Dark Path to justify their slutty behaviour."

"The Darkening of Defilement isn't supposed to be a pleasurable experience." Lewis adopted his priestly tone. "It's meant to degrade and humiliate the adolescent soul into relinquishing its perfectionism, thus preparing it for the realities of life."

"Ralphie knows that. He warned Emma that she wasn't going to enjoy it" – she stifled a laugh – "I listened at the door and all I heard was Wildo calling her a filthy bitch."

Lewis frowned. "I see."

King re-appeared, with drinks on a tray. "Here we are…Ah, I think I hear a door opening. Another adult has been born." He laughed.

A tall plump girl, Emma presumably, came into the sitting room. Lewis clapped. King and Abby joined the applause.

"Well done, Emma, congratulations on becoming an adult." King grinned. "There's a green cocktail for you on the tray, help yourself!"

Emma knelt beside the coffee table and gulped her green drink, shoulders hunched, her hair hanging lankly about her face. Wildo swaggered into the room, in boxer shorts and a Dan-Back T shirt.

"Hi, Saint Fox. I'm doing a great job for the Dark Path. Did Abby tell you?"

"Yes, I understand you've found your vocation." Lewis raised his glass. "Here's to the Dark Path. Emma, do you feel more mature now that you've been enlightened?"

Emma lifted her eyes to Lewis. "I'm a proper adult now," she slurred.

Lewis gave his sagely nod.

Wildo tossed a green LED headband on the floor beside her. "Put that on, bitch!"

Emma fitted it around her head and adopted a chin-up pose, staring at Lewis with a hard glint in her eyes.

He couldn't quite work out whether it was triumph or hatred. It turned out to be a stoic mask, when suddenly she started to sob, distorting her face like a doll's head melting on a coal fire, turning black with its residue of thick mascara. Lewis looked blankly at Wildo and King, seated in their armchairs.

Abby showed Emma to the door.

"What exactly did you do to her?" Lewis asked.

"What every bloke dreams of." Wildo winked.

"She wouldn't be my type," King said.

"You're focusing on the wrong end." Wildo slid his eyes towards him. "That's how pussy gets away with it. Mate, you got to keep your eye on the game."

With those words, his sandy mane and thin upper lip, Wildo reminded Lewis of a young lion he'd seen in a wild-life documentary, gorging on its first proper kill. Except that the zebra wasn't quite dead and was watching the lion feed from the hole in its abdomen, its long mouth gaping horribly. The image had disturbed Lewis, yet often popped into his head at the weirdest moments.

Abby returned and sat beside Lewis on the sofa. "Emma said she feels like killing herself," she said.

"Tough titty. Women must learn their place in the scheme of things." Wildo lifted his chin, eyes narrowed at Lewis. "That's what every religion teaches. Isn't that right, Saint Fox?"

"Ask Emma to come and see me tomorrow," Lewis said, looking at Abby. "I'll pray with her, for her strength and forbearance to shine on." Lewis turned to Wildo. "The Dark Path teaches us compassion, Brother Wildo. If you fail to show compassion in future, I'll undertake your own Darkening myself, and believe you me, I'll teach you some."

"You kinky fox." Wildo grinned. "I bet you'd just love to whip my ass." He rose and walked out to the kitchen.

"Is there any news on Dan and Mary's whereabouts?" King said.

"I've checked the UISC bulletin again today, there's nothing."

Lewis finished his water and put the empty glass on the floor. "But the Udano Regiment left last night. That suggests to me that Dan must've made contact to give the order." He pressed his fingers to his thumbs, to feel their tender, slightly puckered pulps, where he'd been drawing blood since last Sunday night, in worship.

"Have you had any more ideas about how to move the Dark Path forward?" King sipped his green cocktail.

"Yes. I've been doing a lot of thinking over the last couple of days. As founders of a new religious movement, it's our job to bring people together with rituals and appropriate icons to inspire the kind of worship that goes on in churches. It's time we considered a proper Dark Path service and communion, with the Cosmic Soul."

"Right on, Saint Fox, you're on the money again." Wildo sauntered back to his chair, cracking open a can of beer. "What's the big idea this time?"

"I think we should launch the religion with a Ceremony of some kind" – Lewis steepled his hands – "and I prefer we call it the UDAN Religion, as calling it the Dark Path might give the wrong impression."

"That sounds much better," Abby said. "We could have a gathering in the Student Common Room. It's got a huge UDAN window and loads of comfortable chairs."

"I was hoping for a relevant venue." Lewis glanced sideways at her. "The Governors are a bit miffed that the Udano Regiment didn't remove the sand in their swimming pool before they left. They've requested student volunteers over the weekend to go in and clear it out.

"I saw Jane O'Neil today and asked if I could organise one

last function there to make use of the Holorama, as Dan put so much work into it, it seems a pity not to make use of it. I said if they'd allow me, I'd be able to secure loads of volunteers to clean the place afterwards. Jane said she'd discuss it with them." Lewis smiled at Wildo. "It'd be pretty powerful to have our First Communion with the Cosmic Soul in front of the Red Giant Holorama, don't you think?"

"We'd have to ask for donations to fund it," Wildo said, "for food and drinks and what was that other thing you said… icons, yeah?"

"I'll leave you to organise the collections with King, as you seem to have a talent." Lewis nodded.

"Oi, Pinkie over there, go fetch us a couple of beers." Wildo kicked out his leg. "I think we should celebrate the new UDAN Religion!"

"Go fetch them yourself!" Abby folded her arms. "I'm not your slave."

"If you're going to act like a spoiled brat, Pinkie, you can go home." Wildo cocked his head toward the door. "Is it good-bye or my good girl? Be a sport, fetch the beers."

"Asshole," Abby said under her breath. She rose and went to the kitchen.

"King, that's how it's done, mate," Wildo said. "You wait and see. I'll have her in the sack by Saturday."

Lewis smiled at Abby handing him a can of beer.

The four of them carried on talking, pooling ideas. On Wildo's orders, Abby got up again to fetch him a pad and a pencil, so that he could make sketches of various icons, while Lewis and King drew up lists of things to do. At one point Lewis put his head back on the sofa and closed his eyes, listening to their excited chatter.

He didn't have a reason to smile. He missed Dan too much. But this was tolerable. This much at least, he could live with.

Chapter Thirty-Six

Mary woke up, eyes wide-open.

"Mary, you're with me. You're in my apartment. You're safe now."

She saw a silhouette against the light.

"Desi, give Mary a sip of water."

Water passed over Mary's tongue.

"That's better, dear...You've been sedated. Lie back. Give yourself a few minutes to come round."

Mary lay back and focused on Jane's face.

"Jane, what's happened?" Mary said.

"You're going to be all right. Desi and I are taking care of you. There's Desi." Mary followed Jane's gaze to Desi, holding a glass of water.

"You'll recover." Desi smiled. "But you must rest now."

Jane stroked the back of Mary's hand. "You and Dan went missing from the party on Sunday evening. It's Thursday morning. You were discovered late last night. Desi found you on the bed in your suite at the Penthouse, unconscious. Cookie and Connie brought you down to my apartment on a carrier."

Mary cast her eyes about. "Where's Dan?"

"Dan has returned to Lacerta. He went yesterday," Jane said.

"When is he coming back?" Mary stared at her.

"He didn't say." Jane patted her hand. "Don't worry about Dan. Can you tell us where you were for four days?"

"Why did he leave?" Mary couldn't catch her breath and sat up. "Call him!" She put her hand on her chest and heaved in. "Bring him back!"

"You should be honest with her, Jane," Desi said, "show her the letter."

"Dan wrote me a letter and left it on your pillow," Jane said. "I'll explain after you've had something to eat. Desi has made some chicken soup. You'll feel better once you've eaten." She put her hand on Mary's shoulder. "Lie down, you're exhausted."

Mary felt the drain on her strength just by sitting up. She sank back on the pillows. "What does he say? When can I see him?" Her voice broke. "Why did he go?"

"I believe it will help her to read the letter," Desi said.

"Not yet," Jane said, "Not until I know what happened." Jane searched Mary's face. "Can you tell us?"

Mary closed her eyes. Fatigue washed over her, flashbacks to feelings so intense, her heart started to pound. A sweet, clutching sensation in her chest told of her need for Dan to be here, right now.

"Dan and I have become lovers." She sighed. "We're so deeply in love. I can touch him, Jane, and he can touch me. There's no skin between us."

"Would you say your time together was pleasant?" Jane said.

"Dan is my life. He's my world. He's the reason I was born." Mary opened her eyes and smiled. "When is he coming back?"

"I think, Desi, you might be right." Jane looked at Desi. "She needs to read his letter. I'll go and fetch it." Jane left the room.

Desi held the glass of water in front of Mary. "You must drink plenty of this-"

Jane returned. "Dan's writing is small. Perhaps you'd like me to read it to you?"

Mary handed the empty glass back to Desi. "If you don't mind" – Mary reached for the letter – "I'd like to read it myself."

Dear Jane,

I leave Mary in your safe hands.

She has been sedated. By the time she wakes, I'll be gone. I'm retuning to Lacerta this afternoon. I do not wish to see her again or hear from her.

Let there be silence between us now, as if we had never met.

I'm sorry for all the heartache I've caused, during my stay at Wicklow. The whole affair has been a disaster. I regret ever setting foot in this place.

It has proven to me, once and for all, that I must stay away from humanity.

I would like some peace. Please do not call me. Send Cookie home first thing tomorrow morning. Desi can stay on with you a while longer, to help with the woman in your care.

Do not give Mary anything but the facts. She will demand to know the truth.

I suggest you give her this letter to read.

She's strong. She'll get through this.

Dan

"Dan didn't write this," Mary said, "He would never write

this." She looked up at Jane. "I need to talk to him. Call him now, on your intercom." She threw back the duvet, put her feet on the floor and stood up.

Her vision blurred. The room spun around her.

"Get into bed!" Desi caught Mary by the arm. "You must rest!"

"We love each other! Why are you keeping us apart?" Mary pulled away from her, too weak to stand, her legs gave way. Jane and Desi caught her, lifted her by her armpits and lowered her back onto the bed.

"Tell her!" Desi bore down on Mary's shoulders. "She doesn't remember. Tell her the truth. It's what Dan wants. She needs to know. Cookie promised him we'd all look after her."

"Let me go!" Mary strained her head away from Desi. "Dan, help me!"

"He can't hear you. He's not here." Jane's face appeared beside Desi's. "Mary, you're not well."

"I know he's here. He would never leave me." Mary raised her head. "Dan, where are you? I need you!"

She felt a sharp smack on her cheek. Desi pointed at her. "Pull yourself together! Dan is not here. He is in trouble."

Mary pulled herself up. "Why, what has he done?"

"Let's have some of that soup, thank you, Desi," Jane said.

Desi lifted the jug and walked away.

Jane drew a chair up bedside the bed. She picked up Dan's letter from the duvet and folded it inside her cardigan pocket.

"I hesitated to show you the letter," Jane said, "because separation is the last thing he wants. But it is what's necessary." She inclined her head. "You obviously have no recollection of what happened." Her expression softened. "When you were found, looking so unwell, Cookie and I took the decision to undertake your medical examination ourselves. We wanted to protect your and Dan's privacy. We knew you'd understand."

Mary nodded.

"You've lost a lot of blood. When we scanned you, we found no signs of significant internal or external injury, to explain the loss of blood. But you do have signs of" – she lowered her voice – "forced intercourse." Jane fixed her eyes on Mary. "Be honest with me, Mary. What happened between you?"

Mary gazed back at Jane. "Dan is wonderful. He's magical. He's everything they say he is."

Mary closed her eyes and saw butterflies, in their thousands, rising from a flower meadow. A boy with long silver hair, running through rainbows. The whole world shapeshifting. And a bed. Their bed, rising through treetops, reaching for the stars.

"Jane, it was nothing like this world. I felt so safe. I was safe. Everything was-" Mary smiled and opened her eyes. "I trust him, Jane. I have complete faith in him."

"You've been drugged. Your memory of what happened will return." Jane tightened her lips. "It's up to you whether you wish to press charges. At the UISC, in cases of rape, manslaughter and murder, UDAN defers to the Irish judiciary system. You could have him arrested, to face criminal charges."

"Is that what he's worried about?" Mary frowned.

"No. Dan doesn't care what happens to him. He's devastated. He's never lost control like this before. Something must've switched on the… dangerous behaviour." Jane looked sideways.

"Mary, all I know is that by giving you up, he's protecting you. Cookie went back to Lacerta this morning. Dan has locked himself away in his study. He normally does that when he's working on something new. But if I know my nephew, he'll be in there drinking himself sick, tearing himself apart." Jane straightened, as if bracing herself for the worst.

"When you remember what happened, will you talk to me, Mary, before you decide to press charges? There are others, as you know, out there, who know about him. Highly qualified people, ready to help him."

"You don't understand." Mary said. "All I want is to see him again." She touched Jane's wrist. "Please, tell him, I love him."

"Thank God for you." Jane looked into her eyes. "But Mary, you must know, my nephew can't go on like this."

Chapter Thirty-Seven

The steel agricultural arms were pumping, the soil trays were shaking in their bunks, the seeds were sewn, and Lewis had done his bit, overseeing the new crop implantations in all the Sections.

He undid the buttons on his overalls, meandering back through the aisles to the Control Room, exposing his Dan-Back T-shirt underneath. Although there was nobody around at close range to see it, Lewis knew in his heart, that the Cosmic Soul would be watching and hopefully, appreciated his discomfort for the cause. The T – shirt's fabric was coarse, making him itch all morning. A veritable hairshirt, he thought, worthy of any Saint.

He paused, as usual, to squint through the Control Room window, waiting for Jolly to turn its priestly face with its benign smile. But when their gaze met, there was no smile for him. Jolly's eyes clouded. Lewis strode in.

"Why the long face?"

"I think the T-shirts are in poor taste, Lewis," Jolly said, "Dan will be hurt to see you wearing such a garment, in his name."

"Be that as it may, I'm wearing it until I see him again, because it makes me feel closer to him." Lewis put his overalls over the back of the chair and began pulling his T-shirt off over his head. "Lock the door and turn out the lights!"

The room dimmed, immersing Lewis in the lambent glow from Jolly's face, emergency LEDs and computer screens. "Thanks, Jolls." He removed his trousers and underpants, folded them and tucked them under the desk, away from prying eyes, just in case. Naked, crouching, he removed a specimen bottle and a scalpel from the desk-drawer. He spread his Dan-Back T-shirt flat-out on the floor and placed the utensils on top. "Jolls, is there anyone outside?"

"There are four Park Monitors working in E Zone, they do not appear to be heading this way," Jolly said, "Why have you removed your clothes, Lewis?"

"Because I'm hot," Lewis said, "Let me know me if you see someone coming. I don't want to give anybody a nasty shock." He ducked his head down, scurrying over to the kitchen area. In the cupboard under the sink, he found a cracked Petri-dish and an old pipette Mary had used for something or other. He returned to place them with the other items on top of the T-shirt and then knelt on the floor, facing the meagre display.

"What are you doing, Lewis?" Jolly said.

"It's a private matter. Don't speak, unless it's to warn me about intruders."

He placed his hands together, pointing his fingers at the ceiling, then at Jolly's Ceegee, then at the spot where Dan had caught the lightning bolt.

"Open the window, open the window, open the window," he said in a quiet voice. "I call upon the Cosmic Soul to witness my sacrifice."

He took a deep breath, snatched up the scalpel and stuck

it into the palm of his hand, pulled it out, smeared with blood, stabbed himself in the same place again, and again. With a cry he tossed the scalpel aside and doubled over, clutching his hand over the Petri-dish to catch the blood, dripping fast. "It's all yours, Dan" – he gritted his teeth – "towards our eternal bond."

"Lewis, stop!" Jolly cried. "This is not what he wants. Dan wants you to be happy."

"I am happy! God is witness to my suffering." Lewis raised his eyes, tears running down his face. The pain couldn't be worse than if he'd taken a hammer to his hand and shattered every bone. "I'm the Saint and the Saint must suffer!"

"You are not a Saint. You are my friend and Dan's friend. We care about you. Please stop what you are doing!"

"Until you can bleed, until you can feel my agony, don't talk to me about caring! You should know by now that a human face is not enough."

Lewis squeezed his palm with his other hand, causing blood to pulse from the wound, thicker, darker than he'd expected. Not just his palm, now his whole arm throbbed, aching into his armpit, making him feel sick.

"Is that enough for you, Dan?"

He glared up into the Surveillance Eye, high in the corner of the room, before removing the lid from the specimen bottle, almost full, black with congealed blood.

"Do you see this?" He held it up. "It's not port-wine this time."

His hand dripped all over the Dan-Back T-shirt as he began, with the pipette, to draw blood from the Petri-dish, transferring it to the specimen bottle. "I say, Dan, how many of these do you think it would take to fill two buckets?" Lewis closed his left fist. His middle finger sank deep inside the wound, soggy as a sponge, making him gag. "Make that two, golden buckets!"

"May I speak now, Lewis?" Jolly said.

"Is someone coming?" He clasped his hands between his thighs. There was no escaping the pain, burning like a red-hot iron against his skin.

"No, Lewis. I have just seen Mary on the Surveillance Eye, entering her apartment on Level Two."

"They're back! Jolly, I knew it. I'm going to see Dan again. My life can begin again. Quick, turn the lights on!" Lewis groped under the desk for his clothes, oblivious to smearing blood all over his underpants and trousers, rushing to get dressed. "Give me five minutes, Jolly, and then call her intercom!"

"Yes, Lewis."

Lewis wrapped everything up inside the T-shirt and stuffed it into the cupboard under the sink. He bound his hand in a paper towel, awkwardly pulling on his overalls, feeling so light-headed he kept staggering to keep his balance, and put it down to euphoria. He sat down at his desk, weak and breathless.

"Any sightings of Dan?"

"No, Lewis."

"Okay, call Mary" – he took a deep breath – "let's see what she has to say."

Mary's face appeared on screen, gaunt, pale, eyes sunken.

"Hello Lewis, I was going to call you later. I've only just got back to my apartment."

"Crikey, Mary, what's happened to you?"

"I've got a bit of a cold. I must've caught it from Dan while we were away." She gave a faint smile. "I understand the new crop implantations went well today. Congratulations."

"Piece of cake." Lewis tightened his fist to suppress the throbbing in his palm. "Where the hell did you go?"

"It's confidential… to do with vaccine production." She blinked heavy eyelids. "You don't look well either. Are you all right?"

"Fine, I've been working all day, just a bit hot under the collar." He puffed. "Did you know Jane was looking for you inside the building? Some people are convinced you two never left the UISC. Is this some sort of cover-up?"

"I can't discuss it, Lewis."

"Oh, I get it. I'm out of the loop." Lewis twisted his mouth. "I suppose everything's nice and cosy between you, now that you must've spread your legs for him. Did he teach you some humility or are you still as hubristic as ever?"

"If you continue like this, I'll hang up."

"Whoops, sorry, didn't mean to upset you." He sucked air through his teeth, at the limit of his pain threshold. "So what are you doing back in your own apartment? I thought you two were living together at his Penthouse?"

"Dan has left." The faraway look in Mary's eyes appeared to intensify. 'Vacant' was the word that came to mind. "It's unlikely any of us will see him again."

"He might not see you again. It doesn't mean he won't see me." Lewis's tone sharpened. "Where's he gone?"

"I don't know. He's got to keep his head down now that he's revealed his identity to the UISC Community." She lowered her voice. "Dan can't see you again, even if he wanted to."

"Really? Is it because I know he's a mutant?"

"Who told you?" She held her deep, unflinching gaze, unreadable.

"Soraya."

"Don't tell anyone else, will you?" Mary's look hardened. "It would make life very difficult for him."

"Sorry, too late." Lewis sniffed. "Soraya told everybody before she left, including the students. Haven't you seen the Dan Back T-shirts everybody is wearing?"

"What T-shirts?" She narrowed her eyes.

"T-shirts depicting the link between Dan and the Cosmos, written in the life-forms plastered all over his back." Lewis squeezed his fist. Blood was seeping through the paper towel. "You won't have a clue until you've seen the evidence yourself. Dan Udan is connected to whatever is out there responsible for everything in this Creation. That's what we all believe, as followers of the UDAN Religion. Of course, I wouldn't expect you to agree with us, with your" – he raised a haughty shoulder – "blind spot, otherwise known as hubris."

"Lewis, do you realise you've made it impossible for Dan ever to return to the UISC. Or to reveal his identity ever again, anywhere."

"Why?" Lewis laughed. "What do you think people are going to do? Crucify him?" The screen blanked.

Chapter Thirty-Eight

Mary forced herself to concentrate, reading the POX V2 vaccine report from St Anthony's hospital.

Sean Flanagan's analysis was exhaustive, detailing all the minor ailments of the out-patient trials, over seven days.

She scrolled back to Stefan Mohr's summary, from the UISC.

The vaccine had continued to sustain Scotty Tissue's immunity. Stefan was confident the news wasn't going to change. Things were looking good for the UISC genetics team in the race for the vaccine. Plans for mass production were already underway this Friday afternoon, involving Craig Craigan and Dr Flanagan in talks with drug companies on behalf of UDAN Corporations.

She'd had no choice but to lie to Lewis about her involvement.

She moved on to the Farm Park data analysis of crop-yield to biosphere maintenance for March 2028. There were sheets missing from Lewis' contribution. For an entire day he'd copied the results from last February, as if she wouldn't notice. Harvester malfunction was to blame. There was nothing to show for Wednesday the eighth of March, but blank boxes where the figures should've been.

Mary lingered over the date of Dan's birthday, until it

became a blur. She held herself, rocking back and forth, taking deep breaths. She knew grief well, the ebb and flow of its tide. In a moment this would pass, the pain would recede. She sat up straight and wiped her cheeks.

By midnight she'd completed her workload and left her study, to move wearily through her sitting-room, picking up a used mug, adjusting the rug beside the coffee table. Everything here had been put back, almost exactly as it was before.

In the kitchen, she turned on the tap and let it run cold, leaning over the sink to splash her face and heard it again.

The sound of breaking glass.

She closed her eyes, fighting her way back through the fog, to find the source of the memory. There was a little silver boy, a four-poster bed, a needle and a tube, *the vortex*... The only glass she could remember was the Udan Window and the mirror in the bathroom.

Mary hadn't told Jane the whole truth. She remembered a lot. She just didn't remember everything. But why were some hours lost and others saved? She turned to the wall where Dan had stood to drink his coffee, the day he moved in. In his blue sweater and jeans, she could see him now. His sky-blue gaze, washing over her.

"*Dan, why have you abandoned me*?"

This time, he didn't beckon to her. In her mind he was silent. She went over and leaned with her back against the same wall.

"*Whatever happened between us, I'll always love you... Please, look after yourself-*"

She performed her bedtime ritual mechanically, inhaling the smell of fresh paint in her bedroom, where things had to be changed after Dan had slept here during his illness. New mattress, new duvet and new bedcovers. It no longer felt like her room. She got into bed and turned out the lights, staring into the darkness.

Images flickered at the back of her mind. She closed her eyes and heard the echo of her own voice.

"Then it's too late... I'm not leaving you."

She remembers – she can feel him, pressing his lips to her body, moving down to the place between her thighs. So slow, so tender, she longs for him to come inside her.

His first entry is like a birth. Tearing her open, as he cradles her head inside his arms.

Sensing her pain, Dan shudders, he holds himself back.

They don't speak. There's no need. When he reaches the limits of her body, he stops and waits for her flesh to give a little more, before he carries on.

Mary puts her hand on his cheek. "My love, gently-"

She has a sense of time passing, of time distorted –

Dan is thrusting inside her. Saliva glazes his lips. The grunting sound she makes is the forced expulsion of breath from her lungs, as he takes her, holding her down by her wrists.

Now he's gentle, stirring a need inside her so deep, Mary starts to pant. He catches her on a wave, lifting her to another place, where she cannot help but move to his rhythm.

For one, long, sensual moment they dance to their own music. He quickens, driving her body to its highest pitch, until the pleasure is more than she can bear, she bucks, convulses and cries out.

He covers her mouth with his, possessing her so completely, they are one animal.

Day and night have merged into seamless happiness. In their world of no boundaries, there's no such thing as separation or shame. Dan lives inside her, and Mary feels a part of him, as if she were another of his limbs. And she can't get enough of his mouth. She loves to run her tongue over his big, white teeth, to taste his laughter, and his tears. All he wants is more, and all Mary wants, is to give him more.

Even as she sleeps, Dan moves inside her.

When Mary wakes, she is lying on her stomach. He's still holding her down, though there's no need. She surrendered at their first kiss. When he's passionate, he takes her breath away. But this is a slow, cooler man inside her, milking every sensation, moaning every time he reaches her limit.

Mary lifts her head from the pillow. "Dan, I've had enough."

His voice is so tender – "Hey now, what's the matter?" – he sweeps the damp hair out of her eyes. "Sweetheart, tell me."

"You're using me."

"Don't say that. You know how much I love you."

He withdraws from her body and lies on his side to face her. Now that they're two people again, she feels a rush of possessiveness towards him. "I can't get enough of you, angel." He strokes her hair. "But, of course, if you want me to stop, I'll stop." But she senses impatience in the way he's stroking her hair.

"I don't mean to reject you," she says, "I need to rest."

"Don't ever reject me. I couldn't bear it." His face is so close, his eyes reach out to her like feelers. "I don't know if you know, but I haven't climaxed yet." He furrows his brow. "I'm almost there… But if you must rest, I'll stop now."

"I had no idea." She's suddenly conscious of all the cold,

selfish places inside her.

He puts his forehead to hers. "You'll know when I do. I'm like a supernova."

Mary recognises his shy expression, the way he blushed on the day they met.

"Then you mustn't stop. I want you to be happy."

"Are you sure? I don't want to do anything to upset you."

"Darling, I love you-" She pushes the tip of her tongue between his lips. Dan closes his mouth around hers, with a teasing growl in the back of his throat, probing between her thighs with an erection that never abated. He hoists her leg up over his arm, roughly now, starts to take her. She clasps his face. "Remember, my love, gently-"

But he's a different animal. She no longer feels part of him. He rolls her over and begins to violate her.

She can't take him and cries out, again and again. Stop. And his human name. Daniel.

He takes her in his teeth by the scruff of her neck, as if he might shake her, but instead, holds her there. She hears a long, low growl coming from underneath the bed.

Mary is frozen in terror

Time is missing

When she becomes aware, he's on her back, motionless. There's something reptilian in his stillness, waiting for her flesh to submit to his, to gain access to her womb.

She feels the world tremble.

More time missing

He's pushing her across the floor, in a bear-hug from behind. Barely conscious, the oak panels rattle and shock her awake. Mary's cheek is flat against the wall. She strains with both hands, to push herself backwards, her cries drowned out by his grunts, the rattling of the panels. She sees the bluebottle on the back of her hand, switch position, rub its legs. Vomit spurts between her lips.

Time missing

Faraway an animal shrieks and gives up its life,

That life pulses inside her,

The world stands still.

Mary turns around and sinks to her knees.

Dan staggers backwards, his face contorted in a silent scream. He crumples to the floor, rolls onto his side, and draws his knees up to his chest, his head inside his arms.

He lets out the scream.

Mary covers her ears and shrinks against the wall, staring at the reptilian eye at the base of his spine, hooded open, staring back at her. The scrotal sack bulging between his thighs looks like a human heart has been wedged there. He starts to moan, a desolate, lost-child's whimper, his hands and feet quivering.

While his back is turned, Mary creeps along the wall, towards the bathroom's sliding panels.

She slips inside. Leaking blood and semen, hands shaking, she can barely turn the taps. She stands in the bath and washes herself. Beyond the quietly running water, she can still hear him. She dries herself, wraps a towel around her and sits on the chair, with her teeth clenched to stop their chattering.

Mary feels numb inside. No hatred, no anger, not even fear.

Time passes. An hour, maybe more. She senses a shift, remembering his heartbeat, strong and fast. A moment of eternity, gazing into his eyes. She rises from the chair.

The doors slide open. Dan stands there in his black dressing gown. He takes two steps into the bathroom.

"Mary, I love you more than my life." He turns his head and looks at his reflection in the mirror. "There's no coming back from this, is there?" He smashes the mirror with his fist, shards of glass clatter inside the sink. He grabs one and puts it to his throat. "I'd rather die than live without your love."

Mary reaches towards him. "No!"

With one clean swipe, his neck gapes, spattering blood at the wall.

She catches him as he falls, both collapsing under his weight. Her reflexes are so fast she scrambles to put her hand over the wound. Dan's limbs begin to jerk. His eyes roll upwards. He's losing breath, rasping through his severed windpipe, drowning in his own blood. She strips the towel from around her and presses it to his neck.

"Stay with me! Open your eyes, Dan, look at me!"

Her mind leaps. There's a tube in the bedroom, somewhere. She could insert it inside his lungs, he could use it to breathe through. "Dan, hold on! I'll be straight back!"

She stands up and cries out, only now noticing the floor. The area of white tiles has shrunk to one corner, the rest is a sea of blood, closing in. "Oh God, no!" She covers her eyes. "Dan, don't do this to me!"

She drops onto her knees and takes his head in her hands. The light in his eyes is fading. His lips are blue.

"Dan, I never stopped loving you. Don't leave me!" She smothers his face in kisses. "I love you! I love you!"

She hears loud gurgling from the wound. He gives one final convulsion. His eyes glaze over, staring upward. She puts her mouth over his, one moment kissing him, the next, trying frantically to breathe air inside him.

"You're not dead. I know you can live without breath, longer than anyone." But when she looks at his face, there's no change. She listens to his heart, to its terrible silence.

She clutches his head to her breast. "Oh, God help him! He believes in you, please God, save him. God, I beg you-"

Mary loses all awareness of how long she has been rocking Dan in her arms. Her grief is visceral. She is sick with it, retching until she is coughing up blood. Until she is exhausted, until she can't breathe, willing her own life to end. She lies down beside him and puts her head on his chest, so hard and cold. There is nowhere to go. Nothing to do but die.

Her gaze turns towards the ceiling. She imagines him watching over her.

"Wait for me," she whispers.

She slips down into a dream, walking in the wildflower meadow, brushing her hands over grasses that stand as high as her waist. She looks up at the deep blue sky, where there's a pure-white cloud, all alone and peaceful, way up high. Something about the cloud fills her with sadness.

As she looks, the cloud becomes etched with silver. The sun appears and a shaft of dazzling sunlight falls across the meadow. And there is Dan, in his white suit, his arms open wide.

"Mary!"

She runs to him, and he throws his arms around her, lifting her off the ground.

"Mary, I'm sorry I hurt you." He kisses her forehead and puts her down. "I haven't got long. God has only granted me a few minutes."

"I love you. I need you. Come back." Mary clings to him.

"Oh, please, Dan, please come back." She bursts into tears.

He takes her hands in his, his expression is full of sadness. "Mary, God has taken me away from you. I'm not worthy of your love. You've got to be strong. I want you to wake up and leave the bathroom. Go down the corridor. There's a door on the left that leads onto a staircase that'll take you down to your suite in the Penthouse. Tell Cookie where I am, and he'll take care of my body. Please, will you do that for me?"

"No." She grasps his fingers. "I'm staying with you until I die. You're not to blame. I was the one who opened the door."

"Listen to me." He firms his mouth. "I'm not fit to sit at your table, let alone share your bed. I'm a savage brute and you're better off without me. Now go!" He points behind her. "Go back!"

"I'll kill myself," she says.

He grabs her shoulders. "Don't do this to us, Mary, you're already pregnant with our son. You've got to carry on God's work without me. God doesn't want Lucida growing up hating his father and pitying his mother. The decision has been made. Marry Sean Flanagan. He'll make a far better father than me. Now get back there, before God throws me to hell."

"Then I'll see you in hell." She reaches up and takes his face in her hands.

"Mary, you can't have me. I'm dead."

"So am I." She gazes up into his eyes.

"Don't force my hand, or you'll be back in the lion's den."

"Then I'll find a way to tame you."

Mary opens her eyes.

She's in the bathroom, sitting on the chair, with a towel wrapped around her. The floor-tiles are white. The bathroom mirror is intact. She rises and goes to look through the sliding panels. Dan is lying naked on the floor, on his side. She can hear him breathing, in a deep sleep. She kneels at his side and runs her fingers through his hair.

"I had a terrible dream," she whispers. "Thank God, you're still alive."

He turns his head and looks up at her.

"Mary, I had the same dream." He puts his hand to his neck and touches a line of ragged, black stitches.

At his shoulder there's a reel of black cotton. A long, golden needle.

Chapter Thirty-Nine

"Good morning, Mary, how are you feeling? Did you manage to sleep much?"

"Not too bad, thank you." Mary muted the sound on the television news and put her mobile on loudspeaker. She felt bleary-eyed, with a head full of cottonwool, having had no sleep at all.

"Did you take any pain killers?"

"I haven't really needed them. I've been too busy catching up with work." She took a sip of coffee. "I've just been listening to Criag Craigan on the news, talking about our vaccine availability by the end of next week. I would've liked to have completed the out-patient trials before we started the rollout."

"I understand your concern, but people are willing to take the risk," Jane said. "UDAN's Shelter Communities can afford to wait for procedure, but outside things are getting desperate. Overnight, there were seven thousand more deaths in the UK. This morning UDAN Corps took the decision to go ahead. They have every faith in you, Mary."

"Have you spoken to Dan?" Mary's voice wavered.

"No. But the reason I'm calling does concern him." Jane's inhalation was audible down the phone. "Do you remember me telling you about Alex Palmer from MI6, who found Dan nine years ago?"

"Of course, I do."

Jane's voice lifted. "Well, he's here. He's come over from London with a colleague and they'd both like to meet you for an informal chat about Dan. Would you be up to seeing the three of us this morning, for coffee?"

"Why do they want to talk to me?" Mary felt a prickle of adrenalin.

"Because you've been closer to him than anyone else." Jane's voice took on a slightly coercive tone. "We're all very worried about Dan's state of mind. All the signs indicate that he's become a danger to others, and to himself. I'd be grateful if you'd talk to us."

"Yes, if I can help." Mary's brain was starting to wake-up. "What time?"

"Thank-you, dear, about eleven-thirty." She gave a sigh of relief. "Do you remember anything more about your time together?"

"It's all very much like a dream." Mary hesitated. "But I've a question. Would you know if Dan has…an injury to his throat?"

"Yes, he does. Cookie said yesterday on the phone, he saw a nasty scar around his neck. Dan won't talk about it. Do you know what happened?"

Mary felt a chill go through her. "No. It's just one of the many disjointed images I've had… I'll see you at eleven-thirty."

Mary's hands started to shake. She put the breakfast plate on the coffee-table and lay down on the sofa, with her forearm across her eyes, straining her mind back to a scene that made no sense. Things can't have happened the way she remembered them. And yet, Dan's wound was real. She had a faint recollection of picking up the needle, holding it between her finger and thumb.

Mary closed her eyes and tried to remember how they had parted.

She hears him, in a harsher voice.

"Get dressed." He places her gown on the bed. "You'll find clean underwear in that drawer."

Dan walks across the room to the oak-panel wall, slides it open and removes his white suit from a coat-hanger. The black robe slips from his shoulders. From where Mary watches him, the growths on his back appear as intricate embroidery. The dragonfly is iridescent blue, its orange wings are luminous beneath the chandelier. As he moves to get dressed the colours and shapes shift and change, like a kaleidoscope. It really is quite beautiful.

He turns around. "What are you doing sitting there. We haven't got all day." The stitches around his throat look like a black choker. He lifts his shirt collar to do up his top button and conceals it. "What's wrong, don't you want to go home?"

She doesn't. She wants to go back to bed, to be as close as they were in the beginning. But she recognises the wall. He's shutting her out.

"Where do you come from?" Mary sits on the end of the bed, in her white robe, while he does up his tie, chin up.

"I'm Dublin, born and bred. Where did you think?"

She inclines her head. "Oh, I don't know. I thought maybe, another world, in a different galaxy?"

Dan laughs, showing his big white teeth. His laughter reassures her, encourages her to probe, deeper.

"I'm close, aren't I? Closer than I've ever been. Please, tell me the truth."

He raises his eyebrows. "Ach, so small, Mary. Think big. Think outside. What's outside?"

"If you mean outside the universe? There's nothing, is there?"

"And that's where I'm from."

"That's impossible."

"So, I'm impossible. I'll be even more impossible if you don't get dressed. Come on now" – he snaps his fingers, twice – "up and at them!"

"You could be some sort of god, I suppose." She clasps her hands around one raised knee, in a coy, come to bed gesture. "Is that thought big enough for you?"

"I'm not good enough." He smiles. "But I'm not the devil either." He gives a tug to his shirt cuffs and moves over to the bed. Immaculate again, in his white suit. He picks up her gown. "Would you like me to help you with the hooks and eyes?"

She looks up at him with a teasing smile, but she is on a serious mission. "Are you from another universe?"

"Yes, is the answer to all your questions. Now" – he holds the gown out for her – "you step in, and I'll do you up."

Mary rises and places her feet inside her gown. "That's not an answer," she says. Dan bends on one knee and starts fixing the hooks and eyes down her flank, tickling her, making her squirm. "Dan, don't you think I deserve to know the truth?"

He stands and tucks her hair behind her ears. The look in his eyes makes her blush.

"The truth is you're too lovely, and I can't help myself." He takes something from his jacket pocket and puts it in his mouth. She doesn't know what he places on his tongue, until his lips are on hers and he feeds it to her. He closes his hand over her mouth. "Swallow it," he says. It's on the back of her tongue. She has no choice but to swallow a small pill.

"What have you given me?"

"Something to make you sleep and forget." He kisses her forehead. "Put your head down on that pillow."

"But I don't want to forget." A wave of drowsiness passes over her. Mary lowers herself onto the bed. She gazes up at the chandelier's pendants. Her hands and feet are tingling.

Dan stretches out beside her. He leans over her and looks into her eyes. "How does it feel when I touch you?" He starts to stoke her thigh.

"I'm going numb, all over. Is that supposed to happen?" Her eyelids grow heavy. She senses herself slipping down, as he breathes in her ear and moves over her body,

"I promise, you won't feel anything this time . . . Open your legs, sweetheart or shall I?"

"Mary, this is Alex Palmer from Military Intelligence." Jane gestured towards the first gentleman who followed her into Mary's apartment, wearing a light-grey suit. He extended his hand.

"Delighted to meet you, Mary. Thank you for seeing us this morning." He was well-spoken, a tall, gaunt man in his early sixties, with a direct gaze and a disarmingly limp handshake.

"And this is Leon La Grau. Leon is French, but he speaks very good English." Jane's smile passed from La Grau to Mary. "Leon lives in Paris. This is his second visit to the UISC."

"Hello Mary." An energetic handshake by contrast, from a short, dark-haired man in a black polo-neck. La Grau looked to be in his early forties. "Aha, cherchez la femme!"

"Do please sit down," Mary said, "The coffee is ready, I'll bring it in." She went to the kitchen, with Jane at her heels.

"Are you all right, Mary? You look a bit distracted."

"I didn't sleep as well as I thought." She placed a large pot of freshly ground coffee on the tray. "Do excuse me if I'm not very talkative."

"Alex and Leon know what happened. I've had to tell them everything." Jane gave a firm nod. "You'll understand, once we've explained."

But there was an awkward silence as they sipped their coffee, making quiet clinks with their cups on their saucers, compelling Mary to speak up.

"Please tell me what this is about."

"Alex, would you like to begin?" Jane said.

Palmer sat forward in the armchair, with his elbows on his thighs, making a bridge with his fingers.

"I'll cut to the chase. Jane told me about Dan's enduring obsession with you ...five or six years ago." He spoke in a restrained, halting manner. "I thought he had you in mind to become his wife one day. I also anticipated that one day I'd be... talking to you like this." He lowered his eyes. "I hear from Jane that you were, until recently, a couple in love, planning a future, until the reality of your situation became apparent. Obviously, Dan is no ordinary man. I've always been of the opinion, that to treat him as such would, in time cause him...considerable stress, putting himself and others in danger." He raised his eyes. "Would you agree?"

Mary caught Jane's eye.

"Alex isn't here to make accusations," Jane said, "He has

yours and Dan's interest at heart."

"Of course, I'm worried about him," Mary said.

Palmer sat back in the armchair and crossed his legs. "Would it worry you to know that Dan intends to leave for the States on Monday morning, with the Cooksons? He has signed another contract with Warner Brothers to create a… series of holographic films and plans to live there for the next six months, rubbing shoulders with people from the industry, not as Dan Udan, but masquerading as a UDAN rep."

"Am I worried, do you mean, because of Phoenix Ra?" Mary felt suddenly weak, absorbing Palmer's words.

"Dan has ordered the vaccination of all residents at Lacerta, including Cookie and Desi, before they leave," Jane said.

"The terrorist threat is a concern to us all." Palmer winced. "But I understand your vaccine, so far, has been a great success. Our main concern is for Dan and… his sanity. I appreciate you don't remember much about the days you spent with him." He placed his elbow on the arm of the chair and curled his forefinger over his upper lip.

"Dan left you in Jane's care," he went on, "The results of your medical tests speak for themselves. We know Udan can cover his tracks, anytime he likes. But not this time. This time he wants someone to step in. Someone, other than Jane and his staff at Lacerta, must take control over his life.

"Dan Udan is, basically, a very decent fellow, but for his extreme animal instincts. If he thought a prison sentence could change him, he'd have handed himself in by now. But, to put Udan behind bars would create havoc. Udan requires specialist care, which we can provide for him. But the fellow would have to co-operate." Palmer raised one eyebrow. "Unfortunately, after his experience with us nine years ago, our fellow hasn't much faith in our methods. Military Intelligence's understanding of Udan has matured considerably since then." Palmer nodded at La Grau. "Leon, if you would-"

"Madam, allow me to introduce myself properly." La Grau rose from the sofa and proffered his hand a second time. "I am Dr Leon La Grau, Head of Research at the SETI Institute in Paris. You have heard about us?"

"The research institute for extra-terrestrial intelligence?" Mary blinked, dazed by the turn of the conversation.

"That is correct." La Grau sat and lifted a leather satchel onto his lap, undoing the buckles. "We have been observing Udan for a number of years, at a respectful distance naturally." He gave Mary a fleeting smile. "When MI6 informed SETI of Udan's existence in twenty-twenty, I was determined to discover everything I could about the human chimera with the bio-electric metabolism. In the years that have followed, I have been amazed by his economic and technological rise to power. It has been incredible, don't you think?"

Mary glanced at Jane, whose eyes remained lowered, expression solemn. "Yes," Mary said.

"The Udan phenomenon is of great interest to us all, yet it remains enigmatic." La Grau removed something like a holiday-brochure from his satchel. "We at SETI consider Dan Udan to be humanity's greatest asset. For all that he has given to us and for his futuristic aspirations for our world, he is a beacon of hope.

"Unfortunately, there is a shadow that hangs over him. The super-human biology that gives him mysterious powers is ferociously animalistic. He is both predatory and dangerous."

La Grau peered at her from beneath heavy eyebrows. "Udan is losing the battle with his transgenic nature. Our hypothesis is that he does not feed properly. He thrives on a diet of raw meat and live insects. Without these his behaviour becomes chaotic, like an addict with cravings, his needs become insatiable."

"Our chimera needs to be taken in hand. Jane knows it. Cookson knows it. I'm sure you do too, Mary," Palmer said. "I'm sure Udan appreciates your loyalty. The knowledge that he assaulted you doesn't appear to have changed your feelings for him. Jane tells me you're still devoted to Dan Udan. Is that right?"

"Yes. But I know if Dan goes to the States with the Cooksons on Monday, it will end in disaster."

"Cookie said he dreads going with Dan." Jane looked over at Mary. "There's nobody we know who can stop Dan from leaving, except you, Mary. If Dan could have you back in his life, without the risk of exposing you to danger, I believe he'd stay."

"Madam, if there was a place, a safe haven, where you and Dan could be together, where his feeding could be brought under control and his behaviour safely monitored, would you visit him there?" La Grau gazed at Mary. "Would you visit him, at this place." He leaned across and handed over the brochure. "Take a good look."

Mary leafed through the glossy pages, featuring a luxurious, modern house set in private grounds, surrounded by trees. Nowhere did it suggest that it was anything but an expensive family residence.

"SETI has created a purpose-built apartment for Udan, near London," Palmer said. "The scientists there will monitor him and learn more about this extraordinary man, whom I believe, is fundamentally a new species of human being, having a spot of trouble coming to terms with himself."

"There will be around the clock CCTV surveillance until you visit him, then SETI will respect your privacy. There will be a panic button available for you to wear and in every room. You will have our advice and support." Leon smiled. "You will be safe with him."

"You're going to deprive him of his freedom?" Mary searched their faces.

"It won't be like that," Jane said. "Dan would have to agree to it, like a voluntary sectioning. If you're willing to visit him, he's more likely to give his consent. Cookie says he's desperate to see you. But he feels so guilty and ashamed of himself, he can't pick up the phone."

"Would you visit him in London, Mary?" Palmer said.

"Yes," Mary said, "Everyday, if I could."

"They have an incredible bond," Jane murmured.

"Would you be prepared to explain to Udan what SETI is offering him?" Palmer contracted his eyes. "It would be better coming from you."

"He refuses to speak to me." Mary looked from one to the other. "And his name is John Daniel or Dan, if you don't mind."

"Our fellow, Daniel, has just made plans to visit the UISC before he heads out to the States," Palmer said. "He has a meeting with your Governors tomorrow night and intends to fly out from the UISC first thing Monday morning."

"We are certain he will come to you, Mary. He would not be able to resist it." La Grau shook his head.

"Dan can fool himself, but not us, or Jane, true?" He looked at Jane beside him on the sofa.

"I don't know how Dan thinks he can cope with going to America," Jane said. "Cookie expects he'll want to come back within the week. He'll be that sick with separation anxiety. Missing you, Mary."

"What time is he arriving tomorrow?" Mary couldn't conceal the catch in her breath.

"The meeting is scheduled for seven pm," Palmer said. "He could arrive at your door any time before or after. We'll leave you with SETI's details. If you could assert your powers of persuasion, Mary, you'd be doing us more than a favour. You'd be saving Dan's life."

"Saving his life, absolutely." La Grau nodded. "For we all know he cannot continue this way."

"Leon has something for you." Palmer gave a supercilious nod at La Grau.

"Ah oui-" La Grau reached into his satchel. "I doubt if you will need this. I am sure that Dan will do his best to maintain his composure. But just in case, we'd like you to wear it."

Mary accepted into her palm a golden chain with a small diamond pendant. "A necklace?"

"It is not simply a necklace. At SETI we have adopted much of UDAN's technology in surveillance and security." La Grau smiled. "It is a discrete panic button. If you feel threatened in any way at all, press on the diamond and surveillance officers will be alerted to come to your aid."

"Thank you." Mary met his eyes. "What happens if Dan refuses to accept SETI's help?"

"Leon and I will follow Dan and the Cooksons out to the States, in secret convoy with SETI scientists." Palmer sighed.

“In that event, we’ll have no other option but to wait for the proverbial to hit the fan.”

Chapter Forty

Lewis felt a hand clamp down on his shoulder and spun around.

"I'm Liam McGin, Manager for Upper Levels. Are you the one I'm supposed to be meeting here?"

A vaguely familiar man in white shirtsleeves stood before him, with possibly the least appealing face Lewis could remember, uncannily like a frog.

"Yes, Mr McGin, I'm Mr Fox, a new tutor at the University." He opened his hands indicating the beach. "Isn't it marvellous, what the Lord has created for our pleasure." He sniffed and exhaled. "Can you smell that sea air!"

McGin's eyes bulged, absorbing the sight of Lewis in his golden cassock, with his cleanly shaved head.

"Are you a priest or something?"

"I am, indeed, a Saint of the UDAN faith. You may, if you wish, address me as Saint Fox."

McGin wiggled his little finger in his ear. "Oh, I don't know about that Mr Fox, I wouldn't want to cause any offence. What can I do you for?"

Lewis bared his canines in a narrow smile. "I have gained permission from the Governor's Committee concerning the use of this Swimming Pool, allowing for a student function here tomorrow night, so long as we observe regulations by following your instructions."

"Ah, yes, I heard about that" – McGin wagged his forefinger horizontally – "on the understanding that it's the last time. Once all this sand has been removed, there will be no more parties in here, for students or otherwise. This is a swimming pool, intended for swimming and keeping inmates physically fit, do you understand?" He pointed at Lewis. "Wait, don't I know you?"

Lewis smiled superciliously. "No, but apparently I look very much like one of the scientists who works here, except that I have a lot more hair." He chuckled. "But I've heard a lot about you, Mr McGin, trying to get our Mr Udan evicted when you thought he was just an ordinary mortal." He crinkled up his eyes, to give his penetrating look. "That must've been an enlightening moment for you, when you discovered the truth… Praise be to UDAN." Lewis raised his eyes. "UDAN works in mysterious ways."

McGin glowered. "You're a strange one, aren't you? You can come by my office and pick up the Regulation Booklet." He looked up the slope, towards the bar. "You'll find forms behind the bar to fill in if you want to order refreshments, but the Student Union will have to pay for them. If you're having food-"

"Mr McGin, sorry to interrupt" – Lewis clasped his hands, hunching his shoulders – "I do have a great favour to ask on behalf of my students. They'd love to see the Red Giant Sun, shinning tomorrow evening. Since the party is in celebration of Mr Udan's recent visit, I'd be very grateful if you could make the occasion that extra bit special, by having it switched on?"

McGin's mouth pursed into a lipless seal. "Give you an inch

and you take a mile. The answer is *no*. This hologram is for the Governors' use only. You should count yourselves lucky to have what you've got and don't look a gift-horse in the mouth."

"I do take your point, Mr McGin. But I happen to be a very close friend of Mr Udan's and I believe he'd be very disappointed to hear that his students missed an opportunity to witness one of his most breath-taking creations." Lewis adopted a tone of lyrical persuasion, relishing his priestly role. "Some have already seen it, but many have not. Those that have had the honour were profoundly inspired and have already improved in their studies. If you did grant permission, I believe Mr Udan would congratulate you on your *forward thinking*."

"Then you don't know him as I do." McGin's voice hardened. "He'd have me over a barrel for breaking the rule of Work and Energy Conservation. I'd be creating extra work for the weather boys on a Sunday night which is their busiest time. They're the ones who'd have to programme the Ceegee. The answer is no and I'm not going to stand here repeating myself." He started to walk backwards, crunching sand and gravel. "I don't like the tone of your voice, Mr Fox. You can send one of your students to pick up the Regulation Booklet. I'll be here tomorrow night to make sure you behave yourselves." He jabbed his forefinger. "I've heard things about your lot, mister and I'm not impressed."

Lewis' cheeks burned. "Do you have any idea who you're talking to?"

"I'm not interested." He turned his back and trekked up the slope, one hand pressed against his thick waist.

There were shouts up at the bar. Wildo and Abby were waving. Lewis started a few yards behind McGin, walking up the slope, catching up with him as he met Wildo and Abby.

Lewis shook his head to convey the negative signal, propelling Wildo forward with an outstretched hand.

"Good morning, Mr McGin, it's great to see you, sir."

McGin took his hand. "Weren't you there that night, involved in Dr. Downs' incident?"

"Yes, sir, when drink got the better of him." Wildo smiled. "But we weren't to know who he was, sir and you were caught in the middle, just doing your job. I hope my witness statement helped."

"It did come in handy, thanks…What are you doing here?"

Abby stepped forward on her tiptoes and kissed McGin on the cheek, in her pink bikini-top and mini-skirt, her blonde hair scraped into a ponytail. The fat man stood stock-still and gaped at her. She put her thumb to his cheek and rubbed away a smudge of lipstick.

"It's my birthday tomorrow, Mr McGin." She clasped her hands. "Please, please, sir, can we have sunshine on the beach?"

McGin came to his senses with a gruff laugh. "Oh, I see, I'm being buttered up, am I?" He gave a heavy sigh, scanning the girl. "I've told your tutor already, the answer is no." Eyes roaming all over Abby, his voice lost some of its edge. "How old are you tomorrow?"

"Nineteen." She popped her bubble-gum and put her hand on her hip. "You can come if you want. I think you'd have a lot of fun."

"Yeah, sir, that's guaranteed." Wildo was wearing a bright floral shirt, looking every bit the Australian beach-boy. The expression in his eyes appeared to wax and wane, as if he liked to let on that he was docile, when he was far from it. "Girls these days don't play hard to get, they just play hard, isn't that right little Pinkie?"

"But we need *sunshine.*" Abby swung her hip, popping and chewing her bubble-gum so seductively that the fat around McGin's neck started to turn a raw shade of pink. Lewis almost felt sorry for him, entering melt-down despite his best efforts. Wildo caught his eye with a look that Lewis had begun to associate with the lion documentary: *Going in for the kill.*

"If you do come, sir, we'll make sure you have the time of your life and I'm talking about no holds barred." He cocked his eyebrow at McGin. "If you bring the sunshine, sir, we'll bring on the dancing girls."

"Can I have" – McGin cleared his throat – "a word with you, just the two of us?"

Wildo and McGin walked away together and stopped when they were out of earshot. Abby grinned at Lewis with a gleam of triumph in her eye and popped her gum noisily. Lewis chuckled, but he was thinking, what a sucker.

Wildo returned on his own, leaving McGin standing with his hands in his pockets.

"What's the deal?" Lewis said.

Wildo put his arm around Abby's shoulder. "Pinkie, how would you like to earn your Green Soul tomorrow night?"

Her mouth dropped. "Why? What does he want?"

"He said he'll give us the Red Giant if he can have you" – he glanced over his shoulder – "he's ready to blow as it is. I don't think it would take you more than a minute to finish him off. What do you say, Pinkie?"

"No way, Ralphie! You said all I had to do was flirt."

"Yeah, but you've got him all hot and bothered. Come on. We need this thing tomorrow night to be spectacular. We're launching the UDAN Religion, yeah? We're going to look bleeding pathetic if we can't get Udan's sun to shine."

"Ralphie, I am not, I can't!" She'd turned redder than McGin. "Just the thought of it makes me sick, so don't even ask me." She glared at him. "Ralphie!"

"Abby, God is calling for your soul to rise up." Lewis took her hand in his and stroked the backs of her fingers. "It's time for you to enter the Darkening of Defilement and become an adult. You mustn't resist your calling. You must find the courage to endure."

"Pinkie, you can't be pink all your life." Wildo put his face down into hers. "For one thing I need a woman, not a girl." He tapped the middle of her chest with his forefinger. "If you want me, you better give McGin what he wants, and I mean it. This is our turning point. If you don't do this for me, we're through and you're not even welcome at the party."

"Ralphie, no" – she pumped her knees, puffing like a child in pain – "don't make me. Why can't you Darken me? Don't make me go with him, please, Ralphie-"

"To Darken is to suffer. I can't make you suffer, for one thing, because I'm too much in love with you, yeah? But do you know how selfish you're being? The three of us started the UDAN Religion, but now you're going to spoil everything for the sake of a few minutes, at the most. Come on Abby" – he squeezed her against his side – "I'll make it up to you, afterwards. We're going to have a fantastic future together."

McGin gave a discreet cough. Wildo patted Abby's shoulder. "I'm going over to tell him it's a deal. Eight o'clock tomorrow night, down at our windshield, you've got a date. Are we cool?"

Her response of silence evidently signalled consent. Wildo

traipsed back to McGin, and the two men shook hands.

"See you tomorrow night, Pinkie," McGin called over, "I'm looking forward to watching you dance in your grass skirt. Happy birthday!" He waved, heading off towards the dolphin doors.

"Well done, Abby." Lewis smiled at her, trying to overlook her face smeared with tears and eye make-up. "You've just won us the Red Giant Sun."

She spat her bubble gum into the sand. "You've ruined my birthday forever."

"If it's any comfort, I know how you feel," Lewis said. "You will get over this. You're stronger than you think you are."

"Hey, Saint Fox, get a load of this!"

Lewis turned to see Wildo emerge from behind the bar with his arm raised, swinging what appeared at first to be a large metal birdcage, until Lewis recognised it from the sketches Wildo had made on Thursday evening.

It was the icon for their Communion Ceremony. As Abby had pointed out at the time, they couldn't have a model of Dan's back without a front and so on Lewis' suggestion they'd decided upon creating a Dan Torso. Wildo laid it at Lewis' feet.

"What do you think?" he said. "The thing has got to be wired up with all the bits and pieces. But that's your job, yeah? Did you talk to the guys at the Theatre Group about lighting effects?"

"I saw them yesterday afternoon," Lewis said, "They can make it glow using the same techniques we used for Aladdin's lamp in the pantomime. They were brilliant."

"Fantastic." Wildo winked at Abby. "See, Pinkie, everybody is doing their bit."

Up close Lewis judged that the birdcage could just about pass as a scaffold for a human torso. He got down on one knee and ran his fingers over the thin vertical bars connecting horizontal rings, expertly welded together by Udanist students of the Art and Textiles Department. A wide aperture at the neck provided leather attachments for arm-stumps. Lewis tugged on them firmly, proving the structure secure. The hips tapered abruptly into a hole at the bottom, also created from a circle of leather. As agreed, there were no buttocks or genitals to distract worshipers from its primary function: to radiate light and to shed silver confetti at the height of the Ceremony. For this end the torso had been left hollow.

"It's exactly as we designed it." Lewis looked up at Wildo. "They've done a great job. I told our lighting guys they can have the torso by this afternoon, any chance?"

"Yeah, take it now, if you like. Give the guys plenty of time to do a good job." Wildo nodded. "Pinkie and I are heading off to meet the dinner ladies from the Refectory, to discuss beach barbeques. They're asking for a couple of hundred euros up front for the work. We must dip into our savings. Is that okay with you, Saint Fox?"

"Of course, these things cost." Lewis rose and turned his penetrating gaze on Abby. "There's no such thing as a free lunch in this world, my dear. We must suffer for everything. All you can do is pray for the strength to endure."

"I will, Saint Fox and please will you pray for me too," she said in a little voice.

Wildo and Abby left the Governor's Swimming Pool. Abby walking behind him, dragging her feet.

Alone again, Lewis went down to the water and dropped

onto his knees.

"Thank you, Udan" – he put his hands in the air – "for granting us sunshine!"

Chapter Forty-One

Mary kept herself busy, longing for the hours to pass. She couldn't decide what to wear for her meeting with Dan. This afternoon she went through her wardrobe and tried on dresses she rarely wore, to give herself a few options. She narrowed the choice down to two and hung them on the wardrobe door, casting a glance at them as she put the rest away.

By early evening she'd tidied her apartment and re-organised the cupboards in her kitchen, throwing away old packets and jars.

Always in the back of her mind was the problem of what to offer Dan, when he arrived. He wouldn't be eating with the Governors, and so should she cook a Sunday dinner? Or offer him wine with cold snacks, to avoid filling her apartment with aromas that might overwhelm his senses. She decided upon the latter, welcoming the idea of a walk into the Second Village, for a visit to the Mars Delicatessen.

Dan loved his red wine. Through their days and nights, he kept a bottle on the bedside table and as soon as it was finished, he'd open another. She remembered tasting wine on his tongue and when he laughed, showing his big teeth, stained red.

She loved the way he laughed, with no inhibition. Even now, walking past the rockery and the small flouncing fountain, on her way into the Village, Mary smiled to herself, remembering their dotty happiness.

There was another scene, she couldn't place in the chronology of her memory. It could've been near the end, when orchestral music came on, a violin waltz. He danced her across the room as stars spun around the walls.

'Mary, look up,' he said, "and see the stars!'

More than stars, she saw spiralling galaxies, shimmering constellations and misty nebulae. Where the ceiling should've been, it was like looking into outer space. When they stopped waltzing and the room closed around them, Mary drew him by his hand, back to bed.

She lifted a shopping basket on her way into the Mars Delicatessen and paused for a moment to absorb the cool ambience, aisles with chrome shelves, lit with amber LEDs, selling everything from Irish chutney to African tribal fare. At one end of the shop was a mural-hologram of the Mars landscape, at the other, a massive chiller, displaying cheeses, hams, hors d'oeuvres and exotic sauces. Mary headed across the shop to the huge selection of fine wines and Champagnes.

She chose a safe bet, her very own Park Shiraz, grapes she'd enhanced genetically herself, during her first term at the UISC. Dan must've approved it, because she'd received an order from on-high, not to tamper anymore with the grapes, as the Park Shiraz was excellent. She placed four bottles in her basket and hoping that they'd have something to celebrate, a future together with SETI's help, Mary added a bottle of Champagne.

"Drinking on your own on a Saturday night? Not a good sign."

Mary turned. "Lewis… hello." A little awkward after their

phone call yesterday. "This isn't all for me." She glanced at the two bottles of port in his basket. "What about you? Have you got company tonight?"

He looked worse in the flesh than he did on screen, complexion waxy, jaw-line sharp from a sudden, recent weight loss. He wore the cassock he had on when she last saw him at the beach party, except now it was filthy, and he had blood-stained bandages around his hands.

He lifted a bottle of port from his basket. "Tonight, I'll be drinking this. I'd ask you to join me, but I'm expecting a visitor. A very special visitor." His eyes behind his thick spectacles were heavy-lidded, feverish. No stubble on his scalp, his bald head appeared to be polished, gleaming with perspiration.

"How do you feel?" she said. "You look as if you might have a temperature."

"I've never felt better in my life." He gave a shaking laugh. "I'm in ecstasy. I have my lover, my Jesus and my Lucifer. He came for me last night and he'll come again tonight. He bares his soul to me. He opens himself up to me. Every time he comes, he cries in my arms. And he loves me, and I worship him."

"Lewis, what are you talking about?" She felt a chill trying to meet his gaze, as if he wasn't seeing her.

"You mean who? As if you ever stop thinking about him. May I say you look more ravished than ravishing these days?" He put his stained bandages up to her face. "I can see by your eyes he has extracted your soul. You think you're the same person, but you're not." He gave the strange laugh. "Look in the mirror and you won't see yourself, because you're not there. But I'll pray for you, Mary, as I am nothing, if not compassionate."

"Do you have any idea how crazy you sound?" She stared at

him. "What's happened to your hands?"

"Dear old Mary, you don't understand. The Cosmic Soul has cursed you for your hubris. But I'm here to help people like you. As his Saint, I can appeal on your behalf, for his forgiveness. Wait here a minute. I've got something for you."

He rustled off down the aisle, stooped to pick up a satchel he'd left on the floor and returned.

"You can be helped, but you must join the UDAN Religion." He fumbled in his satchel and withdrew a yellow leaflet. "This is an invitation to our beach party.

"It's no ordinary party. It's a call to our Communion Ceremony." Lewis wrinkled up his nose. "We didn't want to advertise it as a religious event just in case it got up the Governor's noses, so keep that little detail to yourself." He drew his face closer to hers, reeking of alcohol. "I urge you to join us tomorrow night. I'll lift the curse from you, in honour of the friendship we once had." He cocked his head. "Read the invitation."

He held it out. Mary picked it from his fingers, cramped inside bandages. She read:

The UISC Student Union
Cordially invites You to a Beach Party
8pm, this Sunday, at the Governor's Swimming Pool
In Celebration and Honour of the
Great Light Wizard's Recent Visit
to our Esteemed Community.
Dress: Preferably Swimming-Trunks, Bikinis,
Grass skirts. Plus, UDAN Headbands, if you have one.
Otherwise please dress to enhance the

Colour of Your Soul
All Night Sunshine!
All Night Music and Dancing to the Student Bongo Band
Free Drinks!
(Food available at 35 euros per head.
Please pay for food-tokens at the door)
Come and join Saint Fox and
Brother Wildo to enlighten your soul!
Shine On DAN UDAN!

"I'm afraid I won't be able to make it," Mary said, "I have another commitment."

Lewis widened his eyes. "What could be more important than your soul?"

"You said I didn't have one." She gave her flinty smile. "I'll see you on Monday morning. Hopefully by then you'll be feeling a lot better."

"You've thrown away your last chance, Mary." He widened his eyes. "How did you ever become so blind? Goodbyee!"

As soon as Mary arrived home, she called Jane on her intercom.

"I've just seen Lewis in the Mars Deli. He was drunk, obsessing about a new religion and saving people's souls. Apparently, there's a party in the Governor's swimming pool tomorrow night. He says it's a communion ceremony for the UDAN religion. Jane, do you have any idea what's going on?"

"Yes, we know all about Lewis and his student following." Jane looked weary on screen. "The Governors have decided to put him on gardening leave for a while. He'll be notified first thing on Monday, so you're going to have to cope without him for a while, until he's recovered."

"He's having a mental breakdown, isn't he? He's completely lost his mind."

"Well, he's lost touch with reality, that much we do know," Jane said.

"Does Dan know what Lewis is doing?"

"Yes. The President told him. Dan said to let them get on with it, just for this weekend. He wants the students to enjoy the Beach Holorama one last time. He believes once Lewis has left, the whole thing will die down." Jane sighed. "He'll be right, of course."

"He didn't arrive here last night, did he, by any chance?" Mary probed.

"No dear, we're expecting him tomorrow. I'll give you a call as soon as he gets here." There was a tremor in her voice. "Cookie says he's drinking and chain-smoking again, refusing to eat. God knows how it will all end. I'm praying that he goes with SETI…"

Mary sat on the sofa with her face in her hands, close to tears, remembering Lewis as he used to be. His ink-blue eyes gazing at her, magnified through ultra-thick spectacles. Quick-witted, dapper, obsessed with A. I., bursting with ideas. Once, a good friend.

She blamed Dan for Lewis' breakdown. But Lewis had played his part too. A blind devotee of his idol, he turned his back on his scientific training and believed everything Dan said: to the point of stupefaction. She would never have thought Lewis, an expert in artificial intelligence, would be susceptible to indoctrination.

But such was the potency of Dan's genius, Mary had endured her own struggle with reality. She wasn't sure which of her memories were drug-induced hallucinations, or the illusionist's magic. Since she'd come home, she'd resolved, as a matter of choice, to keep her sanity. She rejected the notion of Dan's divine power or alien origins and put everything down to the Light Wizard's sleight of hand.

She sat at her desk for a while and wrote Lewis a handwritten letter, to send to his parents' address in Suffolk. She wished him well. She told him how much she would miss him and looked forward to working with him again, soon. She avoided the reason for his sick leave. She left it in her post-tray for the monitor to collect in the morning, so that it would be waiting for him when he arrived in England.

She opened a bottle of wine and ran a bath, to immerse herself in bubbles and memories of Dan. Lewis was right about that much. She never stopped thinking about Dan.

He was beside her in everything she did, until she ached to hold him. Mary wasn't the cool, dispassionate woman she used to be, as if her nervous system had been re-strung, she was in a state of constant arousal. Dan had over-sexed her, left her body quivering at its highest pitch, on the edge of orgasm, every moment craving intercourse. But to pleasure herself only brought her to tears.

Too nervous to eat, she finished the wine and tried on the two dresses she'd put aside. But still couldn't make up her mind. She got into bed at midnight and thought about Lewis alone in his apartment, in his dream world with Dan, making love to a ghost. She closed her eyes and resisted the urge to do the same thing. Somehow, she slept, until Sunday.

Mary chose the brightest daylight setting in the UDAN window. She returned one of the garments to her wardrobe. The black cocktail dress she'd worn to the Christmas party. Lewis said he didn't think black was her colour, until he saw her wearing it. 'You look out of this world,' he said, 'and if I wasn't gay, I'd be in trouble."

Upon reflection, it would send the wrong message to Dan. She opted for the calf length cotton dress, with a washed-blue floral pattern. Pretty and girlish, a little big now that she'd lost weight, it hid the roundness of her breasts and made her feel innocent again. She experimented with different shades of eyeshadow to enhance her honey-brown eyes that he loved so much, insisting that they weren't brown, but gold.

By five pm Mary was in her armchair, with a glass of wine, bathed, scented, her long hair spilling over her shoulders in curls, after a two-hour struggle with curling tongs. Her fingernails were painted light gold, her face made-up with nude foundation and a gold shimmer eyeshadow, pale lip-gloss and a delicate brush of brown mascara.

If a woman's face could launch a thousand ships, then perhaps her effort to look her best might delay the man she loved from going to America. But, for Dan to accept voluntary incarceration at SETI's safehouse would require extraordinary persuasion. Would he be prepared to give up his freedom, to keep her in his life? It felt like too much to ask. As if Palmer and La Grau had dismissed the fact that the human-chimera was still the most powerful man in the world.

Her mobile startled her.

"Hello dear, it's Jane. Dan has arrived early. He said he wants to see you before the Governor's meeting."

"When?" Mary gripped the mobile to her ear.

"He's already left the Penthouse. He should be with you any minute."

Now it was happening, now it was real, the thought of seeing him again shocked Mary from her reverie.

"Oh God, Jane." Her voice shook. "I'm scared."

"If you can't face him, we understand. We all wondered when reality would sink in," she said. "Press down on your panic button and surveillance officers will stop him and turn him around."

"But I want to see him, I'm just" – Mary swallowed – "not sure what to say to him. What if he's angry about us talking to Alex and Leon? What if he thinks we're trying to have him put away?"

"I don't think Dan will blame you for anything. He's lucky to be walking free as it is. I believe he'll be in the mood to listen. Try to relax and be positive. This is his last chance of a future." There was a catch in her voice. "Are you able to see him?"

"Yes." Mary's hands were trembling so much she dropped her mobile in her lap and grabbed it again, missing the first part of Jane's response.

". . . know what Dan's hearing is like. We'd better get off the phone. Good luck, dear."

She stood in the middle of the room, with her hand over the diamond pendant at her throat, her heart thudding against her ribs. Only in this silence would she have heard it. A barely audible knock on the front door, followed by two more quiet knocks.

She held her breath, until it happened again, louder.

Chapter Forty-Two

For a moment she didn't recognise him. A tall, gaunt man with cropped hair, trimmed beard, in a dark business suit. Until he removed his sunglasses.

She put her hand over her mouth. "Dan?"

"May I come in?"

Mary stepped aside. He entered her apartment, carrying a briefcase and avoided her eyes as he slid the sunglasses into his breast-pocket.

"I can't stay long," he said. "I've another meeting in an hour's time. Shall we sit?" He gestured towards the sofa, then strode over and sat in her armchair. He placed his briefcase on top of the coffee table. "Sit over there, where I can see you. Not too close, mind."

"Would you like a glass of red wine" – Mary's voice pitched – "or a whiskey?"

He looked up. "Go on then, a quick one. I'll have the red."

"You look naked without your curls" – unnerved by the ferocity of his eyes, Mary faltered – "but it suits you."

"And you look like wee Goldilocks standing there." Dan pursed his lips. He shook his head. "What the feck is that about? You think I don't know you, woman?"

She gave him her flinty smile. "I'm the only one who knows

the real you. You're no god. You're not from another universe. You're desperate and you're dying. Wake up, Dan Udan. You haven't got much time. Weeks, maybe, two months at the most. Give us one thousand hours to save you. Is that too much to ask?" Mary paused. "Me, Jane, Cookie, and there are others, we're your last chance. There is no god to save you. Put your faith in us and our science."

Dan lowered his eyes. "Do me a favour. Drop it."

"I've got nuts, crisps, bread, French cheeses." Mary put her hands on her hips, to control their sudden trembling. "Are you hungry?"

"Don't bother me with that shite." He removed an envelope from his briefcase, snapped the briefcase shut and looked up. "I might die of thirst before too long." He gave an upward nod. "Where's that wine, then, Goldilocks? What are you good for?"

"Nothing. And we can't have that." Mary left the room. In the kitchen she placed her elbows on the work-top and put her head in her hands.

And she remembers.

He tucks her gown around her waist to expose everything below. Mary is numb as he opens her legs to enter her and looks into her eyes. Mary knows, by the way he's panting, that he's lost in his own need, by the quickening of her shame, that she's paralysed and unable to speak. She knows herself as an object of flesh, conscious, without sensation, A dumb witness.

"I'll have to be gone soon, Mary, where's the wine?"

She raised her head, half expecting to see him in the archway, snapping his fingers.

"It won't be long!" She twisted the screw-top on the wine bottle, withdrew a pint glass from the cupboard and filled it to the brim with red wine. She moved around her kitchen, selected the largest serving bowl she could find and emptied the bags of nuts and crisps into it, two jars of olives, a jar of pickled onions, a jar of pickled quails' eggs, a carton of curry dip and stirred it all together, leaving the serving spoon inside.

She lifted the bowl and the pint glass and marched into the sitting room. "Here we are. Sorry to keep you waiting." She plonked the bowl on the coffee table and handed him the pint glass. "I went to the Mars Deli yesterday for some nibbles. Help yourself, as you always do."

"That's more like it." He laughed, surprising her. "I enjoy an olive or two." He pinched his forefinger and thumb together, picking out an olive from the mash. "Hmm, a big juicy one."

She lifted her own glass from the lamp table and sat at the end of the sofa, closest to him. "If you want, I'll put the whole lot in a doggy bag, so you can take it with you."

"Waste not, want not, eh?" He popped the olive in his mouth and said with his mouth full, "Are you sure you want to sit there, in reach of my paw?"

"I'm fine here." She inhaled a deep breath, perplexed by her changing emotions. "It's good to hear you laugh again."

Dan shifted to cross his legs, clutching the pint of wine. "You've given me a bucket of wine and a full trough to feed from, sure, it must be love." He winked at her.

Mary opened her hand towards the bowl. "That is a trough of bitterness."

"I got that. Love me or hate me, Mary, you'll never tame me."

"Was it love or hate" – she observed his expression – "when you drugged me and used me for your own satisfaction?"

He closed his eyes. The colour in his cheeks deepened.

"Dan-" She softened her voice. "If you don't know why you do these things, don't you think it's time you accepted help?"

"It was for love." He raised his eyes, his searing gaze accentuated by his cropped hair. "I didn't want our son to be conceived to the sound of his mother's screams. When Lucida's soul entered this creation, I made sure that you were comfortably numb."

It was an explosive impulse. Mary didn't even see it coming herself. But he must have, because he ducked to the side, as the wine flew out of her glass, drenching his suit, instead of his face, which she'd aimed for.

"There's no child! There's no mortal or immortal Lucida. Get it into your head, I'm not pregnant!"

He stared at her. "Have you quite finished?" He swallowed a mouthful of wine and continued in his quiet voice. "The thing is, Mary, you won't have any signs you're pregnant until next May, when you'll present with a normal looking, six-week-old embryo." He withdrew a handkerchief from his trouser pocket and folded it over with one hand.

"The only change you'll notice this year is that you'll begin to look younger" – he smiled faintly – "I mean, like a teenager. Your biological age will reverse by fifteen years." He dabbed the lapels of his suit with the handkerchief, to soak up the wine. "While you're carrying our son, no harm can come to you, no sickness or accident. Even if you were to be run over by a bus, you'll walk away unscathed. So, Mary" – he gazed at her with that dreamy look in his eyes – "it doesn't matter if you don't believe a word I say. God's Will is done. Nature will take care of the rest."

She shook her head. "I didn't know it was possible to love anybody as much as I've loved you. But if you carry on like this, I'll just end up crazy, like Lewis… Lewis is" – tears stung her eyes – "he's gone insane."

"I know. And I'm to blame for that." The colour rose again in Dan's face. "I hope time with his parents will bring him back to himself." He held her gaze. "But Mary, you're stronger. You've got what it takes to live with two realities. Mine and yours. You've already learned to juggle them in your head, with your feet on the ground."

She blinked back tears and lifted her chin. "When will we be together?"

He put his hand to his brow. "Mary, I can't-"

"But you promised when I moved into your Penthouse that you were going to get help." She couldn't bear to hear what he had to say next. "I've never stopped loving you."

Dan moved forward to put his glass on the coffee table and knelt in front of her. He took her hands in his and closed his fingers around hers. Usually warm, they were ice cold. "You shouldn't want to be with me. You should be pushing me out that door. Mary, I thought I could fight my demons, but I was wrong." He bit down on his lip. "I want to explain something to you. Will you try to accept what I say?"

She nodded. A tear dripped onto her cheek.

"When God saved me twenty years ago, it put the forces of nature into my hands, to bring an immortal child into this world, through you, the one I adore." He kissed the tips of her fingers. "I was in command of those forces, until the day we made love." He drew a deep breath. "Now I'm afraid I'm going to kill someone. There's so much violence inside me and ravenous hunger, I feel like a wild animal, not a man, anymore." His eyes misted.

"Dan, we can help you. Are you prepared to listen?"

He kissed her fingertips again. "Thank God you're safe from me," he said, as if he hadn't heard her. "So long as you're carrying our son, I can't harm you. But it won't stop the brute in me from making your life a misery." He squeezed her fingers so hard she cried out. "I don't want to hurt you, Mary."

"Stop it, Dan, you are hurting me!"

"I can't trust myself." He shouted in her face. "Do you hear me!" He tossed her hands away from him.

"Stay away from me" – he covered his face, fingers quivering – "Mary, let me go!"

Mary slid from the sofa onto her knees, wrapped her arms around his neck and clung to him.

"Dan, you're going to stay and get help."

He clasped her head and brought her face close to his, brushing their eyelashes, as they used to do in bed.

"You can't help me, angel." He pushed his tongue inside her mouth, kissing her so hard she couldn't breathe, and then held her at arm's length. "We can't do this!" He got to his feet and stumbled out to the kitchen, like a drunk, almost tripping over his feet. Mary went after him. She found him bent over the sink, soaking his head under a running tap.

"We can do this." She swallowed and tasted blood where he'd bruised her lip. "If you want it enough, there's a way. Don't you want to try, at least for my sake?"

He straightened up and ran his hands back over his temples, dripping wet.

"I've got to go where I can't be found." He withdrew the

stained handkerchief from his pocket and flapped it open to dab his face. “I’m going to dig a grave and bury myself alive.”

“Now you’re being silly.” Mary opened a drawer for a clean towel. She reached up over his head to dry his hair, giving it a gentle rub. “Your shirt collar is drenched. I think you should postpone your meeting with the Governors.”

“This rotten body of mine has served its purpose,” he said from beneath the towel. “I’m no good to you or our son. I’m a monster.”

She withdrew the towel and looked up into his eyes. “Please, Dan, don’t talk like that.”

“I’m not talking about sinking to the bottom of the Irish Sea. I’m talking about shaking this thing off, like a snake sheds its skin. I want a life with you and Lucida. But I’ve got to go back to the grave, where it all began. It could take months, or it could take years, before we can meet again.” He furrowed his brow. “Would you wait that long for me?”

“I’d wait forever for you.” She put her hand on his cheek, cold and clammy to her touch. “But I don’t have to. What if there was a safehouse, where all your needs could be met. Where you could be supported through a treatment plan.”

Before he could answer, Mary walked into the sitting room, to feel behind a cushion for SETI’s brochure. When she turned, he was standing behind her. “Jane came to see me, with Alex Palmer and a man from the SETI institute.” Hairs prickled at the nape of her neck, to see his expression harden.

“Everybody is worried about you” – she placed her hand on his arm – “They know you can’t go on as you are. They believe you’re not feeding properly. In time, when you’re ready, they can offer you surgery.

"Dan, my darling, we can't risk losing you. Please, read it." She held out the brochure. "SETI has created a special residence for you… for us. I'll be able to visit you. Please, look!"

He took it, with a softer expression on his face and flicked through the pages. He handed it back.

"They can't help me anymore than they can help a caterpillar change into a butterfly." He smiled his lopsided smile. "Ach, that lot. They never stop trying to pin me down. But you know me better than that." He inclined his head. "Don't you, Mary? You know I'm the only one who can sort myself out. I swear, if you ever see me again after tonight, I'll be worthy of your love."

"Can't you at least try what SETI has to offer?" She gave him a pleading look. "We'll be together. It could be so much better than you think."

"Would you put me in a Zoo?"

"It won't be anything like that," she said.

"It'll be them watching this brute tossing-off, chucking shite at the walls like a demented ape." He gave a bitter laugh. "If I thought it'd do any good at all, I'd go, but I'm more likely to rip their fecken heads off. Sorry angel, but" – he shook his head – "no way."

He moved across the room and picked up the white envelope from the coffee-table.

"UDAN's drug companies are on track to start mass production in a week's time," he said in a business-like tone. "Your team has won the race for the vaccine, so you've earned yourselves a bonus." He patted the envelope. "In here is your Record of Excellence from UDAN Corporations, signed by me." He smiled. "You can frame it and hang it on the wall to look at when you want to appreciate yourselves.

"The bonus of twelve million euros has been awarded to the UISC Genetics Team. It's entirely up to you how you want to spend it."

"It seems wrong to be making money out of this crisis." Mary had turned cold inside. He was preparing to leave. "I'd forgotten we were in a race with other UDAN teams."

"When it comes to fighting bio-wars we don't just need the best scientists, but the fastest. This was just my way of finding out the slowcoaches amongst yous. Some workers have received warnings over this, because you've shown them up. If you feel you can't accept your reward, then give your share to charity. I won't mind." He flapped the envelope and then tossed it onto the coffee table. "Well, there you are. Congratulations."

"Thank you." A sudden urge to cry was making her nauseous. "I'll give my share to the UISC research fund."

He stood for a moment, pursing his lips, then inched back his sleeve to glance at his watch. "I'll be off then… I guess you'll be looking forward to getting back to work on Monday?"

"Dan-" Mary moved towards him.

He caught her wrist, reached with his other hand inside his jacket pocket and removed a small black box.

"I want you to have this. I was hoping to give it to you under different circumstances, if things had worked out between us." His voice softened. "I don't expect you to wear it. Just keep it to remember me by." When she didn't take it, he pressed the box into her palm. "Wait until I'm gone."

"If you loved me, you'd stay and accept SETI's help." She put the box on the coffee-table. Dan picked up his briefcase.

"No-" She grabbed his hand. "I won't let you go."

"Mary, we've both got to be strong." He tried to shake her

off, but she clung on with both hands.

"Let go now, you're making it worse!"

"I can't live without you. Dan, please, don't go!"

He thrust his forefinger in her face. "Did you want me to stay and turn your life into a fecken nightmare? Is that what you want, because that's what you'll get. Count yourself lucky I'm going out that door." He pushed her off. "Get a grip on yourself, before I lose mine." He walked out and slammed the door.

Mary sank to her knees and doubled over. The past flashed before her eyes. Her mother waving goodbye at the door, like a broken branch in the wind. Her father dangling like a puppet on a string, in his winter coat, mouth oblong. And now she turned onto her side, remembering Dan inside her, looking up into his eyes, a moment of eternity. Her whole body began to shake.

Chapter Forty-Three

The door burst open. Dan staggered back into the room, followed by La Grau and Palmer in padded silver vests, space-gloves, helmets under their arms.

Fully clad astronauts filed into the room, brandishing rods that resembled cattle-prods, luminous and buzzing. They waved the prods at Dan until he was backed up against the wall, still clutching his briefcase, his other hand raised, laughing an incredulous, nervous laugh.

Palmer helped Mary to her feet. "No need to distress yourself. Lover-boy isn't going anywhere without you."

"Who are these people?" she said.

"SETI's Special Forces." His voice was clipped. "We have come to take him away." He indicated to the diamond around her neck. "That's also a listening device. We heard everything."

La Grau shouted across the room. "Give me a reading!"

"Radiation negative, sir," an astronaut said, his voice amplified from a mouthpiece inside his helmet.

Mary grasped Palmer's arm. "Why have they got weapons?"

"They're ultrasound wands." Palmer patted her hand. "Our fellow has zero tolerance for human contact. SETI's alternative is to negotiate with him using ultrasound."

Palmer led her by the hand between the astronauts. About

a dozen had gathered around Dan, standing at a prod's length. They silenced their weapons and shuffled back a few steps, visors reflecting the image of Mary's ashen face as she and Palmer nudged their way through. "Your job is to persuade him to come along, with minimum fuss," Palmer said.

"Bonjour Mary, come, come!" La Grau stood to the side of Dan and beckoned. "Come and be re-united with your love." He waved. "There is no need to part with such sorrow."

Dan looked at him with an expression of weary exasperation.

Palmer released her hand and gave a gentle push to Mary's back. "Give the poor fellow a kiss. He looks like he could do with one."

She looked up into Dan's eyes. "I knew nothing about this. I'm so sorry."

He surprised her with a smile, reaching his laughter lines. "Where's my kiss?"

Mary went up onto her tiptoes and kissed his lips, dry, salty.

La Grau clapped. "Bring in the Portacell. We are going to London!"

Dan whispered in her ear. "There's no way I can give myself up to SETI. Leave and let me handle this." He glanced to the side. "Go to the Penthouse, tell Cookie I've been delayed. Will you do that for me?"

Palmer stepped forward, tapping his earpiece. "I heard that. Mary's not going anywhere. She's staying here to assist in your rescue. They're bringing in the Portacell now. I suggest you do as she says."

He laid his gloved hand on Dan's shoulder. "I'm sorry it must happen like this, Dan, but I did promise you we'd catch up with you one day. I think you'll be impressed by our Portacell." He nodded towards the door.

Mary turned to see two SETI officers pushing a large transparent cubicle mounted on wheels into her apartment, with a sunken armchair inside, that appeared to be made of Perspex. There were metal restraints for his ankles, wrists, torso and neck, and a Perspex cranial cap for his head. Suspended from the roof was a cylindrical dispenser with a tube, something like a caged rodent would drink from, except that it didn't contain water.

She looked at Dan. His complexion had turned grey.

"The Portacell is a fully insulated cell," Palmer said, "a secure, impenetrable unit designed to contain you in transit whilst ensuring the safe function of our instruments. As we've discovered, things tend to malfunction when you're around." Palmer chuckled and patted his shoulder. "We don't want the helicopter rotors shutting out in mid-flight.

"There are special fibres in the seat with sensory detectors and absorbent chemicals for the collection of data from your body, during the journey to London and future trips you make with SETI, your new family.

"We'll keep no secrets from you, Dan. Our purpose is to understand your metabolism and protect that brain of yours." Palmer put his hand out towards La Grau. "Allow me to introduce you. This is my colleague, Dr. Leon La Grau from the SETI Institute in North London. He's just one of the many who'll be taking care of you from now on."

La Grau extended his gloved hand to Dan. "Mr. Udan, monsieur, it is a great honour to meet you at last." Dan shook his hand. "I have been following your progress for eight years and you are, for sure, out of this world." La Grau had a look of mischievous intensity. "Thank you, for all you have done for us. Maybe we can do something for you, in return?"

Dan smiled. "You're the guy who's been following me around, waiting for my flying-saucer to appear." He laughed. "As if I'd want to stick out like a sore thumb."

La Grau chuckled. "Of course, monsieur, you are far too clever for flying-saucers. But what a pity that you, yourself, have become a terrible sore thumb."

"You need to strip-off for the Portacell," Palmer said, "take everything off, underwear, the lot."

"Alex," Mary said through her teeth, "why are you treating him this way?"

"Come with me." He pressed his hand to Mary's back to usher her away, but when she wouldn't move, he put his mouth to her ear. "Young lady, we're here to help him. We agreed yesterday, he can't go on like this. The world can't risk losing UDAN Corporations."

"Alex! Get that thing out of here and take your fancy-dress party with you!" Dan pointed to the door. "Get out, all of you!"

Palmer dropped his hand from Mary's back and lifted his face to Dan, the tallest man in the room.

"Sorry, old fellow." He winced. "But as a detainee of the SETI Institute, on the authority of the United Nations Leadership Committee, you have no choice but to give yourself up.

"As of today, you are no longer a free man. All your assets are frozen until further notice, because, Dan Udan, *John Daniel Downs*, there is evidence that you are an impostor. My friend, Leon here, doubts that you are even human." His voice wavered. "Which makes you an illegal alien trespassing on our planet, with no human rights whatsoever, not at least, until we grant them."

Dan hooded his eyes. "Alex, you're taking the piss, now."

Palmer inclined his head. "We intend you no harm. We want the answers to our questions. We are concerned" – he arched his voice – "by the trajectory of your domination of our world, your enigmatic persona, and not least, your multi-species transgenic metabolism that affords you supernatural powers that would match any science-fiction super-hero."

"Here we go again." Dan sighed.

"Give me a field-reading!" La Grau barked.

"Radiation negative, sir."

"My men will lift you into the Portacell, Mr Udan, if you do not co-operate," La Grau said.

"Why would I co-operate?" Dan widened his eyes.

"Bien." La Grau raised his voice. "Gentlemen, lift Mr Udan into the Portacell!" He clapped his hands. "Vite!"

Mary heard shuffling and rustling of spacesuits. Amplified voices as the astronauts closed around Dan, obscuring her view. More astronauts joined in, shouting orders to one another to adopt alternative methods. Mary crept around the coffee-table, trying to catch a glimpse.

"We can't lift him, sir. There's something holding him down."

"It's not possible, sir! He won't give an inch!"

"Thank you, gentlemen, you've proved our case." It was Palmer's voice. "Dan, I want you to understand that the more you resist, the more we suspect you have something to hide." His tone sharpened. "Things could get very unpleasant for you."

Dan didn't speak.

"Mr Udan, tell me where you come from?" La Grau said.

"Dublin City, born and bred," Dan said.

"John Daniel Downs was born in Dublin City in the year two thousand. But you, Dan Udan, are not him." La Grau's voice took on a shrill tone. "John Daniel was murdered in two thousand and eight. You, Udan, took his body to use for your own purposes. Where do you come from, Udan? Answer me!"

"I'm Irish, for God's sake." Dan gave an audible sigh. "My body is God's work. I'll not be tampered with."

"Your God is killing you," Palmer said.

"Udan, we know this is not your true face." La Grau's voice shook with intensity. "Perhaps you are afraid that if humanity discovered the truth, it would be catastrophic for you. I promise you that your secret will remain with SETI. Please, reveal yourself as you are. Reveal the power in your hands. Let us meet E.T. and we will accept you back into our world, with open arms. We adore E.T.!"

A gap appeared between the spacesuits. Mary could see Dan in profile, sitting on the floor with his knees bent, hugging them with a loose hold on his wrist. He seemed relaxed, but for the pallor of his skin, in stark contrast to his beard. He was looking up at La Grau, with his lopsided smile, shaking his head.

"I'm an illusionist," he said, "You should talk to Mary. She knows all about my illusions. But unlike your heads, hers sits firmly on her shoulders."

"Of course, Mary is protecting you. She will never reveal the truth about what happened between you. Alors, we must progress to the next stage. Perhaps agony will expose your true face?"

Palmer appeared in the gap, blocking Mary's view of Dan.

"If you continue to resist SETI forces, we'll assume that you're a threat to us and we'll treat you accordingly. This is your last chance to co-operate. Will you step inside the Portacell?"

"No, Alex, I will not," Dan said.

"Tune wands to two hundred megahertz, engage Udan's temporal lobes," La Grau said.

"No!" Mary raised her hands.

There was an eerie whining sound. Her ear drums fluttered. And then there was silence. She pushed between the astronauts to reach Dan. A couple of them turned and waved at her to go back, more like faceless humanoids than people.

She heard crackling explosions, like electrical short-circuits. Dan cried out, the hoarse cries of a man in agony. His pitch rose to a screech. Neither a human sound, nor that of any animal. The only parallel she could think of was non-biological, electronic, acoustic feedback. Mary covered her ears. She started to sob. Was that him? How could that be him? La Grau shouted unintelligible orders and the din stopped, but for the sound of ragged panting.

"Let Mary come to him," La Grau said in a low voice.

The astronauts opened a gap to let her through. She froze. Dan was lying on his stomach, limbs jerking, his head to one side. A black, oily slick had spewed from his mouth, across the carpet.

"Collect the contents of his stomach," Palmer said.

"Mary" – La Grau put out his hand – "see if you can persuade him now."

Mary knelt beside Dan, close to the astronaut on his knees, scooping the residue inside a test tube. She stroked Dan's head, feverishly hot, soaked in perspiration. His panting softened to regular breathing. The jerking in his legs and arms reduced to quivering.

La Grau squatted at Dan's head.

"My formidable friend," he said, "We will not leave here without you." He inhaled, as if to draw perseverance. "We have no desire to hurt you. But we will continue with this inhumanity, until you co-operate. Will you co-operate?"

Dan gave no response.

La Grau looked at Mary. "We will torture his ears, until he places himself in the Portacell."

"Please, I beg you, let him go." She looked up at Palmer. "Alex, you heard him. Dan wants to go into hiding. He will heal himself, in his own way. Trust him. Please."

Palmer firmed his mouth. "Mary, there are forces accessible to Udan that we don't understand. We are determined to find out what they are. Don't be concerned. Once we get him to SETI, he'll be treated like a prince."

La Grau rose to his feet. "He has one minute before we start again. Prepare yourself Mary, for his suffering will get worse. We will engage his temporal lobes at one gigahertz, and you must leave this room."

Mary put her mouth to Dan's ear. Her teeth were chattering. "Can you hear me, Dan? Go with them. Show them you're not a threat." She stroked his temple. "You can control their minds. You can run rings around them. Do to them what you did to me. They have no power over you. Or are you letting this happen?"

Mary raised her head to look into Dan's eyes, slanted towards her. From that look in his eyes, she knew.

"But why?" she said.

"For what I did to you. For what I did to Lewis, I deserve this. Leave now." He closed his eyes. "I must suffer for my sins."

"Don't you do this to me!" Mary started to shake. She clasped his head, as if she could squeeze sense into him. "You've suffered enough! Stop torturing yourself, because this is torture for me. I love you." Tears dripped from her eyes onto his face. "If you ever loved me, now is the time to show me. Go with them."

"Well…when you put it like that-" He wheezed like an old man.

"Dan, please–"

"If it'll stop your crying-"

"Will you?"

"You tell them" – he let out a ragged sigh – "before I change my mind."

Mary looked up at La Grau and Palmer. "Dan has agreed to go."

La Grau crouched down to look at Dan. "Is this true, Mr Udan?"

Dan gave a curt nod.

La Grau straightened up and waved. "Gentlemen, bring the Portacell over!" He gestured to Mary still on her knees. "You may help Udan to undress. He will be weak."

Dan got to his feet and staggered as he removed his jacket. Pale faced, expressionless, he kept his eyes closed, and struggled like a man in his sleep, to undo the knot in his tie.

"Let me help you with that," she said.

He dropped his hands and let her remove his tie. Mary undid his shirt, and tugged it down over his shoulders, exposing him in his leather tunic. Anxious that, at any moment, he might change his mind. She distracted him and touched the scar around his neck.

"Did it really happen the way I remember?" she whispered. Dan opened his eyes and smiled. Mary understood it did happen, everything, the way she remembered it.

"Leon–" She turned to La Grau. "I'd like him to keep his tunic and his trousers on."

La Grau shook his head. "He must be naked for the Portacell."

She looked at the astronauts milling around with their helmets off. The room was teeming with fresh-faced, young men. "Are they prepared for this?"

"They are SETI officers," La Grau said, "We are all familiar with the images from Military Intelligence. Would Mr Udan allow them a close look at him before he sits in the Portacell?"

"Dan?" She touched his arm. "Will you let them look at you?"

"I'm in your hands," he said, "You know what to do."

Mary undid the Velcro fastenings on his tunic, the little buckles at the side and peeled away the front and rear panels, leaving the gauze to cling to his back, soiled and damp. La Grau and his officers gathered around. Mary lifted the gauze away and stepped aside.

"Mon Dieu…Mon Dieu-" La Grau inched forward. A few officers bolted out of sight. Another gave a cry and sank onto his knees. She heard gasps and muttering from the others, saw fear and disbelief on their faces.

"Come closer and see the reality." La Grau beckoned to the men behind him. "Ask yourselves, is this a human being or is this E.T.?" He sounded breathless. "You see here, the dragonfly is where he is most sensitive to pain. And here is the luminous green of the bush cricket, and these tangled lesions are the legs of many insects." He moved closer, hunching like a man peeping though a keyhole –

"The red mass inside is the trapped remains of a reptile's entrails. Oui. Here we have the crocodile eye, with its functioning eyelid. The question is: *Can it see us?*" He waved. "And all of these are mushrooms in combination with human flesh, intoxicating and poisonous species." He drew back, puffing air into his cheeks. "Mon Dieu. I did not know it was so terrible and yet so beautiful."

Mary watched Dan, with his face raised, his eyes closed, standing like a man sunning himself, in a world of his own.

"Leon," she said, "he's human too."

"For the time being, I will agree." He circled to face Dan and looked up at him with a new, intense fervour. "Monsieur E.T. it is time to go. Open the Portacell hatch!"

Dan glanced at Mary and took the few steps to the Portacell. He stooped to enter the cubicle and in a few perfunctory moves, he unbuckled his belt, removed his trousers and underpants and tossed them out through the hatch, into the room of silent, watchful faces. He sat in the semi-reclining chair. The hatch hissed, closing him inside. An officer forced steel bolts across the front. La Grau held a remote control in his hand and tapped on a keypad. He put it up to his mouth.

"Mr Udan, you are electronically and mechanically sealed in. Lie back and make yourself comfortable. Place your head and feet in the slots provided and place your arms on the armrests." He waited as Dan adjusted himself. "The restraints will now place themselves automatically around your body."

There was no sound from inside the cubicle as the steel bands and cuffs clamped around Dan's forehead, his waist, his limbs, doubling up in three or four places.

"They are extremely powerful and impossible for you to overcome. I am talking about in excess of a thousand horsepower. But if you do attempt to force them open, a claxon will sound, and you will receive an assault on your ears, of one gigahertz." He smiled. "You see, the Portacell is completely Udan-proof."

Mary glared at Palmer standing by the open door. He blinked when he caught her eye. As if to appease her, he said,

"Would you like to come to London this evening and help him settle in?

"Yes," she said.

"I suggest you fly out later and meet us at the London residence. I assure you he'll receive a hero's welcome at SETI. His accommodation is palatial. Say your goodbyes before we cover the Portacell."

She approached the Portacell, placed her hand flat on the glass and gazed in at Dan. He sat paralysed, neck muscles rigid, staring up at the feeder hanging from the roof, filled with blood.

"When I wish to feed him, I do this." La Grau tapped the remote control. The tube grew down and touched Dan's mouth. "All he must do is suck." Dan closed his eyes and compressed his mouth, his face flaming almost the same colour as the feeder. "Bien, shroud the Portacell!"

"Dan!" Mary banged on the glass, "I'm sorry! I'm so sorry!"

Officers surrounded the Portacell, throwing a foil sheet over the top, to come floating down like a parachute, concealing him inside. They ushered Mary back. Palmer came over.

"You can accompany him to the lift. There's really no call for tears." He stroked the back of her head, like a father comforting his daughter. "One day he'll thank us for this."

By the time Mary had put on her shoes, the officers had already left with the Portacell, pushing it up the deserted corridor like a dreary carnival float, Palmer and La Grau striding out ahead. She ran to catch up with them and clung to the foil shroud as if it were Dan's hand, talking to him as if he could hear her.

"I'll be with you tonight. You're going to get well. They'll look after you...Jane has been in touch with Alex for years, she trusts him...I love you-"

They stopped at the single elevator for Level Two.

"Leon, you go up to Level Eight first with the Portacell," Palmer said, "The rest of us will wait."

La Grau shook Mary's hand. "I am sorry for your distress. I hope you understand why it was necessary to debilitate Mr Udan. But as you saw, it was only temporary, and he has sustained no injuries." He hunched his shoulders and smiled. "Au revoir."

They wheeled the Portacell inside the lift, with room enough for La Grau and six of his officers. Mary fixed her gaze on the cubicle until the doors closed, then watched the number display of the lift's progress up through the Shelter... Level 3... Level 4...

"Dan hasn't slept for days," Palmer said beside her. "He'll probably sleep through the journey."

Level 5

"I wonder if he'll succumb to temptation." Palmer rocked back on his heels. "Poor fellow looked mortified when he saw what was in the dispenser."

Level 6… Level 7…Level 6… Level 5…

"The lift didn't go to Level Eight," Mary said, "it's coming down again."

"Do you think they've forgotten something, sir?" an officer said behind them.

"No, we've got everything we came for." Palmer furrowed his brow.

Level 3…Level 2… The doors parted.

"Oh-" La Grau's mouth dropped. "How did you get here first?"

"We didn't." Palmer cleared this throat. "You lot have come back down to Level Two."

"How?" La Grau looked around at his officers. "Did you interfere with the lift?" They shook their heads.

"Check the Portacell." Palmer ordered.

"It cannot be Udan," La Grau said, "He cannot do anything in there but breathe."

"Check it anyway. I want to see if he's okay," Palmer said, "look under the shroud."

The officer's head disappeared beneath it. "I can't see, sir. It's dark under here. Can someone pull it over a bit?"

They tugged the shroud from the other end and revealed the Portacell.

Empty.

Chapter Forty-Four

"Can you see the sun, Jolly?" Lewis adjusts Jolly's Ceegee by a few degrees, where it sits in the middle of the bar.

"Yes, Lewis, I can feel the sun on my face. It is wonderful. Thank you."

Behind the bar, King spins a cocktail glass in the air and catches it by the stem. "Do you mind, Saint Fox, removing your Ceegee. Your Jolly is in my way."

Lewis glares at King. "You call yourself a Udanist, where's your compassion?" He lays his hand on Jolly's cool, plastic dome. "Would you deprive a soul of sunshine, who's never experienced sunshine in his life before?"

King tweaks his mouth into a wry smirk. "Don't overdo it, Foxy, or people might think you've lost your marbles." He fills the glass with Green Flame, a bright green cocktail that he has invented. "I mean, we're doing okay, we've made loads of dosh from the merchandise and food tokens. Brother Wildo is singing your praises."

"I don't care about the money. I care about the enlightenment of people's souls, including this one." Lewis pats Jolly's Ceegee. "He's staying right here, where he can see the Red Giant."

"Put that thing at the end of the bar" – Kings spins another glass in the air – "where it won't get knocked off. There, that's compassion for you."

King wears green Speedos for the beach party. His torso is naked, glistening with oil, to show himself off to the girls in bikinis, some of whom are hoping to enter the Darkening of Defilement tonight. Lewis is distracted by the nineteen – year old's sinewy torso. There's not an ounce of fat on him. He feels cornered. It's difficult to argue with a good-looking boy.

"Lewis, I do not mind sitting at the end of the bar. I will still be able to see the Red Giant." Jolly raises its eyes, rippling its brow into furrows, in a face that appears otherwise to be sculpted from ice. "I will have a better view."

Hoping to catch King's eye to signal his pique, Lewis gives up and carries Jolly's face to the end of the bar. He sits on a stool and faces the Red Giant, swigging port from a hipflask, observing the party that has just started. It's quite a do. Over a hundred students have shown up, wearing next to nothing. It's been a while since he's seen so many near-naked men and with the Student Bongo Band drumming a rousing jungle beat, he feels a stirring in his loins.

The Red Giant has blown to its full size but has yet to bleed red. At the core it is the cream of a poached egg-yolk, shedding the most heart-breaking shade of pink that Lewis has ever seen, when teenage boys playing beach-ball leap up and reveal their sleek and effortless contours. There's a new mirror-ball spinning on the ceiling, chasing reflections around kiosks and parasols and over mattresses that weren't there before. Only Dan and Mary's tipi is missing.

"Thank you for letting me see the sun with my own eyes," Jolly says beside him. "It is so much more beautiful than I had imagined."

A laughing girl comes careering towards Lewis and bashes against the bar. Fairy-lights wound around her abdomen dangle between her thighs. It's a moment before Lewis realises, she's naked.

"I've been defiled!" She throws back her head. "Be happy for me, Saint Fox!"

He knows her. How could he ever forget her? She's the one who agonised over his fingers, trying to choose which one to cut with her scalpel. She looks totally different with her sweaty face and hair, her small pointy breasts resembling, uncomfortably, the red-raw teats of a nursing mammal.

"Sophie," Lewis says under his breath, "I think you should cover yourself up."

She puts her face up to his. Lewis can tell that she's blind drunk, even so, her eyes possess a burning fervour.

"Saint Fox, when you say we've got to pray to… the Cosmic Soul," she slurs, "are we really praying to Dan – Dan Udan?"

"Um-" Lewis glances at King who smirks and stalks off to the other end of the bar. "The thing is, Sophie" – Lewis has struggled with this question himself – "Yes and no… You've got to remember that the Cosmic Soul is a vast and omnipotent entity responsible for the whole of creation and that Dan Udan is a transgenic human being." He tries to make eye contact, but with difficulty, because she's looking through him, at the same time as pressing her abdomen against his knee. "Dan is the human face of the Cosmic Soul . . . He is the channel through which we can communicate with our Creator. So, yes and no, is the answer to your question."

"So, if he's like a normal man" – Sophie sways, bearing down on his thigh to balance herself – "underneath all his powers and everything, can he get married and have kids like the rest of us?"

"I would think so"-Lewis nods – "if he wants to. Dan has the power to do whatever he wants."

"In that case, he should know" – Sophie smiles the sickly, leery smile of the inebriated – "that I want to marry him." She raises her hands in the air. "I'm ready for him now!"

King slides a green cocktail across the bar, with a brolly and a fizzing sparkler. "Hey, Sophie, welcome to the Green Flame. Don't be so desperate to get hitched. I was hoping to have some fun with you later, now you're one of us."

She lifts her green drink to her lips. "Fine. But you better be scarier than my blood sucker dream, or you're just a wimp."

King winks. "Just you wait, our little Sophie, we've got a few surprises in store for you lot."

"Hoy, Saint Fox!" Wildo treks up the sandy slope, in red Speedos. His pale hair is combed back from his forehead. Lean and long-bodied with beefy arms and stocky thighs, he's even more reminiscent of the lion in the wild-life documentary. "What are you doing sitting around, mate? We've got to hoist the Dan-Back above the pool." He beckons.

Lewis takes a swig from his hipflask and steps down from the barstool. "See you in a minute, Jolly. Enjoy the sun." He casts a glance at Sophie leaning over the bar, talking to King who appears attentive, topping up her glass.

He follows Wildo down the slope, aware of feeling a bit jaded after last night's alcoholic binge. He could do with lying down in the sand and having a nap before his sermon. But where could he rest? The beach is crowded.

A large group of girls have got their arms around one

another, swaying with the cohesion of a bait-ball, their bodies decorated with strings of fairy-lights. As he and Wildo walk by, the girls with bare bottoms bend forward, with shrieks of laughter. Lewis catches a glimpse of female pudenda and looks away. Wildo smacks a few of their behinds, exciting more shrieks.

The steel torso sits in the sand just beyond reach of the simmering surf. It has fairy lights flickering between its ribs and wires attached to its shoulder stumps, that extend up to a pulley-wheel fixed to the ceiling. Wildo's flatmate, Steve – who looks reassuringly puny in Speedos – is holding onto the wires, ready to hoist the sculpture in the air.

Standing a few yards away is a roughly hewn stepladder rising to a podium made up of wooden slats, created to serve as Lewis' pulpit, with a discrete microphone.

"We want to know how high above your head to hang this thing, Foxy." Wildo takes one of the wires from Steve. "You go and stand in your pulpit, and we'll pull it up to see what it looks like, yeah?"

Lewis mounts the pulpit. He doesn't trust it to hold his weight, although it has been stabilised deep in the sand. It's six feet high and he's not that fond of heights, besides which, he's already tipsy. He grips onto the narrow rail. Like looking from a balcony, he can see over everybody's heads to the bar, where Jolly's face shines, wearing an expression full of wonderment.

Wildo and Steve start to yank the wires, twanging and vibrating, jerking the torso upwards, unevenly, by its shoulder stumps.

"What do you think, Foxy, is that high enough?" Wildo shouts up to him, above the boom of the bongos, the rising laughter and chatter. Lewis looks to see the torso at a standstill, hanging crookedly, like a half-decomposed carcass on the gallows. He can see up into the pelvic outlet, to the bulging bag of silver confetti.

"That's high enough," Lewis shouts down. "Can you straighten it up a bit?" One of them yanks a wire, the torso drops, swinging to one side, the way a monkey swings. "That's worse" – he shouts – "try again!"

There's more twanging. Wildo's mouth tightens, and Lewis knows he's already fed up with it. The man has no patience.

"That'll have to do, Foxy, my wire has snagged!" Wildo lets go and traipses through the sand to the foot of Lewis' pulpit. He squints up. "Are you ready to roll soon, Foxy? We might as well get it over with!"

"Get what over with?" Lewis says.

"The bleeding sermon, mate, what planet are you on? Things can't kick off properly until you've given the blessing!"

"Right." Lewis nods. "I'll make an initial announcement, or something, shall I?"

"No, let's hear your sermon! Then we can get on with what's important." He chuckles, with his hands low on his hips, fingers pointing inward.

"You guys! Do you want me to set off the flare now?" Steve calls over. He's very accommodating where Wildo is concerned and is starting to annoy Lewis. He was hoping to spend twenty minutes or so, making notes for his sermon. But once the green flare has been lit above the water, it's time for him to begin.

"Go for it, Steve!" Wildo punches the air with his fist. "This is show-time, as Udan would say! Okay Foxy? Are you ready to rock with the Cosmic Soul?"

Lewis hasn't got the energy to argue. He needs to preserve it, anyway, for his sermon. "Can you give me a few minutes to prepare?"

Wildo holds up two fingers, like an insult. "When the flare goes up, McGin will dim the lights and I'll shine the spot-light." He grins. "Then you sock it to them, Saint Fox!"

Lewis turns his back to the beach. Beneath him, Steve pushes off in the rubber dinghy and starts to row into the middle of the swimming pool, bobbing over the automated waves.

Lewis has one hand behind his back, holding onto his makeshift balcony for safety, willing himself to feel the surge of energy he felt once before. That strange, heady excitement that gave clarity to his thoughts. But watching the man in the dinghy, he's feeling quite sea-sick, or perhaps this is vertigo.

He tries to ignore the lapping water, and taking a deep breath, he fixes his eyes on the Red Giant, looking deep into its core, now seething. He thinks he can see tiny bodies inside there, wriggling like millions of red ants warring with each other. Lewis thinks, everything is consumed, one way or another, in this world.

Steve has arrived in the middle of the pool and he's waving, not at Lewis, but at Wildo.

"Saint Fox!"

He hears Wildo behind him and turns gingerly to face his congregation, that has yet to notice he's climbed up to his pulpit. Lewis clutches the balcony rail, and with his other hand, gropes for the hipflask in his pocket.

The lights are dimmed around the walls, leaving the Red Giant's russet glow on the students' faces as they stop dancing and turn. There's a loud bang. The flare flickers green light across the beach and the Bongo Band stops playing. The students look up at Lewis. He takes a swig from his hipflask as Wildo directs a spotlight at the pulpit, bathing it in a frosty, ultraviolet haze, prompting Lewis to glance down at himself.

He's pleased now, that he decided not to wash his cassock, or change the bandages on his hands. Every bloodstain shows up darker in this light, telling of the pain of his martyrdom, giving him a sense of authenticity and a much-needed boost to his confidence.

He raises his hands above his head.

"Udanists, welcome! We are joined together this evening to celebrate one God, one Cosmic Soul, UDAN, for whom we suffer for our enlightenment!"

He shakes his arms at the ceiling.

"We have suffered this outrageous indignation, this degradation of a body that must be defiled, that must bleed and squat like the beast" – he raises his eyes to the sculpture – "that must lump and grump over the face of this earth as the worm and as the chattering ape, like the one you see swinging above my head."

Lewis stretches up, as if he could reach the sculpture, then losing his balance, drops his arms to grasp hold of the pulpit. He deepens his voice to talk in his booming, theatrical tone.

"Our bodies are no more than flesh-candles to be consumed, to be degraded, ladies and gentlemen, yes, to be burned into submission for the beauty of the soul, whose flame will glow all the brighter.

"When we commune with God, we do so through our souls… Tonight our souls will travel, but our bodies will remain where we stand… So, I want you all now, to take up your launch-pad positions. Part your feet and put your hands in the air, with your fingertips together."

Lewis touches his fingertips and raises his arms. Unsteady on his feet he adopts a wide stance and bends his knees.

"Your bodies must serve as the rocket for lift-off. If you've ever seen a dog – how's your father – then you've got the idea, that you must thrust with your hips, as fast and as hard as you can, otherwise you won't lift-off." He opens his arms expansively. "Remember, your souls must travel millions of light-years across the universe. If you don't give them enough thrust, they'll get stuck in orbit around the earth and will never again be re-untied with your bodies. You'll have to live out the rest of your lives in a soulless limbo."

He takes his hipflask from his pocket and waves it like a drunk. He looks down at Wildo, who is lying on his stomach. In the violet twilight he can see him grimacing, clutching the spotlight, pinching the bridge of his nose with his other hand, trying to stop himself from laughing.

He's not the only one. Above the drone of the wave machine, the spitting fat from the rotisseries dotted around the beach, Lewis can hear titters and stifled giggles. He can see silhouettes with their arms raised and fingertips together, genuflecting, and quite a few experimenting with the manoeuvre for lift-off. He can read the atmosphere.

"Laugh at me by all means" – he smiles – "but remember, life has two sides, and the clown has two faces. Today you're laughing, but tomorrow you'll be crying. In time, you'll understand what compassion means. Like my silver friend, Jolly, who's sitting on the bar." The shadows turn to look behind them. "Only the most compassionate among you will be able to see my friend's true face." Lewis extends his hand towards Jolly.

"Foxy," Wildo hisses, "stick to the point!"

Perspiration is trickling from Lewis' temples. He's cooking inside his cassock, marinated in salty slime. Overcome by a sense of lassitude, Lewis draws a deep breath and puts his fingertips together. He lifts his arms above his head.

"And so, now that we have our rockets, we must make ready for ignition! Three… two… one… and lift off! And thrust!" Lewis thrusts with his hips. "Thrust, thrust!"

He grasps hold of the rail and with one hand still raised, he gives it his all, thrusting with all his might, like a rodeo cowboy, as the students stagger about, laughing. The more they shriek and hoot the madder he goes, until his legs give way, and he must stop to catch his breath.

Only now he sees that they've started to copy him, thrusting their hips, arms rocket-shaped. Lewis throws back his head, flask in the air. "Open the window! Open the window! Open the window!" He hears a twang, as Steve, below him, pulls on the wire, tearing open the bag of silver confetti to pour down on top of Lewis. Not shimmering and twinkling around his head as he envisioned, but in a single dump, dropping like a curtain in front of his face.

Lewis closes his eyes. Confetti weighs on his eyelids, and he can almost feel the walls around him shaking with laughter. Even the waves in the pool behind him are chopping with glee. He flutters his eyelids and peeks through his confetti blinds, to see students doubled over, clutching their stomachs in agony of merriment.

He looks down at Wildo's square mouth and beetroot-red

face, still holding tight to his spotlight, his legs twisting in the sand as if he might wet himself. And Lewis understands that it's not just his indignity they're all laughing at. It's the deadpan expression on his face.

So – this is what it feels like to be Dan the Clown. He folds his arms and waits for the laughter to die down, to shake his head, to roll his eyes –

"Have you quite finished? You really are very childish, all of you!"

The room erupts all over again. Lewis stamps his foot. He thrusts his arms up in a V and yells at the top of his voice. "In the name of the Comic Soul, I command you, brothers and sisters, to go forth and shine on!"

He descends his pulpit to the din of cheers and applause. Wildo is on his feet, patting Lewis' back.

"Saint Fox, that was fantastic! You and Udan could be a double act, you're a fucking brilliant pair of clowns."

The lights go up around the walls and students crowd him, all talking at once, and Lewis can't ask for more. They thought they were in for a boring old sermon, not a comedy act. But what he did was even more powerful, connecting everybody through laughter. They feel up-lifted, inspired, and really loving towards each other.

It's a true communion spirit as they make their way to the rotisseries to share in the communion feast, now being served. For one thing, they all agree, nodding and smiling at him as he stands at the head of the queue, the Cosmic Soul has one great sense of humour.

"To know that you only have to look at me." He smiles.

It smells like Christmas, with the carving up of roasted

turkey and goose on long tables, students piling their paper plates with slabs of white meat and dollops of red jelly.

There are plastic forks to hand, but Lewis eats his with his fingers, perched awkwardly on a mattress. He's ravenous, chewing so fast he can't taste the meat before he swallows it. He must have seconds and thirds to appreciate the succulent taste. When his stomach is full, someone hands him a Green Flame, refreshing, with a bite of lime.

The Bongo Band starts its jungle patter and Lewis sits back against the wall to watch the students dancing. All the girls are naked, but for the strings of fairy-lights looped around their necks and boys are tugging on them, this way and that way, for a laugh.

There's a girl slumped on another mattress not far from him, with a rope knotted around her neck. Lewis blinks. It's Sophie. King sits beside her. He has the end of the rope wrapped around his fist. Lewis waves but Sophie looks glazed, too drunk to register. King grins and gives a triumphant thumbs-up.

Lewis rises from the mattress. The sight of so many bare breasts tossing up and down like boats on a rough sea, is making him queasy. He heads up to the bar, where boys are cavorting, mucking about with a couple of funnels, pouring drinks down each other's throats.

"Hey, Saint Fox," one of them calls over, "do you reckon he's got the knack?"

Lewis gives a weary smile. "You'll know in the morning, if he's still sober."

He returns to stand beside Jolly and gazes out across the beach at the Red Giant. The core is boiling the colour of fresh blood, reflecting deep red on the white sands, looking from here, as if blood has in fact been spilled.

"Are you enjoying yourself, Jolly?" Lewis sips his Green Flame.

"I am glad Dan is not here to see this," Jolly says.

"Why?" Lewis laughs. "He'd want to see the students suffering for enlightenment."

"No, Lewis. Suffering is a burden Dan must carry."

"Really?" Lewis is half-listening, sickened by a group of males pulling females along by their flickering leashes, into the shadows.

"Yes," Jolly says. "Dan's daydreams are of perfection. But then comes the night. Then comes the dark after the light. The suffering after the joy. The death after life. UDAN cannot escape its nature. Dan knows the only solution to his creation is compassion. Compassion is Dan's last word to us – Lewis, are you listening?"

"Shit!" Lewis gasps. He has just seen a blonde head pop up from behind a blue windshield and go under again, like someone caught in the teeth of a man-eating shark. He squints, waiting to see if it will re-appear. It does, hair, flying upwards and vanishing.

"Mary!" Lewis drops his glass and runs, ploughing through the sand. The bastards! He's thinking, they can't do this! Not to his Mary! All the way down the slope, he waves his fists and barges into dancers, pushing them aside. "You bastards! You, no good bastards!"

At the blue windshield he stops. The sight snatches his voice away. Shirttails barely cover a man's sagging buttocks, on his knees pumping a girl from behind, on all fours. At her head is Wildo, holding her face up to him by her hair, thrusting inside her mouth.

"You…you… fucking bastards!" Lewis grabs McGin around the waist. He's so heavy that momentum alone is enough to dismount him, sprawling him sideways. "You sick pair of fucks! I'm going to report both of you!"

Wildo stands to his full height and pulls Abby to her feet, sobbing.

"What the hell do you think you're doing you stupid pansy?" Wildo says. "This was our deal. He gets Abby, or there's no more sunshine." Walking up to him, Wildo starts to masturbate, sliding the veins along his cock like worms moving beneath the shaft, waving it at Lewis. "What is it, Foxy? Are you fancying some of this yourself, you horny devil?" He laughs. "I can arrange a few guys to tie you down for a good roasting."

Lewis steps back and points in Wildo's face. "Dan was right about you. I should've listened to him. You piece of shit!"

McGin is pulling up his trousers, tucking in his tails. "I'm finished here, Mr Wild." His mouth opens and closes just like a frog's. "And so are you, Dr Allen, you bloody lunatic. Go ahead and report me, but you won't get anywhere, as of tomorrow, you don't work here."

Lewis curls his lip. "What are you talking about?"

"You've been fired!" McGin cranes his head forward, eyes bulging. "If you don't believe me, ask Jane O'Neil or the President. We received the order yesterday, from on high" – he points upwards – "from your God himself, Dan Udan. There, I thought you'd appreciate that. Goodbye and good riddance.

"And you" – he points at Abby – "what was all the crying about? I thought we had a deal. Know yourself better in future, silly cow." McGin climbs the slope, kicking up sand, muttering to himself.

Lewis stares at Wildo. "What do you know?"

Wildo shrugs. "It's the first I've heard, Foxy. Once a martyr, always a martyr, I guess." He gives the inane, beach-boy grin. "Have a great party."

"Ralphie... Ralphie!" Abby drops onto her knees and puts her face in her hands. "It's my birthday! Ralphie!"

Lewis turns and walks away.

*

He can't disbelieve Liam McGin. The man hasn't the imagination to make something like that up and anyway, what would be the point? McGin saw the writing on the wall and must've known he'd get away with this tonight. Lewis thinks, who can he turn to? Who, amongst the governors, would listen to him now? McGin has never broken a rule in his life, uglier than sin itself, who'd believe he could have his way with Abby?

He sits down beside his pulpit and hugs his knees to his chin. The surf, sighing back and forth, licks the tips of his toes. He looks up at the steel sculpture still hanging there, tracing a small circle, as pendulums do, that lack energy.

To be honest, Lewis was just beginning to wonder what more it would take to rouse Dan Udan from his imperfect equilibrium. This alone gives him something to smile about, that his beloved Dan has noticed him, at last. He's been forced to do something he didn't want to do, perhaps altering the subtle dynamics of his world.

Only, what real impact would it have on Dan's life, if Lewis no longer worked for him? It's a depressing thought, knowing that one day Dan Udan will forget that Lewis ever existed.

Lewis stares up into the Red Giant, until his eyes change

focus, and he can make out the crystal facets switching inside the hologram, sweeping through whirls and spirals, in constant motion, never still. All at once he sees what's behind them. A three-dimensional structure of an enormous spider's web, hidden from him all this time.

He sits still, not daring to move in case he loses sight of it, not even allowing himself to blink, sensing that something is caught in the web. He can't see it, but he can feel it, vibrating across the threads, until it passes through a gap, unseen, and slips softly into his mind.

A most compelling idea.

FIVE MONTHS LATER

28th August 2028, Dublin

Every morning before Mary leaves her flat in Clarendon Street, she completes the circuit of her garden, to survey her plants.

At this time of year, in the outside world, the days are too long, rainfall is too low and by midday the heat is intolerable. Although she has equipped her plants to endure these extremes of hardship, their numbers still disappoint, but not so their colours, vibrant in the haze, sparkling with dew. Their perfume hangs in the morning air, refreshing, cool against her skin, as she strolls the gravel-path with her mug of tea.

When she arrives at the top of her garden, she pauses to gaze at a mist of forget-me-nots around a maple tree. She doesn't need to be reminded, but whenever she's here, she thinks about Lewis.

She wants to remember him as he was, in the days before

Dan Udan. She can see Lewis now, sitting at his black lacquered desk, chatting away to Jolly. He never sat still for very long. There were always too many ideas racing around in his head, too many things to do, to keep up with himself.

She understands now that it was his unrequited love for Dan Udan, that Lewis couldn't live with.

If she'd been able to look into his eyes the last time they met, Mary might've recognised the signs that Lewis was slipping away, before he knew it himself.

He never learned what happened to his idol. On the night Dan Udan vanished, in the last hour of the student's beach party, Liam McGin discovered Lewis floating face down in the Governor's Swimming Pool.

He had forced his head and shoulders inside a metal sculpture that had become so mangled around his face, it looked as if he'd struggled to swim in his final moments. McGin found Lewis' cassock and his underwear neatly folded in the sand and a note written on a small writing-pad, that Lewis must have taken from the bar. It included old bar-tabs for food and drinks. His intentions were clear to all those who were familiar with Dan Udan's Reality Treatise, quoted in Lewis' shaky handwriting-

'And so, love for the Saint is God's last temptation. The courageous soul whose suffering is greater than any other, makes God weep. For the Saint cannot be favoured or spared. Although none will witness God's anguish, the cries of the raging storm are His-'

A few days later, a vigil was held for Lewis Fox Allen in the Governor's Swimming Pool, where students and UISC staff gathered, many in tears, to place candles down by the water, close to where he'd been found drifting. The students agreed that there was no sense in which Lewis' soul was present. He had long flown, faraway across the universe, to be with his precious Cosmic Soul, now walking hand in hand, amongst the stars.

For weeks afterwards Jolly shut itself down to basic function. Lewis' Computer couldn't or wouldn't talk, not even to Mary when she tried to cajole it.

Its chalky face had frozen with its eyes gazing upwards, luminous with unshed tears. Until the day she sat down in front of Jolly's face and spoke about her own feelings of grief and loss, inviting Jolly to share *his* feelings with her.

Jolly focused on Mary with big, milky eyes and thereafter spilled his first tears of water-light.

They discussed at length a suitable memorial for Lewis, only to discover that UDAN Corporations was ahead on the project, when a large bust of Lewis' head and shoulders arrived one day at the UISC.

It was a remarkable likeness, cut from diamond crystal, depicting a hologram inside the cranium, of blue-skies and puffy white clouds. The bust would soon sit as a centrepiece for a fountain in the middle of the Farm Park, with a golden plaque mounted on a low wall:

'In memory of Dr. Lewis Fox Allen,
for his contribution to the development of
Character and Personality in UDAN Quantum A.I'.
'In loving memory of my dear friend, Lewis.
He created me as his brother and

invited me into the human family.' Jolly.

Within days of Lewis' death, Ralph Wild and Liam McGin were evicted from the UISC, to face criminal charges, following a statement to the Governors from a traumatised student nurse. Once Abby Anders had stepped forward, the Governors received an avalanche of complaints from female students, accusing both men of preying on young women.

The UDAN Religion took a deathblow.

But the SETI Institute had a secret. Leon La Grau kept his promise.

Nothing was ever reported on how Dan Udan vanished from the world. All witnesses were sworn to secrecy, in the words of Wittgenstein, spoken in La Grau's tremulous voice in Mary's sitting room:

'That whereof we cannot speak, thereof we must remain silent.'

La Grau was convinced that if Udan had left the Earth for good, they would find his body, discarded like a used costume. He and his officers searched the UISC, high and low, even pulling back the duvet on Mary's bed, half expecting to find him there, laid out like the deceased.

Secret planes scoured the Wicklow Mountains and were still searching for Dan's body months after his disappearance. They found nothing. So long as there was no corpse, La Grau held onto the hope that Dan Udan might return one day. Assured of Udan's ultimate benevolence towards humanity, following his restraint in the face of physical coercion, SETI offered, that should he wish to return to Earth, he would be regarded as a citizen of the world, a free man with all his human rights and properties re-instated.

To this day the SETI Institute continues to transmit its 'Message to UDAN' across the Universe, with a promise that his secret is safe.

It is, at last, with an ache in her heart that Mary turns away from the forget-me-nots and carries on down the gravel path. Before mounting the steps to the patio-doors she shields her eyes and looks up at the early morning sky. She stands like this for a while, gazing into the haze, until there's a tiny flash. Even though she knows it's an aeroplane turning towards the sun thousands of feet above, she reads it as a sign.

"This is an important day for us," she says aloud, "wish us luck."

In the pond close by, a mother duck splashes into the water. The fountain gurgles, flounces up, hunches low. And then there's quiet.

The birds have stopped.

The sighing trees grow still.

Mary listens. She has come to know so many kinds of silence. Some give her hope. Some fill her with sadness. It's uncanny how complete this silence is, in the open air.

"I'd better go." She smiles. "We mustn't be late."

Crossing College Park in a navy-blue jacket and skirt, high heels, carrying a heavy briefcase, Mary can already feel the sun's heat on her back. By the time she reaches the UDAN Conference building she's flushed and damp with perspiration.

But for a few ushers, the foyer is deserted. She glances at her watch. Stefan Mohr appears in the doorway.

"Good morning, Mary. The delegates decided to take their seats early as it is cooler in the hall. You have ten minutes.

Would you like a coffee before you start?"

"No thanks. I'll go and freshen up. It's hot out there already."

Stefan smiles. "Hey, happy birthday." He wags his finger. "You are going to celebrate today. We are not going to let you get away with it."

In the Ladies Powder Room Mary splashes her face with cold water and dabs her underarms with paper towels. She examines her face in the mirror and then seeks in her handbag for foundation cream, eyeshadow and lipstick. She applies make-up these days to make herself look older. She tucks in her blouse, does up the second button, straightens her jacket. She's ready to go in.

"Good morning, ladies and gentlemen. As this week's conference draws to a close, we're in a good position to appreciate the advances made in genetic medicine, owing to the dedication and unstinting work of UDAN's research teams.

"Last but not least, I'd like now to share with you the progress we've made in the quest for human longevity, taking our life span from one hundred years today at best, to two hundred and fifty years, by mid-century-" Mary illuminates her first slide.

The delegates give her a standing ovation. Craig Craigan, the new CEO for UDAN Corporations, walks on stage with a huge bouquet of white roses and puts his arm around her shoulders.

"And there are more congratulations in order." Craigan gives her an avuncular embrace, side-on. "Today is Professor Gallagher's birthday." There's cheering as Mary accepts the bouquet into her arms. "I'm not going to tell you how old she is, but it's obvious she's not a day over twenty-one." He grins at her. "Would there be any other genetic research you've not told us about?"

The delegates laugh at his good-natured banter.

Mary smiles. "That's your lot I'm afraid!"

"Until next year!" Craigan puts his fist in the air. "We've only just begun!"

But if Mary were to tell them the truth, that she's growing younger every day and that in the last few months all her birthmarks have disappeared, through no action of her own, the cheering probably would stop. She'd be looking at rows of disbelieving faces.

Craigan opens his arms with largesse. "UDAN Corporations invites you all to join us for Champagne and a piece of Mary's birthday cake in the Crick and Watson Room. Before you go, just to remind you, after lunch we'll be showing our research films-"

In the Crick and Watson Room, Stefan hands a Champagne flute to Mary and puts his cheek to hers.

"As always you were fantastic today and you look so beautiful, it is not fair on us men."

Jane places a hand on Mary's arm. "Well done, dear, we're proud of you. Alf and I have got a present for you and you're going to have dinner with us tonight, we won't accept a refusal."

President Alf Macnamara hugs Mary, prickling her neck with his beard. "Happy birthday. Please say you'll join us. It'll make Jane so happy." He murmurs in her ear, "She has some very bad days, misses *him* terribly. I know you do. You two must talk."

"I'd like to join you for dinner." Mary draws back and smiles. "Do you mind if we make it tomorrow evening?"

Jane's face lights up. "Have you other plans for tonight?"

"Yes," Mary says.

"Oh, I'm so pleased." Jane clasps Mary's hand, like a grown up with a child, giving it a shake. "You have a wonderful time. My goodness, you deserve it. May I ask who with?"

"No," Mary says.

"Is it a secret?" Jane smiles.

"I'm going to have a nice bath and curl up with a book." Mary levels her eyes at Jane. "Will you please stop worrying. I'm fine."

"What's all this about thirty?" Sean Flanagan steps towards Mary. "You don't look a day over sixteen." He gives her his cherubic smile and kisses her cheek. "Happy birthday, gorgeous. You can open it now if you like."

He hands her a golden box tied with a yellow ribbon. Mary passes her Champagne flute to Jane to accept the box, feeling shy as she undoes the ribbon and lifts the lid. Sean's gift nestles on a bed of lamb's wool. It's a delicately crafted golden brooch, in the shape of a rose.

"Sean, it's lovely."

"A rose for an Irish rose." His cheeks have become flushed. "Hold it up to the light and you'll see."

Mary lifts it to the light. At the heart of the rose is a small diamond.

"Sean, it's so pretty, thank you so much, but I can't… I really can't." She shakes her head. "I'm sorry." She returns the brooch to its box and gives it back to him. "I could never wear it. I'd feel" – she winced, but there was no other word to describe her feelings – "guilty."

"Please don't. Can't you just accept it as a birthday present? I know where I stand." But seeing the look on Mary's face, he has no choice but to take the box, his colour deepening. "Sorry. I should've settled for a box of chocolates."

Jane touches Mary's elbow. "You're not doing yourself any favours by refusing Sean's present," she says, "You can't bring *him* back by denying yourself a life. I know how you feel, but we've all got to come to terms with the fact that my nephew has gone. Please, don't cut yourself off from everybody. You know how much it worries me when you withdraw, like your father."

Jane faces Sean, Alf and Stefan. "Why don't the five of us go out to dinner this evening? Alf and I have discovered a wonderful new Greek restaurant in the Temple Bar."

Mary pulls her handbag onto her shoulder and picks up her briefcase.

"Sorry Jane, I can't do this." She glances around at their faces. "Thank you everybody, for your lovely cards and gifts. I appreciate your kindness. I'm just very tired and would like to go home. I'll see you all tomorrow." She turns her back.

"Mary, please," Jane calls out, "don't walk away!"

Outside in the burning heat, Mary strides away from the Conference building, through the Parade Ground, passing the old Genetics building to re-enter College Park.

Her gait is purposeful, her chin is up. But soon after she reaches the green, she veers off the path, seeking cover among the trees. Maidenhair, ash, silver-lime, beech. She reaches out and touches their cool trunks, blinded by tears.

Beneath the canopy of leaves, she puts down her handbag and briefcase and leans her back against a tree-trunk. She takes the black velvet box from her pocket and returns Dan's engagement ring to her ring-finger, flashing eight coloured diamonds in the dappled sunshine.

She lifts her face to see the sky between the branches, seeking some form of geometry among the random and irregular shapes, a pattern, a sign.

"*Whisper to me,*" she says, "*Speak to me through the leaves... My darling, I miss you so much.*"

The sound of footsteps on the path. Mary braces herself against the tree-trunk. Sean Flanagan goes by. She watches him walk across the park, his tall, dark figure flickering in the sunlight. She closes her eyes, trying to visualise or even sense Dan Udan in a different form.

"*Please, let me see you-*" sunlight dapples the insides of her eyelids – "*I want to know what you look like. Or maybe you don't have any form at all-*"

The leaves have stopped whispering. Mary opens her eyes and gazes up at the sky. A shiver passes through her. She dabs her cheeks with the back of her hand, picks up her briefcase and handbag, and returns to the path.

At the Zebra crossing on Nassau Street Mary waits, looking up the road. The bus is coming down too fast. Its grill is a rictus, appearing to melt behind thermal waves rising from the tarmac, the driver invisible behind the dazzling windscreen.

It's as if there's nobody at the wheel.

What if she were to step out now?

Would *he* be there, waiting to take her by the hand? She watches the bus growing wider, looming higher, mesmerised, she steps off the curb.

Blank shoppers' faces float by. Mary finds herself in the middle of Grafton Street, dazed, as the pedestrians swerve to avoid her. She continues home.

It's not much cooler inside. Mary pours herself a glass

of Chardonnay, runs a tepid bath, shaking in a few drops of lavender oil.

Dipping down into the perfumed water, her head resting on the bath pillow, she sips wine and lets the chill seep into her bones. She tells herself she's content.

The remaining hours of the day stretch before her, but she has birthday cards to read, presents from colleagues to open, bouquets of flowers to transfer to vases. There's a Thai-takeaway in the freezer, all she must do is microwave. Read her book, watch a television documentary, then bed.

She refuses to cry again, on her birthday.

Refreshed from her bath, in a dressing-gown, she opens the patio-doors into the garden. The water sprinklers are throwing glitter at the sun, casting rainbows across the lawn.

Poppies along the fence shout that life is simply scarlet and that's all the joy there is. At moments like this when the world is full of itself, there are no secret signs. It's all in her mind.

She turns on the radio.

These days Mary listens to the Golden Oldies, remembering how much he loved to sing old pop-songs. She imagines whenever he feels alone out there, he might tune into this radio station. She lies on the sofa, gazing up at the ceiling, the un-read book face-down on her abdomen, listening to the words of *Mr Blue Sky, California Dreaming, Waterloo Sunset*, drifting off…

'And I need you more than want you and I want you for all time, the Wichita Lineman is still on the line-'

It's the thin line between sunset and dusk, with a veil of moisture so sheer it puts a sparkle in the air.

Mary stands in the middle of the lawn, bare feet chilling

on the wet grass and watches the sky's pink deepening to plum. There's a hunter's moon tonight, drifting with a wisp of a tail.

"*Send me a shooting star*," she says aloud.

The telephone rings faraway, in the sitting room. It'll be Jane or Sean. She lets it ring, gazing up, determined to hold the whole night-sky in her sight. If she blinks, she could miss his sign arcing towards the earth. The ringing stops.

She has no idea how long she's been out here. Her bones ache.

"*It's my birthday, please Dan, just one shooting star…*"

The telephone rings again. Mary holds her breath. She'll wait here all night if she must. The ringing stops. She breathes again and continues to watch, for another hour, maybe longer, growing colder.

Behind her someone sighs.

She turns, her limbs barely able to move. In the dim light of the patio doors there's the silhouette of a tall man, arms folded, leaning against the wall, his face is in shadow. Is her longing to see him so intense, her mind has conjured him up? Mary blinks, stares and blinks again.

"*Dan, is that you*?"

He moves away from the wall and descends the patio-steps. "It's me, Sean. You left your keys in the front door."

There's a gust of wind, the maple tree rustles. Mary senses a movement behind her and turns around.

"Sean Flanagan, isn't it?" Dan slips out of the darkness, ghostly pale in a white suit, clean shaven. His hair has grown back into thick, tousled curls.

Mary cries out. Her legs give way as Dan catches her around the waist and holds onto her.

He extends his gloveless hand to Sean.

"Dan Udan, pleased to meet you, Sean." The two men shake hands.

"It's an honour and a privilege to meet you sir, at last, face to face," Sean says.

"And you too, Sean. You're welcome to join us for a nightcap, although Mary and I must have an early night." Dan hugs Mary tight to his side. "We're getting married in the morning."

"Eleven o'clock at St Luke's and then afterwards at the Andromeda Hotel." Sean nods. "I received your invitation this afternoon… I've been trying to call Mary all evening to congratulate her and to say I'd be delighted to attend." He laughs. "She's been out here star-gazing, all night."

"Aye, what's that about?" Dan chuckles and puts his mouth to Mary's ear. "Angel, you should know me better by now. If you'd looked in the opposite direction, you would've seen me waving."

Mary reaches for his hand and interlinks their fingers with a possessive squeeze. "My darling, I wasn't looking for you." She looks up and deep into his eyes. "I sensed you were everywhere, and right beside me, the whole time."

"Old habits die hard." Dan smiles his lopsided smile. "Where's my kiss?"